SAXON

SAXON

He's the one man I can never have,
but the only one I crave…

Saxon Gray has reason to hate me. He spent five years in prison after saving me from a brutal violation at the hands of a rival motorcycle club – and he paid for that rescue with his freedom. I've never been able to settle the debt I owe him…until now. The menace of that old rivalry is flaring up again, and as president of the Hellfire Riders, Saxon is the one man who can keep me safe. But I want more than his protection. I want his heart.

LOOKING FOR CONTENT WARNINGS?
FLIP TO THE END!

To avoid putting spoilers up front where readers might accidentally see them, I've listed the content warnings on the very last page (the printer will likely insert a blank page at the very end, but you will find CWs on the final printed page.) If you are browsing through a "Look Inside" feature and can't flip to the end, please feel free to visit my website and look for the content warnings link in the menu.
www.katiwilde.com

SAXON

THE HELLFIRE RIDERS

KATI WILDE

SAXON

Also by Kati Wilde

*The Hellfire Riders
(Discreet Cover Editions)*

SAXON

BLOWBACK

GUNNER

BULL & DUKE

STONE

*The Hellfire Riders MC Series
(Original Covers & Ebooks)*

THE HELLFIRE RIDERS: SAXON & JENNY

THE HELLFIRE RIDERS: JACK & LILY

BREAKING IT ALL

GIVING IT ALL

CRAVING IT ALL

FAKING IT ALL

LOSING IT ALL

(Turn the page for more...)

The Dead Lands
Fantasy Romance

THE MIDWINTER MAIL-ORDER BRIDE

THE MIDNIGHT BRIDE

PRETTY BRIDE

THE MIDSUMMER BRIDE
(COMING SOON)

Wolfkin & Berserkers
Shapeshifter Romance

BEAUTY IN SPRING

HIGH MOON

TEACHER'S PET WOLF

SHERIFF'S BAD BEAR
(COMING SOON)

Other Romances by Kati

GOING NOWHERE FAST[1]

SECRET SANTA

THE KING'S HORRIBLE BRIDE

ALL HE WANTS FOR CHRISTMAS

THE WEDDING NIGHT

EVIL TWIN[2]

---

[1] Includes cameos by the Hellfire Riders
[2] Set in the same world as the Dead Lands

CONTENTS

FOREWORD

In the summer of 2014, I went camping with my mom and sisters—along with my daughter and all of my nieces—on the Oregon coast. We were having a girls' weekend, and while my younger sister sacrificed a Barbie over the campfire (don't ask), I was inside a tent with my laptop, giving myself permission to write whatever I wanted to write.

So I drafted the first few chapters of Saxon & Jenny's romance, and it turned out that this book was the one I *needed* to write.

The year 2014 was not a good year for me, for a whole lot of reasons—but one particular reason was that I'd completely burned out, professionally and creatively. I've always loved writing. Simply loved it. But I hit a point where I could not make any story work, and the frustration and loss became overwhelming.

So that weekend, I gave myself permission to write anything—and so I wrote a werewolf romance, except I set it in an alternate universe where werewolves didn't exist; and instead of a pack of shapeshifters, they were a pack of bikers. And instead of fighting monsters or vampires, they were fighting white supremacists and sex trafficking clubs.

I know, I know. It sounds like ridiculous mental gymnastics. But it allowed me to put the story far outside of reality, and at the time, that was what I needed: just letting my brain ride free.

And quite frankly, that might have saved me.

I'd written other books before—stories that I love and that other people loved, too—but those particular stories weren't coming anymore, and it terrified me. With the Hellfire Riders, however, I didn't worry about anything but the story I wanted to tell. And eventually, my burnout fueled a brand-new creative fire.

So I hope you enjoy the heck out of this series, which began in a tent on the Oregon coast and finished seven years later (at the beginning of the pandemic and what would be another couple of bad years for everyone...but that's a story for another time.)

Until then, happy reading!

—Kati

A NOTE ABOUT READING ORDER

The Hellfire Riders series was originally conceived as a series of novellas for readers who want heat, emotion, and a happy ending, but who don't have the time to read a full-length book. Saxon and Jenny's primary romance is featured in three novellas: *Wanting It All*, *Taking It All*, and *Having It All*. They are also the main characters in a holiday romance, *Giving It All*, which can be read as their epilogue story.

The first three novellas were originally collected together in *The Hellfire Riders: Saxon & Jenny*, and *Giving It All* was published as a separate book. In this edition, I've collected all four novellas featuring this couple—but please be aware that *Giving It All* takes place chronologically after Blowback's book and concurrently with Gunner's book. So if you are a stickler for reading in proper order, you will want to read the first three novellas in this edition, skip to *Blowback*, and then come back and read the final novella in this book.

WANTING IT ALL

ONE

As soon as I step through the Wolf Den's doors, the noise in the bar pounds into me like a fist. Heavy metal. Male voices shouting over it. Bursts of raucous laughter. The crack of billiard balls.

It all lulls as everyone sees me. Hard eyes look me up and down. Others turn away from me. The wings of fire and wheels of steel emblazoned on the back of their leather battle jackets serve as a warning—they're all Hellfire Riders.

And my father leads the Steel Titans. There isn't any bad blood between the two clubs—not any more—but there are rules. Territories. Even though I don't ride with the Titans, and I'm sure as hell not one of their old ladies, I'm not supposed to be here.

Not right now, anyway. I come often enough during the day, when the business behind the business of selling liquor is conducted. When the tavern is quiet, and even the locals will stop in for lunch. But nights are something else. The nights belong to the club that rules this den.

I know better than to march farther inside without a welcome. That welcome will come. Still, it's nerve-wracking waiting with all those eyes measuring me. I'm pretty sure some of them are measuring the lengths of their tables, too, and deciding just how far I would stretch across it while they tear off my pants and teach me a lesson about intruding on Hellfire territory.

My stomach roils sickly as I imagine it, even though I know these guys won't do anything like that. Some of them might think it, but they won't do it. There are rules about that, too. The Hellfire Riders don't hurt women unless the women really like it. Unless they ask for it.

Not everyone I've met has followed the same code.

At the bar, a big biker slowly rises from a stool and comes toward me. Short blond hair, long easy stride. His name's Aaron, but everyone calls him Stone Wall—the Riders' enforcer. The casual attitude he always wears is just a sheep's skin. He'll tear apart anyone who threatens the club or its members. As far as I know, he already has. His face has seen better days. He took a bad beating a few years back. I have no idea who laid it on him. But his nose isn't so straight anymore. The deep slash of a blade cuts through his eyebrow and traces a ragged path down his cheek. His lips are scarred as if they've been smashed between his teeth and a fist too many times.

But I remember when those lips were perfectly shaped. I remember him throwing kisses at a roomful of giggling preteens during one of his sister's sleepovers. Every girl in junior high would have sworn Anna's older brother was the hottest thing that ever prowled the streets of Pine Valley, Oregon.

That was a long time ago. Some things haven't changed. I'm still friends with Anna. I don't giggle much now, though.

And these days, the Stone Wall isn't the hottest thing to prowl these streets. Not because of his face. Anna's brother is still hot in that primitive, dangerous way some of these guys have, and the scars only add to it. But there is one man who could outsteam any other in this town. In this state. Maybe the whole damn world.

I've just walked into his den. I don't see him now. I don't know if I want to.

Being anywhere near Saxon Gray is always heaven. And it's always hell.

"Jenny." Stone stops close, a bottle of Budweiser dangling from his long fingers. "You all right?"

He asks me that because he knows I wouldn't have stopped here at night if I'd been able to help it. But I'm all right. Now. I just don't want to go back out on the road anytime soon.

And I don't want to tell him about it. I know what it might lead to. Fights. Blood. One man dead. Another man in prison. It happened before. I don't want to see it happen again. Not now, when my dad is so sick. When I don't know if he would live through a fight, let alone anything that might follow.

So I shake my head and say, "I just want to see Anna."

Stone takes a swig of his Bud, studying me over the length of the bottle. Doubting me.

"And to save you from drinking that shit," I add.

He grins. "A working man can't afford your golden piss. Not for everyday drinking."

"Then I'll buy you one."

With another long look at me, he finally nods. His head jerks toward the bar. That is my welcome. He walks with me as I make my way through the tables. And so it begins. I won't take another step without a high-ranking Rider at my side. Even with no bad blood between the clubs, toss in enough liquor and chest thumping, and the danger of someone doing or saying something stupid to me rises exponentially. So Stone will stop any trouble from coming my way before it begins—and if he has to bail for any reason, someone else will take his place.

Maybe Zachary Cooper, since the Riders' sergeant at arms is already sitting at the bar, his elbows braced on the counter as he watches us come. All the Hellfire men are tight, but there are few tighter than Zach and Stone—and their brotherhood began long before they'd straddled a motorcycle. Both former marines, they served together in Iraq. Stone returned to Pine Valley after his tour ended; Zach came with him, though he didn't grow up around here. I don't really know where he's from. Chatty, he isn't. Instead he just watches everything. Me, right now. Usually, he seems to be watching Anna, but only when she isn't looking back at him.

She looks often. There isn't any touching, though. She made a move once and he shut her down. After that, she always seems to look despite herself. I can't blame the girl, though. It's hard not to look. Wherever Zach Cooper comes from, they grow 'em big and pretty, with thick black hair, chiseled jaws, and glacial blue eyes. They probably have a sign: Welcome to Sexyville, USA. Population: One brooding guy who will never touch my best friend because she's the sister of *his* best friend.

What a sad little town that is.

I head for the short leg of the L-shaped bar. Stone claims his seat next to Zach—near enough to talk to me and run interference if needed, but with a few empty stools between us.

At the other end of the bar, Anna is popping the caps off a half dozen beer bottles, and she throws me a curious glance as she places them on a tray. Her dark hair is up in a simple ponytail, which means she probably crawled out of bed just before starting her shift.

"Hey, gorgeous," I call as she comes closer. The music isn't going to allow any real conversation, which is fine by me.

She leans in, forearms on the counter. "What's going on?"

"I'm looking for a good beer. You got one? I'm buying for your brother, too."

Lips compressed, she tilts her head and waits.

Damn it. "I just didn't like the look of some guys riding behind me is all. So I came this way."

Her eyebrows pinch together. "The Eighty-Eight?"

"I don't know."

Such a lie. After pulling into the Den's parking lot, I waited until the bikers rode by. Their emblems were hard to mistake—an eagle over a death's head. Supremacist fuckers. They call themselves the Eighty-Eight Henchmen, though there aren't eighty-eight members. The number is a nod to their buddy Adolf.

Face troubled, Anna draws back. I catch her hand.

"Look, it's nothing. Okay? Just bad luck that they were passing through this way. They probably didn't even realize I was ahead of them. And they rode on."

They hadn't swarmed my truck. Hadn't hooted and shouted about how they were going to force my thighs open and get in line.

They hadn't this time, anyway.

"Really," I say, squeezing her hand. "Nothing. But it will be something if you mention it."

Because every biker in this tavern will ride out after them. But if the Eighty-Eight were just passing through, there's no reason to start any trouble. Especially since her brother will be in the middle of it.

Anna studies my face for a long minute, then finally gives a heavy sigh. "What are you having?"

"Lionheart." My favorite stout—and the strongest ale that my brewery sells. The Wolf Den keeps it on tap. "Along with a shot of Patrón."

Her gaze narrows. "It was nothing, huh?"

So maybe I'm a little shaky. And I have no intention of leaving soon. It's still nothing. "Now that I'm here, I might as well keep you company for a while."

With a roll of her eyes, Anna turns away. Not upset that I'm here. Just not believing a word I say.

I don't have to say much more. Before she finishes drawing my pint, more drink orders come in, and I'm left alone with my tequila and ale. Just as well.

The shot is a delicious burn down my throat. No salt or lime for me. Just the liquor.

I slide the empty shot glass back across the counter and cradle the pint in my hands. Aside from a glance here and there, no one is looking in my direction anymore. They've all gone back to their pool tables and their drinking—and at the shadowed corner tables, some have gone back to their fucking.

None of them is Saxon Gray.

My stomach hot, I look away. So stupid. Rumor is, he

doesn't fuck in public the way some of the others do. But I searched for him in the corners anyway—knowing that if I saw him, it would be a knife in my chest.

That's stupid, too. Saxon isn't mine. He has never been mine. He's never been anything *close* to mine. And if he has any reason to hate someone, it would be me—the girl who didn't have the brains to stay where she belonged. The stranger he spent five years in prison for, because he'd protected her.

Protected *me*. Now I'm taking advantage of his protection again. Maybe bringing trouble to his door.

I shouldn't have come here. But leaving isn't an option yet. Better to nurse this ale for an hour, then roll home.

Home. Maybe not for much longer. I've lived on the ranch with my dad all my life. The ranch isn't a working one anymore, just a big spread of land with the clubhouse on one side and our place on the other, so most of the Titans' business is kept away from the house—and away from the old barn on the property that I renovated when I started up my microbrewery.

But the Titans aren't as strong as they'd once been. I would never say as much to my dad, but I know it. Just as I know that as soon as the Eighty-Eight think that I'm unprotected, as soon as word gets around that my dad is sick, they'll make good on their threats. They have a score to settle with me.

So leaving Pine Valley is beginning to look like the best option. I can just start over somewhere else. It'll have to be pretty far, though. Moving a county away, even a state away wouldn't cut it. A weekend's ride could bring the Eighty-Eight to my door. I'll have to cross half the country before things even begin to look safe.

But moving that far will make starting over a lot harder. I'm doing well for myself, but most of my business contacts are regional. My ingredients are local. I know their flavors, their quirks. I won't be starting over from square one, but it'll be a near thing.

Still. Square one looks a hell of a lot better than what the Eighty-Eight is planning for me.

So maybe it's time to put out feelers. The chances of starting up a new brewery and having as much success are pretty slim, but I can work with someone else for a while. Sell everything here, save up my money, establish a reputation and foothold in another region. Then branch out on my own again.

Alone. Because the entire damn reason for this is the fucking cancer eating away at my dad's chest. Already at stage four when he went in to have it checked out, he'd refused treatment, and he'd refused to fight with me when I told him he had to try. I yelled at him anyway, but even then, a part of me knew he wouldn't budge. Stubborn, stupid man. But he's been alone for a while, too—since my mom died in a car wreck fifteen years ago. There's been just me and him, and the club. Maybe he's been waiting all this time to be with her again, but he just held off until he could be sure that I'll be okay.

Maybe I will be. I just know that it sucks balls to spend so much time worrying about your own future when your dad doesn't have one. Pretty fucking selfish.

Except…knowing that I'll be all right will probably help him through the next months more than any drug will. The one thing that could hurt him, really hurt him, would be knowing that I'm vulnerable and that he can't protect me.

So. Tomorrow. Feelers. Look for someone to buy my brewery here, look for another job back east somewhere. Then just suck up the pain of going.

Or drown it. I signal to Anna, asking for another shot.

Her frowny, worried look is in place as she pours. "You're sure?"

Not asking about the shot. Asking if I'm sure that I'm okay. She doesn't know about my dad yet. But I can't tell her now.

"Just a rough day," I say. "Now I'm working up a good, snotty cry."

Anna grins, because it's the kind of thing I usually say to make her laugh. This time it isn't really a joke. She doesn't have to know that.

Another biker comes up to the bar and she leaves me to get his drink. My throat feels too tight to shoot the tequila right away. I scan the tavern and stop on Lily Burns standing by the pool table, a cue in one hand and a beer in the other. She's looking my way—maybe not looking *at* me, but our eyes meet as my gaze skims the room. She lifts her bottle in acknowledgment. I lift my glass.

Both the daughters of motorcycle club presidents, but we couldn't be much more different. I'm small and dark-haired, and Lily is like a Viking. A Valkyrie. Blonde and tall, and built like an Olympic volleyball player.

The differences don't stop at the physical. I've never wanted to ride with the Titans. The few times I've gone anywhere with them, it was mostly just to be with my dad, and only when I was younger—we clung to each other hard in the years after my mom was killed. Lily wanted to ride from the first, and she had, though her dad hadn't let her join the Riders or wear the kutte.

When she left Pine Valley after high school, I hadn't really known what became of her. I just assumed that she'd gotten tired of being metaphorically kicked in the cunt while knocking at the door of the Hellfire Riders' clubhouse. Then about five years ago, her dad lost a head-on race with a semitruck, Saxon Gray was voted into his place as club president, and Lily came back—taller, blonder, and more Viking-warrior than ever.

I discovered then where she'd been: flying helicopters in Afghanistan. Now she works as a mechanic at a local airfield, taking tourists up now and then—and during the forest fire season, flying chemical suppressants and firefighters out to the burn sites. So many guys in this tavern think they're pretty badass, but Lily outbadasses most of them. And when she made her bid for a kutte and the Hellfire colors, she got them.

Not without raising a hell of an uproar. And not without some members turning in their colors and leaving the Riders. Usually that kind of shit is hush-hush, but since some of the guys came over to the Steel Titans, I heard how it all went down.

Lily found a loophole in the Hellfire Riders' club bylaws. Nowhere do they say specifically that women can't apply for membership. It just never was done. But the bylaws also state that no one who served in the armed forces can be rejected without good reason.

Saxon Gray decided that possession of a vagina wasn't good reason. Apparently when other objections came up—whether she'd be weaker than a man and hold her own—she'd wiped the floor with the first three guys who'd challenged her.

There are times when I wish that I were more like her—I probably wouldn't be thinking of running across the country if I was. But having grown up around a club gives me a pretty good idea of the shit she probably goes through on a daily basis, fighting twice as hard as every guy around her and having five times as much crap thrown at her, and I can't be sorry not to be dealing with that.

I'm pretty sure she sees me the same way, but opposite—sometimes wishing it were easier, but not willing to give up what she's earned just to walk a smoother path.

So I hold her gaze as I down my shot. She grins and takes a swig in return. We aren't good friends. We aren't anything alike. But damn if I don't understand that woman.

"Jenny?"

I'm not expecting a voice behind me—the only thing on this side of the bar is the employees' door that leads to the back rooms and offices—and I'm not expecting *that* voice. Heart in my throat, I whirl on the barstool.

"Uncle Thorne?" Caught by utter surprise, I stare at him. Tall, wiry, and with gray turning his dark hair to iron, he's not really my uncle. Not by blood. But it doesn't matter. As VP of the Titans, he's called my father 'brother' for as long as I can remember. "What are you doing here?"

It's just an automatic question—he won't tell me club business. But if my being here is considered a minor territorial breach, then *his* being here means that something big is going down between the clubs.

"I'd ask you the same." Gravelly voiced and smelling of Marlboros, he pulls me in for a quick hug and a kiss to the top of my head. "But I think I know."

He does? When I draw back, I quickly search his face. No, I don't think he knows. Because if he were aware of the Eighty-Eight on my tail, he wouldn't be looking at me with such concern and affection. Steam would be pouring out of his nose, instead.

So whatever Thorne thinks brought me here, I'll keep on letting him think it.

"Yeah," I say, then he comes around me to grab the next barstool and my heart clutches painfully in my chest.

Heaven. Hell.

Because Saxon Gray is standing behind him.

TWO

My breath stops when I see Saxon. Everything stops. I hate this, hate how I can't process what this man does to me and how he just shuts everything down.

I hadn't seen him that day at the rally, almost fourteen years ago. The first time I saw him was at the trial that followed it. I'd been sixteen, my mom hadn't been dead even a year, and I wasn't paying attention to where I was going. Even if I had been paying attention, I might have gotten lost in that crowded field anyway. But I got turned around after visiting the portable john and ended up in the Eighty-Eight Henchmen's section. They recognized me as my father's daughter. Everyone called me Baby Red then, even though my hair isn't the auburn shock that his was. I was still his girl. Before that day, I loved the nickname.

As soon as I recognized their eagle and death's head I tried to get the hell out of there. But they'd already surrounded me, and the Henchmen's president, Timothy Reichmann, pinned me to the dirt on my stomach.

I don't remember much. Just his voice in my ear—*You got a baby pussy, too?*—and the tearing pain as he shoved his fingers into me. The laughter as he showed the blood to his men. *Baby Red!* they shouted then. Sick with pain and fear, I was fighting and screaming all the while. But when I heard his belt unbuckling, I puked.

Then the world exploded around me. I didn't learn until later that Saxon Gray had roared in and sent Reichmann flying off me with a brutal kick to his head. I didn't know that the rest of the Riders charged in after him. I just knew that Reichmann wasn't holding me down anymore, so I crawled through the chaos as fast as I could, then got to my feet and ran.

But that one kick sealed Saxon's fate. Reichmann didn't wake up. After three days of lying in a hospital bed he was dead. I don't know how the cops tied Saxon to the kick. Most likely, one of the Eighty-Eight broke code and snitched. After a search, investigators found Reichmann's blood on Saxon's boot, and when the time came, Saxon didn't deny it. He just said he'd seen a girl attacked, he'd helped her, then he hadn't given another thought to the piece of shit that Reichmann had been until the cops showed up at his door.

No one named me. The Eighty-Eight said no girl was there. The Riders backed up Saxon but kept their mouths shut about who I was. My dad would have let it stay that way, but I insisted that he let me give my statement to the cops.

It didn't make a difference. Almost a year later, Saxon was convicted of manslaughter, and I watched as the man who saved me from a brutal rape was sentenced to ten years in prison. I watched his mom sobbing in the courtroom as he was shuffled out in chains.

Saxon only served five years. But still. He isn't much older than me—and was only twenty at the time. And just like that, five years were gone. By the time he got out, twenty percent of his lifetime had been spent behind bars. Just because a girl hadn't watched where she was going. Just because he'd tried to help her.

I've never really been able to deal with it. Not the guilt, not the gratitude. But Saxon didn't want an apology or a thank you. He made that clear. When I was eighteen and headed to college—to *college*, and he'd just been sent to *prison*—I wrote to him. I poured out everything. My thanks. My apologies. And a promise to repay him, if it was possible. I knew it wasn't.

He wrote back. A short note in his heavy script.

I still have that letter, tucked away in a drawer beside my bed, tattered by frequent readings. And I tried to do as he said. I tried not to be sorry. But the first time I saw Saxon after his release, he was coming out of the auto store on Main carrying a box of motor oil. Already tall and built, he was even bigger than he'd been in the court-room, as if he spent a lot of those five years pumping iron. His black hair had grown and was pulled back in a thick, short tail. My heart pounding, I rushed up to him and it was the first thing I said. That I was so sorry. And that if he ever needed anything, I'd do everything I could to give it to him, because I could never repay him.

He gave me a narrowed look before nodding—then told me he never wanted to hear it again.

I never said it again.

And it isn't what I want to say now. Nine years have passed. I'm not bursting with guilt and gratitude anymore, though it still eats at me now and then. But life has moved on. I earned my bachelor's degree in organic chemistry and a master's in business administration before starting up my brewery. He bought a hole-in-the-wall dump, turned it into the Wolf Den, and took on the Hellfire Riders' presidency. Through the brewery and the bar, through my friendship with Anna, my path crosses his often enough. But I'm still Red's daughter. Saxon leads the Hellfire

Riders. And there are still rules. Territories. I can't risk stumbling over any lines again. Just coming here tonight walks the tight edge of one.

So it doesn't matter that I feel much more than gratitude toward him now. It doesn't matter that I can't look away. Seeing him standing there is a gift and a punishment all at once. There's no one in the world that I want more. There's no one I'm less likely to have.

Especially now, when I'll soon be leaving town. Knowing this is one of the last times I'll see him is a physical pain, a burning knot in my throat that tangles up with the knot in my chest.

I can't say any of that either. So I force a weak smile and a husky "Hey, Saxon."

He doesn't smile back. Instead his dark gaze falls to my mouth before sliding to the shot glass in my hand. Unlike most of the Hellfire Riders, he's not wearing his kutte now. Just worn denim and a faded black T-shirt stretched over hard muscle. In the past year, he's grown out a short beard. I've never been a fan of beards…until I saw Saxon's. His jaw is a sculpted wonder, and I never imagined he could look even better with it covered, but somehow he does. The beard doesn't conceal the shape of his jaw but just makes it seem even stronger—and the look fits him. Rugged and earthy.

To anyone who doesn't know him well, he probably just looks big and mean. I think he's sexy as fuck.

My entire body clenches as he steps in closer. His

voice is low and deep, with a rough edge, like coarse sheets at midnight. Hearing him speak always leaves me restless and too aware of my skin. "You needed a drink before coming to see me?"

What? I frown up at him. "No."

"Bullshit." It's evenly said. No anger or heat. He holds out his big hand. "Come on back then."

Suddenly warm and lightheaded, I just stare at his hand. I haven't drunk enough to begin imagining things. This is something else. Business I'd forgotten about? I've been in the back office with him before, but our contracts and delivery dates are set. Solid. They have been for a while.

"Jenny," Thorne says beside me. When I glance over, he's watching me with that steely look in his eyes that says these words are important and I'd best listen. "You don't do this for anyone unless you want it, you understand? Not for your old man. Not for me. Not for the Titans."

I don't understand. But I can't think, either, because Saxon's callused fingers slide between mine and he tugs me off the barstool. Every question building in my head is suddenly drowned out by the roar of my pulse.

He hasn't touched me before. Ever. Not even when he saved me from Reichmann.

I can't stop my fingers from tightening on his. Clinging to him, almost, but I can't make myself let go as he leads me toward the door. He could shake my grip so easily. There's so much strength in his hands. His arms. The short sleeves of his black shirt tightly hug his biceps.

My head barely reaches his shoulder.

But he doesn't shake me off. He holds on and I follow, my heart thundering.

A single bulb lights the paneled hallway. Nothing fancy back here. A storeroom. An office. Not much decoration, just a big desk supporting a sleek computer with a wide flat screen, and metal filing cabinets against the wall. Posters for beer festivals and veterans' rights rallies are tacked up beside a barred window overlooking the parking lot. The wall behind me is filled with employee-of-the-month plaques—all of them of Anna. She made them herself, and has been putting up a new goofy photo every month since she began working here. The first is dated almost six years ago.

Saxon closes the door, and the soft *thunk* of wood into the jamb suddenly transforms the pounding of my pulse into a riot of nerves. I pull my hand from his and face him, arms crossed beneath my breasts.

As soon as I meet his eyes, my anxiety increases. There's something different in the way he looks back at me. Not so…stoic. His expression never gives much away, even though you can tell there's always a lot going on behind it. Shadowed by heavy brows, his dark blue eyes are always intense. Always reading your face. Always assessing. When the Riders aren't calling him Prez, they call him by his road name, the Wolf—and his gaze is like a wolf's. Just steady. Waiting. Those eyes are a warning to anyone who meets him, because one look and you know through to your bones that if you make a wrong move, Saxon will tear you apart.

The way he looks at me now, it's as if it's too late for a warning. As if he isn't waiting to come after me, but on the verge of taking me down—and only a leash of sheer willpower holds him back.

Oh, God. Maybe I *have* stepped over the line. Spine rigid, I stare back at him.

He leans back against the door, crossing his arms over his broad chest. Mirroring me—and that's different, too. Usually he goes straight to his desk. Putting space between us or just trying to seem less intimidating by putting all that muscle behind a block of wood, I never know.

His heavy-lidded gaze slides down to my toes before coming back up. Gruffly he says, "You dressed up."

Not really. I'm just not in my usual jeans. I spent the evening wooing a pair of lawyers who are opening a new pub, so I wore heeled sandals and a black capri pantsuit, with my brown hair in a loose braid over my shoulder.

"I had business up in Bend," I tell him.

"You look good. You just got back?"

"Yes."

Slowly he nods. Though his posture is casual, the stillness of his body and the intensity of his gaze aren't. "Did you already decide, then? Or did you want to talk about it first?"

Okay. I've really missed something. "Decide what?"

For a long second, he says nothing at all, but I *see*

the leash on his control tighten—as if he was close to springing, but now is pulling himself back. "Have you talked to Red today?"

"My dad? Why?" Worry immediately shoots into my heart. Why would *Saxon* ask me if I'd talked to him? "Did something happen to him?"

His jaw clenches. He turns his head, not looking at me now, but as if he's walked into a situation that doesn't look anything like he expected and is searching for a new direction.

"Sax? Did something happen? Is that why Thorne is here?"

I hear the rising fear in my voice. He must hear it, too, because his gaze snaps back to mine. "Nothing happened. He's just fi— Nothing happened."

Fine. He'd bitten off the word quick. *So* quick. Because my dad isn't fine. And somehow, Saxon knows it.

I watch him carefully now. "What did he say to you?"

"Fuck." With a heavy sigh, he shakes his head. "You need to talk to him first."

"I'm asking you."

"And I'm telling you, Jenny. Talk to Red first."

Dammit. But even as I try to stare him down, I know he won't give in. Then his eyes narrow, and I realize that real trouble is heading my way.

He pushes away from the door. "If you haven't talked to him, why did you stop by?"

Fuck. *Fuck.* "To see Anna."

"Bullshit." Not evenly spoken now, but like the crack of a whip. "Don't fucking lie to me. Why'd you stop here? You wouldn't. *You* wouldn't, unless you had to. So why did you have to?"

He's still coming at me, all solid muscle and sharp focus. Breath shallow, I back into the file cabinets. The handles dig into my spine. "It was nothing, Sax."

"My house. My den. I decide what's *nothing*, princess." Gaze like iron, he traps me. His big hands grip the edge of the cabinets on either side of my shoulders, his powerful arms caging me in. "Now you tell me what brought you in or I'll fucking make you scream it."

"Bullshit," I throw back, lifting my chin. "You think I'll believe a line like that? Hellfire Riders don't hurt women."

"I didn't say I'd hurt you." Before I can make sense of that, he leans in, bringing his face closer to mine. His gaze softens as it searches my features. "You aren't afraid of me at all, are you?"

"No."

The breathless response probably sounds like fear. I'm trembling, too. Ten seconds ago I was tossing curses back at his face and now it's all I can do to hold his gaze. Because, God—he looks good. Not even dressed up. Just dark blue eyes and broad shoulders and tanned skin that I'd give anything to taste.

His gaze falls to my mouth. "I'd heard you were skittish with men. That you were afraid to let them touch you."

"You heard *what*?" My cheeks catch fire. I don't know

if I'm horrified or angry. It's true, almost every date I have turns into a disaster as soon as the guy touches more than my hand. But I didn't realize people were talking about those disasters. "Who said that?"

He doesn't tell me. Instead he eases his grip on the cabinet, watching my face as his long fingers push aside my braid and his thumb traces a path down the side of my neck. "This doesn't scare you, does it?"

Aside from a shake of my head, I can't reply. Only stare up at him, feeling that touch like a shiver over every inch of my skin. My silk camisole suddenly seems as harsh as burlap, and every panting breath rasps the material against my sensitive nipples, drawing them tighter.

His thumb pauses over my racing pulse. "You're sure?"

"Yes."

Not scared. But I'm not prepared. No matter how many times I've thought about him touching me, dreamed of it, his simple caress quickly undoes everything within me. Unravels my brain. Undermines my strength.

"Then I intend to kiss you, Jenny," he says, and my knees almost give out.

A kiss. *A kiss.* First his touch. Now this. My fingers tighten on his forearms, his warm flesh like steel. I can't even remember reaching for him, supporting myself against him.

He still watches me. The wolf, waiting. "You're not afraid of that?"

"No." Just desperate for it.

Saxon's gaze never leaves mine as his head lowers. His voice is rough. "You're shaking."

"Only because it's you," I say just before his mouth claims mine.

A kiss, he said. Saxon Gray doesn't know the meaning of the word. His big hands come up to cradle my jaw and his tongue strokes between my lips. Tasting me. Devouring me. Need twists me up with that single lick into the heat of my mouth, tearing open a hollow ache inside. The next thrust of his tongue draws a ragged moan from deep in my throat, then a soft cry as he pushes closer, the hard length of his body against the softness of mine.

"So fucking hot," he growls against my lips. "You and me, Jenny. We're gonna burn up together."

His mouth takes mine again. Not a kiss. Possession. His hands slide down to my ass and he hefts me up, wrapping my legs around his lean hips and settling in, rigid and thick and right where I need him most. He rocks against me, slowly at first, then harder, as if he can screw his way into me right through our clothes. The cabinet handles jab rhythmically into my back and I don't care, I don't care. His tongue fucks my mouth in deep strokes and my pussy begins clenching as if he's stroking that big cock inside me, instead. Mindless with need, I grind against him, wishing my pants gone, his jeans gone, and nothing between us but slick, hot skin.

Then he goes still and I whimper in desperate frustration. His fingers push into the hair at my nape and he holds me pinned against the cabinet with my legs circling his waist and my body aching.

"Why'd you come, Jenny?"

His hoarse question barely penetrates. I *haven't* come. That's the problem now.

"Jenny." Long fingers tighten in my hair. "Why'd you stop by?"

My chest seems suddenly squeezed by those same fingers. I look up. Saxon's dark blue eyes are steady on mine. Waiting.

He said he'd make me scream my answer to him. I didn't scream. But I panted and moaned.

Now the ache that fills me isn't need. Just embarrassment. Anger. And the pain of realizing just how stupid I am. That wasn't a kiss. Saxon just wanted my guard down so that I'll tell him what he wants to know.

I should have realized, though. I should have guessed. Where Saxon is concerned, nothing is pure heaven. There's always the hell, too.

"Get off me," I say, but my throat is so thick that barely a whisper emerges.

Saxon must have heard me, because he sets my feet down. I turn away from him, folding my arms over my aching stomach. I don't know if I'm going to cry or be sick.

He's still right behind me. "Why'd you—"

"Just let it go!" I close my eyes against their burning. "Please."

The harsh sound of his breathing fills the silence. Then

he says softly, "Should I go ask Anna, instead?"

"You asshole." I whirl and shove at his chest—and get nowhere, except more pissed. "You wouldn't ever ask any of your brothers to snitch on each other. Don't you put that shit on her, making her choose between her boss or her friend."

"So I'm an asshole. And you're hiding something you believe would be a snitch." He catches my wrists in a tight grip. "Was it the Eighty-Eight? Were they hassling you?"

"No!" Damn it all. He *will* ask Anna. "They were behind me when I got off the highway. So I pulled in here, just in case. But as far as I could tell, they were just passing through. I don't even think they recognized me. So it was nothing."

His eyes blaze. "You know Reichmann's brother is running their house now? You know the shit he's stirring up about you?"

That I'm a cocktease. That I've fucked all the Titans and deliberately put myself in front of his brother at the rally, to start a fight between the clubs, to see him killed. And that I deserve to get a real fucking now.

Saxon is the one who'd killed the man's brother, but Reichmann is either too cowardly or too smart to gun for him. That's probably why Reichmann focused on me— because there is actually some chance of getting to me and taking his revenge.

"I heard," I say quietly.

"You heard." With an enraged snarl, Saxon yanks me

closer. "And you're telling me that it's fucking *nothing*?"

"Yes." I don't know where my sudden calm comes from. Maybe I just don't have anything else left. "Because I'm leaving."

"You just downed two shots and a beer," he says through gritted teeth. "You think I'm letting you drive out of here?"

"No." I wouldn't be that stupid. "I mean that I'm leaving town. So it won't matter what the Eighty-Eight wants to do to me, because I'll be gone."

I've never seen Saxon staggered by anything. I've watched him hear out a guilty verdict and a prison sentence with no more reaction than a tilt of his head and a nod of acceptance. Now he stares at me, his face a rigid mask, his lips edged with white. "You're *what*?"

"I decided today. I'm selling the brewery. And just getting out." God, and my calm is already cracking. Apparently I do have more left inside me—and it all hurts. "Because the cops can't do anything until Reichmann actually touches me, and by that time I'll already have been gang-raped. Maybe worse. So if I stay, either I'll end up hurt, or someone who tries to protect me will."

Expression savage, he shoves his face into mine. "Over. My. Dead. Fucking. Body."

"That's the point," I say on a shuddering breath, and he jerks away, releasing my wrists.

"No." He stares at me, his jaw working. Tightening his own leash again. Finally he growls, "You stay *right* here.

I'll be back in one minute. Don't you fucking try to slip out the back."

I wouldn't. I'm running from the Eighty-Eight Henchmen, not from Saxon. At my nod, he rips open the door and stalks out. I hear him roaring for Stone.

My legs are shaking. All of me is shaking—and tears are far too close. Taking shallow breaths, trying to loosen the thick knot in my throat, I sink into the chair facing the desk and cover my mouth with trembling hands.

So this is it. My life shattered by the abnormal cells going apeshit in my dad's lungs and some supremacist with a grudge. I need to just pick up the pieces and go.

But there are going to be so many pieces missing. My dad, the biggest. Along with Thorne, Anna. They've been a part of my life for so long. Knowing they soon won't be hurts almost more than I can bear.

And Saxon. I don't know why the thought of never seeing him again tears me apart like this—as if I'm letting go. Even though I've never had him.

Except one kiss.

My lips still feel hot and swollen. Branded. As if he marked me as his.

He doesn't need to. I've been Saxon Gray's for a long time now. I don't know how long, exactly. Maybe since the rally. The courtroom. Outside the auto shop, or sometime during all the years following.

Or since the letter. *Don't you EVER be sorry.*

I hadn't done a good job of not being sorry before. I

will now. No excuses. No apologies. Just do what I need to do, the best that I can do it—and never be sorry for it.

"Jenny."

God. Just hearing his voice hurts. Heart aching, I glance over. Saxon stands at the office's entrance. He's wearing his kutte now, and the leather vest makes him look even bigger, meaner. His hands grip either side of the door frame and his arms are tightly flexed, as if he's bracing himself against the wood—or stopping himself from coming through.

His hard blue gaze never leaves my face. "We're running the route back to the highway, then to your place, and making sure those fuckers aren't waiting. When you're ready to go, Thorne will ride with you. A few more of us will follow as escort. All right?"

Throat thick, I nod. "Thank you."

For a moment I think he'll throw my gratitude back in my face. Instead his voice is like dark, rough asphalt when he asks, "You sold your equipment yet? Take any jobs?"

Pain squeezes my chest. "Not yet. I planned to make a few calls tomorrow. I've had offers before."

"Of course you have. You're smart as fuck and any joint that sells your beer knows they'll never have anything better. Only someone with piss for brains wouldn't want you." His fingers tighten on the door frame. "But there's one more offer coming. Maybe another option. So don't make any decisions just yet."

"What option?"

"Talk to Red. You working tomorrow?"

Working? I'm always working. And my mind is scrambling to catch up.

Tomorrow. Saturday. During tourist season. "I'll be at the barn all day. I've got tours and the tasting room from noon to six."

"I'll come for you at six, then."

Come for me? "Sax—"

"You talk to your dad." Abruptly he pulls back. "Then you'll tell me if you want what he lays out. And you need to *want* it. All right?"

And whatever that is, Saxon won't tell me now. That much is clear.

Mutely, I nod. A second later he's gone.

THREE

It's after midnight when I pull up to the house. My high beams catch my dad waiting on the porch. He squints into the glare and I quickly flick off my headlights.

The rumble of Thorne's bike is already fading when I get out of the truck. The Hellfire Riders escorted us to the long driveway leading to the house and continued past, staying on the main road. Uncle Thorne followed me part of the way up the drive, up to the point where our paths split—mine toward home, his to the clubhouse and cabins on the opposite side of the property. Everything else is quiet. Just the singing crickets and the cooling tick of my engine. All the lights are off in the house. The stars are brilliant above, like diamond dust scattered across the heavens. There's nothing as beautiful as the sky over central Oregon on a clear summer night. When I was younger, my dad, my mom, and I used to lie out in the yard on a blanket, content just to look up.

Aside from the years I was away at college, I've lived here all of my life. I love the old ranch house with its white siding and tall gables. It's probably too much house for just two people, but my dad has made it ours over the years, renovating the tight rooms into spaces filled with light and air.

Usually it doesn't matter what sort of day I've had—coming home seems to lift whatever weight I carry. Not tonight. Tension knots my shoulders and neck as I climb the porch stairs.

Dad is only a shadow on a deck chair, but it's so easy to picture what I can't see through the dark. Tall and lean, with grizzled red hair and a short white beard—and wearing the same jeans, boots, and T-shirt combination that he always does. I hear the clink of a bottle against glass.

I sink into the chair beside him, then take the whiskey he offers—and wonder if the drink is to soothe my nerves or his. He isn't usually so quiet.

Which means one thing. "Uncle Thorne called you?"

"He did."

"I was all right."

"Since I'm sitting here instead of tailing you home, you know he told me that, too."

I nod, sipping the whiskey and holding it on my tongue, because if I swallow I'll have no reason not to ask him what this other option is. Better to let him start.

His heavy sigh fills the space between us. "Did you talk to Saxon?"

"Only a little." And kissed him. Wrapped my legs tight around him. But the memory doesn't make me hot now; it only makes my heart ache. "He said I needed to talk to you. I told him I was selling the brewery and leaving town."

His chair creaks as he leans forward. "Do you want to?"

No. Throat suddenly tight, I shake my head. My voice is a strained whisper. "It just seems like the only thing to do."

"Wait for me to die and then go?"

"*Jesus*, Daddy." The tears spill fast, before I can stop them. He's always blunt. But how could he put it that way? "Taking care of you. Then taking care of myself."

"There's only one part of that I give a shit about, and it ain't the part where you're taking care of me."

"And if you think I'm going to leave you alone, then fuck your lungs, because the doctors obviously forgot to look for the tumors in your brain!"

He snorts. "That's my girl. So dry up now. You know I can't stand strong when you're crying. And I need to stand strong now, Jenny."

The husky catch in his voice as he speaks my name almost breaks me again. But I won't let him down. If he can stand strong, then I can, too—so I suck up the tears and down the whiskey, bracing myself for whatever is coming.

A lighter flicks, revealing his face in the glow as he lights a cigarette. He's watching me, his eyes the same pale green as mine.

"Dad," I say softly. He quit smoking years ago.

"It don't matter now, does it? I stopped too late." His right shoulder lifts in a careless shrug, but after a long draw, he grinds out the cigarette. "But the secondhand ain't good for you, I guess. Now, you tell me what you want to do when I'm gone. You want to stay here at the ranch? Or you want to give up the brewery?"

With a sigh, I pull my feet up to the edge of the seat and wrap my arms around my knees. "I want to stay. Of course I want to stay."

"But the Eighty-Eight are going to keep fucking with you."

Sudden fear spears my heart. "You aren't thinking of—"

"Killing every last Henchman? Yeah, I think it. Every single fucking day, I think it. What do I have to lose?" The whiskey bottle clinks against the rim of his glass as he pours another. "But I ain't some fool to risk that, Jenny. Say I get some of them, but not all. The rest will be out for revenge—and not the kind Reichmann is stirring up. That just passes the time for most of them. It's a bit of enter-tainment. None of them except for Reichmann are boiling angry. That would change if I went after them. Maybe they'd even bring in Henchmen from other chapters. Then it'd be all-out war between a national club and us. No question who'd lose. So I'd be hurting you by touching any one of them."

And that pisses him off. His voice has taken on a hard edge I know well. Dad *would* stop the Eighty-Eight Henchmen by killing them, if he could—and he wouldn't care if he spends the rest of his life behind bars for it.

I care. "Promise me you won't."

"I won't promise. But it's not in my sights right now."

"What is?"

He takes his time. Gathering his thoughts, maybe. Or just enjoying the whiskey. Finally he says, "I used to be a Rider, you know. Second to Tommy Burns."

Lily the Viking's father, and former president of the Hellfire Riders. "I know."

"I never said anything to you about it."

"Uncle Thorne did once, after I asked him why there'd been bad blood between you and the Riders."

"Huh." The bland tone is a deceptive one; fifteen years ago, my dad's response would have indicated that Thorne had earned an ass-kicking. Now it just means that he's annoyed. "Did he say why we left and started up the Steel Titans?"

"He said you and Tommy Burns split over a woman."

"Bullshit."

"'Bullshit' because Uncle Thorne wouldn't say that? Or 'bullshit', it wasn't a woman?"

"It wasn't a woman. Not really. Tommy and me had our eye on the same one. Megan Fitzgerald. Tommy eventually got her, and sure enough, I wasn't none too happy about it. I thought I was in love—of course, I didn't know what that was until your mom came along. At the time, though, it stung deep. But never would I have let a woman come between me and my brothers. He got her; I let her go."

"Then what happened?"

"Tommy let her get between us." In the shadows, he shakes his head. "Nah, not even that's right. She didn't get between us. Tommy's prick did. Because me and Megan had been riding together a few times, you know what I mean?"

Oh, God. I prefer not to think about my dad having sex. "So he was jealous?"

"Like a fucking bull. Always snorting in my face. Touching her around me, kissing her. Making sure I knew she was his, though I wasn't likely to forget."

"So *he* was the one who didn't put the bros before the hos."

A laugh barks from him and ends as a ragged cough. "Christ, Jenny. You'll kill me saying shit like that."

He thumps his chest and takes a long breath. It sounds even and smooth, but my own throat and lungs are aching, making it hard for me to breathe. I wait for him to continue.

"Anyway. He decided to marry her, then put some crazy shit in the club bylaws. This was before there was real structure, you know? Nothing real official, no real voting, not like we have now."

"What kind of crazy?"

"Everyone had to watch him fuck her and then join in. That was supposed to prove they thought she was worthy of everyone there; then they'd swear their loyalty and protection." Another laugh runs beneath the statement. No coughing this time. Just a laugh that rolls harder with every word, as if each one sounds stupider than the last. "At the time, it was a kick in the face. But just imagine the whole scene—sitting there as Tommy banged away, while we bowed our heads or some shit—"

His laughter gets in the way of talking then, and it does sound silly, but it's hard to laugh along with him when I can hear the wheeze beneath his breath.

He wipes his eyes. "God damn. But I was so pissed. I left before it ever happened—I just wasn't going to be a part of that. To my mind, Tommy let his dick take over the club. So Thorne and I walked. It wasn't much later that Grandpop left me this place. It's been the Titans' home ever since. That's what I'm thinking of when I'm not thinking of you."

So we're finally getting around to it. "Do you think I'll be upset if you leave the property to Uncle Thorne or the club? Because I won't."

"It's yours, Jenny." His tone tells me not to argue.

"Then they've still got a home. Even if I leave." I can rent out the house, maybe. "And if I don't leave…well, Uncle Thorne will look out for me. You know he will."

"Yeah," says my dad softly—agreement, but with reservations. "Thorne ain't young, Jenny. And the Titans aren't as strong as we once were."

I can't say anything. Not a thing. I can't imagine what it took for him to speak those words. And I know they are true words. The club isn't getting much new blood and they've been losing territory. Not through fights or power plays; it's just slipping away. Joints that were once exclusively theirs just aren't anymore. Such as this one tavern out near the county line—the Barracks. Not so long ago, it was like the Wolf Den. If you belonged to another club, you risked an ass-kicking simply by stepping inside without the Titans' okay. It isn't like that anymore. A rowdy mix of riders—including the Eighty-Eight—usually hang out at the Barracks now. But the Titans weren't *pushed* out. They've just let it go. When the guys aren't out riding, most of them pass the time at the clubhouse on the ranch, instead.

But there is one club that hasn't weakened, and heat shoots up beneath my skin as I suddenly realize where he's going with this. He'd talked to Saxon.

Saxon, who has already protected me once.

And who is president of a rival club. Just because there

isn't bad blood between them anymore—there hasn't been since Saxon stepped into Tommy Burns' boots—doesn't mean that my dad isn't stirring up some serious shit here. How are the Titans going to take the news that my dad went to Saxon for this?

Yet…he must have already talked to Uncle Thorne about it, because Thorne had been at the Wolf Den. I didn't notice any anger there. If anything, Uncle Thorne was just concerned.

You don't do this for anyone unless you want it, you understand? Not for your old man. Not for me. Not for the Titans.

What will I be doing?

"We're going to fold the clubs together," my dad says. "The Titans, the Hellfire Riders."

In the dark, he probably can't see the way my mouth gapes open. "You can do that?"

"If we don't, the Titans won't last long. Thorne will hold them together for a while. But when he's done? It'll fall to shit. We've got good men but there ain't a lot of ambition between them, and the ones who do have ambition don't have a lot of brains. They'll be in over their heads real fast. So you tell me true, Jenny—how are you going to feel having them on the property after Thorne is gone?"

Not so good. I know all the guys. I like a lot of them. But my dad has read them right. It will probably end up a lot like the Barracks. Without a strong presence to lead them, the good ones will slowly drift away, and the only thing left will be chaos. Except this time, that chaos wouldn't be out at the county line but real close to home.

"So you talked to Saxon?" My voice sounds heavy. "You approached him with this?"

"Yeah. He's willing."

I just can't believe it. "Some of your guys walked away from the Riders when Lily joined them. They turned in their colors. He's going to take *them* back? No way."

"I wouldn't either. But I said to him that I knew what it was to walk out in anger—and I knew what it was to see a club change for the better. Maybe he'll give them a chance. Maybe they won't want one. Either way, it's a rough couple of months coming. But Saxon's not just getting trouble in return for this. He wants the clubhouse and use of the land out there."

So close. He'll be so close.

I try to ignore the knot of nerves tightening in my stomach. He's never been *that* far away. Pine Valley isn't exactly a huge distance from here.

But I still don't understand what my part in this is, aside from being a bit safer from the Eighty-Eight than I would be without the Hellfire Riders' strong presence so near. "Is he worried that I'll prevent the Riders from taking over the clubhouse? I won't. He can have it."

"That's not what he's worried about. That's not what *I'm* worried about. Because Reichmann ain't likely to risk riding out here to the ranch, but when you're out there working? Driving around like you were tonight? When I'm gone, Jenny, there's no family connection. He's going to think you're unprotected."

"But Saxon will let everyone know—"

"Just *saying* it ain't enough. Not with fuckers like Reichmann and the way they think of women. If she's got tits, then someone owns her. And if she ain't claimed, she's free game and he won't think there's any retaliation coming. Not from anyone he needs to fear, anyway."

I can hardly breathe. "What are *you* saying?"

"I'm saying that Saxon knows why I'm asking this, and that it's all about you. About making sure you're all right." His voice is grim. "And he doesn't just want the clubhouse. He wants the package deal. But that's up to you."

Up to me. A package deal. So what is it that Saxon wants from me—sex in exchange for protection?

Now I know why he kissed me tonight, after all these years of never showing interest. He was sampling the goods.

I feel sick. Hot tears clog my throat. "Daddy," I whisper.

"It's up to you, Jenny," he repeats and his strong hands enfold mine. "But you always look at him different than other men. You talk about him different. And I also know you wouldn't have ever looked too long, no matter if you wanted to. Not at a Rider, and not knowing what trouble might come of it. So I thought it was worth putting in front of you. Whether or not you take it is your choice."

My choice. To have the man I've wanted for so long. To be safe.

Except I won't be safe. Not really. My body won't be

in as much danger, true.
    But my heart will be.

FOUR

After a sleepless night, I'm up early. The tasting room is open today, so I forego my usual jeans and tee in favor of a short black skirt, a black T-shirt with ripped-off sleeves sporting a worn Led Zeppelin logo, and black shitkickers that lace up to my knees. A costume, basically, but one that fits the brewery's theme—the Black Boots Brewery, serving up beer that kicks ass.

It's all a gimmick, but one that I put a ridiculous amount of research into. It sells particularly well with my target demographics: young urbanites who appreciate the humorous marketing angle—which could include almost everyone I went to college with—and the working class Joe who prefers a craft beer. Black Boots. Solid, dependable, and completely tongue-in-cheek.

Just the thought of giving it up makes my chest feel tight.

I've put so much work into this place, from renovating the barn to securing the loan for the stainless steel brewhouses to hanging up the T-shirts that I sell in the storefront. This brewery started as my baby, but I took it from crawling along to standing on its own feet, and now it's running smoothly. Someone else *could* take over at this point. But it's mine, and I'm so fucking proud of it all. I don't want to see it in someone else's hands.

But if I stay, I'm risking more than my business. I'm risking my life. My heart, too.

That heart feels as heavy as lead as I unlock the doors. I've still got a few hours before I open to visitors, but there's more than enough work to fill the time. No two batches are ever quite the same, so monitoring the progress through brewing and fermentation is a critical part of the job.

When I give tours, people always ask me what the most important part of the process is. Many of them simply like beer and are curious, but sometimes the question comes from home brewers. Some of them don't like the real answer—that there's no one factor that's more important than any other. Even the smallest variable can create significant changes in taste and quality. So after I say that, I tell them that as long as they're starting with good ingredients, then it's down to two things: temperature and time. Too hot or too cold, let it sit too long or not long enough, and the batch goes off.

I'm like a brew going bad today. By midmorning, I'm hot as hell, in a temper and wishing that Saxon would show up so that I could tell him exactly what I think of his package deal. Then I imagine all the things I'd do to him in my bed and that deal starts looking really good. After a while, I'm cold again, thinking of being traded like some piece of property—even pissed at my dad, because he said that was how the Eighty-Eight looked at women and I didn't see any difference between that and what he and Saxon were proposing—but then feeling shitty and ungrateful, because he only wants to see me safe.

But by the time six o'clock rolls around I'm hot and bitter again, and irritated by a group of frat boys who are taking their sweet time picking out their mini-kegs. One of them is hanging by the bar, sampling his way through an ale flight and flirting with me. He's not good at it, and when he comments on the flavors he comes off really fucking patronizing, as if it never occurs to him that the petite girl behind the counter isn't just some monkey trained to sell beer but might actually be the one running this whole show.

He's asking me what time I close up shop when I hear the distinctive rumble of a Harley-Davidson coming up the drive. I'm feeling just mean enough to enjoy the frat boys' unease as Saxon comes in, a big biker with his "President" patch beneath his club tag and road name. The Wolf.

The big bad fucking wolf, boys. I don't know if they can read the other patches. There aren't a lot of them. Unlike some bikers who cover the front of their kuttes with anything that takes their fancy in addition to the patches they've earned, Saxon's is pretty clear, which tells me that the ones he does wear mean a lot more to him. The skull and crossbones is for Timothy Reichmann. Maybe Saxon hadn't intended to kill him with that boot to the head, but he had, and he obviously doesn't regret it. He wears that patch just below his one-percent diamond. A big *FTW* decorates the bottom left side of his vest.

Fuck the world. That's my favorite one. And it's the way I feel right now.

His dark blue eyes catch mine and it's like the whole day just comes back over me all at once. Cold. Hot. Need.

I don't want him to see the hurt that joins it and turn my attention back to the guy sampling the ales. He's quiet now, and I'm grateful that Saxon's presence seems to be hurrying them all along, even though he hasn't done anything but look around the store a bit. His first time here. While the frat boys are filling out the keg deposit form, I draw him a cold one. He offers a gravelly thanks when I give him the pint, and his gaze runs to my toes before lifting to my face. *God.* A man doesn't need to flirt when he looks at a woman the way Saxon is looking at me.

He hasn't seen me in clothes like this before, either, I

realize. It's possible that he hasn't seen so much of my legs since the day Reichmann attacked me. Obviously he likes what he sees.

Maybe he's already thinking they're his. Two legs, included as part of the package deal.

Renewed anger adds to the building heat. I return to the counter and finish ringing up the sale, throwing in a few complimentary T-shirts because no matter how irritating college boys can be, if they're walking around wearing my logo it's free advertising. The bell over the door chimes as they leave. I stay at the counter, closing out the register, acutely aware of every step that brings Saxon closer.

Carefully, he sets his pint on the bar. He's barely drunk any of it. "You talk to your dad?"

"I did." It's sharp. I don't care. I'm burning with temper and fanning the flames, because if I don't only the hurt will be left. "It sounds like you both have it all worked out."

He's quiet for a second. "Only if you want it."

"What I want?" I yank out the cash drawer and slam the register closed before heading to the bar. Glass clatters as I dump his pint and shove the glass into the dishwasher. "You can have the clubhouse, the cabins on the property. We'll work out a lease."

His throat works. He looks away from me and there's something I can't read in his face. Not just his usual stoicism, though there's that. The stone in his expression is harder than ever, but there's a crack through it in the tightening of his jaw and the flattening of his gaze. "If that's what you want."

"It is. And you'll pay me every month in my bed."

All at once his eyes are back on me, narrowed and dangerous. "I'll do what?"

"What?" I throw back at him, wide-eyed. "Are you telling me that selling yourself doesn't feel so good? Because being told I'll be protected in exchange for fucking you feels pretty shitty."

"An exchange? That's what you think I'm asking for?"

"Oh, my dad explained it. You want the package deal. The clubhouse and the land out there. And you'll be claiming me so that Reichmann is less likely to try something." My chest is heaving as I stalk out from behind the bar. "Like I'm just another cabin on the property and you're tagging the walls."

"Tagging the walls?" He's pissed now too, and when he comes for me there's nowhere to go, backing me up against the front counter and caging me in with powerful arms. Teeth clenched, he gets in my face. "If I was tagging you, princess, I'd be jerking off all over your sweet little ass. No, fuck jerking off. I've done that enough thinking of you. So I'd bury my cock inside you, then fuck your pussy deep and hard, and when I'm finally ready to blow I'll pull out and tag you then."

Not a chance in fucking hell. I open my mouth to tell him but he doesn't give me time to even draw a breath before he's on me, a kiss like fire and tasting of beer. Damn him. I want him too much and I can't fight like this. But I try, though I'm surrounded. He's so big, his body like a wall. The counter is behind me. Desperate, I bite his tongue. His head jerks back and he growls as he spins me around, bending me over the counter, pushing me down with his forearm at my back. His stiff cock wedges against my ass.

His mouth is hot at the back of my neck. "You want it like this between us instead of how I offered? You want me to pay with a fucking? It doesn't matter to me. I'll take you any way I can get you. Slide your skirt up and I'll put in my down payment now."

My hands are braced beside me. He could reach my skirt easier than I can. But I realize what he's doing. This will be my choice. If I want it like this, I just have to do as he says. Then maybe he'll fuck me until all this anger and hurt goes away.

But it doesn't matter if it does go away. Because I'll take him any way that I can get him, too, and I've always known that having him would never be easy. Expecting hell, I yank the short hem of my skirt higher.

I get heaven, instead.

"Fuck," Saxon breathes the curse. His fingers are gentle, sliding over the curve of my ass, tracing the lacy edge of my black panties, and all of a sudden he's laughing. "You get me so wound up, Jenny. So pissed that you think this is what I'm here for. But now I've got you bent over, the truth is I'd love to see my cum painting this ass. Jesus,

I could tag you all night."

The pressure against my back eases. He turns me to face him before setting me on the counter, the surface cold beneath my thighs. I realize he's not going to fuck me after all and it's too much. In an instant, everything builds up. My dad's cancer. This shitty day. Having Saxon so close but not *having* him, and I'm fighting so hard not to cry.

Fighting and losing.

"Shh." Voice low, he's kissing me softly. "I know this has all been rough on you. I shouldn't be, too. But I'm a rough man. You'd be better off with someone like those kids that just left. One's going to be a lawyer or some shit."

The thought of it almost makes me laugh. I know a lot of guys like that. Not all of them as irritating as the frat boys. Most are decent, some are even smart and funny and sexy. "They're not what I want."

"What do you want, then?"

So much. "I don't want to lose my dad. I don't want to worry about the Eighty-Eight. I don't want to move away."

Gently his hands cradle my jaw and he tilts my head back until my eyes meet his. They're dark and intense and dead serious. "I can't give you all of that. But what I can, Jenny, I will. Whether you take me or not."

A package deal. I don't know how to answer. But maybe I don't need to. His thumb sweeps across my trembling lips and he lowers his head, his mouth catching mine, and suddenly I feel like crying all over again. Not out of hurt this time, but because he's right here, muscles like steel and his kiss stirring a fire inside me, burning away pain and doubt and leaving behind nothing but need. He crowds closer, pulling me against him until my ass is at the edge of the counter and my legs are wrapped around his waist. Moaning, I lean back, bracing my weight on my elbows and he comes with me, his body flush against mine. He grinds his cock between my thighs and I can't stop myself, I'm grinding back, riding the hard ridge of his erection and wishing it wasn't covered in denim, wishing he was already inside me.

Suddenly he lifts his head, his breathing harsh. "Oh, fuck, Jenny. I meant to be sweet. But I'm not."

Maybe not. But this is the sweetest pleasure I've ever known. Fiercely, I pull him close again. "This is exactly what I need."

Someone rough. Someone to sand away all of the painful edges.

But not *someone*. Just Saxon.

His mouth takes mine again and this time he's not holding back his hunger. He tastes my lips, my throat, then hauls up my shirt and sucks hard on my nipple while his left hand pushes between us. His fingers find lace soaked in my arousal and he groans against my breast before lifting his head.

"You're so fucking wet." His voice deepens. "Tell me it's all mine."

His fingertips are tracing the shape of my pussy through the lace and I can barely form a coherent thought, let alone words. I strain closer, riding his hand, and my response emerges as a moan. *"Yours."*

His. For so long.

"Then I'm going to eat it all up." His eyes gleam up at me and he lowers his head again, softly pinching my nipple between his teeth at the same time his fingers slide beneath the edge of my panties. I cry out, my back arching. Saxon groans and sucks hard at my sensitive flesh, his fingers stroking through my drenched pussy and circling my clit. "God, Jenny. You're already wetter. Even if I lick it up, you'll still make more for me, won't you? And even more when I'm inside you. I can't wait to feel this pussy juice sliding all over my cock."

Sliding. Drowning. I'm sprawled beside the register in my tasting room, skirt hiked around my waist, and Saxon is teasing the entrance to my cunt with blunt fingers, his teeth tugging my nipple to a burning point. The door is still unlocked and I don't even care, let everyone in the world come in, just don't ever let Saxon stop what he's doing.

My body clenches uncontrollably when he pushes his longest finger as deep as he can. Oh, God. My hips jerk, the motion pushing him harder into me, his thumb rubbing mercilessly over my clit and I'm biting the back of my hand to stop myself from screaming.

I'm so wet. I can hear the slick luscious sounds of his finger pumping into me over the noises I'm making, wild little grunts and moans that I can't stop. He's looking up at my face, intense blue eyes seeing everything I can't hide. I'm not like this. I'm never like this. Anyone else touches me and I freeze up, but I'm a volcano with him, heat and pressure rising so quickly, with quakes of need trembling through my burning flesh. I'm working up to an explosion, and I've had that before. I've used toys and vibrators and my own fingers. But it wasn't like this. He's got just one finger inside me and I feel so full, fuller than I've ever been, though some of my toys are bigger. The sensation of something filling my cunt has never felt so vivid before.

I've never felt this vivid before. Every gasp of air is sweeter, my skin tighter, as if my body can barely contain the devastating pleasure that's building inside me with every thrust of his hand.

Suddenly I'm overwhelmed. *All these years.* All these years of dating and all those disasters and all those nights of coming home to my empty bed, where I imagined that every dildo was Saxon's cock, and every vibrator was his tongue against my clit. I thought that was pleasure, but compared to the reality of his touch those sensations were so faint, so *nothing*, and all at once everything that came before feels wasted and worthless.

I was okay before this. Satisfied. Content.

Knowing now what was missing, I never will be again. Not without him.

That isn't something I want to learn. The sudden pain in my heart lends a sharp edge to the pleasure, but even that is better than any pain before. My breath comes in desperate sobs. The inner muscles of my pussy ache from squeezing him tighter and tighter, my body winding higher with every slick thrust, every slide of his thumb over my clit. One finger-fuck in my brewery and I'm ruined, ruined, and I don't even care why he wants me now. I just need him to fuck me harder.

But he's slowing a little. "You all right?"

Before I can stop it my head shakes *No*, but for the wrong reason. He's slowing, and I can't bear it. I manage a breathless, "Don't stop."

He doesn't, but he's still careful, still watching me, and his voice is rough and low. "Is this giving you bad times?"

I know what he means. I don't know if he saw exactly what Reichmann had done to me at that rally but he heard me testify in court, heard every detail of how the bastard had shoved his fingers into me and made me bleed.

This isn't the same. It could never be the same. But to even ask me whether it was, Saxon must have seen my pain. He must have worried.

I shake my head and my response almost slips out. *I'm sorry.*

But I'm not going to be sorry. Not ever again.

And *never* sorry for this. No matter how much it ends up hurting. If I shatter, I can pick up the pieces later. But for now, I'll take the pain in my heart, and love the sharp edges that make my whole body shake with ecstasy, with need as hard and as brilliant as a diamond.

I'll take it all and make it sharper. I look up at him, my

chest rising on ragged breaths, my nipples reddened by the rough ministrations of his mouth. Boldly my hands cup my breasts, thumbs flicking over the taut peaks, and each little tease seems to tug on every nerve between the hardened tips and my drenched core.

Saxon's concern fades. Stark hunger replaces it.

Another blunt finger slides in to join the first, thrusting deep. Helplessly I moan his name, assaulted by excruciating pleasure and the stinging burn of his invasion. I'm too full now. None of my toys stretch me like this—and none make me lift my hips, seeking more.

"Like that, Jenny. *Fuck.*" With one hand pumping into me, Saxon roughly grips my thigh and shoves my knee back toward my shoulder, spreading me wide. I'm still wearing my panties and the lace running between my legs is stretched tight alongside his penetrating fingers and soaked in my arousal. He watches his fingers sink into my clenching heat, his teeth gritted, his face a mask of tension. "Look at you. Not skittish. Just so fucking sexy—and so fucking tight. It's going to take forever to work my cock all the way into you."

Denim is straining over the thick ridge of his erection. I need that hard length inside me. "Please, Saxon. Now."

My breathless plea is answered by a possessive growl and he leans in. He's still holding my legs open, my booted ankle is over his shoulder, and as he bends over to claim my mouth the pressure of his weight between my thighs shoves his hand hard against me, into me. Hot and deep, he kisses me, and I'm trembling and on the edge when he lifts his head.

"You'll take all of me?" His fingers press deeper as he asks, and I cry out, pushing back against him. "Tell me, Jenny. You want my mouth, my hands, my cock?"

I can only gasp "yes" and my fingers slide between us, because he's stopped working my clit and I'm so close. *So close.* But he catches me, snagging my wrist and dragging my hand away, my fingertips slick with my arousal.

"That's mine, princess," he warns and his heated mouth closes around my fingers, sucking away my juices. "My cock is all yours. This pussy is mine."

Sharp frustration bites at me. "Then I want your cock now."

He grins. "It's yours, but I didn't say you get to decide what to do with it."

"You sure as hell decided what to do with my pussy."

"That I did." As if to emphasize his reply, he sinks his fingers into me again, his thumb rubbing over my clit. "Because I'm bigger, stronger, and the first time I fuck you it's not going to be on this counter. So I'm just going to eat you up and watch you come."

Oh, God. "Then I guess I'll let you keep your cock in your pants."

He laughs, a low rumble that dissolves into a groan when he licks my fingers again. Abruptly he lets go of my wrist and palms the underside of my left thigh, holding me open with my knee against my shoulder.

A whimper escapes me as his fingers slide out of my pussy and grip the waist of my panties, dragging the lace down over my hips. But they can't go far, not with my legs spread, until he pushes my right knee up to my shoulder and I feel folded in half, exposed and suddenly uncertain.

Then he bends his head, his mouth takes possession of my needy flesh and I can't feel anything but Saxon tasting me, his tongue sweeping up between the lips of my cunt in long, broad strokes, as if my pussy is melting ice cream and he refuses to waste a single creamy drop.

He slowly licks a path from my entrance to my clit, ignoring my pleas for him to go faster, harder. The grip of his big hands on my legs is immovable, but I can't stop myself from struggling against it—not trying to get away but I can barely breathe, barely think. My knees are raised and spread, I'm completely open to him and he's thrusting his tongue into me now, then sliding up to tease my clit before doing it all over again. The sensations are so intense, whips of pleasure flaying my nerves, and I'm desperate to relieve the building pressure. I squirm and cry out but his hands tighten, pushing my legs wider until my left knee hits the register. The position stretches the muscles of my inner thighs, and when I look down past the skirt bunched at my waist I see Saxon looking back at me, blue eyes fixed on my face.

He holds my gaze as his mouth latches onto my throbbing clit. He sucks hard on the slick bundle of nerves, and that's all it takes. Orgasm hits me like a speeding truck and I scream, back bowing and pussy clenching. Dimly I'm aware of glass shattering when the convulsive sweep of my hand knocks a display of shot glasses to the floor, but the sound is nothing to Saxon's groan of satisfaction. He continues licking but I can't bear it, I'm too sensitive now. Each stroke of his tongue is heaven and hell and pain and pleasure.

"I can't." My breath coming in ragged sobs from the sheer intensity of it, I push at his head, my fingers threading through his thick hair. "I can't. No more."

He eases away from my clit but doesn't lift his head yet, gently licking the length of my slit as if he isn't willing to relinquish his claim on the moisture he's drawn from me. His tongue dips inside my core and another tremor shakes through my body.

"Fucking amazing," he says gruffly, his voice deep with arousal and his mouth hot against my inner thigh. He presses a kiss against its trembling length before rising over me.

I'm still shaking when he tugs me up to sitting and pulls me to the edge of the counter again, wrapping my legs around his hips, my heated flesh pressed tight against the erection straining behind his fly. His mouth finds mine and the kiss is a slow, sweet burn, his beard a soft brush against my chin. My lips cling to his when he finally lifts his head, his blue gaze searching my face. I must look half-drunk. I feel as if I am, my body liquid and warm, intoxicated by erotic bliss and his proximity.

He's hard as a rock against me, but it's not desire sharpening the lines of his face now. Intense purpose fills his gaze. "I told you it'd be like this between us. So damn hot."

"Yes." My response emerges on a shuddering breath.

His strong fingers catch my chin. "Now maybe you'll tell me why you think I'm asking you to whore yourself in exchange for protection."

My heart clenches. So he's done it again. Last night he promised to make me scream the answer he wanted, and I'd been forced to tell him about the Eighty-Eight. Now he *has* made me scream. He can probably still taste my pussy on his tongue and he's already demanding more answers that I don't want to give.

"Fuck." He snarls the word and is suddenly in my face, forcing me to lean back until I'm gripping his biceps for support. "And now you've got something else in your head. So you tell me what the hell you're thinking that makes you look like I just kicked your dog."

My throat aches. "I don't know what you want, Saxon. I just know that in all these years, you've never touched me. Now the clubhouse and the property are on the table and you do. And I think that whatever it is that you want, you'll use sex to persuade me to fall in line."

"Damn fucking right I'll use sex. I'll use anything I have to get what I want." His fingers tighten on my chin as I try to avert my face, my lips trembling, but he forces me to meet his solemn gaze. His voice roughens. "What

I want, Jenny, is you. I want the clubhouse, too, but it's for the Riders—and if I need to I'll go about getting it in the usual way. Rent, lease, whatever. We can keep it separate. But I want you for myself."

Those words are so close to what I've dreamed of that I can't trust they're real. "Want me for what? For how long?"

He tilts his head, studying me. "What did Red say to you?"

"That you want the package deal. The clubhouse and me."

"Then he understood what I want just fine. I want to call you mine, Jenny. You need me to clarify that?"

No. I've been around clubs long enough to know what it means. My breath hitches. "You want me to be your old lady?"

I don't want to be. Some women like being a biker's property—and it means their men have absolute trust in them. But loyalty to the club comes before everything, and I won't put any club before someone I love.

"I don't give a fuck if you are." Saxon doesn't look away from me. "I'm not saying I wouldn't love to see you wearing a patch telling everyone you belong to me, or that I wouldn't feel like a king every time someone saw it. But I told you this isn't about the Riders. It's you and me. And I want you in my bed every night, or I want to be in yours. You got troubles, I want to be the first one you call. I want to be the only man you look at, because you're the only woman I'll see. And I want it for a hell of a long time."

Oh, God. Everything I want. I just have to trust it.

But it's so hard to believe. "You didn't want it before."

"You think so?" The reply is sharp, and there's suddenly new tension steeling his body and a dangerous glint in his eyes. But though I've pissed him off, he's holding it back. "Princess, you weren't knocking down my door, either."

God. My throat is rough as I say, "You know I couldn't."

"Yeah. I know." His voice softens. "And I knew exactly what would have happened if I'd come to you when I'd wanted to—and I wanted to from the day I was sitting in my cell and opened your letter, Jenny. But all the reasons why I couldn't were in every apology you'd written. If I'd come to you, you'd have worried, because of the shit that started when you stepped out of your territory before. You'd have been afraid of what might shake out of it between the clubs, and we both know that Tommy Burns would have gotten onto Red about you."

I hadn't known that. I wasn't that familiar with the Hellfire Riders' previous president. But considering what my dad had said about him last night, Saxon is probably right. Burns wouldn't have passed up the opportunity to crow to my dad that one of the Riders was deep-dicking his daughter. The bad blood hadn't died down between the clubs until Saxon had taken over. But even now there is still tension—mostly because of resentment over Lily and her wearing the Riders' colors.

His thumb sweeps across my bottom lip as he continues, "I knew you'd have two choices: sneaking around with me or putting it out in the open and risk stirring up trouble. And you're not Juliet, dicking around with Romeo like she's got piss for brains and no respect for her house. You're loyal. To your dad, if not to the Titans."

So he has me pegged. "You're no Romeo, either."

"Because I'm not a boy. I didn't want to put that shit on you and force you to make a choice between me and Red. I knew that even if I'd come to you, you'd have told me you couldn't be with me."

And that would have torn me apart. To be offered everything I wanted, and not to take it.

Not taking it now will tear me apart, too.

His fingers catch my chin again, as if he thinks I'll try to escape from his next words. "But I'll tell you this: Lately I've been thinking that I would ask. I've been thinking of seeing whether we could do this without spilling any of my brothers' blood for it. So I was already planning on talking to Red—because if it came from him, you would know it wouldn't cause trouble. It just turns out that he came to me first, and I saw an opportunity that I never had before. You think I'm not going to take it? What, on fucking principle? I'm not that honorable, princess."

He is. In his own way. If he wasn't I wouldn't be here now. But his honor has never been in question, and hearing that he's wanted me just as long as I've wanted him should have eased all my fears, but instead they're only stronger. Because now I have something I never did before: hope. For the first time, I think Saxon could be mine. But I'm afraid that I might want more than he's offering, and I can't hide my uncertainty from his unwavering gaze.

"You're not sure," he observes flatly.

"How can I be? We've never even…" *Dated*, I was going to say. But that's so stupid.

Saxon must have guessed where I was headed. His eyes narrow. "You really think there's anything important that we don't know about each other already? Or do you think this wanting you is sudden? That I'm just sweet-talking you now?"

"No." If he promises to be in my bed every night, to be there when I call, I know that he'll keep those promises. "What if it doesn't work out? If might get ugly, especially since you're trying to bring the clubs together."

"It's going to be ugly anyway." His brief smile doesn't soften the iron determination in his eyes. "But you and me? That'll work. Because you let me in this far. Now I'll do anything to keep you here."

Where I would have everything I want. I just need to take it.

I just need to risk my heart. Not so easy to do.

This man could destroy me—and I don't think he knows it. I'm afraid to let him know it. So I simply stare up at him, hope and fear waging a painful battle within me.

Hope begins to win when he suddenly grins.

"I see I'll have to convince you." Swiftly he kisses my

mouth and links his fingers through mine, tugging me off the counter. "So let's ride."

FIVE

I balk a little when I see Saxon's motorcycle. I'm looking forward to riding with him, but my panties are soaked and this little skirt isn't going to protect me from the grit of the road or the heat of his engine. Saxon doesn't blink when I say that I need to drive up to the house and change my clothes. He just nods and starts up his bike while I climb into my truck. There's no counting how many times I've heard guys—bikers or not—argue against a woman taking a few extra minutes to get ready, dismissing it as trivial or time-wasting. But Saxon doesn't even ask me to explain why or try to convince me that the clothes I'm wearing are fine, and I appreciate that when I tell him there's something I need to do, he just waits for me to do it.

Such a simple thing, but it matters. Because if Saxon and I give this a shot, there will be many times when I'll have things I need to do: taking care of my dad and working at the brewery, just to start. And we know a lot about each other, but we don't know the little things like this—and as far as I can tell, it's often those little things that make or break a couple.

My dad's bike is gone from its usual spot in front of the house. Since nothing is settled with Saxon, my dad's absence is a relief. I'm not really sure what I would tell him.

I invite Saxon in, but he waits outside with his engine idling. From anyone else, that might have been a subtle hint to hurry me along; from Saxon, it's simply respect. This isn't just my place, but also belongs to the Steel Titans' president. Whatever agreement they're working out between the clubs, this is still Titan territory. Even though Saxon is here by invitation, parking his bike and coming into the house is too close to declaring that he's pushing my father out, so I know he'll hold off until the invitation comes from my dad, instead.

He's frowning down at his phone when I come out wearing jeans, my riding jacket, and gloves. His dark gaze skims down my length, stopping at my feet. The cuffs of my straight-cut jeans cover the top of my red cowboy boots. With a round toe and wooden heel, they were designed with another type of riding in mind, but they're great on a motorcycle, too.

He meets my eyes. "Nice boots."

"They're good for kicking ass," I say, but despite the bold words, I'm suddenly nervous. My anxiety doesn't escape his notice.

"You're not used to the idea of me being at your place."

"I'm not used to the idea of *any* guy being at my place," I retort.

His smile is wide and slow. "I shouldn't like that answer as much as I do," he tells me, then gestures to the short stretch of seat behind him, inviting me to sit. "Your cell reception out here is shit."

Worse than shit, usually. I pull on my helmet. "And it's even shittier at the clubhouse's end of the property. Is that a deal breaker?"

I'm teasing him, but his response is swift and serious. He snags my belt and pulls me close. Even though he's seated on his bike, our eyes are almost even.

"Nothing's going to break this deal, princess. *Nothing.*" He waits a second to let that sink in, then lets go of my belt and smacks my ass. "Now get on. And scoot up real close, because your legs in those jeans are the sexiest I've ever seen, and I want them holding me tight."

I grin and swing my leg over the back. My nervousness melts away. I'm suddenly glad I'm behind him and that he can't see my face, because the emotion that replaces the anxiety is warm and full, and would reveal far too much.

It *is* strange to have him here. But it also feels *so* right.

God, and his abs are like steel when I slide my hands beneath his kutte to grip his sides. I've never seen him without a shirt but my fingers tell me that when I do, I'll be looking at slabs of muscle and a six-pack that could make angels weep.

"You know," I call to him as he slowly opens the throttle, "we could just head upstairs to my bedroom!"

I can't hear his laugh but I feel the rumble of it join the vibration of the engine. His big hand comes down to squeeze my thigh before returning to the handlebar. Thanks to my helmet I can't get as close as I want, can't lay my cheek against his strong back and close my eyes. Oh, but I want to. I could easily ride like that for so long.

As it is, the road flies by and I'm barely aware of it. Today was a hot one. Even though it's heading into evening the air is still heavy with the smell of baked dirt and pine, yet it's Saxon's scent that seems to fill my every breath. The leather of his kutte, the fragrance of freshly laundered cotton—as if he pulled a clean shirt straight out of the dryer before coming to see me. And he's so big. So solid. My heart feels tight just being this close. My body feels even tighter, my breasts pushed up against his back and my inner thighs gripping his hips.

All I can think is that it won't be long until he's inside me. Fucking me.

God, I hope it's soon. My pussy is already soaking wet again. I don't know where we're going. If I'm lucky, it'll be straight to his bed, but I'd be just as happy if he stopped on the side of the road and dragged me onto his lap.

But as we ride through town I realize we're headed to the Hellfire Riders' clubhouse—maybe because of whatever message he was trying to respond to on his phone. Though I'd have liked to leave thoughts of the Titans and the Riders behind us for a few hours, I can't be upset. I've got my stuff to take care of and Saxon has his, and I know exactly how much time a club demands from its president.

He told me that he wants me for himself. That this need between us is just about him and me. I don't doubt that. A man's dick doesn't give a shit what colors anyone wears. But I can't pretend for a second that the club won't always be right there with us.

That's not so bad. My mom told me once that a club can be like in-laws. Sometimes easy to get along with, and sometimes you just want to kill them. And they might put strain on a relationship, but if a couple is solid, they'll get through it.

I've seen a lot of the Titans' relationships fall apart, and almost every single time, someone blamed the club. But the club wasn't really at fault; it was just the excuse. Sometimes the guys were dickheads and used the club as the reason to avoid other responsibilities—their jobs, their families. Sometimes they took advantage of easy pussy and cheated. Sometimes the old ladies and girlfriends were jealous of every second their men spent away from them. Little things multiplied into big things and soon they were splitting up.

The club is already a big thing for Saxon, just as my dad and my brewery are for me. If I want to be with him, it'll mean never trying to force him to choose between me and the Riders.

I can't imagine that I ever would. Now that he and my dad are working something out, the Riders aren't a threat to me or to anyone that I love. And I can't imagine Saxon avoiding responsibilities. If I ever need him, he'll make time for me.

He'll be there for me. The question is whether his heart will be there, too.

Mine is. Right here, exposed and raw. He intends to persuade me into taking a chance on him, but the truth is, there's no other choice for me. He wants to call me his— but I already am. The only thing I can do is go into this with my eyes wide open. So before I tell him my decision, I'll take a few days to collect all the little bits about Saxon that I didn't know before, and make sure that my heart is prepared for everything that comes next.

For now, though, I simply savor the feel of him against me.

My hold on him tightens as we approach the club-house. I know where it is, of course—although I don't come this way often, this is a small city. So I've seen the place before. Decades ago, it was a car lot on the outskirts of town, until the owner moved his business up to Bend. Tommy Burns took the property over and established it as the Riders' base. At the time, there wasn't much out this way except empty fields and a few farmhouses. Now a chain-link fence is all that separates the clubhouse parking lot from the neighbors on both sides—a self-serve frozen yogurt shop and a laundromat. Across the street, a Starbucks shares a building with a local pizzeria and a taekwondo dojang. A little farther down, the street is lined by long rows of midsize houses with tiny brown lawns.

The bike slows as we turn into the parking lot. The old car dealership used to have big front windows, but those probably hadn't lasted long. Now the front of the club-house is walled in. Though only a single story, it's a big and boxy structure, resembling a warehouse. Almost a dozen motorcycles are lined up outside the building. Each door of a big three-bay garage is up, and there's a small crowd around the entrance to the first bay.

When Saxon rolls in, all eyes turn our way. That's to be expected. Acknowledging the club president's arrival is standard protocol. But their gazes linger on me, until the focus of the entire group has shifted away from whatever they'd been gathered around.

A motorcycle, I realize—and my lips part on a horrified gasp when I see the state of it. The chrome pipes are beat to shit and the tires slashed. It looks like someone took a sledgehammer to the tank and the front of the frame. And I know that bike. It's Lily's. Jesus jumping Christ. That's not just a *bike* but a custom chopper Lily ordered from

Wheels Up a few years ago. Whoever fucked it up hadn't just destroyed a motorcycle but a freaking work of art.

Tension has turned Saxon's muscles to iron, but his manner is easy when he brakes at the edge of the group. Lily's crouching beside the ruin of her bike. The red around her eyes says that she's been crying. I'd bet anything that not one Rider has seen her shed a tear before, not when she knows they might call her weak for it. But some of the guys are looking a little weepy themselves and no one is going to blame her for crying over this.

Saxon touches my knee, letting me know that it's safe for me to get off. As soon as I do he snags my wrist and pulls me close again. He's still straddling his motorcycle, his booted feet flat on the ground, and now I'm all but sitting in his lap. Everyone is staring. Casually I unbuckle my helmet and try to pretend that the way he's stating his claim without saying a word is nothing, and that my heart isn't thumping through my ribs.

His arm circles my waist, but his focus is on Lily's bike. "I'm guessing you didn't take a bite of the road, Zoomie."

"No, boss." Lily stands and her gaze flits to my face for only a second before returning to his. "Not unless I bit it while riding in the hangar at Tucker's field."

The airfield where she works. "So you were up in the air and it was locked away?" Saxon asks.

"I was. And it was."

"And you didn't see who did it."

Her jaw firms and her eyes are like flint. "I wouldn't

be here if I knew, boss. I'd be busting some fucking heads."

Saxon nods. "We'll find out. You got a ride in the meantime?"

"I'll figure something out."

"Talk to Blowback if you can't. He'll hook you up."

For just an instant, the flint in her eyes sparks, as if she might tell Saxon to shove that suggestion right up his ass. But whatever set her temper off, she quickly swallows it. "I will."

"All right. If you see my veep, send him up to the Crib. I'll be there until I'm gone," Saxon tells them, then gives my ass a little smack, a signal for me to get up again.

He seems to like spanking me. I don't really mind it, either. In front of everyone, it's not really a turn-on—it's just kind of fun, and I love that he's treating me as if I've been hanging around the clubhouse longer than five minutes. As if it's completely natural for me to be there and there's no reason for everyone to keep staring.

Threading his fingers through mine, he leads me through the garage. Not a bolt or a tool is out of place. The concrete pads practically gleam.

"Are you the hard-ass in here," I ask quietly, "or is someone else?"

He grins. "I would be. But I don't need to. Blowback gets on them if they leave shit lying around."

The Hellfire Riders' vice president, Jack Hayden. I know him by sight, but I don't think we've ever exchanged a single word. I'm not really sorry for that. Saxon looks big and mean; his veep is just big and scary, built like a tank and always wearing an expression that said he'd just as soon kill you as look at you. "Why is he called Blowback?"

"Because he's the hell that rains down on your head when you fuck up."

"Has he ever rained on your head?"

He glances at me. "A few times. But that's what veeps are for."

Uncle Thorne does the same for my dad. Never in front of the other club members, always in private—and my dad lets him because he trusts Thorne over any other living man. I suspect that Blowback is the man Saxon trusts.

"He's kind of terrifying," I say as we enter the main building. "Is he really like a giant, gentle puppy on the inside?"

Saxon's deep laugh echoes through the big, open room. "Not even a bit."

That's good to know. But I don't reply, because curiosity has taken hold and I'm looking everywhere at once. The outside of the clubhouse tips toward the side of ugly, but they've got a nice setup inside. There's a couple of seating areas with plush leather couches and big screen televisions. A galley-style kitchen with stainless steel counters and a well-stocked bar take up one wall. A pair of pool tables stand at the far end, and through an open partition is a weight room filled with equipment. Doors in the back wall probably lead to bunks or showers.

There's a pair of women sitting at one of the dining tables. A blonde and a redhead. I recognize their faces but don't know their names. They both fall silent as we come in, their mouths rounded in surprise and their eyebrows raised high. Saxon doesn't look that direction at all but I give them a little wave and smile. Even if I'm not around the clubhouse much, starting off wrong with the old ladies is a guaranteed way to make my life a living hell. It's a relief when they grin and waggle their fingers at me in return.

Everyone else seems to be gone. Probably outside crying over Lily's bike or over at the Wolf Den drinking their Saturday night away. Saxon leads me to a staircase built against the south wall. The clubhouse is only a single level, but they've constructed a spacious open loft over the weight room. The Crib, I'm guessing—and probably off-limits to everyone but the club's officers and the people they've explicitly invited up.

In the corner of the Crib stands an office with walls and a door. There's another beside it with a heavy lock. Maybe the treasurer's office, or where the club's weapons are stored.

Instead of a desk, a conference table fills the corner office. Saxon leaves the door open and takes the chair at the head of the table. He doesn't have to ask me even once before I'm straddling him. My mouth quickly finds his— and, *God*, his kiss unravels me so fast. But there's already a little thing rearing its head. I don't even want to bring it up. I need to, though.

My breath is coming in sharp pants when I raise my head. "I don't want it here."

He palms the back of my neck, guiding me down again until our lips are only a whisper apart. His voice is a low growl. "You don't want what here?"

"Sex. It's not…private. Even if the door is closed."

His mouth claims mine, and I feel the possessive heat of his kiss down to my toes. A whimper escapes me, and I can't stop myself from rocking against him. He's thick and hard and in another minute I might not even care that the door is open.

He groans and pulls back. Big hands slide down my spine before gripping my hips. "No fucking here," he agrees roughly. "Because I don't want to share you with anyone. That includes sharing what you look like after I've had my cock deep inside you, or what you sound like when you come. I'm not into making it public."

Neither was I. "Good. So we're just waiting for Blowback?"

"Not just," he says, and grinds up against me, until I'm writhing and biting my lip against my moan. "I'm here to persuade you."

My response is a breathless laugh. "I *knew* you'd use sex."

He offers an unrepentant grin. "This is just because I like getting my hands on you. But that's not why I brought you."

"You heard about Lily's bike."

"I was going to bring you here, anyway. To show you what we've got. What *I've* got. Fuck, I can't think when you're on me." All at once he lifts me onto the edge of the table. He leans back, looking up at me. God, he is *such* a man. From those intense eyes to his iron stomach to the thick bulge behind his fly. "You know about the Den. You can probably see that I'm doing all right there. I'm not making a shitload of profits, but business is steady."

I stare at him, trying to make sense of that. He's talking about his pub. I'm just not sure why. "All right," I say.

"Now, this place—when Burns was killed, the property went to his widow. Blowback, Stone, Gunner, and I bought it from her. But this location is shit."

"You get complaints?"

"Not a fucking week goes by without one. Our bikes are too loud, we're bad for business, and the good citizens down the road are just waiting for us to rape and pillage. It doesn't matter that we were here before they all moved in and built their shit."

"So that's why you want the clubhouse out by my place."

"Yes. No. Fuck." He leans forward and wraps his hands around the back of my calves, just beneath my knees. "I'm talking about persuading you. So I'm telling you that we've been discussing moving to another location anyway—but we don't intend to give up this place.

Instead we're thinking of renovating it into a gym. Weights, a fighting ring, personal trainers. Pine Valley doesn't have a real one yet, just that shitty little club off Main. It'll be a good investment."

It probably would be. But it still didn't explain what I'm being persuaded to do. "Why are you telling me this? You want me to invest, too?"

"Just in me." His dark gaze holds mine. "Because if you agree to this, I'm thinking long term. And you, Jenny—your brewery is doing pretty damn well, isn't it? You're smart and you've got a lot of drive, and you won't be happy with someone who's just coasting through. So I want you to know that I'm solid, too."

Long term. My chest is tight again. "I already knew that."

"You do." His voice flattens. "Then what's holding you back?"

"From going all in on the package deal?" At his sharp nod, I tell him, "Because it's a big investment that includes a hefty amount of risk. No matter how good it looks, I'd be a fool to jump in without taking my time to consider the angles and doing a little research first."

His eyes narrow. "You think it looks good?"

"I think it looks really good."

He likes that. Easing back in his chair again, he regards me with renewed determination. "Where's the risk? I'll minimize it."

I have to laugh. "You can't. Just making that offer

increases it." On a deep breath, I tap my fingertips over my pounding heart. "The risk is here."

His frown tells me that he doesn't immediately get it—as if maybe I'm pointing to my tit. Then his gaze shoots to mine and he says gruffly, "You get over here."

I do, straddling his lap again. His fingers tangle in my hair and his kiss is hot and fierce.

He pulls back but keeps hold of me, his big hands cupping my face. I can't look anywhere else. "You're safe with me. I'm a rough man, and I'm not promising I won't ever fuck up, but I won't do anything that would bring hurt onto you. All right?"

With emotion clogging my throat, I can only nod. It's enough for now.

He tastes me again but it doesn't last long. I don't hear any footsteps. Only the subtle tension in Saxon's body tells me that someone is there.

Jack Hayden, looking as big and as scary as always. Despite the heat of the day he's wearing a black long-sleeved shirt under his kutte, but it doesn't conceal a single heavy muscle. I start to climb off the chair, but Saxon simply grips my waist and resettles me, sitting sideways across his lap. Blowback doesn't blink, just watches us with a cold, dead stare.

"You hear anything yet?" Saxon asks him.

"Spiral says he passed a van heading toward the airfield road, and the driver was one of the little shit prospects for the Eighty-Eight. But he was a few miles out and couldn't say for sure that was where the fucker went. I'd put my money on them or the Titans. Some of them are still pissed that you brought Lily in."

My body stiffens. No way in hell would anyone in my dad's club do that. Only a bunch of cowards would trash someone's bike when its rider wasn't around to defend it. But although I keep my mouth shut, my reaction doesn't go unnoticed by either man. Blowback's eyes are like dark knives, slicing right through me, seeing everything.

Saxon's hand smooths over my hip. "They're pissed, but if it came to that, they'd go after her. Not that bike."

"We'll look at the prospect, then." Blowback's cold gaze slides over me again before meeting Saxon's. "You're going to have to deal with the First Lady clause."

Now Saxon's every muscle is steel. "Fuck it."

"I'd let you. But some of the brothers won't. Just so you're prepared."

His jaw clenching, Saxon nods. "You got a ride for Zoomie?"

"I'll see if I can round something up."

"I've got one," I offer and both men look to me. "Mostly it just sits in our garage but my dad keeps it up. Lily could use it until her insurance comes in and she's able to buy another."

Saxon and Blowback exchange a glance.

"It's not a sissy bike," I add. "She won't be embarrassed by it. The Riders won't be, either."

"All right," Saxon says. "But we'll hold off on that until

we've got our other business with the Titans squared away."

Meaning that he hasn't told all of the Riders that he'll be folding in the Titans. So Lily can't accept a motorcycle from Red's daughter yet.

Blowback nods. "Got anything else for me?"

"That's it. Let me know if you track down that prospect."

Obviously the other man has no doubt that he will. "You'll be getting a call."

I wait until Blowback is gone before asking, "What's the First Lady clause?"

Aside from something that obviously pertained to me.

Saxon all but snarls his response. "It's nothing to worry about, princess."

Sure. That's why mentioning it makes him look like he wants to shove his boot up someone's ass. But he must think that he can take care of it. So whatever it is, I'll trust that it truly will be nothing.

His jaw hardens again before his expression clears and he smacks my ass. "You feel like riding up to Bend?"

"What's in Bend?"

"A good steakhouse, and your thighs holding me tight for thirty miles."

"All right."

He grins. "You're easily persuaded."

I can't even pretend to be chagrined. Because when it comes to Saxon? I really am easy.

Saxon checks his phone as we're leaving the steakhouse and by the tightening of his jaw, I suspect that Blowback has found the prospect—which means I won't be going home with him tonight. I'm disappointed, but thirty miles of holding on makes up for a little of it.

My dad's at home when we roll in, but he remains scarce while I get my feet on the ground. Still seated, Saxon pulls me close. "You're working tomorrow?"

"Always."

He nods. "We've got a ride scheduled. I expect we'll get back into town by eight. Are you free?"

"I'm having dinner with Anna at six, then we're heading out for drinks. You want to meet up with us?" I give him a saucy little grin. "You can drive me home and take advantage of me."

His eyes flare with heat. His voice is a low growl. "I'll do that, princess."

He tugs me down, and his kiss is a blistering promise. I'm dizzy with need when he's done, my nipples tight and my pussy clenching. Jesus. Tomorrow night can't arrive fast enough.

My dad comes out as I'm climbing the porch stairs. His gaze scans my face and settles on my smile. "You're all right, then?"

"I am."

He looks to Saxon. "Thanks for looking after her."

Saxon returns his gaze steadily. "I always will."

My dad nods. Then Saxon is gone and I'm staring

after his taillight. Soon the crickets are louder than the fading sound of his engine.

When I look back at my dad, I find him watching me, and there's both hope and sorrow on his face. Probably hope that I'll be safe, along with the sorrow that he can't guarantee that safety himself—and for all the days he won't have. "So you got it worked out?" he asks.

"Not completely." My heart aching, I slip my arms around his lean waist and squeeze him tight. "But I think we're getting there."

SIX

We're heading to the Corral, because Anna wants to go anywhere but the Den. I expect we'll be there a while.

I text Saxon as Anna and I are leaving the restaurant. His reply comes less than a minute later.

Tell her she's fired. See you in 1 hour.

"Your disloyal ass is fired," I tell her, and toss my phone into the console between our seats.

"Again?" She flips down her visor and checks her lipstick in the mirror. "But I'm his best employee. I've got almost a hundred plaques to prove it."

My phone buzzes again as I pull out of the parking

lot and into the road. Since I'm driving, Anna reads it for me.

"Saxon says, 'I hope your pussy is ready.'"

I almost run up onto the curb. "What?"

"Just fucking with you. It's your freaking Twitter notification. @beaverfan84 says that he's chilling by a campfire with a Black Boots stout. And I still can't believe you're banging my boss."

As she's already said about a dozen times tonight. "You can't? Really?"

"Let me amend that. I still can't believe it took you *so long* to start banging my boss."

"I haven't banged him."

"Yet."

Yet. I can't stop my grin or the hot anticipation sliding across every nerve. Energy is buzzing through me when we arrive at the Corral. It's packed. There's live music tonight, some overloud country-rock hybrid with a lead singer who's practically oozing sweat through his leather pants. After shouting our orders at the bartender, we snag a booth in the corner just as another couple is leaving it, then head out to the dance floor. The music's so awful that it doesn't matter that my dancing is worse.

Anna and I are both laughing when we head to the bar for another shot. I force myself not to check my phone, to look at the time. The minutes will only crawl by more slowly if I do.

I sit out the third set, because I'm loose and warm and

some cowboy fake-lassoed Anna out on the dance floor, and she allowed him to pull her in for a slow dance. I peek at my phone and my heart thumps. The hour is almost up.

A big body slides into the booth next to me. My heart gives another wild jump—then freezes in my chest when I glance up.

Reichmann. Terror locks my every muscle. His eyes are a pale milky blue. His head is shaved bald and an auburn goatee frames his thin mouth. He's smiling at me, but there's nothing nice about the curl of his lips. Just triumphant and cruel.

He pushes closer, crowding me against the wall. I tell myself to scream, to kick, but I can't move, can only stare at him in disbelief and horror.

"So here you are, Baby Red."

Baby Red. I cringe and try to stop the memories that flood in. Try to stop feeling those rough fingers shoving into me, making me bleed.

As if relishing my fear, he grins and leans closer. "I couldn't believe my luck when I saw your truck outside. Now I'm even luckier, because you're here all alone."

No. But I can't see past him, and I don't know if anyone can see in. The booth is in the corner and the seat shadowed. I pray that Anna noticed him come in. If she did, she'll get help.

"Look at me, Baby Red," he says sharply, and against my will, I do. "You know I know people. One of those people works in a medical lab, running tests. And you know what she told me? Your daddy's going to leave you real soon."

Rage and pain blast away the terror. "Get the fuck away from me."

"Or what?"

I try to scramble up onto the bench, to get up, to get out, to be seen. Hard fingers grip my upper arm like a vise and Reichmann slams me back against the wall. The wail coming from the stage drowns out my scream. I kick, but though I'm wearing boots with a solid toe, I'm angled the wrong way and I only glance off his shin.

It must have hurt, though, because his fingers tighten. He shoves me harder into the corner and gets his face up in mine.

"You little bitch. You want to play rough? Let's play rough. And let me tell you what we're going to do as soon as your daddy's dead. Me and my brothers, we're going to spread your legs and you're going to pull a train. Every single Henchman is going to blow his load up your cunt. When we can't use it anymore, we're going to start in on your shithole. And while they're fucking away, I'm going to make you choke on my dick." His sour breath washes over my mouth and nose. "Right now I'm going to give you a little taste, so you can start looking forward to it."

His hand clamps around my thigh, fingers pushing up beneath my skirt. Bile shoots up my throat. Retching, I flail for something to grab onto—and find a pint glass. Swinging as hard as I can, I smash it against the side of his head. I hope that it shatters, that the shards pierce his brain, but it just *thunk*s hard enough to send splinters of pain through my hand. Blinking rapidly, Reichmann shakes his head, as if for an instant he's stunned. Screaming again, I pivot in the seat and ratchet my knee up before slamming my boot heel into his chest.

He doesn't fly back. Grunting, he doubles over, and when he looks up at me with his fists clenched, I know I'm in for a lot more hurt than he originally intended to lay on me tonight.

Chest shuddering, I brace myself for the pain heading my way. It doesn't come.

Saxon does.

He appears at the end of the booth and his face is already tight with rage. There's no hesitation, no surprise. Before Reichmann even realizes he's there, Saxon has a steely arm locked around the Henchman's neck and is dragging him out of the booth. Eyes popping wide, Reichmann claws at Saxon's arm, but the choke hold only tightens. The big man's boots pound the floor. Suddenly the caterwauling singer falls silent, and the music follows suit one instrument at a time as the band notices what's happening.

And what's happening is that Saxon is going to kill him. What's happening is that no one will stop him, because there's three other Riders forming a wall at his back and they'll prevent any attempt to interfere.

New terror clutches at my throat, because I see it all

happening again. One man dead. Another in prison. And I can't lose him now. I can't. "Don't. Saxon—don't!"

He looks at me, still cringing in the corner of the booth, my cheeks wet with tears of pain. I know that what he sees isn't changing his mind. It's only making him more determined.

"Please." My voice trembles and my vision is blurring. "Too many people will witness it. It'll be more than five years."

"I won't be sorry for a single fucking second of it. Not even if it's the rest of my life." Each word is harsh, deadly.

"I know." My tears slide over. "But I've loved you for so long—and after all this time, you're finally mine. I can't bear losing you now."

His body stills. His teeth are clenched, a muscle in his cheek jumping. My heart seems to beat a thousand times before he abruptly nods, then bends his head and speaks directly into Reichmann's ear. The man's face is purple, his eyes bulging. I'm shaking with sudden relief, and though I can't hear what Saxon is telling him, I can guess.

If Saxon ever catches Reichmann without any witnesses around, he'll make sure no one ever finds the body.

He throws the Henchman to the floor like he's nothing but a sack of shit. Even as Saxon comes for me, Blowback and Stone haul Reichmann up by his kutte. Zach Cooper is holding Anna back. She's fighting against him, her eyes wide and terrified.

His gaze never leaving my face, Saxon holds out his hand to me. I scoot forward across the bench and slide my fingers through his, and the moment I'm close enough he scoops me up against his chest. There's a shift in the crowd as I come out of the booth, as if until this moment they thought they'd been witnessing a handful of thugs attacking some innocent man. But my tears and the way Saxon is cradling me in his arms tell a different story, and now most of them are looking at Reichmann as if thinking he deserved what he got.

I don't think they realize he hasn't gotten it all yet.

As Saxon carries me past them, Blowback asks quietly, "You want me to take this motherfucker to Lily, since he's the one that ordered the prospect to trash her ride?"

"She's already taken hers out on the prospect," Saxon says. "What you give to him now is coming from me. Just make sure he's alive to deliver my message back to his club."

"Will do," Stone says and they start shoving Reichmann toward the door. Getting out of here before the cops showed.

Saxon glances at Cooper. "You see Anna home."

White-faced, Anna doesn't even argue. "I'll come see you tomorrow, Jenny."

My throat in a knot, I nod; then Saxon's carrying me out into the warm night air. His motorcycle isn't far from Reichmann's. So that was how he'd known. He'd recognized the other man's bike and charged in to save me.

Again.

"Can you hold on?" he asks me quietly, and his voice is rough. "Or do you want me to drive your truck?"

"I'll hold on." Forever, if I can.

"Is your gear in the cab?"

"Yes."

He takes my keys from me and finds my helmet and jacket. I'm slowly steadying as I put them on, and by the time I'm zipping up the leather, I'm no longer shaking.

I haul in a deep breath. "Thank you."

"Don't," is all he says before leading me to his bike, and as soon as I wrap my arms around him everything is all right again.

I don't know if Saxon is. He usually sits easy as he rides, but I can feel his tension, a steel wire strung tight. Still raging because I'd been hurt? Still pumped with adrenaline? Or wishing that he was the one pounding on Reichmann now?

Maybe all of the above.

The wind whips at my skirt and chills my bare legs. I hold him tighter, then gasp as he suddenly swings off the two-lane blacktop. The flood of his headlight reveals a dirt road, the path deeply rutted and barely wide enough for a car. A forest service road or an old logging track. Within a minute, the pine trees have swallowed us up. I can't see the main road. When Saxon slows to a stop, shutting off his engine and his lights, we're surrounded by utter darkness. The click of the kickstand is loud in the sudden quiet.

I know what's going to happen now. I know. And I'm already wet and trembling.

"Jenny." His voice is low and taut. "You going to be all right if I touch you?"

"I won't be if you don't."

"Then get your ass up here," he commands, but doesn't wait for me to swing all the way off. Bracing his feet, he snags his arm around my waist and drags me forward over his hip until I'm sitting in his lap. I'm already reaching for him, finding his mouth in the dark.

With a possessive growl, he demands entry and I give it, opening to the penetrating thrust of his tongue. A groan tears from his chest when he tastes me. Suddenly he pulls away, tugging at the buckle of my helmet, ripping away his own. Then his fingers dive into my hair and he's devouring my mouth, stealing my breath.

"*Saxon.*"

His name is a ragged moan when he tilts my head back, tasting the length of my throat. Panting, I struggle out of my jacket. My eyes are adjusting to the dark, to the faint moonlight streaming through the trees. His expression is harsh with his arousal. Even as he palms the back of my neck and claims my mouth again, his big hand jerks at his belt. Desperate whimpers escape me when he frees his cock. He rips open a condom packet with his teeth, then his fingers slide under my skirt to find me wet and swollen with need.

"Fuck." He groans the curse, then he's gripping my

waist, lifting and repositioning me with my thighs spread wide over his. His thumb strums my clit, and I'm crying out, my hips bucking with every slick stroke. "Next time I'll go slow, princess. I'll be sweet."

I don't care what he is. Wrapping my arms around his neck, I push closer. Roughly he captures my mouth again, his broad hand flat against my back. Wild, needy moans erupt deep in my throat as he slides the blunt head of his cock along the seam of my pussy, parting me, his tongue thrusting past my lips in possessive strokes as his body begins to claim mine.

And, God, he's big. I try not to stiffen, but his sheathed cock feels enormous, stretching my sensitive tissues to the edge of discomfort. Saxon seems to realize it, gentling his kiss and pushing his hand between us. His long fingers brush my clit and we both moan as my inner walls clench around his thick shaft. New sparks of pleasure ignite and flare across my nerves, and the ache building inside my core isn't just from taking his length in but from my desperation to be filled.

With a subtle rock of his hips, slowly he fucks deeper into me, and I'm winding tighter and tighter with every inch. I begin to move with him, and my head falls back on a strangled cry when he suddenly catches my hips and pushes me down over the full length of his cock. Excruciating pleasure spears through me. He's so big. So deep. But he's finally mine, and there's no hell in this. Simply heaven.

My back arches on the next deep thrust. With a ravenous groan, Saxon lowers his head. His hot mouth covers my breast, teeth catching my beaded nipple through my shirt. My body begins to shake, incoherent sounds spilling from my lips.

Saxon tugs hard at my nipple before groaning against my breast. "You're so fucking beautiful, Jenny."

His fingers slip between us again, stroking my clit and ecstasy shatters through me all at once. I can't even cry out, every muscle locking into place except for the exquisite convulsions around his thick cock. With a tortured grunt, Saxon fucks harder into my clenching flesh, then slows as the orgasm releases me.

I cling to him as I come down. His kiss is rough and deep and still hungry. He hasn't come yet. With his cock buried inside me, he lifts his head. The faint moonlight glints in his eyes. Gently he pushes my hair from my face.

"Can you take more?"

"I can take everything you give me."

His fingers tighten on my hips. "I need you hard, Jenny. So hard."

A shiver races through me. His voice is hoarse with need and my own is rising again to meet it. "Then take me hard."

Abruptly Saxon stands, lifting me up with him. "Turn around and kneel on this seat, then reach up and grab those handlebars."

God. The seat is just wide enough for my knees. I

can feel Saxon behind me, straddling the bike as I grip the handlebars. The motorcycle's long body forces me to stretch forward over the tank—and when Saxon stands with his legs on either side of the bike, his erect cock is on level with my entrance.

His callused palms run up the length of my trembling thighs and drag my skirt up over my ass. Anticipation tightens the muscles along my spine. He's not saying anything, just letting his fingers trail over my skin, and in the dark his touch seems almost reverent.

Then his hands grip my hips and he surges forward, burying his full length in one slick thrust. Shock and pleasure erupt beneath my skin, and I cry out, my fingers clenching the handlebars in a death grip. God help me. He felt big before, but now my thighs are clamped together because I'm kneeling on the seat, and his long thick cock stretches me tighter, plunges deeper. Before I can catch my breath he pushes into me again. I moan helplessly as my pussy grips his steely length.

Saxon's groan sounds like part ecstasy, part torture. He grinds against me as if trying to get deeper, but there's no deeper, and the sensation of his cock screwing inside me is just making me clench harder around him.

"So fucking tight." His voice is a growl. "It's like you're sucking me in."

"Please." It emerges on a sobbing breath. I'm begging, begging, don't even know for what, but Saxon gives it to me in a powerful thrust that jolts me forward, my breasts

swaying heavily beneath me, my nipples hardened to throbbing points.

Another jolting stroke, then another, then Saxon grips my waist and fucks me at a relentless pace. My skin is hot, burning, slick with sweat and between my thighs I'm drenched in my arousal. The slick sound of his cock pistoning into my wet pussy joins the slap of his hips against my ass, and my inner walls are tightening around him, each stroke seeming deeper and deeper, until it's too tight, too much. I rock forward, trying to relieve the unbearable tension, but his hands clench on my hips and drag me back, and the orgasm slams into me with the length of his cock. I scream, trying to jolt forward again, but he holds me still and fucks me and suddenly I'm coming again, or I didn't stop, and when I'm done my body sags and I can barely hold on. Behind me, Saxon groans, grinding deep, and the pulse of his release sends little aftershocks through my flesh.

I'm limp and shaking, my body boneless when Saxon seems to collapse onto his seat and drags me onto his lap. His chest heaves against my back. He buries his face in the side of my neck. His breath is a ragged rasp across my throat.

"All right?" he finally says.

I can barely nod, and for the longest time he just holds me. Slowly, my trembling stops and I relax against him. "Just in case it isn't clear," I tell him softly, "you've persuaded me."

His rough laugh shakes against my back, but it soon quiets, and his deep voice is solemn when he finally responds. "These next few months are going to be rough, Jenny. With Red sick, and trying to fold the clubs together, and this shit with the Eighty-Eight."

"I know."

His arms tighten. "Just hold onto me. I'll get us through. And I won't give you any reason to be sorry that you're with me."

I shook my head. That's the one thing that could never happen—and he's the one who taught me that.

Lifting my mouth to his, I promise against his lips, "I won't *ever* be sorry."

TAKING IT ALL

ONE

JENNY

Saturday evening at the Wolf Den, yet the Hellfire Riders' favorite watering hole is as quiet as a Sunday morning. I know the club isn't out on a weekend ride, and considering how hard its members like to drink and play, there's only one possible reason for their absence now.

I belly up to the bar and sling my bag onto an empty stool. "The club's meeting isn't over yet?"

"Nope. And a good thing, too, because Marie was sick today and none of the prep was done." Behind the bar,

Anna glances up from a pile of lemon wedges. A brunette with delicate features, she often looks sweeter than she is. She has a pixie's face but a harpy's temper, and that dark side makes its appearance now when her eyebrows shoot together in a frown. "You look like shit, Jenny. Are you all right?"

Damn it. After spending a good part of the afternoon crying, my eyes are still puffy. I slathered on concealer, but Anna's been my best friend since we were little. Makeup might fool some people, but it can't hide anything from her.

I can't hide this from her any longer, either. "Not really."

"Why? Is it Saxon?" Her expression tightens. "Or the Eighty-Eight?"

"No. To both," I say, but it's no surprise those are her first guesses. Less than a week ago, Luke Reichmann—who leads the Eighty-Eight Henchmen MC—attacked me while I was out dancing with Anna at a local bar. Saxon Gray, the president of the Hellfire Riders, almost killed him for it before handing Reichmann over to his men. I don't know how badly they fucked him up. Probably pretty bad. Saxon told them to leave Reichmann alive, but there's a lot of hurt that can be dealt out before hitting the line between living and dead. Eventually the Eighty-Eight will probably retaliate. I haven't heard anything from them yet, though. Reichmann's probably still licking his wounds.

And Saxon…just thinking of him makes my heart tighten. I've wanted him for so long, but we've only been together since the night of the attack. Only a week. It doesn't feel real yet. Almost like a dream. But if it is, it's the best dream I've ever had.

Except for one thing.

"My dad's sick," I tell Anna on a shuddering breath.

Her lips part as her gaze searches my face. "You don't mean the flu."

All at once my eyes fill with tears. "No."

"Oh, Jenny." She puts her knife down. I know she's going to come around the bar and hug me, but if she does I'll just lose it.

I hold up my hand, stopping her. "Don't." My voice is hoarse. "If you do, I'll start bawling."

"Maybe you need to."

"I already did." More than once over the past few weeks. I take the glass of water she gives me and try to get my emotions under control. "It's cancer."

Two little words, and she suddenly looks almost as devastated as I feel. Anna's known my dad forever.

She reaches across the bar and grips my hand. "I'm so sorry, honey. You know I'm here."

Nodding, I squeeze her fingers. "I know."

"You want something stronger than water?" she offers. "It's on the house."

I don't really want anything, but I know she needs to do something for me. "A shot would be great."

After pouring two shots of tequila, Anna lifts hers with a solemn "Fuck cancer" and we pound them back together. At least now I have another reason for the burning in my eyes.

Knife in hand, Anna starts in on a bowl of limes. "So what's going to happen with the Titans? Has he told them yet?"

The Steel Titans. My dad is co-founder and president of the club—and has been since he had a fallout with the Hellfire Riders' previous leader and turned in his colors. That blowup happened before I was born, and long before Saxon Gray had been voted in as the Riders' prez. For years, the bad blood between the clubs meant that I could look at Saxon, but never think about touching him. Even coming into this tavern was off-limits to me. Saxon owns it, and the Wolf Den is Hellfire Riders' territory. My dad and the Titans have their own territory, and the center of it is on the ranch spread where Dad and I live. The Titans' clubhouse sits at the opposite end of the property. It used to be, Saxon wouldn't come out there, either.

But for the past week, we've both been crossing territory lines. He's been coming out to my brewery; I've been staying nights at his place. Anna hasn't asked me about that, though she must be wondering. But it doesn't matter. The answer to the question she's asking and the reason I'm comfortable coming into the Wolf Den now is the same.

"The Titans' club meeting is tonight, too." And for the same reason Saxon and the Riders are still at their own clubhouse instead of here. "I don't know if Dad's going to tell them how sick he is—but I know he's going to propose folding the Titans and the Riders together into one club."

Anna suddenly looks up at me, wide-eyed and disbelieving. "What?"

Sometimes I can hardly believe it myself. "My dad went to Saxon. He knows that Uncle Thorne can hold the Titans together after he's gone, but the club isn't as strong as it was. And once Thorne is gone—"

"Then it all goes to shit," Anna guesses. "And you've got a rowdy bunch of bikers on your property without anyone to reel them in."

I tap my finger against the end of my nose, because she's right on it. "And he's worried about the Eighty-Eight coming after me when he's gone. But Saxon wants the clubhouse, and if the Riders are out there, there's not so much to worry about. He'll keep everything in line."

"Yeah, he would." Anna laughs and makes a circling gesture, as if to indicate the bar around us and everything Saxon keeps in line here. "He doesn't put up with any shit, that's for sure."

"No, he doesn't."

And he's mine. Big, sexy, mean as fuck—and by some miracle, all mine. Just thinking of Saxon Gray makes me feel warmer, lighter, helping to ease the solid ache that an afternoon of worrying about my dad left in my chest.

But Anna is giving me an odd little hesitant look. "So

is that why you two finally hooked up—because Saxon will be taking over the Titans?"

"Kind of." We hooked up because I wanted him and he wanted me. Merging the clubs just opened up the opportunity. But now Anna is biting her lip, which means she wants to say something but isn't sure she should. I frown at her. "Why are you looking like that?"

She heaves out a heavy breath. "I thought you both gave in *despite* the club rivalries and shit. I mean, you've been crazy about him forever. And anyone who ever saw him look at you knew it wasn't one-sided. But doesn't it bother you that, for all these years, he always chose the Riders over you?"

That's like a punch to the throat. I stare at her, hurting so much it takes a few seconds to answer. "He didn't."

"What would you call it, then? He never made a move because it would have caused trouble between the clubs. But if he'd just quit the Riders, there wouldn't have been any trouble. He chose to stay with them instead of coming for you."

Just quit the Riders. I know she's only saying this because she's worried for me, but I'm still getting pissed. "That's like saying that *I* should have told my dad to go fuck himself. That I should just toss any loyalty I have to him into the trash, because he's president of the Titans and my relationship to him was getting in the way of my going to Saxon. Screw that. Just because I didn't go to Saxon doesn't mean that I wanted him any less."

"Okay, okay." Her mouth pulls into an apologetic grimace and she quickly holds up her hands. "I'm sorry. You're right."

"I know I am." And I can't freaking believe that she thought otherwise for even a second. "What the hell, Anna?"

"I'm sorry. I just… Okay, this is my shit. Not yours. I shouldn't have laid it on you."

"Laid what on me?"

She just shakes her head. I've got a sudden inkling, though. We haven't seen each other much this week, but when she came out to my brewery the day after the attack to check on me, she seemed a little down. I assumed that she was still rattled, or feeling guilty because she'd left me alone for a few minutes—just long enough for Reich-mann to corner me.

Now another reason occurs to me. Saxon carried me out of the bar, but as we left, he ordered one of the Riders to make sure Anna got home all right. That escort was Zachary Cooper—also known as Gunner, the Hellfire Riders' sergeant at arms…and who'd shot her down once before.

Oh, shit. "Did something happen with Zach?"

Her jaw works before she answers. "I kind of kissed him. He pushed me away and said I was drunk."

"You *were* drunk."

"Yeah, but—" She shrugs. "He sees me a lot when I'm not."

So he did—here at the Wolf Den and at the house Anna shares with her brother. Stone and Zach have been tight since serving together in the Marines, tighter now that they're both Riders, and I assume that friendship is what's holding him back.

"And you think that he's choosing your brother over you?"

"I don't know. I just know he's not choosing me." She braces her hands at the edge of the counter and meets my eyes. "It's nothing. I'll get over it. I'm just sorry that I said anything about Saxon not choosing you."

"It's okay."

"I mean, he's gotta be in love with you, right? He almost killed someone for you. Right in front of everyone."

"Yes," I say, though in truth, that doesn't mean much. I know that better than anyone, because fourteen years ago, Saxon *did* kill someone while trying to protect me… and I was a stranger to him then. I was just a girl unlucky enough to stumble into the Eighty-Eight Henchmen's territory at the wrong time. Saxon was unlucky enough that the kick he aimed at the head of the man trying to rape me—Luke Reichmann's brother—fatally injured the bastard. He spent five years in prison for manslaughter, and told me that he didn't regret a second of it.

Protecting someone didn't mean that Saxon loved them. It just meant that he wouldn't stand by while a man hurt a woman, and that he'd accept whatever consequences came afterward.

So what really mattered wasn't that he'd been ready to kill Reichmann last week, but that he stopped when I asked him to. Because the whole nightmare was unfolding in front of me again, and with so many witnesses, Saxon wouldn't be spending five years in prison; chances were, he'd be going away for much longer. But he stopped when I told him I loved him and that I couldn't bear to lose him—and because he'd promised not to hurt me when I'd told him that being with him risked my heart.

He kept that promise, and *that* means something. I don't know if he loves me. He hasn't said so. But I know that he'll be with me in every way I need him. We burn up the bed together—and there's a hell of a lot of admiration on both sides.

One day, he'll love me. He has to. I can't bear forever if he doesn't.

Forever is a long way away, though. Until then, even if I don't have Saxon's heart, I have *him*.

That's enough for now.

SAXON

"To look at these bastards, you'd think they feel worse about Zoomie's chopper getting trashed than they did when her dad busted his brain bucket on a semi's radiator grille," Spiral comments as he passes me a beer. His easy tone says he's joking. The flat look in his eyes says he's not.

I twist off the cap and wet my throat, watching the brothers return from the garage. The meeting is running long, so when we broke for fifteen minutes, most everyone filed out to cry over the damage the Eighty-Eight's prospect did with the sledgehammer he took to Zoomie's custom bike. Now they're heading back in to grab a drink before settling down to conclude our business.

Spiral's not wrong. To look at them, you'd think Zoomie's bike mattered more than Zoomie's father—even though he was the prez and founder of the Hellfire Riders. Lucifer used to sit where I am now, and when word came down that he'd been killed, a lot of club members were just quiet. Either in shock or disbelieving. Others sat and drank themselves stupid. There wasn't any of the rage the Riders have been showing since Zoomie first rolled her bike in.

But Spiral's not right, either. Losing Lucifer stabbed the Riders more deeply than seeing Zoomie's bike trashed did. The difference is, no one could have done a damn thing to help Lucifer after he rode straight into that truck. Nothing could change it.

We can do something about the Eighty-Eight. And every one of the Riders is ready to. Even now, Picasso catches one of our prospects in a headlock and mimes a punch to his face—showing Knucklehead how he'd have taken care of the Eighty-Eight's little shit.

He won't need to. Zoomie already handled it. A week ago, I stood under the moonlight in Hamilton Quarry and watched while she held a sledgehammer and let the prospect choose which part of his body she was going to hit. The prospect chose a forearm. He should have asked for a thigh—thicker bones, more muscle mass. She'd have broken his leg but probably not shattered it. At least he had the brains to choose his left arm, but he's not going to be a problem again.

The rest of the Eighty-Eight won't be, either. Because I'm not going to stop until they're gone.

Spiral eyes me. "How's your girl doing?"

My girl. My woman. Finally, *mine.*

The fierce possession swelling my chest is only matched by the burning rage, remembering how Reichmann shoved Jenny into the corner of that booth a week ago. Remembering the fear and anger on her face. I'd sworn to protect her but that motherfucker still got his hands on her.

Swallowing the anger with another icy swig, I say, "She'll be doing better after we run off the Eighty-Eight."

"Word is, we might have some help with that. That we're bringing in the Titans. There's rumors flying."

"Are there?" Unconcerned, I finish off the brew and toss the bottle into the empties bucket. I asked my enforcer to start those rumors so we could get an early gauge on the brothers' reactions. "I think we've got a second half of a meeting coming up and those rumors might be addressed."

His eyes are flat again. "I'll be glad to see some of our brothers back. But you know this will stir up that old shit between all of us. I'll stir some myself, if I need to."

"I'm counting on it."

Spiral nods and heads to the leather couches we pulled together in a rough semicircle at the start of the meeting, where he sprawls with his boots out and his usual easygoing look on his face. He's a pain in my ass. Has been since I was voted in as president five years ago. But he's the kind of pain that's good for you. The kind that keeps you from getting lazy or starting to think too much of yourself. If I ever pop off like Lucifer did, Spiral would probably be the next to sit in the prez's seat. He'd be the right choice for the Riders, too. But he's not gunning for my place. He doesn't want the responsibility. For now he just makes sure that I'm earning my right to sit here.

My veep does the same. Blowback just does it a lot harder than Spiral would.

And he does it for me and the Riders as much as he does it for himself. Blowback needs to keep everything around him in line. He needs control. I've never seen him lose his, not even while administering an ass-kicking. I've seen him snap the neck of a man who'd killed one of our brothers without a change of expression. I suspect I never want to see that ice break—and none of the other brothers do, either.

I catch his eye and he signals to Gunner. The sergeant at arms is tasked with keeping order during meetings. Now he calls out that everyone has exactly one minute to get their asses into their seats.

Once they're there, I get started. The rule is, everyone keeps their mouths shut while the prez speaks, so I lay out the deal without interruptions. We'll take on the property and clubhouse on Red Erickson's ranch. Any Titans who want to come over to the Riders will receive a patch and a place within our ranks. They've only got fifteen men, but that will put our own numbers at around fifty bikers. We're already the strongest club in the region. Adding the Titans will only make us stronger and we'll be able to expand our territory, pushing out the Eighty-Eight. I don't try to soften it up. This move means a lot of shit will be coming our way in the next months—or over the next few years, depending on how hard the Henchmen fight back. But the Riders never back down from trouble. We ought to be running toward it.

I can see that most of them are convinced even before I open up the floor for questions, but a few are holding back. When Gunner nods to Spiral, giving him the go-ahead to speak, I already know what's coming.

"So you're gonna let the three brothers who walked after we let Zoomie join us come back?" he asks. "You're gonna give them another patch?"

"I am," I tell him—though it sticks in my throat to even say it. Five years ago, when Zoomie made her bid for a patch, some of the brothers couldn't tolerate the thought of someone with a pair of tits riding with us. But the club's Constitution says that anyone who served in the armed services can't be rejected without good reason. Tits aren't a good reason.

I could have changed the Constitution so that *anyone who served* became *any man who served.* From the day he founded the club Lucifer held onto as much power as he could, and all the rules he wrote into the Constitution are still there. As the president now, I'm the only one who can rewrite the bylaws—and unlike some clubs that vote in their presidents annually, I'm in for life or until the executive board unanimously votes me out.

But I didn't change the laws, Zoomie was voted in, and three of the Riders turned in their colors and joined the Titans.

I hold up my hand, quieting the disgruntled rumble that started in response to my answer. "It'll be with conditions," I continue. "Because I'll tell you true—it pisses me off that they turned their back on the Riders just because pussy walked in. That's not loyalty."

That pisses them off, too. Some, because they're agreeing with me—and some, because they're friends of those former Riders, and I've just insulted those men by calling them disloyal.

Zoomie's more pissed than any of them. Her cheeks are pale with anger and her voice tight as she calls out, "Hey, boss, it might have escaped your fucking notice, but I'm not just *pussy.*"

"That's the point," I say to her over the noise, then sweep my gaze over the rest and that's enough to shut them all up. "I'm willing to let them back because they thought Zoomie would bring the club down. I didn't believe it then and I don't believe it now. But I know some of you did. You came to me then and you told me I was making a mistake, but you stayed. And now we've had years—*years*—that she's been with us. So I want a show of hands if you think the Riders are weaker now that Zoomie's riding with us. It's no secret that some of you used to think so, so nut up and be honest now, too."

Utter quiet. And not one damn hand. Not even from Beaver or Burnout or Knucklehead, who were the most vocal about it at the time.

All right, then. "So I'm willing to accept that they walked *because* of loyalty to the club and they couldn't stand to see it weakened. Now they'll see we're stronger than ever—but if they can't see that, they can just keep on walking. I'll at least give them the chance. Anyone have any argument with that?"

No one does. I look to Gunner and he points to Burnout.

"Prez." The slur at the end of the word and the flush on the man's face says that the beer he grabbed during the break isn't the only drink he's had this evening. "I got a question about this deal you worked out with Red Erickson."

I glance at my veep and see him giving Burnout a hard look. Coming to a meeting intoxicated or high will earn a brother an ass-kicking at best. At worst, he'll have his colors stripped. Blowback will find out if Burnout deserves the best or worst.

"What's the question?"

"Well, it seems like we got a clubhouse and some nice property, but in the past week you've also been hooking up with his daughter. So I'm wondering if she's part of the deal—and do we all get a piece of that, too?"

A piece of Jenny? Rage slams into me, the urge to rip his drunk ass apart, but I only look at him. His hands fly up in surrender, his body pressing back into the couch as if to put distance between us.

"I was just wondering, man! I didn't mean nothing by it."

I grit a response through clenched teeth. "Jenny is *not* part of the deal."

"But we do all get a piece of her," Spiral says so easily the words don't immediately sink in. "At least, that's what the First Lady clause in the club's Constitution says."

This time the rage that rams through me is cold. So fucking cold. "And you're going to enforce that clause, Spiral?"

"I shouldn't have to. What was it you said when some of these guys were asking you to change the bylaws before? You told them, 'If the Hellfire Riders' laws aren't good enough, then you can walk.' And some of those Riders walked." He glances over at Zoomie, who's watching him with narrowed eyes. "You know I was all for you patching in, Lily. And I don't want Jenny—I like my women a little curvier. No offense, Prez. But you can't just enforce some laws to the letter and ignore others."

"He should ignore them when they're as stupid as the First Lady clause," Zoomie blasts him.

"A stupid rule let you in," Goose pipes up from the back.

Gunner looks to me, silently asking whether he should shut them all up. I shake my head. Let it play out.

I'm too fucking pissed to get a coherent word in now, anyway.

Zoomie whirls on Goose. "You think serving our country is stupid?" Meth has rotted a few holes out of Goose's brain but he knows better than to answer that, because she won't be the only one he's up against. When he remains silent, Zoomie says, "The First Lady law is only there because my dad was trying to stick it to Red Erickson by fucking my mom in front of him. That law has *nothing* to do with the club and everything to do with his dick. Just ask the Dubs."

The four W's—Wiggs, Walker, Whistler, and Widow-maker, the Riders' secretary. Along with our treasurer, Old Timer, they're the last of the members who joined the first year the club was founded and who are still around. As president, I outrank them, but not once have I ever talked over them. There's respect that's owed the club's officers and then there's *respect*. Anyone who doesn't show the proper amount to the Dubs and Old Timer is just looking for a beatdown.

Everyone focuses on Wiggs, the brother closest to

Lucifer before the old man died. As it's a meeting day, he's wearing the same denim kutte that he wore during his first years with the Riders. The vest is so ragged it's practically held together by the patches sewn onto it. Half the Riders would give their left nut for a kutte that's seen so much history and ridden so many miles.

"Zoomie has it right," Wiggs says slowly, as if he's reluctant to touch on this topic at all. "But whatever Lucifer's reasons, the clause is there now, so if this situation applies it'll have to be dealt with."

"All right." Speaking evenly requires sheer willpower. I look to Widowmaker, who's sitting at the bar and taking minutes. "Why don't you tell everyone what we're dealing with?"

I know what it is, of course. Blowback warned me it might come up and I know every word of the damn clause.

Widowmaker doesn't bother with the formal language used in the Constitution but just lays out the basics. "When the prez claims a woman—not just screws her, but intends to make her his wife or old lady—his choice has to be approved by the club, because the Hellfire Riders' president is only as strong as those who have his back. And we all know that when a woman's behind a man, she's just as likely to stab him as she is to stand strong."

"For fuck's sake," Zoomie mutters and earns a glance from Gunner. He'll toss her out on her ass at the next interruption.

Widowmaker continues, "So the woman he claims

has to prove herself worthy. First she'll do that by showing us that she's taking him and that she's doing it willingly. The prez can't even touch her because that can be read as coercion. He's stronger, bigger, and maybe it's not so willing if his hands are on her." He scratches his nose and tosses an apologetic look at me. "And by 'taking him' it means that she rides his cock until he comes inside her. The wording is detailed. Even down to the position she's in."

Really fucking detailed. She'd be spread open over me, her back against my chest, her pussy and her tits exposed to every club member.

Pure bullshit. Jenny told me once that she doesn't want to fuck in front of the club, so I'll *never* let it happen. But I bite back that response and acknowledge everything he's said so far with a short nod. "Go on."

"The prez can't touch her, but the brothers can"—he glances at Zoomie—"and our sister, too, I reckon, as we'll be showing admiration for his woman and our support for his decision. That means kissing her, touching her, fucking her. Whatever we ask. And by accepting us, she's showing her trust in the prez and his club, and her belief that *we* are all worthy."

Worthy? Fuck that shit. Not even *one* of us is worthy of Jenny. Including me.

"So that means we start with the first question: Does this situation apply?" Wiggs asks and looks to me. My temper is riding a thin edge now and I don't much care if they can see it. "Are you claiming her?"

I just have to say no. I just have to say that she's a casual fuck, a little pussy that I'm getting on the side.

Even with a gun to my head, I couldn't speak that lie. "She's mine."

"So the clause needs to be addressed. We'll put it on the agenda as new business for the next meeting." The expression on Wiggs' weathered face is hard, as if he doesn't like this any better than I do. "You want to give them all something to think about until then?"

Yeah, I do. This shit shouldn't have to be spoken but apparently needs to be. "Just a reminder that the Riders have another rule in the Constitution: We don't force women and we don't hurt them. And fifteen years ago, the prez of the Eighty-Eight Henchmen forced my woman to the ground with his whole club watching. She fucking *bled* because of what he did to her. Now we're going to ask her to ride a cock in front of another club? We're going to ask her to take us all on?"

In the brief pause I let fall, Beaver speaks up. "And she freaks out when someone touches her." Heads swivel. I hold up my hand to stop Gunner from going after him as Beaver babbles on, "C'mon, you all heard the rumors about her. But I know it's true. We went out to dinner once, one summer while I was home from OSU. I tried to kiss her and she just got all deer-in-the-headlights. She didn't push me away but she was a second from running. Ah, fuck." He spreads his hands, his suddenly wide eyes fixed on my face. "I didn't get any further, man. I'm just backing you up now."

I know he is. But as I'm still struggling to answer without blowing up, Spiral says dryly, "So here's another reason not to see this law enforced. Our prez will kill any of us that show our admiration by touching her."

Fucking right I would. "Then how about you all show your admiration by having a little respect for what she's been through and letting this one go. She *is* skittish. This isn't about ignoring one rule and enforcing another. This is about recognizing that we have two rules in conflict, and we have to decide which is more important: not hurting women or observing this First Lady clause. But that'll be decided in the next meeting. New business now is the Titans. Anything else on them?"

Goose's hand shoots up. "Will you be appointing new officers and drawing from their ranks?"

That's another power Lucifer held close—the president personally appoints every officer, from VP to treasurer. He also chooses the handful of non-officer members who sit on the executive board. "I'm giving Blowback the title of Warlord and bringing in Thorne as my new veep. You know him?"

Nods all around and some quick glances toward Blowback, whose expression hasn't altered from the flat cold stare he always wears. Some will see this move as a demotion but it's not. As warlord, he'll only answer to me—and his role won't include the responsibilities that never sat easy on him. It gives more freedom than he had before.

"Thorne's solid," I say. "He's been the Titans' veep from the beginning. With him acting as my right hand, this integration should go as smooth as it can. I'll also pull one or two of their men onto the executive board, so that we're more likely to catch on to any friction before it turns into something bigger. To that end: Does anyone here have an issue with an individual Titan? And don't bring up any petty shit that you might have with any brother. I don't care if a Titan fucked your mama or your girl. I'm talking the kind of shit that breaks this deal."

When nothing comes up, I tell them, "All right, then. Next week we're holding another meeting and we'll vote to bring the Titans in or not. If we do, we'll walk out of here with more than a dozen new brothers."

Knucklehead raises his hand. "Are we voting on whether we're following through on the First Lady clause, too?"

So they're going to fucking push this? But there's no other answer to give. Jaw clenched, I nod.

"Good thing," Knucklehead says, holding my gaze. "Because it's not her, Prez. It's that you held to the letter of the law when you let Zoomie in. I didn't like it, but I went with it. I took it. Now you've got to take this to the letter, because I want a fucking president who stands by his word."

"The day my word is shit is the day I'll walk." I raze

all of them with a furious look. "Any fucking doubts about that?"

A chorus of "No, boss" comes back. Damn right.

"Anything else?" I only wait one second. "Then this meeting's adjourned. For those of you heading to the Den, we're riding out in ten."

Because I need to see my woman.

TWO

JENNY

The deep rumble of motorcycle engines announces the Riders' arrival. Anticipation and a bit of worry tighten the back of my neck. It's late. I've been shooting the shit with Anna for almost two hours now, so the meeting probably didn't go as smoothly as Saxon hoped it would.

One look at him and I'm sure it didn't. Saxon walks in ahead of the others, a big, dangerous package of muscle and doesn't-give-a-fuck. He's a hard man to read, never giving much away, so the anger I detect in the clench of his bearded jaw and the tense line of his shoulders means that he's *really* pissed.

His intense blue gaze zeroes in on me.

Shit. Nerves tangle in my stomach. An angry Saxon is intimidating as hell. I love him like crazy and I know he won't hurt me, but this is so new, and I have no idea what my role is right now. I'm not sure what's expected of me.

Something is expected. That much is clear. The bikers who come in behind him all look my way and they're not just the same curious stares that have been cast in my direction since Saxon and I got together. The stare that says, *What the hell is Red Erickson's daughter doing in Rider territory?* This is different. Some of Saxon's officers seem grim. Blowback, the Riders' VP, always looks that way, but their enforcer Stone Wall is with him, too. I'd call Anna's brother a good friend, and usually he's got a grin for me, but now he's showing the same hard, angry edge that Saxon is. And a few of the members I don't know so well… God, their eyes are crawling all over me like they expect me to strip naked right here. What the fuck?

I don't know what's going on. Something obviously went down at the meeting. Maybe it involved me—or maybe it's just spillover, if some of the Riders objected to taking on the Titans. Maybe some shit got tossed around and my name came up.

Whatever it was, there's only one thing to do now: straighten my spine and take whatever Saxon gives. Then give him what he needs, too.

Saxon's long strides carry him directly to the bar. I barely have time to smile up at him and say "Hey—" before his big hand clasps the back of my neck and he's scorching my lips with a kiss.

God. Instantly lust shoots through my veins, warming everything that a few drinks haven't already loosened. Moaning low in my throat, I tilt my head back, loving his taste, his possessive grip, the primitive way he simply takes what he wants. I know there's more to this. He's never kissed me like this in front of the others before. He doesn't like participating in public displays. Yet he's clearly staking a claim right now. Making a statement.

Jenny Erickson is mine.

I am. Completely his. And I love it.

My heart is racing and my nipples are throbbing when he lifts his head. His gaze holds mine and for a long second there's no one else, just Saxon and this passion between us.

"You look so damn pretty, Jenny." Low and deep, his voice rasps over my skin like an abrasive tongue. I shiver and he brushes his broad thumb over my kiss-swollen lips. "And you look like you want me to eat your sweet cunt. Do you?"

Five minutes ago I wasn't even thinking of sex. Now my pussy is wet and aching and empty, and his blunt words make my inner walls clench with uncontrollable need.

I silently nod, my breath shuddering across his thumb.

"Good," he says roughly. "Because I need to make you come."

His long fingers slide through mine and he tugs me off the barstool. Suddenly I'm aware of all those eyes again, watching as he leads me to the employees' door that opens to the back offices and storerooms. My face heats but I stubbornly lift my chin. I want Saxon. He wants me. What happens between us is none of the Riders' fucking business, but they're making it theirs by watching us like this—as if millions of people aren't getting it on every single day. As if half the guys in this bar wouldn't stick their dick in a woman right out here where everyone can see them. It's not like he's carrying me out of here with my legs wrapped around his hips and his tongue down my throat.

Saxon pivots to face the crowd behind us just before reaching the swinging door. He pushes through it backward, his expression like carved granite and his hard gaze sweeping the assembled bikers. Suddenly everyone has somewhere else to look.

In the hallway, Saxon shoves me up against the wall just as I hear the first *thwap* of the door swinging closed. Urgency takes over. Rucking up the hem of my skirt, his big hands grip my ass and haul me up. God, his strength. It's as if I weigh nothing. He simply lifts me and in the next second, his thick cock is a solid ridge grinding against my heated flesh, with only denim and silk between us. My moan is lost in his hungry kiss. My body strains closer, my mouth parting beneath the wicked onslaught of his tongue. Every breath is filled with his scent—leather and the summer wind and a long hot ride.

A disappointed whimper escapes me when he breaks the kiss. But I know he has to. Anyone can come across us here and we burn each other up so fast that if we continue, it won't be long until his cock is pumping deep inside me. He doesn't move yet, though, simply holding me with his weight pressing me into the wall and his face buried in the crook of my neck and shoulder.

"God, Jenny." His voice is harsh. "Coming in here, seeing you waiting for me—walking into the Den has never felt so damn good."

My heart suddenly feels tight, so tight. I stroke my hand down the back of his neck. His muscles are rock hard with tension.

"It didn't go well?" I ask.

Immediately his head comes up, blue eyes narrowed. "Just the usual nitpicking shit. Nothing I can't handle, and nothing for you to worry about."

I'm not worried. There's probably very little that Saxon Gray can't handle. "Have you heard anything yet about the Titans' meeting?"

"No. But even if the Titans tell Red to go fuck himself, it doesn't make any difference to *this*." He catches my chin and his gaze is fierce on mine. "You and me. This stays, no matter what goes down between the clubs. All right?"

"I'm not arguing."

"You'd better not." His attention drops to my mouth,

and I gasp as his hips rock between my thighs, sending ripples of aching pleasure through my core. "Screaming my name is a better use for that tongue. Christ, I need to fuck you."

But he won't. Not here. Not even in his locked office, because an interruption could come at any time. Having most of the Hellfire Riders out in the bar means having no real privacy—and as the president of the club, he can't just tell them to fuck off until he's done. Business won't get handled that way.

Business has already wound him up, though. I can feel it in every stiff muscle against me. "I've got a better idea," I tell him.

"There's nothing better than filling you up with my cock, princess." But he's not really arguing, just leaning in with a lazy smile. "A close second is licking up all those sweet pussy juices. Is that what you're thinking?"

"No." I trace his smile with my forefinger. A thrill zings through me when he gently bites down on my fingertip, then flicks his tongue across it. I feel that lick all the way to my clit. Breathlessly I tell him, "I think you should let my tongue do really dirty things to you."

His eyes gleam. "Oh, yeah?"

"Yeah." I tighten my legs around him. "And that way if an interruption comes, you'll be the one hurting. Not me."

His laugh is a deep rumble. "I *did* promise never to see you hurt."

"You did."

"But I still like my idea better," he says, then he's kissing me again, carrying me down the hall into his office—and, oh God, this is already a fight. With his left arm wrapped around my waist, his right hand sneaks up between my thighs. I can't stop my surprised squeal as his fingers slide beneath the drenched silk of my panties and head straight for my clit.

Bucking against him, I tear my mouth from his. "No fair."

Saxon grins. "My place, princess. I decide what's fair. When we're messing around at your brewery you can call the shots."

Right. Aside from a few demands I've made like *harder* and *fuck me now,* I didn't call any shots the couple of times this week he's come out to the brewery to pick me up after work.

As he kicks the office door shut behind us, I give him a narrow stare. "Really?"

"Hell, no," he says and my laugh becomes a ragged moan when he pushes two blunt fingers inside me. My inner muscles clamp down, drawing a hoarse groan from his chest. "You're so fucking ready for me. Tell me you don't want me to lick you all up. Tell me you don't want me sucking on your hot little clit."

I do. God, I do. And I can't help myself—I'm riding his hand, my breath coming in sharp pulls, my pussy so wet that the slick sound of his pumping fingers seems to echo in my head. I lose my mind so fast with him. In just a second he's going to have me spread across his desk and his mouth on my cunt and everything else in the world will be gone.

But he always sees to my pleasure first. This time, I want to give before getting. "I'd rather find out if I can suck your big cock down my throat."

His body stiffens. "Fucking hell, Jenny," he groans.

"You can eat me up after I've swallowed every drop of your cum." I grip his steely shoulders and lick his firm bottom lip, then tease him a little. "I want to see if you can take it or if you'll lose control and fuck me again."

And that easy, I win. He softly chuckles before capturing my mouth in a slow kiss. I played a little dirty, saying that—because in the last week, every time I've gone down on him, after just a short taste he hauls me back up and fucks me hard, as if the feel of my mouth wrapped around his cock breaks his every restraint. Now I love that he's laughing, not offended at all by the challenge…but I also know Saxon won't back down from it.

Still holding me, he sits on the edge of his desk, his powerful legs braced apart and boots flat on the floor. "All right, then."

I'm straddling his hips with my knees supported by the desk's surface. I need to slide down but not yet. Not yet. Because my heart is suddenly so full of that crazy wild love that has been crashing over me all week, squeezing my chest so hard I can't speak. For a long second I just look at him, overwhelmed by the knowledge that he's mine. Not a dream, but here, flesh and blood, everything I've ever wanted—and wanted for so long.

Emotion trembles through my body as I lean in. I don't know what Saxon sees in my expression before my lips meet his, but his response is fierce and rough, his fingers coming up to fist in my hair as he takes control of the kiss. When he releases me, I can't stop touching him, kissing my way along his bearded jaw and down the tanned column of his throat until I hit the collar of his black T-shirt.

I want his clothes off. I want my hands all over his skin. But that can come later. Right now, the president of the Hellfire Riders is jacked up with tension after a difficult night, and he's going to be wearing his colors as I help him release it.

But I can't resist touching him. My hands slide beneath the sides of his leather kutte. God. Through the warm cotton of his shirt, his pecs are like carved slabs of stone and his stomach is ridged with muscle. I love his body. Strong and so fucking big. When I slip my feet to the floor and stand up straight, I still have to look up to meet his eyes, even though he's sitting back on the desk.

His expression is hard now, almost cold—but I know he's not. It's just the leash he's tightening on his control, and as I tug on his belt, his face becomes granite. Oh, but his eyes. His arousal burns through dark blue.

Holding his gaze, I pull the leather through the buckle and start in on his button fly. His hot, steely cock is like a brand against the back of my hand but I don't look away from Saxon's eyes until I've completely unfastened his jeans. His breath shudders as my fingers grip his thick length. My fingertips don't even touch. I haven't had a lot of luck with sex in the past, so my hands-on experience with dick isn't that extensive, but I've seen plenty of big cocks online over the years. So many of them seem sculpted by long-fingered artists, with tapered shafts and flaring heads. Almost elegant.

Saxon's cock is blunt and primitive by comparison. A broad head crowns his meaty shaft, all of it long and massive, as if created for one purpose: To fill my pussy as deep as I can bear, stretching my inner walls with his heavy girth until I'm riding the fine line between pleasure and pain. It always falls on the side of pleasure when he's pumping this thick length inside me, but I don't know if I could take him if he were any bigger.

At the first stroke of my hand, his fingers tighten on the edge of the desk, knuckles whitening.

I slyly glance up at him through my lashes. "It's fortunate the woods were so dark our first night, because if I'd been able to see this monster, I'd have taken off running."

His short laugh is strangled by a groan when I give the head of his cock a firm squeeze. Arousal roughens his voice. "I'd have caught you."

"Yeah?" All kinds of scenarios suddenly tumble through my imagination. "What would have happened then? Maybe you'd have forced me to my knees and made my pussy take every…single…inch."

His breath hisses through his teeth as my fingernails gently scrape a path up those inches. "No." His big hand suddenly tangles in my hair. "I'd have forced you to your knees and seen how much your mouth could take."

The air between us seems to thicken. My gaze raises to his. There's no amusement in his expression now. He's hard and utterly in control.

And now he's going to see how much my mouth can take.

Anticipation and need quiver through my legs as I sink to the floor. His grip on my hair tightens and he fists the base of his cock in his left hand, angling his shaft down toward my upraised lips.

"Look what you've done to me, Jenny. I'm so damn hard I'm already dripping cum."

He is. The head of his cock glistens and a thick bead clings to the tip. The evidence of his rampant need sends a pulse of lust through my core. Whimpering softly, I squeeze my thighs together, but the motion only makes me more aware of the aching emptiness of my cunt. It's not going to be filled. There's only one thing I'm going to get now. Hungrily I focus on that creamy drop.

Saxon commands, "Lick it up."

Bracing my hands on his heavy thighs, I lean forward. The head of his cock is smooth and hot against my lips. A moan vibrates low in my throat as the salty flavor bursts across my tongue.

"Fuck." His body stiffens, muscles rigid beneath my palms. Teeth clenched, he pulls me away, his biceps bulging as if dragging me off his cock is like lifting a great weight. "Your sweet little mouth just makes me harder. I'm already dripping more cum. You want it?"

More than my next breath. "Yes."

"Then wrap your lips around me." His fist in my hair guides my mouth back to his cock. "You suck on the head, you lick up each drop of my cum, then I'll feed you more of my dick. And if you suck nice and hard I'll tell you why this makes me so fucking crazy for you."

Oh, God. I'm crazy for him, too. Eagerly I take his broad crown into my mouth, my tongue frantically working the slick surface. Saxon's groan, a long and drawn-out *"Fuuuuuuuck,"* spurs me on. He's looking down at me, his eyes heavy-lidded and his teeth gritted. I try to swallow more of his cock but his hand in my hair holds me back, allows just the thick tip between my lips, so I suck hard and the hiss of his breath tells me that it's just right.

"Fuck, yeah." The tight leash of his control strains through his voice. "Just like that. Keep going, then I'll feed you more."

I need more. Moaning, I slick the tip of my tongue over the little slit still dripping pre-cum, loving the heavy flavor and the quake that runs through his rigid muscles every time I do it. Never have I imagined craving cock, but it's not even that—it's *Saxon's* cock, and his taste, and his reactions. I can't get enough. Every small crack in his stone expression. Every catch of his breath. Every new drop of cum. It's all mine.

"All right, princess. Open up a little more." His hand tightens in my hair again. His blue gaze is feral. "Take me in. Ah, *fuck* yeah. Like that. Suck me deeper. Can you suck all the way down to my fist?"

I can't. I try, but there's at least an inch between my lips and the fingers wrapped around his thick shaft when he hits the back of my throat. Suddenly my gag reflex kicks in; my chest heaves. Saxon immediately eases up, pulling his cock out of my mouth. His hand leaves my hair to gently stroke my jaw. I stare up at him with tears shimmering in my eyes.

"It's all right, Jenny. You're all right?" His thumb wipes away the moisture at the corner of my eye. "This just from choking?"

"Yes." My voice sounds raw. "I'm okay."

"Is your pussy wet?"

Wet and aching with need. "Yes."

"Good." Bending forward, he lifts my hand and licks my two middle fingers before sliding them into his heated mouth. Desire shudders through my body as his tongue slides up the seam of my fingers as if he's parting the lips of my cunt. Eyes gleaming, he releases me. "Now I want those fingers in your pussy. I want you to fuck yourself nice and slow while I fuck your mouth. Can you do that?"

I'm already slipping my hand into my panties. The silk is drenched, my pussy hot and swollen with need. My flesh greedily grips my fingers but it's not full enough. It's not Saxon.

True pleasure comes when he cradles my face in his big hands and pushes his broad thumb past my teeth. Immediately I begin sucking on it, tasting his skin, and loving how the gentleness and concern in his expression has hardened to stone again. "You got those fingers deep?"

I moan my response, nodding, then moan again when he urges me closer to his straining cock, the taut skin flushed and the thick vein throbbing.

"Christ, Jenny. The way you're so hungry for it is just so damn beautiful. And your mouth… That fucking mouth." His voice deepens to a growl. "Suck me in now. Take as much of my dick as you can and then I'm going to fuck your mouth real slow."

His teeth clench when I do, his expression darkening. All at once he looks angry, his lips drawing back in a snarl, but I know it just means that he's holding onto his control by a thin thread.

"Your *mouth*." His fingers fist in my hair again. "Christ and fuck, you don't know what it's done to me all these goddamn years. A week out of my cell and I run into you on Main Street and you tell me that you're sorry that I went to prison for protecting you, that you'd do anything to make it up to me. And all I could think was that I wanted you on your knees right there, sucking my cock down your throat."

God. I would have. And loved it. I moan and he

pushes deeper, sliding over my flattened tongue.

"But you were Red's daughter." He almost reaches the back of my throat and begins to withdraw, groaning as I suck hard. "So I can only look. I can't touch. But I don't see everything I want to. I don't see your tits or your pussy or your ass. I see your mouth, though. I know exactly what it looks like. Those sexy pink lips. And I picture them wrapped around my cock so many damn times. I jack off to them until I'm almost raw."

His heavy shaft slowly thrusts deeper again. Greedily I arch forward to meet him but his hands tighten, holding me still.

"And there's never any damn relief. I always see you with Anna." *Thrust.* "And you start up your brewery." *Thrust.* "And you come in here and sit right across from me, and all I can fucking do is watch your sexy lips while you talk about contracts and deliveries, but I want you on your knees. Just like this. But now you're here and it's better than I ever fucking dreamed."

He pushes deeper again and stops, holding my gaze. I know what he wants. And, God, I want to give it to him. Breathing deep through my nose, I relax my throat.

"Jenny." He grinds out my name from between his clenched teeth as he slides forward. My body almost revolts but I fight my instinctive reaction as the bulbous crown pushes into my throat. It burns, but I love it, because the expression on his face as he watches me take his cock so deep is stark, agonized bliss.

"Oh, fuck," he groans. "Oh, fuck. Look at you."

Suddenly my throat works convulsively, as if swallowing, pulling him even deeper. Grunting, he withdraws from my throat and I drag in a desperate breath around his cock, tears leaking from my eyes.

He brushes them away. "All right?"

Better than all right. But with my mouth full of his cock, I can only hum my response around his shaft. *Mmm-hmm.*

A shudder wracks his big body. "Christ, that feels good. You still playing with your pussy?"

Mmmm-hmmmm.

"I'm going to lick it up in a minute. Breathe deep, princess." As soon as I do, his fingers delve back into my hair and his cock pushes into my throat again. His body is rigid, his face dark and mean.

Excitement rips through me as I realize he's close to the edge. Moaning, I work my fingers faster. His cock is a burning knot in my throat until he withdraws; then I'm gasping and already hungry for more. He gives it to me, sliding deep again, until I hum. My mouth and throat reverberate all around his thick shaft. Abruptly he pulls out of my throat and his lips draw back in a snarl.

"Suck it hard now. *Fuck.*" His hips jerk, fucking my mouth in quick, shallow strokes. "Harder, Jenny."

A long and low groan sounds deep in his chest, and I know what that sound means. I've heard it so many times this week when he's pounding into me, just before he comes.

Desperate to taste him, I suck harder, pushing closer and forcing him deeper into my mouth with every stroke. His jaw is clenched, the tendons in his neck straining. Then his fingers tighten all at once, holding me still, but he can't stop my mouth. I'm still sucking as the first pulse throbs through his meaty shaft, my tongue sliding around the broad crown. His body stiffens and shakes. Hot and thick and salty, his seed jets to the back of my throat and I swallow it down, sucking his cock deeper.

"Jesus fucking Christ." His voice is hoarse, almost pained. His breath is ragged, his fingers gentle as he pulls me away. His big dick glistens from the wet of my mouth and it's the hottest thing I've ever seen.

Drawing me up, he bends his head and kisses me, deep and slow and sweet. When he finally lifts his head, his dark blue gaze searches my face. "That *was* the better idea."

Still breathless, I laugh. "I think it was."

"Yeah." His big hands run down my back to grip my ass, and all at once his face is hardening again. "Did you come?"

Almost. But it wasn't my fingers that brought me so close. It was the absolute pleasure of feeling him come undone. "No."

"Good." Suddenly he lifts me and lays me back on the desk, hands pushing my knees apart. He groans when he sees the wetness painting my inner thighs. "All this pussy juice. You got this hot from sucking my cock?"

My back is arching, my pussy already tightening in exquisite anticipation. "Yes."

"Then I'll make you suck on my dick all the time." His head dips, and he licks a trail from my knee up to the edge of my panties. Another groan tears from his throat and he settles in, his massive shoulders spreading me wide. "So fucking sweet. You ready for me to eat this pussy? You ready for me to lick your sweet clit?"

God. I'm so desperate I can't even answer, only lift my hips in mute supplication.

His mouth lowers. Through the soaked silk of my panties, his breath is hot against my cunt. His voice is a hungry growl.

"My turn," he says.

THREE

JENNY

My legs are still trembling as I head into the employees' restroom. The rhythmic thunder of heavy metal thumps through the walls and echoes the pounding of my heart. God. My lipstick is gone. Mascara has dried in streaks beneath my eyes. A flush brightens my cheeks. My loose braid has come almost completely undone, my hair falling in thick brown waves over my shoulders. I look thoroughly fucked and Saxon only used his *mouth*.

I'm splashing cold water over my heated face when a

knock comes, followed by Anna's voice. She slides through the door when I crack it open.

"Saxon said you'd need this."

My bag. I intend to stay with Saxon tonight, so it's got a change of clothes and everything I need to fix the mess on my face. Gratefully I take it.

In the mirror over the sink, I see Anna lean back against the wall, watching me with her lower lip trapped between her teeth. *Uh-oh.*

I meet her eyes in the reflection. "What?"

"I heard some of the shit that went down at the meeting."

Of course she did. Working the bar, she probably hears more of the Riders' business than they'd be comfortable knowing. "Something to do with me?"

"Yeah." She bites out the response. Her fingers come up to play with the delicate gold chain around her neck. Not just bothered by something. Working up to being good and pissed. "You ever hear of the First Lady clause?"

"I've heard it mentioned." Only last week while I was sitting with Saxon at the clubhouse. His veep referred to the clause, but when I asked Saxon about it, he said it was nothing. "I don't know what it is."

"It means you have to fuck him in front of the entire club. Oh, and they get to fuck you, too."

My stomach seems to jump into my throat. "What?"

"Yeah. It's some old rule. But apparently it came up at the meeting."

Some old rule. I grip the edge of the sink, desperately trying to think over the doubts crowding my head. *Saxon said it was nothing.* And he told me that some nitpicking shit came up during the meeting, but there was nothing for me to worry about. So it won't happen.

"I think I have heard of it," I say slowly. "From my dad. It's why he left the Riders all those years ago."

"You think Saxon will walk?"

An ache forms in my chest. No. I don't think he ever would. "Maybe he'll just shut it down. Nullify the clause."

"You should probably ask him."

I nod and push away the doubts. "I will."

SAXON

I'D LIKE TO BE BACK in my office and tasting Jenny's pussy all night, but since that isn't an option, the beer she brews is the next best thing. Her smile when she sees what I'm drinking is even better yet. Christ, but she looks good. So damn pretty when I came in tonight, her dark hair braided and wearing a flowery little dress. Fucking beautiful with her mouth wrapped around my dick. Now sexy as hell in the red boots and tight jeans she always puts on before we go riding together, and her hair loose around her shoulders. She'll be leaving here on the back of my bike; then I'll have her in my bed and her juicy little cunt squeezing my cock.

That can't be soon enough. But it isn't coming yet.

She slides onto the barstool beside me. I don't like sitting while I'm out front. Instead I stand next to her with my back up against the bar, watching the brothers drink and play. Business is never just in the meetings. I expect most of them will come up to me at some point tonight, sharing their concerns or support or whatever else is digging at them.

Jenny touches my arm. Her fingers are like live wires against my skin, a burn in the best way. But when I glance over she's not wearing that teasing expression I've gotten to know this week. Instead she's looking hesitant, her green eyes shadowed and worried.

Instantly everything else in the bar is gone. There's only her. "What is it?"

She leans closer so I lower my head. The music's too loud for soft conversation, but I hear her clear enough.

"I heard about the First Lady clause," she says.

Fuck. I catch her chin with my fingers, hold her gaze steady with mine. "It's nothing. All right? I'll deal with it."

The worry clears. She smiles and glances at Anna, and her friend's face goes from pinched to relieved. "All right."

Just like that. My chest suddenly tight, I turn my attention back to the brothers but I don't see a damn thing. Everything Jenny gives me is just like that. So swift. No doubts. I don't fucking deserve it.

I tell her I'll be soft and sweet. I never am. Our first time, not twenty minutes after Reichmann shoved her into that corner, I had her kneeling on the seat of my bike while I pounded her pussy from behind. Each time I mean to go slow and easy and instead I go rough and hard. Even tonight. She's so pretty and delicate and yet I'm grabbing her hair and shoving my cock down her throat until she chokes on it.

She should be with someone better. Someone who doesn't lose his head, who'll treat her gentle. I know this all the way to my bones.

But I'll still never let her go. I can't. Even if I could, I wouldn't.

She gives me everything I could ever want. Just *gives* it. She doesn't like other men touching her. She got hurt bad all those years ago. Not just because she bled when he had her on the ground, but because the fear never went away and she freezes up. But with me she's always hot and sweet and ready. That first night she said she loves me, and maybe she does, but love isn't some magical switch that can turn a body on and off like that. It's only trust that can—and she's trusted me since I kicked that raping asshole's head in.

I don't deserve that from her either. But I've got it. And I'll never betray her trust. Not even for my brothers. I'd do anything for them but that. Let them touch her, knowing how she'll react? No chance in hell. Not at the clubhouse, not here, not for any reason. They can look all they want to. I don't know how any man wouldn't love looking at her.

Just don't fucking touch.

Blowback comes up. If I'm looking as mean as I feel, he's probably the only one who would dare right now. He doesn't have more balls than the others. He just cares less about his continued wellbeing.

"Burnout?" I ask. Drunk at the goddamn meeting.

"A family barbecue this afternoon. He says he lost track of how many he had."

"Fine him. One-fifty. Next time he loses track I take his patch."

Blowback nods. His flat gaze is on the others as he says, "Goose is buying again."

Meth. I don't much care what the brothers get into on their own time. My veep doesn't either. We've had to bail out Goose before on that shit and worked to clean him up, but that's part of being brothers. We have each other's backs. So there's only one reason he'd bring it up now.

"Was he wearing his kutte?" Cops are just itching for a reason to raid our place. Goose will earn worse than an ass-kicking if he's caught selling or buying while boasting our colors.

"Word is. I didn't see it."

"Whose word?"

"The prospect that Lily busted up last week." When I look at him, he shrugs. "I paid him another visit. I wanted to know who the Eighty-Eight's dealers were. He said we should be asking Goose."

"We're not taking that little shit's word over Goose's."

"No. But I'll be watching."

"Give him a warning."

"Already done."

I nod and he heads off. Jenny's slim thigh presses against mine. I glance down but she's talking to Rita, who's parked on the barstool next to her. Not trying to get my attention, then. Just keeping me close.

Then she looks over with the teasing glint back in her eyes, and that gets my dick's attention. Shit. So this is how it's going to be. A damn long night—and hard as a rock every time she looks at me.

But that look is worth it.

I end up watching her as much as I watch everything else going down. We haven't been out together much and having her at the Den, by my side, is new for both of us. But she's got a real easy way with people that would make a body think she'd been hanging out here awhile. She's quick, too. Some of the brothers come up and they just want to pound fists and talk shit for a bit. Sometimes she joins in. But when they come up to talk business she seems to pick up on it without my saying anything, and she turns away to leave us to it. Probably all those years of living with the Titan's prez. Her dad likely had club business carry over to their house from time to time.

Probably not exactly the same, though. I eye the brothers fucking club pussy in the back corner. I recognize some old ladies and some local girls who like a good time. But more and more, new faces have been showing up, most of them driving down from Bend. Some even from up in Portland. I don't know what they're expecting or what they're hearing about the club, but too often they get right in over their heads. Stone and Gunner keep a lookout for anyone in trouble, so I encourage the brothers to keep the fucking inside. It's easier to see if a hookup is going wrong when it's right in front of us.

Some closer than others. From around the pool tables, a cheer rises over the music. It's loud enough to get Jenny's attention. She swivels on her stool and looks in that direction. There's nothing to see yet. Just Old Timer and Spiral chalking their cues while Hashtag racks the balls. Most activity in the bar is slowing, though. At their tables, brothers are shutting up and settling back to watch the show.

Jenny glances up at me. "What happened?"

I shift closer, my leg pressing up against the edge of her seat. "Old Timer just put in his old lady."

Her dark brows shoot up. "A bet?"

"Yep."

She laughs a little. "Am I wrong in remembering that Old Timer plays the big tournaments pretty often? He's been written up in the *Observer* a couple of times, right?"

The local paper. "You remember right. But he doesn't always win while he's here."

"Spiral is that good?"

"No." When her green eyes narrow, I explain a little better. "Sometimes Old Timer throws the game. It depends on whether he's punishing Helena or not."

Her frown is swift. "Punishes her by handing her over to someone else?"

"Punishes her by *not* handing her over."

Her pink lips soften in surprise and her gaze shoots to Helena. With curly red hair and tits that don't quit, Old Timer's old lady always looks good when she comes in on his arm, but tonight she's wearing a little red skirt, a white shirt that stretches the scooped neckline with every breath, and red heels like stilts. Her fingers are curled around Old Timer's thick biceps and she's giving him a saucy grin. No doubt Helena knew what she'd be getting tonight.

"You should come by on her birthday or around Christmas!" From the other side of the bar, Anna calls out over the music. "Then he lets her have five or six guys. We have to put a towel down!"

Jenny's hand shoots up to cover her laugh. She glances to me for confirmation. When I nod, she looks to Anna, who grins at her and moves farther along the counter to take another order.

"Well, then. All right." Still smiling, Jenny sips her beer and focuses on Helena again. "God, I hope I have her body when I'm that age."

"You can have hers as long as I've still got yours." And the fifteen or twenty years that Helena has on Jenny won't nearly be enough for me.

She snorts and bumps her leg against mine. I'm hard as hell again and need to taste her, so I bend my head and catch her mouth. So damn sweet. She lets me right in and her green eyes are bright with need when I let her go. Her breath is coming fast. Her gaze slides out to the pool tables again and she casually takes another drink, but by the way her butt squirms in her seat a little I know she's aching as much as I am.

It isn't going to get any easier. Old Timer wins the break and begins clearing the stripes from the table. There's just one left when he looks up at Helena. She looks back at him, then a wide smile curves her red lips when he sinks the eight ball. Shouts and cheers rise from the brothers. Old Timer just straightens up, watching as she bends over, bracing her hands on the edge of the pool table. Spiral waits for a nod from Old Timer before moving in.

Beside me, Jenny's eyes are wide and she gulps about half her pint.

"All right?" We can get out of here if it isn't.

She nods without looking away. There's been hookups going on all night, and she hasn't paid much attention to them. I can guess why this one's different. It's Helena. Not the high heels or the big tits, but the blissful anticipation that settles over her face when Spiral pushes her skirt up, revealing her round ass and a red thong. It's the way her entire body shudders and her eyes lock with Old Timer's when the man behind her slicks his fingers between her legs and holds up his hand to show everyone how wet she is. When it's so strong and true, a woman's pleasure is a mesmerizing thing and it's hard to take your eyes from her.

Fuck knows that's part of the reason I can't ever look away from Jenny when she's with me.

I like watching her just as much now. She put some glossy makeup on her mouth that I thought would taste like sticky cherries or vanilla when I kissed her, but there was just Jenny's flavor—and the gloss stayed on after. The sexy bow of her mouth glistens as her lips part and she draws in a ragged little breath. I don't need to look over to know that Spiral has just filled Helena's cunt with his dick. Jenny's thighs are pressed together tight, the same way she squeezes my wrist when I'm fingering her pussy, the same way she clamps around my head when I'm fucking her with my tongue.

Christ, my cock has never ached so hard. "You like watching?"

"I guess I do." She glances up at me. "You?"

"Hell, yeah."

Her gaze drops to the erection trying to bust through my jeans and her glossy lips widen into a smile. Taking a sip, she looks back toward the pool table. "Have you ever done this?"

"During my first year with the Riders." High as a kite and all too happy to swing my dick around. But fucking while people looked on got old real fast.

She nods and her gaze runs over the brothers. Most everyone's watching. "But it really is nothing to them, isn't it? Just not a big deal."

Thinking of that First Lady clause again, maybe. "To

most of them it's nothing," I tell her. "It's nothing to Spiral. But it's not nothing to *them*."

Old Timer and Helena. Jenny looks to the older man, then to his old lady. They're holding each other's gaze as Spiral slowly pumps into her and, judging by their faces, they're both getting more out of this than the man fucking her is. And yet Helena's still not getting enough, though Spiral's going deep. Her cunt honey shines the full length of his dick. With every stroke, he almost withdraws before leisurely sinking in up to his balls again. Biting her full lower lip, she tilts her ass up higher and her arms flex as she pushes against the edge of the pool table, trying to force him faster, harder. He only grabs her hips and holds her still for the long slide of his cock.

She raises pleading eyes to Old Timer. He gives a shake of his head and she responds. Maybe cursing him, maybe begging. I can't hear a word over an old Guns N' Roses ballad that's the worst accompaniment to a screwing I've ever heard, but her frustration is clear. She's right on the edge but Spiral's not pushing her over yet. Instead he catches her arms when she shoves against the table again, pulling her wrists to the small of her back and holding them in his left hand while he takes hold of her thick hair in his right. She's bent over at her hips, back arched, and he uses his grip on her wrists and hair to drag her back over his dick. Still so fucking slow, and every time he pulls her back all I can imagine is Jenny in front of me, her pussy a hot vise around my cock. Then as Helena suddenly writes and shakes, her mouth falling open, there's only the memory of Jenny's cunt milking every inch.

Jesus. I chug a few swallows to cool my blood and glance at Jenny. She's flushed and squirming.

Still staring at Helena, she says, "I want to do that when we get to your place."

"Fuck, yeah." Trapping her wrists and hauling her back over my cock. "Slow or hard?"

"Both."

"You'll get both." The way my cock feels, she'll get both a couple of times over. But now I can only bend my head and taste her mouth. I don't want to let her go. My fingers stay clasped around her nape when I straighten again. Spiral hasn't finished. He looks to Old Timer, who signals to Hashtag. The prospect doesn't waste a second before scooting around in front of Helena and freeing her tits. His mouth latches onto one of her fat nipples just as Spiral starts pounding into her. Her eyes glaze over and pure bliss slackens her lips.

And screw this shit. If anyone has more business they can bring it to me tomorrow. Helena's a pleasure to watch but my woman is in need, and there's no one more beautiful than Jenny when she comes.

I sweep my thumb down the side of her neck. When she looks up, I ask, "Ready to get the hell out of here?"

She's off the stool almost before I finish. "Yes."

I grab her hand and head to the door. But it's never that easy. There's more business already waiting outside.

With her blonde hair hanging down her back, Zoomie is in the corner of the lot, tinkering with the guts of a crotch rocket under the flood of a streetlight. Next to the other bikes, it's an emaciated video-game shit-stain of a ride.

Fuck. I can't ignore this. Her custom chopper was trashed but better to ride around in a cage than on that piece of shit. Still holding Jenny's hand, I cross the lot. It's still hot as hell outside, though it'll start cooling off fast around midnight. "Zoomie!"

Her spine stiffens before she looks over her shoulder. She knows what's coming but she plays it off like nothing. "Yeah, boss?"

"You rode that here?"

"Mostly." She gets to her feet and the look she gives the crotch rocket would have made most men back up a step. "The engine cut out on the way."

"Were you wearing your colors on it?" A fucking embarrassment to the whole club.

Her blonde eyebrows shoot together. "Hell, no. I came over like this."

In a black tank and jeans. So I won't be kicking her ass. Instead I might be kicking my veep's. "Blowback gave you a bike that doesn't run? A fucking *Honda*?"

"No. I borrowed it from a friend."

"He was supposed to find you a ride."

"And I told him to shove it up his ass," she says and because she's talking to me, her voice stays even, but every line of her body tells me how pissed she was when Blowback came to her. "I'm not taking anything from him. Next thing he'll be saying I need handouts or some shit. That I can't pull my weight."

No, he wouldn't. She only thinks so because back when she was making her bid for a patch, Blowback got tired of the brothers focusing on the fact that she had tits and he spoke up on the only point that really mattered: He asked whether she could hold her own when she's throwing down. Zoomie read that as him believing she was weak and Blowback never corrected her. I'm not going to, either. That's their shit to work out.

But this is my shit. "*I* told him to get it for you."

She flushes a little. "And I'm grateful, boss. But I don't want it from someone who thinks I'd be better off hanging up my kutte and become a fucking old lady. No offense, Jenny."

"None taken," she responds easily and I like that a hell of a lot. Jenny doesn't want to be an old lady, either—but she doesn't correct Zoomie's assumption and say that she doesn't belong to me. "We all know you'd never fit."

Zoomie snorts. "No, I wouldn't."

"And as long as you don't mind a cage for the night," Jenny adds, "you can take my truck. If you pick me up at Saxon's place in the morning, we can head out to the ranch. I've got a ride you can borrow."

Face blank, Zoomie glances at me. I know what she's asking—whether a Hellfire Rider can even think about heading out to the Erickson's ranch right now, let alone borrow a ride from the daughter of the Titans' president.

"You can take a look," I tell her. No matter what came out of the Titans' meeting, Red wants these clubs together as badly as I do. He won't throw shit over this.

She glances at Jenny. "Then I'll see you tomorrow. What time?"

"No later than eight."

Not a lot of time. Because she's got work at her brewery—and tonight I'm going to have her bent over in front of me and dragging her back over my cock. I'm not wasting another second. I wait just long enough for Jenny to hand Zoomie her keys and then I'm sweeping her up, carrying her to my bike while she laughs. Before I start up the engine, she slides her hands around my waist and says huskily, "Don't forget: slow *and* hard."

I ride like hell for home. Sweet and slow, I remind myself. Just like Jenny deserves. But when we get there, slow turns to rough and hard real fast—and a little rougher every time she comes.

FOUR

JENNY

I wake up alone in Saxon's big bed, with the breeze from an oscillating fan sweeping over the single sheet covering my naked body. There's no air conditioner in the house, so Saxon leaves the window open overnight to let out the heat that builds up during the day. The pale light peeking around the edge of the curtain tells me it's just after dawn. Not much noise is coming from the cul-de-sac outside, not this early on a Sunday morning. Just a few twittering birds. The world is in bed, except for Saxon.

And me. I'm still tired, but I know I won't go back to sleep. It hasn't been coming easily lately and probably won't come at all without Saxon beside me.

I steal a big T-shirt from a shelf in his closet and go in search of him. He can't be far. The house isn't big, just a one-bedroom bungalow. He lives alone—but doesn't seem to *live* here that much, though I know he moved in about six years ago. No pictures hang on the walls. No rugs cover the wood floors. He's got a couch and a bookshelf in the living room, but no TV. Only a small table with two chairs sit in the kitchen, and there's nothing but a bed and a fan in the bedroom. The house just seems to serve as a place for him to eat and sleep.

But even though it's just a pit stop, he keeps it clean. Much cleaner than I expected from a man living on his own. Saxon tells me that I give him too much credit, that he has a housekeeper come in once a week, but he makes her job easy. I've never seen him leave anything lying around. From his toothbrush to a drinking glass, as soon as he uses it he puts it away.

The hallway is dark. Both the living room and kitchen are empty but now I hear a faint *whump whump whump* through the door connecting the kitchen to the garage, where he keeps his motorcycle and his exercise equipment. Aside from the bed, it's the one place he seems to spend any significant time while he's here.

The noise tells me what I'll see before I open the door, but I still stop in my tracks. A woman can't be expected to keep her brain cells running when Saxon is stripped to the waist and pummeling the heavy bag hanging from the garage's ceiling. He's facing away from me. I don't see his naked back often. My fingers have gripped those massive shoulders so many times now, clinging to his solid flesh as he pounds into me, but I haven't had much opportunity this week to simply *look*. When his shirt is off, he's usually above me or behind me.

Now my eyes are greedy, drinking in every inch and returning for seconds. Thirds. I'll never get my fill of him. Sweat gleams over tanned skinned. The Hellfire Riders emblem is tattooed across his broad shoulders and with every punch, his muscles flex smoothly beneath fiery wings and give life to the ink. His heavy arms are ripped; his biceps bulge and his triceps look carved from stone. His gray sweatpants hang low on his hips and I just want to lick my way along the taut, defined lines of muscle that lead beneath his waistband to his perfect ass.

And this beautiful man is mine. For a second I can't even breathe, my heart is so tight.

Saxon pauses, his chest heaving. Without looking over his shoulder he says, "Get over here."

The concrete floor is cold beneath my feet, but only a few steps carry me over to the black gym mat that covers the back half of the garage. A rack of dumbbells and a tree of Olympic plates stand against the wall behind his weight bench. He tosses his boxing gloves onto the bench as I come. His big hands are wrapped and he slides his fingers into my hair, pulling me in for a kiss. It's not deep and hot, just a sweet "good morning" but it still sears me to my toes. God, I love the way he smells and all this sweat just makes his scent stronger.

He begins unwrapping his hands and his dark blue eyes narrow as he looks down at me. "You ought to be in bed still. When did you finally fall asleep—an hour ago, maybe?"

Maybe. I didn't keep track. But if Saxon did, he must not have been sleeping, either. "You're up," I point out.

"Yeah, because my woman was lying awake all night, even though she should have been fucked into exhaustion hours ago. Is that First Lady crap bothering you?"

"No. Is it bothering you?"

"Only that it came up and gave you even a second of worry. That clause is bullshit and everyone knows it."

I nod, watching the flex of his pectorals as he unwinds the handwrap from around his wrist. "Actually, I was thinking of your business plan for after you move the Riders out to the ranch and turn your old clubhouse into a gym."

"Yeah?"

"Mmm-hmm. I think you should put a big window in the front of the building and do your workouts right there. With your shirt off. You'll bring in so many new customers that—"

He shuts me up with a kiss, laughing against my lips. "I'm not into making that public, either. Now make yourself useful and ride my back for a few minutes."

"What?" But it becomes clear when he drops to the mat in a pushup and waits. "Seriously?"

"Your weight will give me just enough resistance to make these interesting again. C'mon. Sit your little ass right between my shoulder blades and then hold still."

Crazy. Gingerly I lower myself, tucking the long length of the T-shirt between my legs because I'm naked beneath and suddenly my face is burning red. But he just waits, solid as a rock beneath me. When I'm balanced with my knees bent and my toes on the mat, he pushes smoothly up. I almost fall but grip his shoulders, giggling all at once. God. He goes down again. As far as I can tell, he's not making any real effort, despite lifting an extra hundred and twenty pounds.

"If you're trying to impress me, it's working," I tell him.

I feel the short laugh rumble through his chest, then he's all business again. I can't be. Lightly my fingers trace the top edge of his tattoo. He's got another high on his arm—a grinning skull and crossbones. Some bikers wear skulls on their skin and it doesn't mean anything. But Saxon wears a similar patch on his kutte, and it does mean something: he killed someone.

"Is this for Timothy Reichmann?" The man who attacked me all those years ago—and the reason the Eighty-Eight Henchmen have it in for me now. The Eighty-Eight's current president is Reichmann's younger brother.

A grunt serves as Saxon's answer. *Yes.* Maybe it's not as effortless now that he's hitting fifteen or twenty of these.

"What are these numbers in the teeth?" In the skull's upper teeth, a gap separates a one and two twelves from a six, fifteen, and eighteen; ten, five, fourteen, another fourteen, and twenty five are inked into the bottom teeth.

He lowers onto his stomach. "It'll come to you. And don't move, because I'm going to do another set in a minute."

I study the numbers. The two on top might be dates. "When did you get the tattoo?"

"The first year I was out."

Of prison. So he got it nine years ago. If the numbers represent a date, I can't figure out what it refers to, and I'm distracted now, anyway. A thick scar runs from beneath his underarm and up toward his shoulder blade. It's straight, but the edges are ragged.

I can't imagine what caused it. "What is this from—an accident?"

"Shrapnel. Part of a Humvee's door panel got wedged up in there."

A Humvee? My fingers sweep over the pale ridge. "You served? When? Where?"

Not as long as I've known him, and he was only twenty when the jury convicted him of manslaughter and sent him away for five years. I know for certain he didn't enlist afterward.

"Kosovo. And it was right out of high school. I joined

the Marines, went through basic training, got assigned to my unit, and we were deployed about three months later. A peacekeeping mission, but inside a week, we were hit by insurgents. I was sent home on disability."

"Disability?"

"Yep." Smoothly he pushes up again. "I couldn't lift that arm high enough to aim a rifle. I couldn't for about three years."

Softly I say, "You were in prison by then."

"With nothing to do but rehabilitate it." Up and down. "And it's why I kicked Reichmann instead of pulling him off of you. I still barely had any strength in that arm."

My gaze slides over to the skull inked into his shoulder. "So I guess you can blame killing him on the insurgents."

"No." He pauses with his elbows bent, his triceps like sculpted bronze. "I blame Reichmann. The fucker got what he deserved. But he might not have gotten it if my arm had been working right. I'd have just beat his ass and walked away."

"I guess." With a sigh, I smooth my hand over the skull. His muscles flex rhythmically beneath my palm. "Did you like being in the corps?"

Another grunt. *Yes.*

I'm not really surprised. "The club's the same in some ways, isn't it? At least it is for a lot of the Titans." Many of whom are ex-military. So are most of the Riders. "There are just different rules."

But it's still all about loyalty and brotherhood and

serving a purpose. The purpose is different, sure. At the core it's all about freedom, though. The corps defends it and the clubs embrace it.

"A lot of different rules. But I won't argue. You're not all right but you aren't wrong, either. Now lift up." When I do, Saxon turns over and lies with his back on the mat, then brings me down so I'm straddling his stomach. "I'll tell you true, Jenny, I was in a pretty bad place when I came back. I liked being in the corps, liked serving, then I was out. Like I hadn't been able to hack it. So joining the Riders felt like a second chance to be a part of something like that again." His gaze shoots to my thighs, spread over him and with the long T-shirt hiding everything between. "You wearing panties?"

I shake my head.

"Is that your pussy getting wet all over me?"

Grinning, I brace my hands on his wide chest and wiggle my ass a little, rubbing my heated flesh against his ridged stomach. "Maybe. And I've got you trapped. Now tell me why you're up so early."

His hand catches the back of my neck and he hauls me down, until my breasts are flattened against his chest and our mouths are just a whisper apart. His voice is rough. "You think it works like that?"

"It seems to work for you." Slowly I rub against him again and watch lust darken his eyes. "Every time I try to hide something from you, you just fuck it out of me."

"Then what are you hiding now, princess?" His free

hand slides up my thigh. "Why couldn't you sleep?"

My throat tightens. Suddenly I don't feel so hot and sexy. Saxon frowns and rolls onto his side, carrying me over. His big hands cradle my face.

"Jenny?"

"I'm not hiding it." My voice has thickened. "I'm just trying not to think about it."

"Your dad?"

My breath shuddering, I nod and he tucks my head against his shoulder. "He's been seeing his lawyer all week," I tell him. "And yesterday afternoon he came in with a stack of papers for me to sign. Putting the property in my name, adding me to the bank accounts, making all the arrangements for…after."

"Because he doesn't want you to have to deal with that shit when you're grieving."

"I know." Though if it hurts this much now, I don't know how I'll get through it anyway. "There wasn't a living will—you know, for when he's so sick that he can't…" I can't finish. Shaking my head, I say, "All those papers, and no living will. You'd think it would be the first thing the lawyer would give him."

"Yeah." The response sounds full of grit. "It was the first thing we got for my mom."

Because Saxon has gone through the same. He never mentions it, but it's a small city, so I remember hearing when she passed six or seven years ago. Breast cancer, I think.

I come up on my elbow. He's wearing that stoic expression again. This time I can't read past it but I probably don't need to. I lost my mom, too. "I'm sorry. I didn't know her well." By sight, and mostly I just remember her crying in the courtroom after he received his guilty verdict—a tall, dark-haired woman with soft eyes and a quiet way of moving. "She seemed very sweet."

That makes the corners of his mouth kick up. "Nah, she wasn't. She was a tough old broad."

"Really?"

"My dad ran off when I was three, so it was just her and me. She cleaned rooms up at the Pine Valley Lodge until her back got messed up, but even after she couldn't work full-time there was always food on the table, always a roof over our heads. She always pulled through." His smile fades. "Until she didn't anymore."

"I'm sorry."

He shakes his head and focuses in on my face again. "You're thinking there's a reason Red didn't make out a living will."

"Yes." My lips press together and a long second passes before I can continue. "I don't think he's going to wait until the cancer takes him. I think he's just going to take a ride and he won't come back from it."

His thumb brushes my trembling lips in a soft caress. "I would, too. I'd fight it. But when there's nothing left to fight? I'd get everything settled and hold out until waiting any longer means that I couldn't steer my bike. Then I'd take that ride, too."

Tears spill over when I nod. "I know. And my head gets it. But here?" I thump my knuckles over my heart. "It's not so easy. And last night I was just thinking: He's all alone out there. And what if he goes tonight? Or what if he's sick and needs help and I'm not home? He's not at that point yet, but I just…I…I feel so guilty."

Saxon catches my face and rolls me onto my back, looking down at me with his brows drawn. "Because you're with me instead of at home?"

"Not because I'm with you. Because I'm not there."

"You want to start spending nights out at the ranch again?"

My breath shudders. What I want doesn't matter much right now. And I *do* want to be with my dad. But even that's not as important as being there *for* him. "I think I should."

"Then you should. You and me, we've got lots of time. You and your dad don't. So take as much as you can and I'll be here when you need me. Or out there, if you need me there. All right?"

God. Thirty seconds ago, I thought I loved Saxon Gray. But that was nothing, *nothing* to what I'm feeling now. My chest hitches, then I'm reaching for him, my fingers sliding into his dark hair. His kiss is hot and sweet and too short. He lifts his head and wipes the tears from the corners of my eyes.

"It's going to be hard, Jenny. Real hard. I put more

miles on my bike when my mom was sick than I did all the years before or since." On a deep breath, he shakes his head. "You just let me know if you need a ride. Or whatever is the same for you."

"You're the same for me," I say hoarsely. "Being with you."

"So you like a ride, too," he responds, and I give a watery laugh before he's kissing me again and lifting me from the mat. "You want me now?"

"Always." I bury my face in his neck, feeling cherished as he holds me in his strong arms and carries me through the kitchen. More pale light is filtering through the windows now. "So why were you up? What's eating at you?"

"You." In the bedroom, he lays me in the center of the mattress and follows me down, his heavy weight settling between my thighs, his upper body braced on his elbows. His voice is like gravel but his mouth is gentle as he kisses the length of my throat. "And how I'm always so rough with you."

"I like rough."

"But you deserve slow and sweet. And I will be this time, princess. I swear it."

I don't need it. But I'm not going to complain when he softly coaxes my lips open. The slow thrust of his tongue against mine is matched by the easy rock of his hips into the cradle of my thighs. A warm hollow ache opens up inside my chest, and a hotter ache stirs below. God, the way he kisses me. I've never been kissed like this before. As if I'm precious and beautiful and needed.

My eyes are burning as his heated lips journey down my throat. The fan's cooling air sweeps over my skin when he moves away for the brief moment needed to slide the T-shirt over my head. I shiver, then he's back over me, solid and warm, the hair on his chest teasing my stiff nipples every time he rocks against me.

It's still gentle and sweet and I almost can't bear how much need is building. My body arches beneath his.

"Saxon." It's a helpless plea. "Inside me. Be slow inside me."

He groans against my lips and reaches for the condoms stashed beneath his pillow. His left hand slips between my legs. His breath hisses through his teeth.

"This is always when I lose my head. You're so damn wet." His thick middle finger pushes into me. "So damn tight."

I cry out as his thumb slides over my clit. He's looking down at me, his eyes feral but his movements controlled as he sheds his sweatpants and rips open the packet.

"Put it on me."

I barely can. His finger is pumping into my pussy. I can't stop my hips from moving with him and my hands are shaking as I smooth the condom over his jutting erection. Expression hard, utterly in control, he positions himself at my entrance. His mouth lowers to mine.

"Wrap your legs around me, princess." He kisses me

gently when I do, and his voice is taut with strain as he says, "Slow, all right?"

God, yes. "And deep."

"Real fucking deep," he says and begins pushing into me.

I suck in a breath. Whether going rough or easy, this part is always slow. He's just so big, so deliciously long and thick, and no matter how wet I am, my sensitive flesh burns and stretches to accept his girth. After a few initial thrusts he'll be able to slide right in, but within a few hours I'm always as tight as if it's our first time again.

His mouth takes mine, tongue slowly thrusting past my lips as his cock tunnels deeper. I whimper into his mouth with every short push. He's all around me. All I can taste, all I can smell, all I can feel. His ass flexes beneath my heels and suddenly he's almost completely inside me, stopping to let me adjust.

Oh, God. Not enough. I rip my mouth from his. "Deeper."

He groans, his body rigid above me. "I bottomed out, Jenny. There's no deeper. I've got more cock but you don't have more cunt."

"I do." My back arches and my legs hug him closer, trying to pull him farther in. "When you're fucking me hard, you're deeper. You're in me all the way."

"Yeah, I am. Buried balls deep." Gripping my hip, he pushes against me and yes, yes. Oh, fuck. I cry out against his mouth and he curses, shaking his head and easing back.

"I'm not deeper," he says hoarsely. "I'm just punching my cock up into you. *Jesus.* Have I been hurting you every time we fuck?"

"No." Tightening my legs, I try to haul him closer again. "Please."

"Jenny." He groans my name but pushes deeper—slowly, watching my face. His heavy length fills me, right to the edge of pain, but it's good. So good. I'm panting as the crown of his cock hits the end of my need-swollen channel. It's pure pleasure, but then the pressure increases and suddenly it's all *more,* ecstasy radiating through every nerve, and all I feel is Saxon and his big cock stuffed inside me and my pussy clenching around every thick inch.

"You're squeezing me like a fist." He grits out the words. Braced beside my shoulders, his arms are like steel. "So you want it like this?"

Clinging to him, I all but sob the answer. "Yes."

"It doesn't hurt?"

My head thrashes in a wild *No.* It aches deep inside, but it's not a hurt. It's all just more intense, pleasure on a razor's edge.

His hand cradles my face as he licks his way past my lips and into a devastatingly thorough kiss. His thick shaft withdraws but only a few inches before he's sliding deep, each thrust slow and deliberate. The intensity never lets up, each sensation building on the last, a spring winding tighter and tighter around his big thrusting cock. I need more and harder because it's too much, I need him to jolt me over, I need to come. He doesn't let me. His face is hard and mean, that look that says he's in control, that he's not going to give in. My pleading cries fill the room. I can't move. He locks my wrists over my head and his weight pins me to the mattress as his cock fills my pussy again and again, so slow, so deep.

I can't bear it. My whole body is burning and writhing and pulled too tight, and the pleasure never stops, but usually I'm being pushed along, riding a wave of sensation. Now I'm just drowning in it, and every kiss, every thrust drags me deeper. I'm at the black bottom when the pressure finally breaks and my orgasm wracks every nerve, every muscle. Release, but I can't even breathe. He's still so deep and I can't stop coming, can't stop breaking again every time he pushes into me.

Then he groans, that low and deep sound that means he's going to come. He lets go of my wrists and his hips thrust in hard jerks, his cock pounding into me. Freed, my fingers slide over his sweat-slicked shoulders, loving the feel of his skin, his strength.

Abruptly his lips capture mine. His kiss is hot and deep and wet, and he's groaning into my mouth when his big body begins shuddering over me, his thick shaft pulsing against my inner walls.

I can't stop kissing him. Not when he slowly withdraws, tossing the condom over the side of the bed. Not when he rolls onto his back, carrying me with him. Not when the alarm clock on my phone trills, telling me that it's time to get up.

But the insistent ring eventually forces me to let him go, rolling over to swipe at the screen. With a sigh, I return to his side. He holds me close, his big arm around me, my head pillowed on his shoulder. Idly, my fingers trail through the dark hair on his broad chest, then swoop in to circle his flat nipple.

"Slow wasn't half bad," I finally say.

His body shakes with his laugh. Grinning, I look up and that wild emotion crashes over me again. My eyes burn and suddenly his laugh stops; then I'm on him, kissing him with my whole fucking heart on my lips.

"I love you," I tell him hoarsely.

His hands fist in my hair and his face goes dark as he pushes me over again. This time it's hard and rough, yet the pleasure of his touch still drowns me in pure sensation. I cling to him until I break, screaming his name.

And that's not half bad, either.

FIVE

JENNY

Lily shows up promptly at eight. My hair's still wet from a hasty shower, so I twist it up in a clip and grab my things. At the front door, Saxon gives me a kiss and swats my ass on my way out.

Lily has the driver's door open and she's standing there with her eyebrows raised, as if asking whether I want to drive. Since I'm in a state of so-tired-I'm-punch-drunk, I head around to the passenger side.

It takes me about a second to realize she's in the

same state. Her eyelids are heavy. Her long blonde hair is mussed and she's still wearing last night's clothes.

She yawns and starts the truck. "Starbucks?"

"God, yes. No, wait. Just head to Minnie's—that drive-thru espresso hut in the Safeway parking lot. We won't have to get out."

"Good thinking. I like your lazy-ass ways."

She reverses out of Saxon's drive. Her kutte is neatly folded on the seat between us. No biker I know wears their colors while in a vehicle. I pull my seatbelt across my chest and notice a scrap of red lace wedged next to the buckle. Pinching the fabric, I drag out a thong.

The panties look about my size but they aren't mine. And Lily's six feet tall, at least. She's lean, her muscles long and defined, but there's no way she's an extra small.

"Whoops." Lily grins and snatches the thong, stuffing it into her front pocket. "I guess Sasha missed that."

"I guess. Do I need to hose anything down?"

"Just the gearshift," she says, and I don't stop laughing until we pull up in line at Minnie's. Lily rolls down the window and tosses the red panties into the trash container sitting beside the hut. She catches my surprised look and shrugs. "No point in making the effort of washing and returning them. I'll see her at the Den again, but she wasn't there for me."

"She left with you."

"Only because I raise her hotness level."

The car in front of us drives on. We pull up to the

window and I have to wait until Minnie takes our orders before I can ask, "Her hotness level?"

"Yeah. No, I got this." Lily waves away my money. "Sasha's with Beaver, mostly. But he still fucks around, you know? Half the brothers basically think they're living in Porno World. So the hottest girls are the ones who suck cock and take it up the ass and fuck two guys at once—preferably in front of everyone else. They don't really give a shit about the girl, just what she'll do."

Ah. "And what's hotter than girl-on-girl action?"

"Right. So Sasha figures she's going to make Beaver more interested by fucking me. A lot of the club girls do. And it usually works to turn their guys on, at least for a while. I think the guys probably just ask what it was like and then stroke off to it." She shrugs. "I don't care. There's never any dick at the Den that I can get with, because they're all brothers and I'm not touching that. So I get laid and it holds me over until I can get up to Portland for a weekend and find some dick that's never heard of the Riders."

"So you'd rather have the dick?"

"If I've got a choice." She passes my coffee over and sticks hers into the cup holder. "It's just, you know, like the difference between a crotch rocket and a Harley. The crotch rocket can go fast and riding one can be fun, but I'd rather have some power and a big engine between my legs."

"Yeah."

"Whoa." She looks to me with widened eyes. "That 'yeah' sounded a lot like 'I know *exactly* what you mean' and not just 'I understand the words you're speaking.'"

I flush—but, hell. It's Sunday morning and she's confessing TMI everywhere. I might as well, too. "You've probably heard about my issues."

Because apparently everyone in town has. Lily proves to be no exception. "I might have heard something like 'skittish' and 'freezes up with men.'"

"That's me. So in college I tried it without men." And found out I'm as straight as a board. "It was nice but the burn wasn't there, you know? And I can get 'nice' with a vibrator. So..." I trail off with a shrug.

"Yeah," she says, but she's suddenly frowning.

Crap. Did I just stick my foot in it? "Not that a woman and a vibrator are the same," I quickly add. "I just don't look at one and think, 'Damn, I need you now.'"

"I get it. I'm just wondering how the hell we started talking about this." She frowns at her coffee cup. "Am I still drunk? How the fuck did we get on this?"

"You hooked up with club pussy and her panties were stuffed in my seat."

"Oh, yeah. Shit. Good times." She grins again. "So what kind of bike are you hiding out there?"

It's a ten year old softail with black and silver paint accented by gleaming chrome. Pretty, if standard. Nothing like Lily's custom chopper was.

"It's mostly stock," I say as Lily pulls on her kutte and crouches beside it. "My dad tweaked it a little, but I don't take it out much, so—"

"*Shh*, Jenny. This girl and I are getting to know each other." She rubs the leather seat. "Hey, baby."

I shake my head but I get it. My dad's the same way. I like bikes, but I don't love them. Lily does.

She glances over at my dad's custom ride. "Do you think he'll care if I get close?"

"God, you're cheating on mine already? Go on. He won't care."

"Oh, my heart." She spends a long time simply circling it. With a sigh, she looks up, her gaze running the length of the garage, lingering over my dad's equipment. I don't come out here much, but even I know it's a sweet garage. "I want to live out here."

"Maybe you will. Or at least you won't be too far if the Riders move to the clubhouse."

"Aw, yeah. Moving out to the ranch. You know, I always thought I should have been a cowboy—kicking sparks out of stone with my bare toes and making lassos out of rattlesnakes. I'd have been the toughest leathery bitch ever." She bats her eyelashes. "You could be my girl."

"Until a big horse gets between your legs."

She snorts out a laugh but her smile fades as she looks past me. I glance over. A big man with red hair that's going gray, my dad's standing in the doorway connecting the garage to the house, holding a coffee mug in one hand.

Though he's wearing a T-shirt and jeans, he's still in his bare feet so he hasn't been up long.

"Lily," he greets her easily.

"Sir."

Her response is stiff. I don't know why, but I suppose there could be a hundred reasons. She's a Hellfire Rider in Titan territory. But more likely, it's because of the bad blood that used to flow between her dad and mine. God knows what she's heard about him all her life.

He looks to me. "I was just about to cook up some breakfast. You heading out to the barn?"

My brewery. I renovated an old barn on the property and that's what we'll probably always call it. The barn. "In a few minutes," I say. "Lily's going to borrow my ride. So if you see her, don't chase her down and beat her up or anything."

His mouth kicks up in amusement. "I'll try to control myself." His gaze slides over to Lily again. "I heard about your bike. A damn shame what that little punk did."

"I took care of him, sir."

"I heard you did. You have any trouble with this one, give me a holler."

"I will."

He nods. "You riding out to the Barracks tomorrow with the rest of us?"

"I am."

They lost me. "The Barracks?"

That's an old Titan joint out by the county line. Mostly

only the Eighty-Eight frequents the place now.

My dad and Lily both look to me but don't answer. So it's club business and none of mine.

"All right, then. I'll leave you ladies to it," he says but pauses before leaving. "That kutte fits you well, Lily. The Riders were right to let you in."

Her expression tightens as if she's been punched in the gut. Her voice is strained. "Thank you, sir."

He nods and closes the door. Lily's still standing there with a white face.

What the hell? "Are you okay?"

She swallows hard. "My dad would never have said that in a million years. Shit." Suddenly turning away, she drags her hands through her hair. "My mouth just keeps running. I'm going to go sleep it off. Thanks, Jenny."

"Any time," I say.

"Fuck. Fuck." She pivots back around, her gray eyes fierce. "You mean it, don't you? Any time."

"I do." Why wouldn't I?

"All right, then. You did me a solid, letting me borrow this bike. I'm going to do you one. Normally I wouldn't ever talk about club business but this is about you, too, so—You heard about the First Lady shit?"

My gut tightens. "Yes. Saxon said it's nothing to worry about."

"I don't know if he's right about that but he's right that it's all bullshit. Anyway, he told them the First Lady clause is in conflict with our rule that we don't hurt women.

And because of your issues, following through would be hurting you. So we're voting on whether we're going to make him follow through on it or not."

So they're all deciding whether I should fuck him. My cheeks are burning. "Okay."

"I'm not telling you to embarrass you. I'm just telling you where the talk you might hear is coming from, because I heard some of the brothers' conversations last night. Now some of them are saying that the rules aren't in conflict but *you* are. We're supposed to approve any woman the prez chooses. So the solution some of them came up with isn't to let the First Lady clause slide, but to tell Saxon he needs to find another woman. One who isn't…damaged."

She looks pained as she says it, so I know it isn't her word but something she heard. It still punches me in the throat.

"Oh," I whisper. There's nothing else to say.

"They're fucking wrong," she says, her cheeks sporting flags of angry color. "I will have the back of any brother. But that doesn't mean I don't think some of them are assholes."

Dad says the same thing about some of the Titans. "Okay."

"I just wanted you to know, so that if you hear this shit being tossed around, it doesn't catch you by surprise. Saxon never would think it, okay? And I've seen that thing you do. You put your chin up and walk on like you don't care if they're looking or what they're saying. Just keep on doing that."

By her tone, I don't think she's only talking to me—or that it's the first time she's said those words. "Is that what you do—just keep on going like you don't give a fuck?"

"Yeah, I do. So you're all right?"

"I am. And I appreciate the heads-up." Though my head is still spinning as she straddles the bike. The rumble of the engine settles me for a second. I lift my voice over the noise. "Lily."

She looks up at me.

"Sunday night, Anna and I usually go out. Kind of a girls' night with dinner and a few drinks. You want to join us?"

Her gray eyes narrow. "You're already swaying and now you have to work. Will you even be on your feet tonight?"

I tap my fingernails along the side of my coffee cup. "There's a lot more caffeine where this came from."

She smiles a little. "All right. See you tonight, then."

"Tonight," I reply, but it's lost in the roar of her engine. I watch her leave, tires kicking up a long cloud of dust down the drive. I go upstairs and change, then e-mail Anna—asking her to keep her ears peeled about this First Lady thing.

Because I don't think it's nothing anymore.

SIX

SAXON

I meet up with Jenny on Sunday night after her dinner with Anna and Zoomie, but she's running on empty. I follow her out to the ranch to make sure she doesn't fall asleep at the wheel and kiss her goodnight at the door. Tonight the Titans and Riders are running out to the Barracks, so I probably won't see her until tomorrow—and that's only if other shit doesn't come up.

She only spent a week in my bed. Two days without her and I'm ready to drag her back into it.

I don't hear from her until I'm in the clubhouse's parking lot, waiting for the stragglers to get their shit together so we can ride. There's always someone who forgets to gas up. Today there were three.

It takes me a second to recognize the picture that comes through on my phone. It's just a photo of a store-front counter—the one in her brewery.

Because that's the counter I bent her over last week. That's where I tasted her cunt for the first time.

My dick is hard as fuck as I straddle my bike. Because of a counter. Jesus H. Christ. I text her back.

Tits or pussy next time.

I want a dick pic first.

I turn my phone's camera toward Stone. The Riders' enforcer frowns at me until I say, "Jenny wants a picture of a dick."

He grins and points two thumbs toward his chest.

I click and send.

OMG. Hahaha! Okay, pussy shot coming.

Where are you? Not at home or the brewery. Cell reception is shit at the ranch. I don't get many texts while she's working.

At the end of my driveway, deciding which way to go. You going to be back in town later?

Real late.

Then I'll probably head up to Bend and catch a movie.

You need an escort? I worry about the Eighty-Eight every damn time she's on the road alone.

I'll be okay. You going to be around tomorrow?

I think so.

She responds by sending a photo of an ugly-ass striped cat with ragged ears. It must be a picture she already had on her phone. Taken at night, the flash of the camera gives his eyes an evil red shine. *This is Henry. He hangs around the ranch house and sleeps on the pillow next to me.*

That's going to be my pillow. *Henry the Devil Pussy needs to find a new spot.*

Aw, he's a good pussy. The best kind. He licks himself.

I grin like a fool and realize the others are waiting on me. Shit. *Heading out. Be safe.*

I push the phone into my pocket. It vibrates, signaling her reply. I roll out, but only make it to the first stop sign before I look at it.

You, too. See you tomorrow.

One more day. Feels like forever. Jesus. Everything with Jenny feels like forever. I've loved her forever. Admired her. She's smart as hell and so fucking sweet, yet has a core of steel, especially when she's standing up for someone. I've known for years there was no other woman for me. I knew I wanted her by my side. I knew we clicked. She knows my world and the sex is blazing hot. I always knew it would be.

But I've never been as close to her as I have in the past week. I love her but I had no idea I'd be so crazy about her.

A tiny woman completely owns me. That's not a new development. I told her the truth about being sent home from Kosovo and how I hit a bad patch afterward. I didn't tell her how rough it got.

I fucked up all through high school and didn't care. Not messing around—just not being in classes half the time. After she injured her back, my mom couldn't get out of bed and her meds were expensive. I worked two jobs and my classwork suffered. The military was a light at the end of the tunnel. With my size, I could have played sports, maybe done well and eventually made some money, but that would involve a hell of a lot of luck. The corps was a guaranteed way to send money home. Then *I* got sent home. The money was still coming in but I wasn't worth anything anymore. But I could ride, so I threw myself in with the toughest motherfuckers I could find, hoping to feel like a man again.

Instead I just got into all kinds of shit. The day I saved Jenny from being raped at the rally I was coked up out of my fucking head. I didn't care when the cops showed up afterward, didn't care that they found evidence on my boot. I was so fucked up that even though my being arrested hurt my mom, I figured it would be better for her if I was gone.

Then Jenny came in to testify for me. She didn't have to. But she sat in that witness chair and laid out everything that bastard did to her in front of a jury, then looked at me like I was a fucking hero.

She looked at me like I was a man.

I spent the next five years in prison cleaning myself

up and becoming one. I read more books than I ever did in school, worked on making myself strong again—so that she would never know how wrong she'd been.

When I got out, I kept at it. I worked my ass off and bought the Den, fixed it up. Everything I did was for Jenny—and I didn't even have her then. Didn't have much hope of having her, either. I just needed to know that Jenny Erickson thought I was worth something. And every time she looked at me with those big green eyes and offered her sweet smile, I knew she did.

There isn't anyone who'd say I'm worthless now—except for me, if she was gone. Everything I've done was to live up to that look in her eyes. If she ever goes, everything I did means nothing.

And she almost went. When the Eighty-Eighty threatened her, she came so close to going without my knowing. It would have destroyed me if she had. Because I need her, need to know she's all right, even if I can't call her mine. But, Jenny—she's the most terrifying kind of woman. She's someone who doesn't need anything or anyone, not really. She would have taken off and she'd have been just fine.

She loves me. That makes me feel like a fucking king, but in the end, it's nothing. I've seen plenty of people who love each other, yet they stay apart for some reason or another. Hell, I loved Jenny and she loved me, yet we were apart for years.

Need, though? That pulls people together. I could

have gotten down on my knees when Red showed up at my door and told me she needed my protection. Need dropped her right into my lap.

That need is growing—not her need for protection but her need for *me*. I could get on my knees for that, too, because when we get rid of the Eighty-Eight, she won't need my protection anymore. But if she needs my mouth and my cock, that's good enough. If she needs me at her side, I'll be there.

I'll always be there. Needing her twice as much.

I ARRANGED TO MEET UP with the Titans in a neutral spot—a rest stop a few miles out of Pine Valley. We aren't waiting there but a few minutes before Red rolls in at the head of his pack. All fifteen Titans are with him. A good sign. This has got to be rough for them. They're going to feel like we're moving in, taking over, and that they're losing everything. But that's the point of this ride—to show that together, we're all gaining something. We're all stronger.

I get off my bike and go to greet Red. The Hellfire Riders are the stronger club and he should be coming to me, but this is more important than the size of my dick. I'll show respect for what he's bringing to me. Egos don't belong here now if we're going to be brothers.

That was always where Lucifer went wrong. His ego was always in play.

The rest of it goes smoother than I thought it would,

and it's not my doing. Old Timer and the Dubs used to ride with Red and Thorne before they broke away from the Riders and formed the Steel Titans, but there's still friendship there and the younger brothers take their cue from the elders. I like seeing Red make a point of talking to Zoomie—she's going to be a sore spot for some, but he helps smooth it over. The brothers who left the Riders when she joined look tense and uneasy, but I make a point of going to them, too.

Next time, they'll have to come to me. I'm willing to put that shit behind us. Whether they can do the same is up to them.

After the meet and greet is over, we ride.

The Barracks is a dive over on the county line. It used to be Titans' territory but they let it go. No one claims it officially now, but drive by on any night and most of the bikes outside belong to the Eighty-Eight.

It's not yet busy when we roll in. A stripper is working a pole up on the stage. Watching her are a few nomads and a pair of Blue Coyotes. Stone goes to talk to them. That club's all right but next time they'll need to secure permission from the Titans or the Riders before coming in. Red and I head into the back. The place is a shithole but Red tells me it wasn't always. The owner just got tired of fixing all the shit the Eighty-Eight broke.

That owner is Pete Schmidt, an old grizzled bastard who's built like a bear and who keeps a shotgun and base-ball bat behind his bar. We find him cleaning a grill in the kitchen. He shakes a gloved fist at Red as we come in. "If you fucking walk in here, Red Erickson, you better be fucking staying."

"We're staying. Me and the Wolf." Red gestures to me and uses my road name. "We're thinking of doing a little cleaning over the next few weeks. Exterminating some vermin."

Schmidt near bursts into tears. He rips off his gloves and his big hand shakes mine, then he pulls Red in for a rough hug. "Only this morning I was standing over there with a match and thinking of burning this place down. But it turns out that today is my lucky fucking day. You go out and sit. I'll send some girls out."

I don't have any interest in the girls but it's going to be my lucky fucking day, too. I left Blowback watching the door and as Red and I return to the main room, my veep finds me.

His flat stare meets mine. "Reichmann and about a dozen of the Henchmen just rolled up."

Reichmann. Anger is cold and sharp. He'll see our bikes outside but if he runs now, he's ruined. His club will mark him as a coward and they'll turn on him like the rabid dogs they all are.

I stay at the bar with Red as Reichmann comes limping in. I grin. My brothers worked him over good last week. He must have come in a cage because his arm's in a sling and a cast surrounds his left foot. His sunken lips tell me his front teeth are gone. His face is still a swollen mess. Flanked by two of his Henchmen, he heads over to a booth. I nod to the brothers sitting there, who look at me as if wondering whether they should stake their claim now. They move out.

The music is loud but there's not a word being spoken. The other Henchmen are looking at the tables, each one taken by a Rider or a Titan. The Henchmen want to assert their ownership over the place, ordering my brothers out of their seats, and I can see them weighing the chances of getting their asses kicked against the size of their dicks. Not all of them are stupid. They head to the bar.

I nod to Red and we head toward Reichmann's table. I point to the two bikers sitting with him. "Get the fuck out. We're having a regional presidents meeting."

Reichmann's trapped and he knows it. He gestures for them to go, but his face is pale, his skin tight over his shaved skull. Bruises still ring his throat where I had him in a choke hold.

I slide in next to Reichmann and Red takes the opposite bench. I get my first look at Red's face since Reichmann came in and suddenly I'm surprised the Henchman is still living. But maybe Jenny asked her dad not to spend his last months in prison. That's all I can imagine holding Red back from killing him now.

Red wouldn't go to jail if it went down here. Not one fucking member of the Eighty-Eight would make it out and there'd be no one to talk about it. But if we're going to shed blood, I want to do it all together as Riders. Not while we're still separate.

"A presidents meeting, huh?" Reichmann's gaze zeroes in on Red. "Some of us won't be a president for much longer. I hear they're measuring your coffin."

"Better than the hole in the ground you'll get. As long as I live long enough to see you in it, I die a satisfied man."

"If I get your daughter on her back, so will—"

My hand shoots out and grips the back of Reichmann's head. I slam his face into the table. The impact is as loud as a gunshot. Everything around us goes quiet as I hold him there. "Shut your mouth. Now."

Blood's streaming from his nose when I let him up. Red tosses him a napkin.

"Now this is simple," I tell him. "You're done here. A Henchman crosses the county line, he's going to find himself in a hole. You deal your shit across the county line? We'll come out and burn your kitchen down."

The stupid fucker laughs. "You think it'll be that easy? There's giants out there who have a vested interest in our supply. They'll squish you like an ant."

"And you're gonna call for help? Have them bring in muscle from other chapters?" I grin. "Go ahead. First thing they'll do is see that your house is weak as shit. They'll cut your throat and throw you to the fucking pigs."

"It ain't my house that's weak. It ain't me that's needing to bring in a dying club." He laughs again and spits blood onto the table. "And it ain't me who can't fuck my woman how and where I want. I sure as hell don't need a fucking clause to make her take it from my brothers."

Red leans in. "You talking about Jenny again? Because that's a bad fucking idea."

"I'm just saying that if you want her to fuck an entire club, Daddy Red, you should have just let us go at her."

He just doesn't know when to shut his trap. This really is my lucky fucking day.

I grab the back of his neck. "My brothers messed you up pretty good, didn't they? And here you are now, stuck in a booth with me. Just like Jenny was with you."

"You going to suck my dick? I'd have made her suck mine." He shakes his head. "What you going to do? You won't kill me. Because she *loooooves* you and can't lose you. Fucking pansy."

My grip tightens. "No, what I'm thinking is that my brothers didn't mess you up enough. Because you still have every fucking finger you used to touch my girl. Red, you want it?"

I do, more than anything. But this is respect, too. I'll defer to her father, this once.

"Yeah," he says. "I fucking want it."

Reichmann tries to bolt. He's not going anywhere. I slam his wrist against the table and shove a wad of napkins in his mouth when he begins to howl. Red's bowie knife is already out of his boot. He's fast. Faster than I would have been. He leaves Reichmann his thumb and little finger.

Schmidt's already at our table, bringing a towel and our drinks and a plastic cup full of ice.

I grin at Reichmann, who's shaking and sticking his bloodied fingers into the ice. "I love a fucking presidents meeting. Shall we call it adjourned?"

And get out of this booth before he pukes on me.

"I say so," Red seconds my motion and we return to the bar.

I down a beer and wonder how long it'll be before Reichmann leaves. Not long. He staggers out a few minutes later. The rest of the Henchmen follow him, breaking some random tables and chairs on the way. Jolly as all fuck, Schmidt looks on like it's Christmas.

Red's still pissed. He turns it on me, but keeps it quiet. "Is that clause Tommy wrote still there?"

"I'm dealing with it."

Jaw tight, he shakes his head. "I trusted you to take care of her."

"And I'll cut off my own hand before I hurt her. I'll cut out my fucking heart."

"You won't need to." He leans in. "Because if you ever do hurt her, I'll cut it out for you."

"Then we're understood." When he nods, I say, "No one's brought up that clause for a long time—not until the Riders' meeting this weekend. No one knew about the clubs merging, either. So who the fuck was talking to him about our business?"

His eyes sharpen. "I'll check my house. You check yours."

CHECKING MY HOUSE MEANS LOOKING at my brothers one by one. It takes time and patience and means that I don't see Jenny. But we don't flush out a snitch. Instead I find myself in Stone Wall's garage two days after our visit to the Barracks. A body is wrapped up in a blanket in the back of his truck. I pull back the cover.

Goose.

I stare at my brother's waxy face with the rage inside me spinning in all directions. The others are quiet. Just Blowback, Stone, and Gunner are here. "How?"

"A needle in his arm."

But if Stone brought him here instead of leaving Goose where he was found, that means this is something the Hellfire Riders are going to take care of. It's not just an overdose. "Who found him?"

"His old lady," Stone says. "He was out in their back-yard shed. She called me."

Cheryl. "Where is she?"

"I took her to stay with Old Timer and Helena."

Where she'd be both protected and under watch, if she had anything to do with this. I cover Goose's face. "A needle? He smokes his shit. When did he start shooting up?"

"He doesn't. And that's not all." Blowback looks fucking grim. On him, that expression means this is all worse than I thought. "He had crank in his stash. I expected that. There was also $50K of heroin."

Goose is too small-time to have that amount stashed

away. Which means it was planted. The back of my neck tightens, as if I can feel an enemy creeping around behind me. If Cheryl had called the cops instead of calling Stone, the Riders would be undergoing a real hard look from the authorities right now. "Did you go through the clubhouse?"

"Yeah. Had the brothers clean it out. There's nothing that they couldn't personally account for."

"The Den?"

"I found more heroin in the freezer. Just a little. But I bet it's the same batch."

So the Eighty-Eight isn't just going after the Riders now. They're specifically targeting me.

And they already got Goose. I look into the truck. "What are we doing for him?"

"Cheryl says he always talked about a Viking funeral. A boat burning on the water."

"Get it for him. Let's take this out of here."

We head out into Stone's back yard. The sun is hot as fuck, and the bright shine feels like an axe blade right between my eyes. Dropping into a deck chair, I pop a beer and ignore the splitting pain. "Was Goose the one talking?"

"He was," Gunner says. "Cheryl gave us his phone. He was sending regular messages about where we were going on runs, when you left the clubhouse, all kinds of shit."

Anger boils in my gut. He betrayed us. That's fucking hard to take. "And he kept the messages?"

"They were twisting his arm. He apparently owed them money. Maybe he was keeping track of what he was paying back."

Blowback fills the chair opposite. "They went after him."

"What do you mean?"

"They saw his weakness—his addiction. He was clean, wasn't he? Then he was using again. I'm guessing they targeted him. They don't have the fucking balls to come after us. They go for the weak spot." My veep leans back, shaking his head. "I told him I was watching him. Gave him that warning. He passed it on to them, let them know he had to be careful."

And his usefulness to them was suddenly gone—except as the star in one last play. Now I have to decide how to spin it around. "How many know that he was passing on info?"

"Just us."

And Red knew someone was leaking info, but not who. I could smooth this out with him.

"No matter what Goose was doing, he was ours." His fate might have ended up the same but it should have come from us, his brothers—not the fucking Eighty-Eight. "They're going to keep trying to take us out in these little fucktwit ways. It's not enough to push them past the county line; we're going to have to raze their house. But we need the Titans for that and I don't want this shit about Goose raising doubts about Rider loyalty."

"We're with you on that, boss," Stone says and Gunner nods.

Blowback adds, "It's not the only doubt."

The ache in my head grows. "Don't you fucking say a word about the First Lady clause. Not now."

"Someone's going to say it. They're going to put it up for a vote and decide whether it matters, and if you get even one holdout saying you've got to follow through—and then if you *don't* follow through—that's going to undermine every decision you make from here on out. It'll just take one vote."

"So I'll rewrite the fucking Constitution."

"It doesn't matter now," Gunner says quietly and I know he's right.

The anger in my gut rolls into something heavy and sick. My head is fucking pounding.

He continues, "It doesn't matter which way you go, the talk is going to twist the other way. You had most of them after the meeting. The two clauses are in conflict. Then just one fucker says that it's not the clauses in conflict, but that your woman isn't worthy."

"Fuck that."

"We're not arguing," Stone says. "But it's not even just Knucklehead or Burnout anymore. It's just fucking talk, but it's growing. You change the Constitution, your word is no good. You ignore their vote to see the clause through, your woman is no good—and if you stay with her after, that means you're ignoring the Constitution. And if you can say 'fuck the rules' then they will, too."

"If they say Jenny's not worthy, I'm going to walk." I

say it quietly but it hits them hard. I don't fucking care. I'm going to lay it out now. "But it won't matter because there won't be anything to walk away from. She's Red Erickson's daughter. It's going to be rough enough bringing the Titans in. They're going with it now but if we say Red's daughter is unworthy it'll blow the whole fucking deal. And what'll we have left? Three dozen assholes who are squabbling over seeing a woman get fucked. You think the Eighty-Eight won't pick up on that? Find someone with enough resentment to stick a few kilos of coke in our house? To poison the taps at the Den? To build a fucking bomb? They'll pick us off one by one."

"You're not wrong," Blowback says.

"You're not," Stone agrees and shoves his hand through his hair. "Have you put this in front of Jenny?"

I stare at him. "You mean ask her to do it?"

"Would she?"

"It doesn't fucking matter if she would. I'm not going to lay this on her. Her father's fucking dying, you know that? She's spent months terrified and watching her back, because Reichmann's after her. Now I'm going to tell her that my brothers have their heads so far up their asses that I need her to save my club by fucking me in front of them?"

"You think she'd walk?"

Pain rips through my chest. I don't know. She loves me. But she doesn't need me as much as I need her. And she doesn't need this shit piled on top of everything else she's dealing with. She'd be better off going than sticking with me—and I wouldn't blame her if she did. "You start spreading the word that we'll lose the Titans if anyone says she isn't worthy. You use Goose to rile them up and make them understand that if they really want to see the Eighty-Eight bleed, we need to be as strong as possible. Maybe they'll have enough sense to let this go."

Gunner nods. "We'll spread it."

Yet I see their doubt. Not doubting me, but thinking that in our next meeting when we vote on whether I'll need to observe the First Lady clause, there's going to be some holdout who says he's standing on principle when he's really standing on a pile of shit. Someone who doesn't give a fuck about that clause, but who just wants to be right and it won't matter that there's no sense in what he's standing behind. I stood behind Zoomie joining because her service to this country meant something. The First Lady clause doesn't mean anything; it was just Lucifer stroking his dick.

And I'm going to lose my club over it.

My brothers here see it. They're all fucking pissed by it. But there's not a fucking thing that we can do about it that we haven't already done.

So I'll take care of business and clean up my house, leaving my brothers in as strong a position as I can give them. Then I'll take the ride that doesn't bring me back.

At least I'll be riding toward Jenny.

There's nothing else left to say. I finish my beer and take my leave. My bike is parked out front and my gut feels hollowed out as I walk through Stone's house.

And she's here. Jenny. Pulling up in her truck with Anna in the passenger seat.

Her smile is bright and beautiful as she bounds out of the rig and comes for me. "Hey! I didn't think I'd see you for another day!" Her smile fades as she nears me. Her step slows. "Is everything all right?"

I can't answer. Catching her against my chest, I kiss her long and deep, until the ache inside me eases. My throat feels like sandpaper when I let her go and my voice is hoarse when I ask, "Can you stay with me tonight?"

"Yes. Of course, yes." Her worried gaze searches my eyes. "What's going on?"

I bury my face in her hair and breathe deep. "I just need you," I say.

JENNY

I shouldn't be doing this.

Hayden's Auto sits in front of my idling truck. It's early. I haven't slept and that might be why I'm contemplating something so stupid.

But something's not right. Saxon's a hard man to read but I don't think I mistook the bleak pain that flattened his eyes every time he looked away from me. Goose is dead, but I don't think that's the reason he's hurting. At least, I don't think it's the only reason. Instead I think it's closer to something Anna mentioned.

Lily was right. The talk had shifted. Anna heard the brothers question whether I'd be worthy. But in what she was saying, I heard something else: They were questioning whether Saxon would keep his word.

I've been around MCs for a long time. I know what it means when doubts trickle in. No matter how small they begin, they roll on top of each other like a snowball loaded with shit and boulders. Everyone in its path either gets crushed or comes out stinking.

But I know what Saxon would say. *It's nothing.*

I think Blowback will tell me whether it really is or not.

Steeling my spine, I make myself leave my truck. Blowback has an apartment over the garage, but I'm glad when I see a light downstairs. I knock on the door to the reception office and Blowback opens it a few seconds later, his hands black with grease and his eyes as empty as death.

I'm not comfortable with him. Not afraid—though maybe I should be. But the way he just looks through me makes me want to squirm. I know what he sees right now, though: A woman who was fucked all night by a man desperate to touch her. A woman who left him pounding a heavy bag and sweat dripping down his back. A woman who wonders why the man she loves looks as if he's about to lose everything.

When I was in my truck, I'd been trying to imagine how to begin—to try to acknowledge that Blowback wouldn't talk club business but ask him to anyway. But all of that doesn't really matter. Only one thing does.

"Do I need to do it?"

He studies me again, as if I've surprised him and he has to reassess. "Can you?"

With Saxon, in front of others? Yes. I don't know if I'd really enjoy it or get past my embarrassment, but if I'm with him, I know I'd feel safe. Could I let the others touch me, though?

A cold tremor rolls through me as my body instinctively rejects the thought. But I've done it before. I wasn't a virgin with Saxon. When I was younger, I thought I could just force my way through the terror. That magically the fear would go away if I just let a guy fuck me. So twice— once about twelve years ago, and again a year later—I made myself lie there and bear it. I can bear it again.

"Yes," I say and I don't think Blowback believes me. I don't care if he does. "Is he going to lose the club if I don't?"

He doesn't want to answer that. But he finally responds. "Sooner or later. Probably sooner, because he'll walk."

My eyes are burning. The club made Saxon feel a part of something when he was injured and in a bad place. But I know that's not the only reason it matters to him. They're his brothers. Some might be assholes, but leaving the Riders would be like ripping out part of himself.

"Are there any other options?"

Blowback nods. "He leaves you."

Shit. *Shit.* All at once I'm crying and I can't stop it.

"He won't."

"No."

"Because he'll keep his word. They're fucking saying he won't, but he'll go with me even if he'd rather stay."

"Yes."

And then what? Oh, God. Despair suddenly rips me open and I'm bawling into my hands, just fucking bawling while Blowback looks on as if I'm folding laundry. If Saxon walks away so that he can keep his promise to protect me, how long before he begins wishing that he never had?

But it doesn't matter. It doesn't matter. Because it won't happen. I'm not going to let him walk.

I lift my head out of my hands. My breath comes in hot shudders and my chest feels hollowed out. Empty.

Determination is slowly filling it. "Will they have a leg to stand on if the terms of the First Lady clause are fulfilled?"

There's suddenly a glint of life in that flat gaze. Surprise? Admiration? I don't know.

"No," he says. "It'll cut their legs out from beneath them."

I nod and take a deep breath. "All right, then. What exactly needs to happen—and when is the next meeting?"

SEVEN

SAXON

Blowback is texting while the hands go up on the Titans vote. Unanimous. If the Titans vote the same way, they're in. It's what I wanted and yet right now I'm not celebrating. I'm five seconds away from slamming my fist into my veep's face. Texting as I call for a vote. Showing such fucking disrespect. On today, of all fucking days, because as soon as the next item of business is finished the First Lady clause goes up to vote, and I'll probably be walking away.

Widowmaker begins reading the next item on the agenda. I rub my eyes and pinch the bridge of my nose. My head is pounding. I can barely fucking hear him. Then I realize he's not talking. He's just silent. Everyone is silent. And they're looking toward the entrance leading from the garage.

Jenny is standing there.

My heart slams right up against my ribs. Why the hell is she here? Is she hurt? Being chased by the Eighty-Eight? I come up off my stool but she doesn't look afraid. Her chin is up and she…

Looks fucking amazing. A black dress with two tiny shoulder straps fits her like a glove from her tits to her upper thighs. She's wearing heels that make her legs seem endless. Her hair is loose and hanging down in thick waves, and I've never seen her eyes so smoky or her lips so red.

She focuses on me and starts coming. My brain lurches ahead like a choked engine. She's here, looking like that. And Blowback was just texting.

Letting her know when to come in?

Anger slams through me like a runaway train. I whirl on him, fists clenched. "If you said a fucking word to her—"

"She came to me," he interrupts evenly.

This isn't going to fucking happen. I push away from my seat and head her off. Her eyes are on me, her shoulders back, and she walks past the club members as if she doesn't give a fuck, but does she think I can't see how nervous she is?

I meet her halfway. She grips the edges of my kutte and smiles up at me but I don't let her get a word out. "Come with me."

"Saxon—"

"My house," I snap out and I've never been this ripped up. So pissed. So fucking overwhelmed. She would give this to me? I would *never* ask for it. Yet she just offers it as if it's something I deserve. "You're quiet until we're upstairs and we can talk about this."

She seems suddenly twice as nervous. Her teeth catch her bottom lip as she nods. I know I'm being too rough but I can't deal with this. Not here.

I lead her toward the stairs climbing to the loft that serves as the executive board's private space but I don't miss the grins that flash across some of the brothers' faces. They're watching her walk away. But not looking at her ass, I realize. She's got four words embroidered down the back of her dress.

Property of Saxon Gray.

Jesus Christ. She's going to fucking break me.

JENNY

I'M NOT GOING TO THROW up. I'm not going to throw up.

It's been my mantra since I woke up this morning, yet I'm more nervous now that I was walking into the clubhouse. Saxon's expression burned with rage when he turned on Blowback, but now it's the dark and mean look that says he's barely holding onto his control. And since he's taking me up to the loft to talk—not just hustling me away from the clubhouse—I'm not just nervous but feeling guilty. I should have warned him I was coming. We should have talked it out before I sprung this on him.

I know why I didn't, though. I was afraid that he would say the clause was nothing and that I would let him persuade me that was true. I was afraid that I'd take the easy way out.

He leads me into the conference room and shuts the door. With a sigh, he asks, "What are you doing, Jenny?"

"Cutting the legs out from beneath anyone who intends to hurt my man."

His eyes gleam a little at that. "They aren't doing it to hurt me."

"They're just stupid, then?"

A short laugh breaks from him but it deepens into a groan. He pinches the bridge of his nose and shakes his head. "Maybe. Fuck."

That sounds resigned, not angry. "You're not just going to forbid it? Or tell me it's nothing?"

"I was going to. I was going to say that there was no fucking way this was going to happen." Dark blue eyes steady on mine, he crosses his arms over his broad chest. "But I'll lay it out, Jenny. It's easy for me to sit out there and let you ride my cock. And I'm not one to pass up an opportunity. I would never have asked for this from you, but I'm not going to throw this gift back in your face. I'm also not going to make this decision for you."

"Thank you."

"Don't thank me." His voice sharpens. "I've done nothing worth thanking. There's no negative for me here—unless it hurts you. Unless you're scared. Then it will be fucking torture for me and worse for you."

Swallowing hard, I nod. "I know. And I don't think it'll be easy. But I've got a plan—I'm just going to suck on your cock until you're about to come, then get on until you do. It'll be quick."

He doesn't look persuaded. "You're nervous as hell."

"Yeah, well." I can't really do anything about that. "I just keep reminding myself that it's nothing to them. We're just another couple having sex. The only people it really matters to is you and me. So I'm just going to pretend they aren't there and only think of what we want. And if they, you know, want to show their admiration—"

"They won't touch you." His gaze holds mine. "I swear to God. The whole thing stops if they try to."

Relief sweeps through me. My legs shake from the strength of it. "I would have forced myself to—"

"No." He's shaking his head. "Forced yourself? Fuck, no."

"Okay." The pressure in my chest is suddenly over-whelming. This *is* going to happen. "Okay, then."

"Any second you want to stop, we do." He tugs me close, lowering his mouth to mine in a sweet kiss before saying again, "Any second."

Heart thundering, I nod. With my hand clasped firmly in his, he opens the door. The loft is like a smaller version of the downstairs clubhouse with sofas, flat screen TVs, and tables. There wasn't anyone up here when we went into the conference room but now Blowback is waiting for us, along with Stone, Gunner, and Spiral. Only Blowback is on his feet and looking at us, though. The other three are sitting on the sofas and poking at their phones.

Saxon frowns at them. "What are you doing?"

"We had a conversation downstairs," Blowback says. "If the Riders' president is going to fulfill the First Lady clause, then we agreed it isn't necessary for every club member to stand witness. I asked them if they're going to doubt the word of the executive board and they aren't. So you can perform it up here, just in front of the officers, instead of down there."

So many fewer people watching. My hand squeezes Saxon's. "You're missing some officers."

Blowback shrugs. "Old Timer elected to remain downstairs because he doesn't want to watch anyone but his old lady. Widowmaker elected the same, claiming that participating might cause conflict between him and his wife, and he persuaded the other board members with wives or old ladies to stay below, as well."

But someone has to stand witness. So the single board members remained.

All of that couldn't have just happened spontaneously,

though. Blowback must have been planning that 'conversation'—and likely enlisting the help of the elder bikers to pressure the others to fall in line.

Saxon seems to realize the same. He clasps Blowback's forearm, and his voice deepens when he says, "Thank you."

The veep nods and his flat gaze falls on me. "We have also decided that, in order to remain in compliance with our Constitution, we will respect your woman's history and we won't bring any hurt on her—so we'll only show our admiration if she invites us to do so."

"I might kiss you for this," I tell him.

A smile touches his mouth. It doesn't make him seem any less scary. His gaze returns to Saxon's. "We *will* make sure you're in full compliance. They're taking our word. You can't touch her. You can't help her. She has to take you. You have to come inside her. That means no condoms."

Saxon frowns. "We won't make liars out of you. But we can't risk—"

I stop him. "I took care of it. The birth control, anyway." When he looks at me, I tell him, "I already had an appointment. I got an IUD. Are you okay for the rest?"

He suddenly grins. "Yeah. Went in for a test the day after you showed up at my Den. I wasn't sure what I'd need to persuade you to take a chance on me."

"Then we're good."

"Real good if I'm getting into you bare." Saxon tugs me toward one of the sofas. "Let's get this done."

I kick off my heels on the way. God, so much better. I

assumed that I'd have to come in and be all sexy in front of everyone. I was thinking of Lily and how she said that so many of the guys lived in Porno World, and if my worth is going to be judged by my hotness level—no matter how stupid that is—then I won't give anyone a reason to say I'm not good enough for Saxon.

He sinks down onto the leather, big and sexy and this isn't going to be so bad. I can't even see the guys behind me. Saxon sits back and locks his hands together behind his head—so that he doesn't forget he can't touch me, I realize. Otherwise it's a casual position, purely masculine, with his knees apart and his boots planted solidly on the floor.

"On your knees, woman," he says, but not in that hard way he usually has. He's teasing me. Trying to put me at ease.

And I need to be put at ease because I'm still shaking a little. With a tremulous smile, I kneel between his feet. My hands slide up his denim-covered thighs. He's not even hard yet. The bulge behind his fly is just his package, not an erection. That's new. Usually I don't even have to touch him. I look up.

His teeth are clenched. "You're fucking trembling."

"I can't help it." My hands go to his buckle. "But you've got to get into it, okay? Because you have to come."

His jaw tightens before he nods. His eyes close.

"You better be thinking of me," I say and his mouth twitches.

"I am, princess. I'm thinking of lifting you up over my face and sucking all the juices from your wet cunt."

And that apparently helps. His dick is already stiffening when I finish unbuttoning his jeans and spread his fly. Even partially soft, his shaft is thick and heavy, lying against a dark thatch of hair that narrows as it arrows up to his navel. God, I just love his cock. I stroke his burgeoning length before leaning in to swirl my tongue over the head. His body tenses. A few more licks and he's fully erect and his breath hissing between his gritted teeth. *Yes.* I swallow him as deep as I can, then somewhere behind me leather squeaks as if one of the guys has shifted position on his sofa and every muscle in my body freezes.

"No, princess. No." Saxon's voice draws my gaze up. His blue eyes are intense and locked on my face. "They're not looking. All right? It's just you and me."

I nod and suck again, but now I can only feel my ass, because I'm bent over Saxon's lap and it's like a thousand eyes are staring at it, even if none are. Even if it's still covered by my dress. I suck and suck, and now my face turns red with every slurping sound, and when I try to go deeper and choke, I wonder why I ever thought I could do this. Only a few days ago this was the sexiest thing I've ever done, taking him deep into my mouth, into my throat, and now my hotness level is hovering somewhere around zero.

"Hey." His face dark, Saxon abruptly leans forward, cradling my jaw in his hands. "Are you done? You want to walk? I'll walk out of here with you, Jenny."

"No." My voice is hoarse and I'm fighting not to let the tears filling my eyes spill over. "I can do this."

He's battling himself. I can see it. Maybe deciding whether to say fuck it all. But he finally nods. "Why don't you come on up into my lap. You'll take my cock in real deep and we'll get this going."

Real deep. That always sounds nice.

"Hands, boss," Stone says quietly behind us.

"Fuck off," Saxon snarls back, but he lets me go and fists them beside his thighs. I crawl up onto the sofa, preparing to turn around and straddle him in the reverse cowgirl required by the clause. I pause when he shakes his head. "Face me and kiss me first."

I can do that—and it's exactly what I need. Swinging my leg over his lap, I center myself over his erection and claim his mouth. He tastes so good, and heat slides down my belly like a good shot of whisky. My tension and shaking slowly ease as I lose myself in him, and I keep going back for another taste, another lick.

"I think I'm okay now," I say softly against his lips.

His voice is rough. "And so fucking beautiful, Jenny."

I smile and step back off the sofa, holding his gaze as I reach up under my dress to tug down my panties. Only my breasts and genitals have to be exposed for this—ostensibly so that everyone can easily see that I'm really taking his cock, but I suspect that Lucifer was just a pig—so I don't need to get naked. I'll just hike up my hem and pull down my top.

The nakedness won't be so bad, anyway. I'd rather parade around nude than share something as private as sex with Saxon.

It's just him and me. Him and me. But although the others aren't looking, I can see them when I turn around. They all appear as stiff and uncomfortable as I am. This must be the worst public sex they've ever seen.

Or not seen.

I sigh and slide over Saxon's lap, his hard chest against my spine. He can't hold me, but I love feeling so much of him pressed against me.

His voice is low in my ear. "All right?"

"Yeah." I reach down between my legs. Dry as a fucking bone. I rub my clit and close my eyes. "Are you going to lick me later?"

"Damn right, I'll lick you. I'm going to eat you all up." His teeth catch my earlobe and I shiver. "Tell me how wet you are."

"Um…"

"Jenny." It's a pained groan. "You're always wet."

"Now you know how I felt when you weren't hard."

"I am now." He kisses the side of my neck. "So fucking hard. I keep thinking of how you're going to feel when you get your pussy around me. I haven't fucked you like this before, but when this is all done, I'm going to get you home and sit you over me like this again. I'm going to bend you forward and spank your ass every time I fill your cunt. You want that?"

"Yes," I say and this is helping, too. I'm not really wet but I'm getting a little moisture worked up.

"Give me your fingers."

He sucks them into his mouth and that's better, too. Sliding my wet fingers through my pussy, I lift up and fit the head of his cock against my entrance. I can't even get him in. This time I lick my own fingers and try again.

"Jenny—"

"It's okay. I can do it."

"You're not ready."

I'm ready for this to be done. Biting my lip, I press down. *Oh, fuck.* I can't stop my whimper. Saxon curses behind me and his arm wraps around my waist, lifting me off him. His breathing is harsh and ragged but he doesn't say anything, he just holds me tight against his chest, my legs spread wide over him, my knees pressing into the sofa cushions.

"It's not going to happen like this," he finally says. "Not when you can't relax. You're just going to get hurt."

"Saxon—"

"Kissing me was good, right?"

I sigh. "Yes. But you can't do anything else. You can't help me."

If he could I'd be standing on the sofa cushions and shoving my pussy into his mouth.

"I can, princess. You just have to trust me. You close your eyes, and I'll get hands and a mouth to help you out.

It'll be me, telling them what to do." His voice is soft. "Will you be able to do that?"

"I don't know." Because now more nervousness is curling in my belly. "But I can try."

"Someone else you trust. Stone, maybe? You've known him a long time. Stone! I need you over here."

Anna's brother looks up even as I shake my head. "It's too weird, Saxon. We've known each other *too* long. I've seen him light his dick on fire, for God's sake."

"Gunner, then." The sergeant at arms is looking our way now, too. They all are. "He's real pretty."

Gorgeous, and even more so when he grins—he must have heard Saxon's comment. "It would hurt Anna if she ever found out."

That gets rid of Gunner's smile. Asshole. It's not like he doesn't know how she wants him.

I can almost feel Saxon eyeing Blowback but I stop him before he can ask whether his veep still scares me. We've been going the wrong way, anyway. I don't freeze up with Saxon…and I don't freeze up with women.

"Lily," I say softly. "Ask if she will."

He doesn't hesitate. "Get Zoomie up here."

Blowback doesn't blink. As he goes to the stairs, I try to relax against Saxon. "I'm sorry," I murmur for his ears only. "I don't know what's going wrong."

"This clause is what's wrong, Jenny. Not you." He pulls me back farther, angling his head so he can taste my mouth. "So don't you ever be sorry for this. The only thing

I care about now is that you're not hurt."

My fingers tighten on his forearm. "Okay."

The sound of boots on the stairs turns my gaze that way. Blowback returns with Lily right behind him, a bottle of beer dangling from her fingers. Her eyes widen when she sees us.

"You needed me, boss?"

"Jenny's real nervous," he says. "You want to show your admiration?"

She blinks as if the words don't make sense—then she suddenly grins. "I'd love to."

Taking a swig, she pushes her bottle toward Blowback. He takes it, his eyes narrowed on her as she saunters toward us. And somehow, it's already easier. I feel Saxon relax a little, too, as if Lily's complete ease and enthusiasm bled into both of us.

Maybe that's all it was. We were both so tense and just wanted it to be over. We just couldn't get into it. But Lily already is.

She drops to her knees between his feet in almost exactly the same position that I was in while sucking his cock. He's not her focus, though. I am. I'm straddling his legs and facing her.

Quietly, she asks, "You're really okay with this, Jenny?"

"Yeah. You?"

"Yeah." Her gaze slides past me. "And you're going to be okay with this, boss? I'm not going to get my ass kicked later, am I?"

She's joking but he answers her seriously. "I'm all right with anything that helps her now. I just need you to be my hands and mouth."

Nodding, she looks at me again, and something changes in her eyes. Slowly her gaze slides down my body, and suddenly she's looking at me like Saxon does. Not with the same intensity and need, but with a hell of a lot of heat, as if she can't wait to eat me up.

Her voice is throatier as she says, "Just tell me where to get started."

Oh, my God. I look up. Spiral, Gunner, and Stone aren't looking at their phones anymore. Instead they're watching us as if electrified. Even Blowback seems transfixed, staring at Lily's back while he downs her beer.

Saxon's arm tightens as he adjusts my position, moving me down and forward a little. His cock is a rigid length against the cleft of my ass. I'm lower now—and he can look down over my shoulder and see everything Lily does.

The movement seems to remind our watchers. "You're touching her, Saxon," Gunner says.

He lets me go, but he's still all around me. I'm leaning back against him and Lily's in front of me…and she's going to be his touch. It's still just him and me.

I close my eyes.

"Her neck," Saxon says and his voice is rough. "Just beneath her ear."

Warmth in front of me. A breath against my skin.

"Right there. Suck on that spot a little, then give it a

little bite. She likes that."

God, so much. A shiver races over my skin as I feel the nip of teeth, then the soothing caress of a warm tongue.

"Are her nipples hard?"

Fingers slide the straps of my dress over my shoulders. Cool air sweeps over my bared skin.

"Not yet, boss."

"She's not real sensitive there at first. You got to suck hard. Make them red as berries. And as soon as they're all roughed up you can go gentle and she'll be squirming all over with every lick. Oh, *fuck.*"

He groans the curse as a warm mouth latches onto the tip of my breast. A shuddering breath escapes me, then my back arches when she sucks my nipple to a burning point. When he does this, Saxon just sucks hard, but she goes after my nipple again and again, suckling and releasing each time with a gentle scrape of her teeth. Then her fingers pinch the turgid flesh and she turns her attentions to my left breast, flicking her thumb in time with each rough bout of suction.

"Jesus, that's beautiful." Saxon's body is like iron beneath me. "Like little cherries. When my cock's in her she clamps right down the second I start sucking on them. She wet yet?"

Warm fingers slip over my heated flesh in a delicate tease. I moan low in my throat, my hips rocking forward.

"Not wet enough."

"You play with her clit, then. Move that damn skirt

out of the way."

My dress is shoved up over my hips, bunching around my waist. My thighs tremble with anticipation as her hand slides back between my legs.

"Rub that little clit. Fuck, yeah. You like that, princess?"

I'm gasping, my hips jerking against the maddening touch. "Yes," I say breathlessly, then cry out when Lily begins sucking hard on my nipple again, her fingers sliding over my clit, gently tugging my delicate flesh with each pass. She moans softly against my breast.

"She's wetter, boss."

"She needs to be fucking dripping. You want to taste her pussy?"

Lily doesn't reply but she's already moving down. Her hands grip my hips and slide me forward a little more, so that I'm sitting lower between Saxon's spread legs and widening my thighs even farther. I hear a deep groan—someone watching, and I don't care. A ravenous ache is building deep inside me and when I realize that Lily's waiting for a go-ahead, I can't stop my plea.

"Saxon." Greedily I lift my hips. "Now."

"You heard her, Zoomie. Lick all the way up her slit. And hold onto her. She'll buck you right off when you hit her clit." Hands clamp over my hips and her warm mouth surrounds my clitoris. A strangled moan rips from my throat. Oh, Jesus. "Fuck me, that pussy. So damn sweet. I never get enough."

Lily's moan of agreement shivers through my aching

flesh. My body is tightening, tightening. Her tongue slides down to my entrance and fucks into me before slicking up to my clit again, and it's all loud, her long and hungry licks like a wet, suckling kiss against my drenched flesh. Sobbing little whimpers escape me and Saxon's voice is filling everything in between.

He gives a tortured groan when Lily shoves my legs wider and backs off for a second, as if making sure he gets a good look. "Oh, fuck, Jenny. That's so fucking sexy and you're so fucking wet. I need you on my cock now, princess."

Shaking with need, I brace my hands and lift up, reaching between us for his shaft. Lily sucks in a breath.

"Damn, boss. I don't know if she's wet enough for *that*."

"She'll take me." It emerges as a low growl. "But we have to go easy. She's so fucking tight we have to take her slow."

"Real slow." Her steadying hands catch my hips again. "All right, Jenny?"

"Yes." Better than all right. Saxon's bare cock is in my hand, and he stiffens beneath me as I slide the fat head through my drenched folds. We've never been flesh to flesh before.

His voice is hoarse. "Jenny—"

His groan strangles my name as I sink onto him. My body tenses, my flesh burning and stretching as my inner muscles yield to the thick crown. Pleasure flares through me, mingling with the pain. Dragging in a ragged breath,

I slowly work him deeper.

Lily's grip tightens on my hips. "Holy shit. Her little pussy is just sucking you in. She's the fucking hottest thing I've ever seen."

"Make her hotter," he grits out, and I'm so focused on the delicious sensation of his cock filling me that I'm not prepared when Lily's mouth covers my clitoris. I almost jolt away from Saxon's cock but her hands are holding me in place, then the sensation rips through me. My scream trails into a sobbing moan as she flicks her tongue. My hips jerk and suddenly he's deeper inside me and she's sucking and Saxon's pumping shallowly up into me, his voice rough in my ear. "You like that, Jenny? You like your clit being sucked while you're being stuffed with my cock?"

I respond with something, maybe a yes, I don't know, because I'm going to come, I'm just going to fly apart. My body's writhing, pushing him deeper and deeper with every roll of my hips and Saxon's sliding down the sofa a little, until I'm half-lying back against him, and Lily's coming up over me slightly, her hands pressing my thighs wider and her tongue lashing against my clit.

"You stay on her when I'm in deep." He sounds hard and mean but Lily just moans, her long hair sliding over my thighs, her mouth so hot.

Saxon surges up beneath me and I scream again as his cock pushes deep, bottoming out and then pressing deeper, intensifying everything but that's too much now, I can't take it. But I can't get away, Lily's holding me still as he begins fucking up into me, slow, so slow, and her tongue is slow now, too, just swirling around my clitoris.

And I can't— I can't—

My body bows upward and I can't even scream, can't breathe, can't do anything but come and come and come. I feel Saxon's groan behind me as my pussy convulses on his cock and Lily's groan as her tongue slides from the delicate flesh stretched around his shaft and up to my clit. My hands are tangled in her hair, but I can't let go yet, because Saxon pumps up into me and I'm coming again and she's sucking on my clitoris, and I'm completely destroyed between them.

I was just supposed to ride him. Just supposed to ride him. Lily grins up at me, her lips swollen and wet, and I realize that I'm saying it out loud, like a breathless chant after a long race. *I was just supposed to ride him.*

"You can now," she says.

My muscles seem weak and trembly as I sit up—then moan as the movement pushes Saxon's cock deep again. He grunts behind me, moving up the sofa so that he's sitting instead of half-reclining. I straddle him again, my knees resting on the cushions on either side of his thighs.

He presses a kiss to my shoulder. "All right?"

"Amazing." And I am. Utterly wrecked and yet feeling so fucking incredible. I look to Lily. "Thank you."

She laughs a little. "Any time. Can I watch the rest?"

"Knock yourself out," I say, because it doesn't matter. I lean against Saxon's chest and reach back to link my arms around his neck. The others are watching but it's only us, only him and me as I begin to ride. Just short strokes, because I can't rise up all the way, yet I'm taking all of him inside me. He's deep, so deep, and he tells me I'm beautiful and then he can't speak, groaning and stiffening as he comes.

I fall back against his heaving chest. His hand fists in my hair and I arch back for his kiss. I'm totally exposed, his cock still buried in my pussy and my nipples red and throbbing.

When he finally releases my mouth, Saxon's arms come around me and he looks over at Blowback. "Good?"

The other man laughs.

Saxon nods, then tugs the top of my dress up and the bottom down. He rises in one easy movement, lifting me with him and cradling me against his chest. "Hold on," he says and carries me to the loft's low wall that overlooks the main floor below. Oh, my God. Everyone's quieting and looking up.

Saxon's face is dark as he sweeps his gaze over them, but it's not his controlled look. Instead it's dangerous and tight with anger. He slides his fingers between my legs, then lets my feet swing to the floor. He holds up his hand and his fingers are wet.

"My cum," he says loudly. "My woman. Your first lady. Anyone have any fucking problem with it?"

My cheeks are burning but I hold my chin up. No response from below except a few hoots and shouts of encouragement.

He silences them. "Only two things matter now: bringing in our new brothers and destroying the Eighty-Eight before they take any more of us. No more of this petty shit or they're going to take us down one by one. So no more."

No more. It's a repeated murmur of agreement that runs through the bikers below.

"All right, then," Saxon says and lifts me up against his chest again. "Meeting's over. Go fuck and ride."

SAXON

I carry Jenny into the conference room. I begin to set her on the table but she squirms free.

Her face is pink. "I can't sit anywhere. There's cum dripping down my legs."

My cum. "That's the sexiest thing I've ever heard."

She laughs and shakes her head. I look her over. She's well-fucked but there's no shadows in her eyes. Lily and I went at her pretty hard but she took it all.

And gave me everything.

My heart swells up and I pull her close. My throat is tight. "What the hell were you thinking, Jenny? And don't tell me it was just undercutting some assholes."

She sighs and lays her head against my chest. "I just didn't want to make you choose."

"Choose what? The only choice I needed to make was whether to walk away, and *they* were forcing that choice, Jenny. Not you."

"But it wouldn't have been an issue if I wasn't in the picture. So I didn't want you to choose between me and the club."

Between her and the club. How could she even think that was a choice? "Did you think I wouldn't choose you?"

She shrugs. "I know you would. Because you said that you'd stay with me and protect me."

I stare at her. She's got her face buried against my chest and I realize she's not just snuggling there for comfort. She's hiding some hurt.

That hurt can't stand. I catch her chin and make her look up at me. Her green eyes are glittering like she's holding back tears. "That isn't why I'd choose you. I'd choose you because you give me fucking *everything*, Jenny. Do you think there's anything I wouldn't do for you? Anything? There's no line I wouldn't cross. Walking away from this club would be *nothing* compared to what I'd do for you. Everything I do is for you. Every single breath I take is for you. Staying with you isn't a choice—it's just the only fucking way I can live. All right?"

That didn't stop her tears. They're spilling over but she's nodding, so at least there's that. I hold her until she quiets, then kiss away the salty drops at the corners of her eyes before meeting her gaze again.

"You got a change of clothes?"

"In my truck." Her voice is thick.

"I'll send out a prospect to get them. And you're all right? We fucked you hard out there."

She suddenly laughs a little. "Yeah."

"No bad times?"

"No. Just so nervous at first. But then…it was really sexy, wasn't it?"

Sexy doesn't begin to describe it. "It was fucking amazing."

"It was." She glances up at me through her lashes. "So…want to go fuck and ride?"

"Hell, yeah." I swing her up. "And I'm going to be real sweet this time."

JENNY

HE'S HARD AND ROUGH. I don't care. All that matters is that I'm here, lying tangled in his sheets, and he's so close to me. My fingers trace the skull on his shoulder, studying the three sets of numbers in the teeth. *1-12-12 6-15-18 10-5-14-14-25*. It'll come to me, he said, and all at once it does.

And it's so easy. So easy. Just a number for a letter. Bikers do it all the time, like the "13" patch that stands for an "M." Some say it refers to marijuana or meth or a Mexican club, but however they use it, the "M" is the same. Even the Eighty-Eight Henchmen are named using a similar code. 88 is HH, for "Heil Hitler."

Lying here, it takes me a few minutes to translate all of the letters. But my heart begins pounding when I hit the last three, and when I finish I'm blinking back tears. *A-L-L F-O-R J-E-N-N-Y.* He got this tattoo nine years ago. *Nine years.*

His voice is heavy with sleep. "You figure it out?"

"Yeah," I whisper. "It says you love me."

His head comes up and his mouth finds mine. It's slow, this kiss. I want it to last forever but I don't mind that it ends. Not when what he says next is so much better.

"You have no idea how much, Jenny."

He'd do anything for me. Considering that I'd do anything for him, I think I have an idea.

His hand slides over my hip, then up over my ribs. I shiver as his big palm cups my breast and my nipples harden. "One more before you go? I wasn't sweet before."

With a laugh, I lift up to meet his kiss. Saxon Gray loves me. Rough or easy, slow or hard, it doesn't matter—as long as he keeps on loving me, each time will always be sweeter than the one before.

"One more," I say.

HAVING
IT ALL

ONE

SAXON

"I say it's time for a beer." Stone tosses the moving pads into the bed of Gunner's truck and slams the tailgate closed. "Let the old ladies fuss over where all this goes. The prospects can muscle around the stuff that's too heavy for the women."

Nodding, Gunner drags up the front of his shirt to wipe the sweat from his face. "I second that. Prez?"

A cold brew sounds pretty damn good. We've been hauling furniture from the clubhouse in town out to the

Erickson ranch for most of the day now, and what started as a cool morning has turned into a hot bitch of an afternoon. But although the moving is done, I'm not.

"Go on without me," I tell them. "You riding out to the Barracks tonight?"

Ever since the Hellfire Riders took over the strip joint and surrounding territory from the Eighty-Eight Henchmen, we've been keeping a strong presence there. Sending a good portion of the Riders in that direction means losing business at my own tavern, the Wolf Den, but I'm absorbing that blow for now. Cutting the Eighty-Eight's legs out from under them matters more than my cash flow does.

Stone's mug hardens, ragged scars whitening against his tan. "We'll be there. Howler and a few other Blue Coyotes are coming in to talk about setting up a ring during the Pendleton rally. You in for that?"

Fighting. I've done it before. My fists earned the down payment on the Den. It could be quick way to make up for that slow cash flow now but I don't need the distraction. "Not this time."

Stone and Gunner exchange a quick glance. Probably deciding whether to try persuading me.

"Not until the Eighty-Eight are gone," I say and Stone nods.

"Fair enough. We'll pin our hopes on Pretty Boy, instead." He jerks a thumb at Gunner.

The sergeant at arms blows him a kiss over the bed of

the truck, then says, "So you don't think the prez is pretty?"

Stone snorts and looks to me. "You're a regular Ken doll, boss. A giant, mean Ken doll."

"Except not blond," Gunner says.

"And with a beard."

"But without the slick suits."

"Or Hawaiian board shorts."

Gunner's eyebrows shoot up. "You know what kind of shorts Ken had?"

"Because I have a sister, asshole. You know how many times I had to put pants on Ken? Made me shrivel every time Anna left him lying naked on top of her other dolls. He doesn't have a *dick*, man. It was my sacred duty as a dude to cover that shit up."

Jesus. I could have gone my whole life without imagining the Riders' enforcer dressing a dickless doll in a pair of flowered shorts. But there's nothing guaranteed to keep Gunner on a topic longer than a mention of Anna—unless she's anywhere near him, then he shuts up real fast. He's good at making his interest appear casual but the pattern doesn't lie. He always follows up any mention of her with a question.

"She had them all naked?"

"Yeah, she was making them do some freaky shit. Which would've been great if it was just the girl dolls, because they had amazing breasts. So perky and the perfect size for rubbing with your thumbs. Although, the first time I saw a real woman, I wondered what the hell her nipples were—"

"Shut it now," I cut Stone off before he can start telling us about jerking off to the plastic tits. "And get the hell out of here before I find a doll to shove up your ass."

They're grinning as they climb into the truck. Jokers, the both of them, until shit starts going down or they're on duty. Then they're two of the coldest bastards currently wearing the Riders' colors.

The tires kick up the red dirt and dried pine needles lying on the ground outside the clubhouse before they hit the gravel drive. We'll need to get asphalt laid down before too long. Now that we're moving out here, we'll be riding that road often, and gravel's hard as hell on a bike. Hard as hell on a biker's face, too.

I can't see the need for many more changes. The clubhouse used to be the main lodge for a dude ranch that Red Erickson's grandfather operated. The property passed to Red just before he started up the Steel Titans. That club has made their home at the lodge for a few decades now, and unlike some MCs, they've taken care of their house—along with the old stable that's been converted to a repair shop and garage. Behind the lodge sits a couple of cabins that the brothers can bunk in if they're too wasted to ride home, or if there's no home to ride to and they need a place to crash for a while.

It's a damn good setup. Not as modern as the clubhouse the Riders had in town, but the lodge is bigger and the property gives us more room to spread out. And there aren't any neighbors complaining about engine noise or fearing that we're going to burn their pretty little houses and rape their pretty little daughters. As if most of us don't live or work right next to them—and as if those daughters haven't been coming to us looking for every kind of ride that a brother can give them. I expect we'll have just as many come looking out here, though they won't come directly. They'll hook up at the Den or the Barracks first. Then their daddies will follow, searching for them. In the five years I've been president of the Hellfire Riders, I've had to warn off more than a few fathers who were coming for my brothers' blood—and stare down the cops they often bring with them.

My inclination is to let the brothers handle that shit, instead. They bang the pussy, they deal with the consequences. The trouble is, more than one Rider is hotheaded enough to make a crap situation worse. Others think with their dicks. So it's better to take care of it myself.

But I won't have time for it over the next few weeks. Not while trying to bring two clubs together and getting rid of the Eighty-Eight Henchmen. Except for the old ladies and the girls we've known a while, best to forbid the brothers from bringing any women around here until everything has settled down. They want to fuck, they can do it in town.

I'll get some pushback from the club, but it's not the fathers I'm worried about now. The Eighty-Eight are cowardly motherfuckers. They won't try to take us down face-to-face. Instead they'll sneak up behind us, or they'll find a vulnerable spot and weasel their way inside, where they'll try to poison everything they find.

A woman can turn into a man's vulnerable spot real quick. So we'll have to look hard at any new pussy that shows up and starts clinging to one of the brothers, just in case she's been sent by Reichmann, the Henchmen's president.

Those Riders that already have women, we'll be making sure they stay safe. Because that's one way the Eighty-Eight will probably come at us. They'll try to hurt our women. They have before. They went after Red Erickson's daughter, and it's the reason behind everything that's happening now—the Steel Titans and the Hellfire Riders coming together, this brewing war with the Eighty-Eight Henchmen.

They went after Red's daughter—and *my* woman. That's when Reichmann and his men fucked up.

Jenny doesn't make me vulnerable. She makes me a force of fucking nature. Unstoppable. Unyielding. There's no line I won't cross in order to protect her. I'll have the blood of every single Henchman on my hands before they *ever* lay another finger on her.

No matter what it costs.

ALMOST FIFTEEN YEARS AGO, PROTECTING Jenny cost me a nickel over at the Snake River pen. I didn't even know her then. I just saw a girl screaming as the Eighty-Eight's president pinned her to the ground and got between her legs. With my arm fucked up by a shrapnel wound I got in Kosovo, I couldn't pull him off her. So I kicked him off, instead.

That boot to the head killed him. I didn't see Jenny again until she was testifying on my behalf at the trial. I still got five years in a prison cell for manslaughter, but I don't regret a second of it. Didn't regret it then, don't regret it now. I'd do it a thousand times over again to anyone who threatened her. And this time, the killing wouldn't be an accident, because if I ever lost her, I'd lose everything. Spending my life in prison would be nothing as long as I know she's safe.

She'll be safer if I'm with her, though. So we're not charging in and killing Reichmann and his crew. Not yet.

We won't wait long. The Eighty-Eight already killed one of my brothers, Goose, then planted enough heroin on him that the feds would have been taking a long, hard look at the Riders if we hadn't found the stash first. I expect more sneaky shit will be coming at us.

But there's another reason it'll all be going down soon—and he's riding his custom chopper up the drive toward the lodge. Red Erickson, the Steel Titans' prez. This is his place. Jenny's his daughter. And in a few months, the cancer eating away at his lungs will kill him. It's why he came to me about folding the clubs together. There are two things he wants before he's in the ground: to know that Jenny's protected and to see Reichmann dead.

I'll give him both.

The sickness isn't showing yet. Red's always been a big bastard, and he's still solid muscle. He got his road name years ago because of his hair but the red's not so bright anymore; his beard is mostly gray. Since Jenny's small-boned and dark-haired, I figure she must take after her mother, who was killed in an accident when Jenny was a teenager.

Red cuts his engine, his gaze sweeping the near-empty lot. "Did everyone head out on a ride I don't know about?"

Because so few bikes are here, even though it's a Sunday afternoon in summer. "It's moving day," I say. "So almost every brother suddenly has a family reunion or a church service to attend."

His grin is like his daughter's—quick and wide. "And I'm suddenly not sorry that Jenny had me checking in on the brewery today. You hear from her yet?"

"About an hour ago." When I was in town loading up the truck. She might have texted me—and Red—since then, but reception out here is shit. "She was just packing up. Says she'll be heading out of Portland by six."

Where she's been tending a booth at a brewer's festival for the better part of the week. A damn *long* week. Every night on the phone, I could hear how tired she was. And now she's got a four-hour drive ahead of her. Chances are, she'll head straight home and I won't see her until she's off work tomorrow.

Red nods. "I'm meeting Thorne up at the house. Why don't you come on by and have a cold one."

The back of my neck tightens. It seems like a simple invitation.

It's not.

BEFORE TODAY, I HAVEN'T STEPPED a foot in Jenny's house. She's invited me to but probably knew I wouldn't come in. Because it's not just her place; it belongs to Red, too. And although he handed over the lodge to me and the Hellfire Riders, this is still his territory. So I wasn't about to disrespect him by going in.

Now it would have been disrespecting him not to. So I'm standing on his deck with one of Jenny's ales in my hand, watching him lay half a dozen bratwurst on the grill. It's a big deck, attached to a big house. He inherited it with the ranch but he and Thorne have done well for themselves over the years, partnering in a construction firm specializing in irrigation systems and reservoir tanks, and he's poured some of that cash back into the house. Every room looks like it came out of a magazine, but they're not fancy or sterile. Just large and open, the kind of place where you imagine strawberry pie in the summer and crackling fires in the winter.

And the entire spread—from the lodge to this house— will be Jenny's when he's gone. Maybe it already is. She's told me that their lawyer keeps bringing around papers for her to sign.

Thorne comes through the French doors carrying a tray of plates and fixings. It's easy to see he's at home here. Years ago, he and Red both used to be Hellfire Riders. They walked away after clashing with Lucifer, the Riders' first president, and started up the Steel Titans together. Thorne has been Red's VP all that time—and they're close enough that Jenny calls him 'uncle.'

As soon as we fold the clubs together, Thorne will serve as my veep, too. So this probably won't be the last time I'm standing here with him.

"You got everything moved over?" he asks me, leaning back against the deck rail and lighting up a Marlboro.

"Everything but what's in the garage. Blowback's taking care of that." My current veep. "He's particular about the tools."

As in, he'll kick the ass of anyone who leaves them lying around or out of place. So best to just let him put them all in their new places.

Thorne grins. "Sounds like Red. He show you his garage yet?"

I've only been through the front door, the main living room and kitchen, and out onto the deck. "Not yet."

"We'll get around to it. He's got his own garage to clean out soon enough." Red looks to me. "You set a date yet for moving out here?"

Into this house. With Jenny.

Something in my chest constricts. Just getting the chance to be with her was like being offered the moon.

Living here with her? That's like being given the sun. But I can't take it yet. No matter how I want it, I can't take it.

And I've waited too long to answer. Though Red's eyes are the same light green as Jenny's, hers have never been so cold. There's serrated steel in his voice when he asks, "You having second thoughts about being with her?"

"No." *Fuck, no.* "Not one."

"But you aren't sure about something." Thorne's tone is easy, but he's white-knuckling his beer as he asks, "Maybe you think moving in here would be pushing Red out?"

"Bullshit," Red says. "The house is big enough, we can both swing our dicks around without smacking each other. So what is it, boy?"

Now he's just pushing my buttons. *Boy.* Another man would be swallowing broken teeth right now. No one calls the president of the Hellfire Riders *boy.*

But I can't say what I need to say as the president of the Hellfire Riders. As prez, I don't need to justify or explain myself—and I sure as hell don't need to earn my place. We aren't talking about the club, though.

"We aren't speaking now prez to prez. I'm speaking to Jenny's father. All right?"

"That depends on who *you* are."

"I'm the man who'd rather be dead than live without her."

"You lived without her for a long time."

"No. She's always been here." Close enough to see, but never to touch. "She just wasn't mine."

Watching me, Red takes a long pull from his beer before nodding. "All right. Talk."

"I haven't earned the right to lie beside her here."

"You think I'm deaf and blind?" He snorts and shakes his head. "She's been in your bed for weeks now."

And if that's all Jenny ever gave me, I'd take it. But it's not the same.

"That wasn't *here*." At this big house she calls her home. "This place means her future lies with mine. This place is for a family. I've got to earn those. I haven't yet. Not until Reichmann's dead."

Because even though I was protecting her, Reichmann still got to her a few weeks ago. Got his hands on her. It doesn't matter that I pulled him off or that he's paid with pain and blood. It's not enough. Not when he's still out there and will still hurt her, given any chance.

"She wouldn't agree you need to earn your place," Thorne says. "She'd say you earned it fifteen years ago when you saved her at that rally."

Red shakes his head. "She'd say he doesn't have to earn it at all. That just her wanting him here is enough."

"All respect to Jenny," I tell them, "but she'd be wrong. On both counts."

And I don't need to explain that to Red. His anger's gone now. He takes another long drink and finally says, "Even if you kill him, you'll never deserve her."

That's a bare fact and one I've known for a long time. But it doesn't mean I'll ever let her go.

"I won't argue that," I tell him.

"Even if you did argue, I don't give a shit about what you deserve. What I care about is what Jenny deserves. She deserves a man who'll lay down his life for her. A man who'll give his heart and his loyalty to her—and not just when it's easy, but when it hurts."

"That's what she has." What she'll always have.

Red nods. "She might need you to move out here before you get to Reichmann."

Because Red's sick and going to get worse, and she won't have anyone else. "If she needs me, I've already told her I'll come."

"That'll do." Smoke billows up when he opens the grill lid. "Now, prez to prez—how do you want to move forward? You want to patch in the Titans right away?"

"I want to wait. There's bound to be friction now that the clubs are sharing the same house. We'll let that settle down, go on a few rides together, let them start to feel like brothers. That way it'll mean something when we give your men their new colors."

"And my role?"

"You're the Titans' prez. I've no interest in pushing you out. The Riders aren't taking over. We're just coming together. So we'll ride side by side until you can't."

He doesn't say anything for a long minute, just turns the brats over. I'm not looking for an answer, anyway.

Except this one. "When the time comes, I'd like to patch you in first. Unless you plan to remain a Titan."

Now he looks up. "I'll tell you what—if Reichmann's in the ground, I'll die a Rider."

Works for me. "You'll look damn good in our colors."

"He always did," Thorne says as he crushes out his cigarette. "So we're down to one problem: How are we taking out the Eighty-Eight?"

TWO

SAXON

Taking out the Eighty-Eight Henchmen won't be the hard part. The hard part is getting to them. The *how* of that is still eating at me later that night while I'm working the speed bag in my garage. Though I've got the main door raised and a fan going, the air's stifling. The muscles in my arms feel like hot iron, but I want the pain. It burns away the frustration of not knowing how to get at the Eighty-Eight, helping to clear my head and refocus on the problem.

And, Christ—I miss Jenny.

I should be hearing from her soon. My phone's sitting on the weight bench. Any time now, she ought to be calling to say that she made it home all right. A week without her is too damn long. Next time she has one of these festivals, I'll try to arrange at least a few days away and go with her.

But not until the Eighty-Eight are gone.

And this is not focused. Shaking my head, I pick up my gloves and move over to the heavy bag. The light in the garage spills down the short driveway. There's no sound from outside but crickets. The street's quiet. My place is on the tail of a dead end, with retirees living on either side of me. The lights in their houses went dark almost before the sun was down. Around eleven, Mrs. Caffee will come out in her robe and wait while her Pomeranian pisses on the Yoder's flower beds. If I'm still out here then and she sees my garage light on, she'll walk by and look in—just checking to make sure I haven't accidentally left the garage door open, she always tells me. Jenny says the older woman's probably just checking to see whether I'm wearing a shirt while I'm lifting.

Fuck. Maybe I should just ride out to the ranch house. I'll see Jenny and get rid of this hollow ache in my gut.

But she's been working her ass off all week. She's *always* working her ass off, yet she's never sounded as tired as she did on the phone. So I'll let her rest—and keep my hands off her until tomorrow.

Anyway, I still haven't earned that spot in her bed. And

never will if I don't focus on the fucking Eighty-Eight.

Their greed is going to take them down. Lots of outlaw clubs get mixed up in shit like they have. The Hellfire Riders haven't—but we don't have clean hands. When we've got a problem, we take care of it and the law wouldn't look too kindly on some of the methods we've used. But we're here to ride. We're here to fuck and fight. We're not here to get rich, and I'm careful about who the Riders ask favors from and who we end up owing.

But the Eighty-Eight started in California with a supremacist agenda and then began chasing the cash, adding chapters in other states. The local Eighty-Eight settled here about twenty years ago. Mostly they cook meth and supply the more powerful chapters. They've probably added other shit—hauling guns or whatever else—but it's the meth that'll bring them down. Because I don't have a single fucking illusion about how brotherhood works in those clubs. If the supply doesn't come, Reichmann and everyone else is dead.

I don't want the bigger chapters to do my work, though. I just need the Eighty-Eight panicking. If I get rid of their cook, their kitchen, and the club's officers, the others will scatter—afraid that they'll be the ones to pay for the shipments that didn't come.

It'll have to be hard and clean and quick. And that's the fucking trouble. The Eighty-Eight has a compound out in the boonies. Word is, there's booby traps laid all around it. Maybe that's just to scare people off, but I'm not betting my brothers' lives on it. Some of the Eighty-Eight's members make Ted Kaczynski look sane. And although we outnumber them, a head-on confrontation isn't going to work. Riding in on fifty bikes is probably just asking to be gunned down from some fortified tower.

Or maybe gunned down from a few log cabins or tin shacks. Because we don't know *what* we'd be heading into. None of the Riders have had eyes on the place.

We've got to get some info before heading in. Because the only other choice is trying to take out the Eighty-Eight somewhere else. Some kind of ambush while they're out riding. But there's too many variables in that scenario. Best to keep it simple. Burn down their kitchen. Take out Reichmann, the cook, and the officers.

I've got to get eyes out there.

My lungs are burning when I stop to wipe the sweat from my face. My arms are like hot rubber. I glance at my phone, then back toward the street when headlights cut through the dark. I squint against the glare before I recognize the rig.

Jenny's truck.

My blood surges. My dick is hard so fast it hurts. I toss my gloves and head out of the garage as she pulls into the drive.

Her interior lights come on and the sight of her is like a punch to my chest. All that dark hair to wrap around my fist and those pink pouty lips already curved into a smile, as if the exhaustion bruising her eyes is nothing. She's got on the black T-shirt and short black skirt that she wears at her brewery storefront, which means that after the festival was over, she didn't even head back to the hotel and change into her regular clothes before coming home.

Before coming home to *me*.

Her green eyes are bright as she opens the door. "Look at you, all sweaty and half-naked. I must be a very good girl to deserve this."

I grin and catch her waist before her boots touch the ground, pushing her back into the driver's seat. "Mrs. Caffee will be coming out in a little while," I say against her mouth. "I thought I'd give her something to dream about."

Her lips part on a laugh and then I'm licking my way in, tasting chocolate and the coffee that kept her alert during the drive. Need is a hot fist in my gut, with fingers reaching up to squeeze my heart. God, this woman. She fucking owns me. I'm standing in my own damn driveway and somehow I'm the one coming home.

Her breath shudders when I raise my head. Her lips glisten.

Arousal hoarsens her voice. "I missed you. So much."

"How much?" I grip her hips and slide her forward. Her thighs widen to make room for me and a hungry little moan escapes her when the hard length of my cock wedges against her pussy. "Because when I get you out of this truck and into the house, I'm gonna have you bent over the kitchen table as fast as I can—and maybe I'll last one minute."

Her small breasts jiggle a little when she laughs. Her nipples are like bullets beneath her tight shirt. "I'm not going to last much longer than that. I was thinking of you the entire way."

"Yeah?" I run my fingertips up the inside of her thigh, watching her lips part. "Were you thinking of me licking your sweet pussy?"

She shivers. "Yes."

"And taking my cock?"

"Yes. You were holding me down and fucking me so deep." Her head falls back as she lifts her hips, grinding against my shaft. "Making me take all of it."

Christ. Only her panties and my sweatpants are keeping me from sinking into her. "Were you wet?"

"I'm wetter now."

And she's trembling and breathless. Fuck. I'm not joking about how quickly I'll have her and how long I'll last. The second she's in my house, I'm going balls deep into her juicy little pussy and filling her with my cum. But no matter how wet she is, her cunt never takes my dick easily; not right away. Better to get her ready now.

"Holding you down?" I grip the back of her neck and she stills, looking up at me. There's no doubt in her eyes. Only need. "On your back or on your knees?"

"My knees. With you behind me."

Standing here with the truck's door open and Jenny sitting on the edge of the seat, I can't get her into that position now. But it doesn't matter. I back off a little, easing the pressure of my cock between her legs, and push my hand between us.

Her panties are soaked. Just fucking soaked. And I'm going to lose it.

"Tell me," I say. It's harsh but I can't help it. I'm barely holding on. Her pussy's so hot and wet and as soon as I get my fingers inside her I know she'll feel like heaven. "Why was I making you take it? You didn't want it?"

"I did. So much. But I shouldn't."

"Why?" I tug her panties aside and slick my middle finger between her pussy lips, plump and swollen with need.

She moans. "Because you're a Rider. And it'll cause so much trouble."

Oh, fuck yeah. So much trouble—at least it would have a month ago. And I love where she's going with this.

My grip tightens on her neck. Her breathing is fast and shallow as I push in to my first knuckle. Her inner walls clasp my finger as if she's sucking me in. "How many times you imagine this, Jenny? The big bad Rider making you take his cock?"

She flashes a wicked little smile. "About every night for nine years."

Since I got out of prison. The first time after the trial that we ran into each other. She's been needing me almost as long as I've been needing her. "And your daddy's the Titans' prez." So I couldn't touch her for so damn long.

"If I make you take it, you don't have to feel bad, do you? You're not disloyal, even when you beg me for it."

Her hips rock forward. "I won't ever beg."

"Even when I hold you down, princess? When I tease your tight little cunt? When I make you come?"

"I won't come. I won't give in."

Her body shakes when my thumb glides over her clit. "You want me to make you come now?"

"I won't."

"I'm going to make you." Her cunt grips my finger as I push deeper and she cries out, her back arching. "I'm going to make you come so fucking hard. Then your hot pussy is going to take every inch of my dick. Tell me you want it."

"No."

"No?" I snarl against her lips. "You're riding my hand, princess. Your pussy juice is all over my fingers. You want more?"

"No," she says and I give it to her, sliding a second finger in, forcing her snug inner walls to stretch, working her clit faster. She clings to my arms, her fingernails digging into my biceps. "Saxon. God. *God.* Please."

Not playing anymore. Her whole body's trembling and stiffening. About to come.

"I'm going to get you inside and fuck you, Jenny." Voice rough, I pump harder into her. "You *are* going to take every fucking inch. Then I'm going to suck on your clit until you come again. You want that?"

"Yes."

Christ, she's so beautiful when she comes. Her green eyes glaze over and her cheeks flush before she curls closer, her mouth hot and open against my neck. Her cry is muffled against my throat. My balls tighten with the need to come when her pussy convulses around my fingers, and I keep pumping, keep sliding my thumb over her clit until her hips buck and she's suddenly pushing me away.

"No more." She's panting. "I can't again."

She will when we get inside. But I ease back for now, slipping out of her pussy and sucking the wetness from my fingers. My right hand smooths down her spine, holding her against me as she catches her breath. Her forehead's pressed to my shoulder and little shudders run through her every few seconds.

Finally she lifts her head and looks up at me. "Well, that was a fun little hello." Her voice is as soft and as warm as the expression in her eyes. "God, it's been a long week."

"Too long." I push her hair back from her face. "You're tired as fuck."

"Then it's a good thing you'll be doing all the work when we get inside; I can just lie there and fall asleep, right?" She gives me another wicked smile when I grin, then tugs at my waistband and runs her fingers over my cockhead. That light tease is torture. "Though I can't say I'm looking forward to dragging myself out of bed and driving out to the ranch later. So I'll make you a deal. You carry in my case and I'll lie there all night."

That's a deal I'll take. I drop a kiss to her mouth and back up. Her overnight bag is in the bed of the truck, strapped in with a bungee cord. As I unhook the cord, movement by the Caffee's fence makes me glance in that direction.

Not a gray-haired woman in a robe. Not a little white dog. Instead it's the dull gleam of a shotgun barrel, swinging up and taking aim.

"Jenny—"

The blast drowns out my roar. My ears are ringing and for a second I'm not here, it's not hot but cold and my shoulder's like crushed glass, and I can smell the burning fuel and my blood and hear Anderson screaming because his leg's been blown off—but it's not a marine screaming. It's Jenny, begging.

"Oh, Jesus, help me. Please, please." She's pulling at my arm and I'm on my knees.

Gotta get up. But my head's spinning and my legs won't steady.

"He's down!" The shout comes from across the yard. "Go grab the girl. The boss wants his whore."

Jenny. Reichmann sent his men for her.

"Get in the house," I tell her roughly. I'll slow them down here. *"Run."*

Tears streaking her cheeks, she shoves her hands under my arms and pushes. "Get in!"

I stagger up and suddenly there's some skinhead fucker with a swastika tattooed into his neck coming around the nose of the truck and looking surprised that I'm alive. Quick, I'm on him, my fist in his gut and my elbow slamming into his back. He's down and I grab his skull and drive his face into the concrete, then my shoulder's on fire and Jenny's screaming, pulling at me.

"Get in!" She throws her shoulder into my gut like a linebacker, knocking me back against the truck cab. "The other one's coming with the shotgun!"

And I'm fading. I slide across her seat and there's blood dripping all over me. Then she shouts "Down!" and the cab's back window explodes, showering glass, and Jenny's crouching low in her seat and shifting into reverse.

We bump across something, the curb or a body and I don't give a fuck. My arm's not moving. I can't lift my head and my neck's raining blood. I fall against the passenger door when she whips the truck around, then she's sitting up, the streetlights racing by in long bright ribbons as she tears off her shirt.

"Hold this against your neck. Saxon! Please, *please.*" She takes a quick glance at the road. Then she's leaning over, cramming the wadded shirt against my throat before taking my hand and lifting it to press against the same spot. "Keep it there. The hospital's only five minutes away. Just hold on."

I'll hold on. Because now she's crying, smears of blood mixing with her tears, and she's not talking to me but just sobbing over and over *please I can't lose him please don't take him too please don't.*

I don't know who she's begging but there's no one who could take me away. I'll never leave her.

But I'll tell her that later, when I can. I'm too tired now. I'm just going to sleep.

It's been a damn long week.

THREE

SAXON

Everything's so fucking bright. The light's drilling into my skull. I squint against it and turn my head, and there's a ragged draw of breath beside me. *Jenny.*

She's leaning over me, her face like a bleached sheet stained by raw pink around her eyes.

"No crying. I'm not leaving you," I tell her and there's a desert in my throat. Nothing but a rasping whisper comes through. "You all right?"

"Yeah." Despite what I told her, those green eyes are

filling again and I can hear the thickness in her voice. "So are you."

That's good. But she doesn't give me a chance to say so, leaning in, her breath hot against my ear.

"*I said I didn't see who it was,*" she says softly, so softly, then her lips press to my cheek and she's lifting her head again. "The sheriff's here to ask you a few questions, and the nurses will probably poke you again, so I'll be back when they're done."

I nod and realize she's holding my hand. She starts to pull away but I tighten my fingers.

"You all right, Jenny?" I think I already asked. I don't think I believed her answer.

She smiles and her tears spill over. "I'm all right."

JENNY

I'm not all right. My chest feels like an iceberg is lodged inside it, heavy and cold. But I'm not numb. I wish I was. Because then I wouldn't be hurting so much. Then I might not be seeing blood explode from Saxon's shoulder and neck every time I close my eyes.

I thought I lost him.

The Henchman used a shotgun, the favored weapon of motorcycle clubs because the ballistics are harder for the cops to trace—there's no rifling on the shot pellets—and you don't have to aim carefully, which is perfect when you're firing while driving by on a bike. You just have to be close to a target for a shotgun to be effective. That probably saved Saxon's life. The Henchman was just far enough away and hit mostly muscle; they had to dig a pile of lead shot out of Saxon's left shoulder. But the pellets also ripped a big chunk out of his neck and there was so much blood. I thought his artery was torn open. I thought he was as good as dead and I was just watching him bleed out.

If the Henchman had aimed just a little more to the right, Saxon *would* have bled out.

And everyone keeps asking if I'm all right. Half a dozen cups of coffee have been shoved into my hand, but I can't get warm and I can't wake up from the nightmare of seeing him bleed and bleed and then pass out.

I thought I was watching Saxon die. He came back from it. Thank God he came back from it.

I don't think I have yet.

"You know what's stupid?" my friend Anna asks. "The whole 'I'm gonna rape you in revenge' thing."

I tear my gaze from the hallway where Saxon's hospital room is. The sheriff hasn't come out yet. "What?"

"The Eighty-Eight and the way they're after you." She says that quietly, so that she can't be overheard. "Because, really, what does anyone get out of that? Especially when you'd be worth so much more for your brain. I mean, think about it. You brew beer and you've got a degree in chemistry. How hard would cooking meth for them be?"

God. "I'm not exactly Walter White."

"I bet you could do it. So if I was a criminal mastermind, I wouldn't want your pussy. I'd just chain you up and force you to make drugs all day and I'd get rich selling them. Then I'd hire a bunch of cabana boys and bang *them*. In revenge."

"Reichmann isn't a mastermind." And he doesn't want my pussy. He just wants to hurt me.

She snorts. "Like I said. 'You know what's stupid?'"

True. But stupid can still be pretty damn dangerous.

Sheriff Landauer isn't in Saxon's room long. He's already talked to me but I'm not surprised when he heads my way again. When she sees him, Anna gets that fighting look on her face, like she's going to tell him to back off or wait until tomorrow or go sit on a sharp stick. I shake my head and she deflates.

"You sure?"

I nod and she gets up, moving across the waiting room to where her brother, Stone, and a handful of other Hellfire Riders are sitting. There were more here earlier, but after Saxon woke up and they got the news that he was going to be all right, some of them started taking off for home.

Landauer folds himself into the chair at my left and caps his bony knee with his hat. He's lean and wiry, with short blond hair salted by gray and sporting a Clint Eastwood jut in his jaw. A scar on his upper lip makes him look like he's always sneering, but he's not so bad.

"You doing all right?"

I can only manage a short, hollow laugh.

"Yep, that's what I thought. I thought I saw Red earlier? I didn't get a chance to say hello to him."

My dad. I don't know if they're really friendly enough to exchange hellos, or if Landauer is just making it sound like they are so I'll relax around him. I've never heard my dad say a bad word against the sheriff—which isn't the case for almost every other cop around the area. "He's picking up clothes for me."

I tug at the front of the scrubs that the hospital gave to me. I came in half naked, with my shirt wadded against Saxon's neck and my shorts soaked in his blood. My suitcase is in my truck but the sheriff has already said I won't be getting anything out of it until they've finished processing the vehicle.

His gaze skims over the assembled Riders, who are looking this way. Maybe thinking they need to extricate their first lady from the cop's grasp. I meet Blowback's eyes. I can handle this. He says something to the others and they've all suddenly got other things to look at.

"You know I always thought your man got a bum deal all those years ago. Crane was a real hard-ass."

The county prosecutor. "I guess."

"He should have dropped the charges when you came forward."

"A jury didn't agree. They didn't seem to think anything I said mattered."

"Well, Crane did a good job of painting him as a troublemaking piece of shit, didn't he?" He leans forward, hands clasped between his knees, watching my face. "Now here we are."

"Where are we?"

"Fifteen years ago he was kicking Timothy Reichmann off of you. Now Reichmann's little brother is president of a biker gang, and word is he's after you. *You*, even though it was Saxon Gray that killed his brother."

Because Luke Reichmann is a misogynist coward who thinks that his brother was just giving me what I deserved—and because he knows better than to go after Saxon. Or at least, he *did* know better. But he still didn't come himself. He sent two of his men, instead.

But, supposedly, I don't know that. "'Word is' he's after me? Who's saying that?"

Landauer doesn't tell me but continues, "And word is, there was an altercation between Gray and Reichmann out at the Corral a couple of weeks ago, and that maybe you were in the middle of it."

I wasn't in the middle of it. I was in a booth and shoved up against a wall with Reichmann threatening me until Saxon pulled him off. But I only shrug. "I was there with Saxon but I didn't see any altercation."

"Word also is that Reichmann came into the ER about a week after that to have three of his fingers reattached. Says he got them caught in a mower. The doctors saved two."

His fingers had been cut off? I don't have to lie about this. "I don't know anything about that."

But I'm not sorry or shocked, either.

The sheriff lifts his shoulders in an easy shrug. "Eh, he lives on a farm. All kinds of accidents can happen, especially if you're mowing at night as he says he was. But it occurs to me that a pattern is forming—and escalating—and that your man might have taken the latest hit tonight. Which means the next hit will be worse."

He's right. I can't imagine that the Hellfire Riders won't strike back hard and fast, and that it'll be bloody. I'm not giving Landauer what he wants, though. "So all these words are flying around—and they're saying I might be in danger—and this is the first time you're talking to me? Why is that? Maybe because until someone is shot or raped, there's not much you can do to help me? That's a little too late, isn't it?"

"I can help now."

No, he can't. Because even if I hand him the men who attacked us tonight and he makes an arrest, those Henchmen aren't going to point their fingers at Reichmann and say he's the one who gave the orders. They're going to keep their mouths shut and nothing will change. I'll still be in danger. Landauer can't protect me. Saxon can.

The only question is how much he'll pay for protecting me. Again.

"I might have run over one of the shooters," I say. "Or maybe it was Saxon's mailbox. I don't know; I was hunched down in my seat because they'd just shot out my back window." All of which he'll find out by looking at my truck; I'm not telling him anything he doesn't already know or won't discover. "You've got my truck so I guess you'll know whether it was a man that I ran over, and if you find a body with tire tracks on it, I guess you'll know whether I killed him. So, what do you think? Is Crane going to come after me for manslaughter because I was in a rush trying to save a man after he'd been shot? Because that doesn't seem much different than prosecuting a man who accidentally killed someone while saving a girl from being raped."

"It doesn't sound much different at all," he surprises me by agreeing. "What does sound different is taking out the 'accident.' Say, if a man trying to protect his woman decides to retaliate instead of just defend. Maybe you think the only difference is the law drawing a line, because protection is protection…but it's a difference that will send a man away for a long time."

I know. And the crushing weight in my chest is suddenly heavier, colder. "I wish I could help. But I didn't see who they were. I was turning to go into the house when he was shot and then I was ducking behind the truck."

"And you didn't hear anything?"

The boss wants his whore. "No. Maybe they said some-thing, but I didn't hear it. I was making a lot of noise, too—I started screaming after the shot went off and I realized Saxon had been hit."

Saxon's neighbors will confirm that.

He gives a deep sigh. "All right. If you suddenly do remember seeing or hearing something, though, you'll let me know?"

"I will."

"Good thing." Landauer slaps his thighs like he's about to get up, then pauses. "Because word is, during that altercation at the Corral, your man was in the process of retaliating…but then you asked him not to. Word is you said you couldn't bear losing him or seeing him in prison again. Which he would be, if he murdered someone."

My throat is a ragged burn. I can't answer.

"I guess I'll just hope evidence turns up that can help me get the bastards who shot at you locked away—along with anyone who might have told them to pull the trigger. Then there will be no one around to threaten you, and no one your man will need to protect you from, you see?"

I nod and he gets to his feet, hat in hand.

"Well, maybe just sleep on it, Miss Erickson. A bit of rest has a way of jogging the memory."

And he obviously knows that being terrified of losing someone you love does, too.

FOUR

JENNY

"I never hated hospitals the way that some people do," my dad says.

It's the first thing either of us have spoken in a little while. The clock reads just after four. Anna's dozing against my shoulder. In a room down the hall, Saxon's pumped full of painkillers and he'll be sleeping until morning, at least—and I can't sit with him, because Pine Valley's hospital is tiny and now he's sharing space with a teenager who fell from a window while trying to sneak out of his house. The kid's parents are sitting beneath the silenced TV mounted in the corner. The mom is sleeping and the dad looks about to nod off. Whatever happened, the kid must not have been hurt too bad. If he was, they'd have shuttled him to the hospital up in Bend.

I don't like hospitals or hate them. But I would have guessed my dad hated them. Especially now, when being here must make him think of everything that's coming for him.

Or not coming for him. Because I don't think he'll wait until he's in a hospital. I don't think he'll make me sit in a room like this. No. He'll take a ride down to Crater Lake, maybe. It was always one of his favorite runs. And the north road winding up around the caldera doesn't have guardrails or a shoulder, despite the sheer drop on the other side of the white line. A sick man could just…fly.

So I can't even ask him why he doesn't hate them. The iceberg in my chest has become a glacier moving into my throat. I just look at him instead. He's not looking back but watching the woman at the nurse's station.

His voice is a little rougher now. "They remind me of your mother."

Who'd been a nurse, too. She hadn't worked here. Her scrubs were a different color. But I guess it doesn't matter.

I take his hand. Years ago, when I'd first gone to college, I started on a medical track mostly because of my mom. Hoping to carry on some kind of legacy for her, because she hadn't got much of a chance to make her own. I ended up majoring in organic chemistry, but instead of heading to medical school, I went for a master's in business admin and started up my brewery. I've never regretted it until now. If I'd gone to medical school, maybe I would have known that Saxon wasn't dying, that his artery wasn't perforated.

Instead I brew a lot of beer. I don't know if I could ever drink enough to make me forget the moment I thought he was dead.

"And you know what your mom would be doing right now, Jenny? She'd be sitting up at that desk and thinking that all of these assholes just need to go home."

"Dad—"

"He's right," Anna mumbles next to me. My pillow of a shoulder has left a big pink splotch on her cheek. She signals to Stone, who nods. "And I need to get going, or Saxon's going to be really pissed and fire me for falling asleep at the Den tomorrow. You want to crash at my place?"

"I'm not going."

She looks over my head to my dad. I don't see what passes between them but she nods and stands, stretching her arms and popping her neck. "God, I'm going to feel this crick all week. All right. Call me if you need me, okay?"

"Okay."

"If he's still here, I'll come back before my shift tomorrow and bring you lunch." She leans down to hug me. "He's fine. You know he's tough and *way* too mean to let this slow him down."

"I know. Thanks."

She's only gone a minute when my dad says, "We ought to get going, too. You need to sleep."

Maybe I do. That doesn't mean I can. "I won't be able to."

"When you came in, they checked you over. Prescribed you a sedative, didn't they?"

One that will knock me out longer than I want to be. If I take it, Saxon will probably wake up before I do. "Yes, but—"

"I picked it up at the pharmacy when I went to get your clothes. Now you listen, all right? These guys aren't going anywhere." He gestures to Blowback, Stone, and Gunner—the three Riders still here. "They're going to watch and make sure that no one gets to him while he's sleeping. He'll be safe."

Safe. How can he be safe? My eyes are burning. "Daddy, you didn't see him. There was so much blood—"

"And it's stopped bleeding. They've given him more. They're taking care of him. But you look like shit and if he sees you like this, it's not going to help him. He'll just worry more than he already is. And I *know* that, Jenny. I know it because I'm feeling the same. I've never seen you look so close to breaking."

Because I've never felt so close. Closer now, because that ragged edge to his breath has returned, the one that comes just before he has a coughing fit and spits a little blood.

"Okay," I whisper. "We'll go home. I'll try to sleep."

He nods and wraps a strong arm around my shoulders, squeezing. "You'll be all right, baby girl."

Maybe. I just don't see how.

SAXON

"SO THEY'RE LETTING YOU WALK out of here?" Gunner asks, and his careful tone tells me that he really wants to say I'm batshit crazy, but he knows better than to speak those words to me.

"I didn't give them much choice." Besides, they only wanted to keep me to watch for infection. There's nothing more they can do to patch me up. But I'm not stupid. I'll take my antibiotics like a good boy and come back if I start running a fever. What I don't want is to hang around here, doped on morphine when Landauer can walk in and start questioning me again. I need a clear head. The pain of moving around will give me that. "How's Jenny?"

"She's holding up. Red pretty much dragged her home around four."

It's only seven-thirty now. I'd have been ready to go earlier but I had to wait on paperwork and the doctor giving me a final look-over. I pull on my jeans and grab the shirt lying folded on the chair. This is going to hurt like a motherfucker. Luckily I'm still floating on the shit they gave me last night.

Carefully I wind the sleeve up my arm. A big padded bandage covers the front of my shoulder. I'm told it looks like ground beef underneath. The chunk out of my neck is the one I'll have to be most careful about, making sure not to rip open the stitches. The one that hurts most, though, is on the side of my jaw, in a spot covered by a measly square inch of gauze. One little pellet hit bone, and opening my mouth makes me want to slam my fist through a wall.

But I keep jawing, because what I have to say is more important than a little pain. "I want either Hashtag or Scarecrow with Jenny every second. And find a way to get the phones working out there. Or get them a sat phone for now."

"We'll do it."

"I've got a list of prescriptions."

"We'll send a prospect to pick them up," Gunner says and looks over as Stone and Blowback come in.

Stone's gaze shoots to the other bed. "The kid's asleep?"

"He's pretending," I say. "And he's going to keep his fucking mouth shut. Aren't you, boy?"

He doesn't open his eyes but just nods. I'd grin if my jaw wasn't aching so bad. There's nothing we've said I care about getting out, anyway.

"What's your name, kid?"

"Thomas James Clark," Blowback answers me before the boy can. By now, he probably knows how much the kid weighed when he was born and which girl in town he's sneaking out to stick his dick in.

Stone adds, "But we're calling him the Defenestrator, because it's much more badass to be thrown out a window than to fall out, right? So you should use that at school, kid. Put it on the back of your jacket."

The boy finally speaks. "I don't even know how to spell it."

"Jesus. I'm gonna look you up in month and kick your ass if you can't spell it for me then."

"Listen to him, kid. He gets real serious about defenestration." Shoving my feet into my boots, I pick up the sling the nurse left for me. "Let's roll. Get Widowmaker on the horn and have him start contacting the brothers. I want everyone who can get there out at the lodge in two hours. My kutte's at the house. So is my phone and my bike. Someone needs to ride it out to the ranch."

It won't be me. Not for a few days, at least.

"I'll do it," Stone says. "Gunner has his rig. You can drop me off and ride out to the lodge with him."

Good. We'll see if the cops are still around my place, too. I won't be.

I haven't earned my place in Jenny's home yet. But I don't fucking care. We didn't expect this move from Reichmann. And we always assumed she'd be safe out at the ranch. I'm not assuming she'll be safe anywhere anymore. Not until Reichmann's a dead man.

But that death will be upon him real soon, because I'm coming for him. And nothing's going to stop me.

JENNY

I didn't take the sedative but I did try to sleep. I did a little, I think. When the alarm I set for eight rang, I must have been dozing, because it startled me awake. I called the hospital to check on Saxon and found out he'd already been released, but he didn't answer his phone when I tried to discover where he'd gone. Then my dad got the message that they're having an emergency meeting out at the clubhouse. So they're all going to make plans to take out the Eighty-Eight and there's a good chance that even though he survived a shotgun blast, I'm going to lose him anyway. If not in this war with Reichmann, then because Landauer knows too much and he'll know exactly who to look at. So Saxon will go to prison and he won't be sorry, because he'll have done it protecting me.

And I can't even breathe, imagining it. Everything hurts. It hurts so much that I'm finally numb, making my way like a zombie through a shower and getting dressed, then eating a few bites of breakfast and taking my dad's truck out to the old barn where my brewery is.

No matter what happens, there will always be work. I'll lose my dad, I'll lose Saxon, but work will always be waiting for me.

I wonder how long it will be before the work isn't enough to keep me going.

I'm only there a few minutes when I hear a bike

coming up the drive. Not Saxon's. I know the sound of his Harley by now. Not my dad's either. I grab the shotgun I stashed in my office last year when Reichmann's threats started circulating and check the window.

Hashtag. One of the Hellfire Riders' prospects, but just because he isn't patched in doesn't mean he's a newbie. I don't know much about him except that Stone was the one who sponsored him. He's a few years younger than me, maybe twenty-six or -seven, and the way he walks, I'm pretty sure he was military once upon a time. Probably pretty recently.

He sees my gun and his hands shoot up. "The prez sent me to look after you!"

Of course Saxon did. I wave him in.

Scarecrow shows up about a half hour later and he looks like his name. He starts making rounds, Hashtag sticks close to me, and he's asking me so many questions about the brewhouse that I don't hear Gunner's truck coming. I just turn and Saxon's there, his arm in a sling and his beard gone. My heart thumps hard and I think the iceberg's cracking, because he's here and so alive, looking mean and hard and just the way I like him.

My hand shakes, making the hydrometer I'm holding clatter against the side of its tray before it slips into place. "Hey."

He looks to Hashtag. "Get gone."

The prospect makes himself scarce. I'm not really sure where he heads. Saxon's coming toward me, his dark blue eyes locked on my face. I can't see anything else, and the iceberg's cracking but it's just bringing all the pain back. Because I don't know where to touch him. I don't know what's going to hurt him.

But I know he'll never tell me what does.

I need to touch him, though. My throat a solid knot, I skim my fingertips down the right side of his jaw. "You shaved."

"The nurse did this morning. They had to scrape off a patch to get the shot out, so she finished it up." His voice is low and rough. His gaze is all over my face. "You're all right?"

God. "Are *you*?"

"I am if you are."

"Then I'm fine." My breath shudders when his big hand cups my face and his thumb caresses my cheek. "Landauer knows it was the Eighty-Eight. I didn't say anything. I didn't *have* to say anything."

"I know."

"He's going to be watching you. Making sure you don't do anything to retaliate."

"I know. But you know I'm going to take care of this."

Because I can't trust myself to speak, because my chest feels like it's being crushed, I just nod.

"You'll be safe, princess." Every word seems cast in iron. "I'm heading out to the lodge now but if you need anything, you just ask. You need me here and I'll come."

"Okay," I manage.

"You gonna work here most the day?"

"I think so. I've got a lot to catch up on after a week away. And I just…I need to keep busy."

He nods and his thumb brushes over my lips. "I'll be staying with you at your house tonight. That all right?"

It's the only thing that is. "Yes."

Something dark moves across his expression then he's bending his head. His mouth catches mine in a kiss that's too sweet and too brief. "I'll see if I can keep you busy tonight—and hope your dad doesn't have a shotgun."

I laugh and for a second, everything inside me lightens. "He has one. So just hope he doesn't have better aim than a Henchman."

His grin comes—then it goes so fast I realize that even smiling hurts him and pain crushes my chest. I hide it, hide it hard, and I must do a good job because instead of asking me if I'm all right he kisses me again. Then he's gone, heading toward the meeting that might take him from me forever.

But I could stop it. I could stop it.

Though if I did, I'd lose him anyway.

FIVE

JENNY

Motorcycle clubs take care of their own shit. You don't go running to the cops. A club member who did would be betraying his brothers. I'm not a Hellfire Rider, I'm not an old lady, but I'm Saxon's. By telling Landauer anything about last night, I'd be betraying him.

But I keep seeing that blood. And I wonder what would be harder to live with: Saxon dead or Saxon not loving me?

I know the answer. Because in the moment last night

that his eyes closed and his bloodied body seemed lifeless, I'd have done anything, *anything,* to bring him back. Even if I never held him again.

Maybe there's another way, though. I don't know what it is. I'm trying to think of one, but Hashtag has moved away from asking questions; instead he's telling me about the night-vision goggles that he and Scarecrow will be using to make sure Reichmann doesn't try to sneak up on us in the dark again. Then he says that everything would be a lot easier if they could just bomb the shit out of the Eighty-Eight's compound, and Scarecrow tells him that he's been fighting overseas too long and forgot about the old ladies and kids that are probably living out there, or maybe he just doesn't give a shit about collateral damage and would like to send in a drone, then they start sniping about the last presidential election and I have to tell them to shut the fuck up so I can think.

But I'm not thinking. I'm just hurting. And now they both keep apologizing, so I tell them to follow me up to the house where I can make us all something for lunch. As soon as I'm there I sit them down in the kitchen, then open the refrigerator and stare at the nothing inside.

A little milk. One egg. Usually one of the Titans' prospects goes grocery shopping for my dad on Monday morning—a perk of being the president of a motorcycle club is that he doesn't ever have to do any of that everyday stuff—but Bottlecap must not have gone today, because he's in an emergency meeting.

Because Saxon was shot.

Because he agreed to protect me.

"I guess we don't have anything," I say dully, then something inside me breaks and I'm bawling. For an endless time, I stand sobbing helplessly in front of the open icebox and I can feel both Scarecrow and Hashtag silently panicking behind me, wondering what to do, but there's nothing they can do.

Maybe there's something *I* can do, though.

I wipe my face and draw a ragged breath. "Don't tell Saxon I did that, okay?"

"Sure thing," Hashtag says. I know he's lying. "It's just delayed shock or whatever."

"Right."

Scarecrow offers, "How about I run into town and grab us all something to eat? It won't take me long."

I've got a better idea. "How about we all just go? I wanted to meet up with Anna sometime today, anyway."

"All right," Hashtag agrees. "I just need to let the boss know we're headed out. You got a magic spot around here so I can send a text?"

Somewhere the phone reception gets through. "Sometimes you can get a bar or two if you're in the window seat in my room. But there's a land line here. The clubhouse is the first number on the speed dial."

"Yeah, that's great, but real talking sucks. Is it okay if I head up to your room?"

I nod and start for the stairs. "I'll show you."

Because I've got a couple of messages to send, too.

SAXON

My shoulder's hurting like a son of a bitch on fire. The few ibuprofen I took aren't cutting it, but the heavy-duty painkillers I've got will fog up my brain and put me half to sleep. Maybe there's no difference, though. There's pain that clears your head and pain that empties your head, and I'm right on the edge of the second.

Luckily I haven't had to do much talking. Instead Red's been laying everything out—who the brothers need to be looking out for and which parts of our asses we need to cover before any cops come poking around. Where the safe houses are if anyone wants to tuck away their family for a bit. The equipment and info we still need before we can head out to the compound.

"The easiest way to get that info is to grab a Henchman and persuade him to tell us about their setup. But Reichmann and the others are likely to be lying low the next week or so," he says. "They got to know that the sheriff's watching all of us real close. Reichmann's as stupid as a donkey's ass, though, so he might want to come out and bray."

"But even if he does, he'll still hide behind someone," I say and the flare of agony in my jaw puts spots in front of my eyes. "He's got two gears: hurting someone weaker than he is, or ordering his brothers to hurt someone stronger. So he's not going to come out alone."

"And if he does come out?" Beaver asks.

"Ride on. You let us know he was out, but you ride on. We're only looking to get one alone." I glance at Blowback. "And we'll make sure he talks."

Picasso frowns. "What about the prospect that trashed Zoomie's bike? We know where he is, don't we?"

"He's gone."

Eyes flat and face hard, my veep answers. Looking at him, most of the brothers are probably assuming that Blowback took the prospect out. He didn't. Blowback got some info from him a few weeks ago—mostly about the Eighty-Eight's meth operation—but the prospect vanished about a day after. We still don't know if he took off or if Reichmann killed him for talking.

"So we need that info," Red says. "We don't want to leave shit to chance. And we don't want to leave anything that'll point to us. So when we burn their house down, we need to be like a dick in a rubber—we go in clean and we come out clean."

Fuck. That's a good one. But grinning makes my head pound and my temper short, so when I see Bottlecap sidling along the wall toward Red and me, the look I give the prospect freezes him in place.

He holds up a phone—*my* phone. The last I saw it I was dumping it in a basket with everyone else's so there weren't any distractions and no one got their asses kicked for texting during the meeting.

"You got a few messages," the kid says.

"Prez," Red reminds him quietly.

"You got a few messages, Prez. I'm on phone duty."

"Bring it here. Everyone else, take ten minutes." Two messages. "You got reception here?"

"No, sir. I was babysitting them out by the bend in the road."

One from Hashtag. *Miss E was crying her eyes out because the fridge is empty. We're heading to PV for lunch.*

Into town. "Who usually shops for groceries?"

"Me, sir."

"You make sure you get them this afternoon."

"Yes, sir."

I read the message again. My chest is tight as fuck. *Crying her eyes out.* Jenny doesn't cry easy. Not over food. She told me she's all right.

She's not.

But there's no message from her, asking for me to come. Just one from Zoomie. According to Blowback, she's not here because she's flying a helitack crew out to a wildfire a few counties over. That probably pisses her off. She's real careful never to give any brothers the oppor-tunity to say she isn't pulling her weight—and some will. They won't say shit about the others who couldn't get off work to come to this meeting. But some will say maybe she's afraid to mix it up with the Eighty-Eight.

It's not about the meeting, though. *Jenny's asking me if I know any aerial photographers so she can make a brochure. BUT SHE DIDN'T WANT TO HIRE MY BIRD. I gave her a few other names but WTF? She wants them by tomorrow. TOMORROW. Is she okay?*

Irritation spikes through me. What's the big fucking deal about tomorrow? There's nothing else going on. And if Zoomie's upset that Jenny wants to hire someone else, that's her damn business. Jenny's not running a lemonade stand. Everything she does with that brewery is based on all kinds of marketing research and she plans everything ahead—

Hell. She plans a lot further ahead than *tomorrow.* That's what Zoomie's getting at. There's nothing particular about tomorrow. It's just that Jenny doesn't run her business that way.

She's usually generous with her friends, too. I've seen it. There's pretty much nothing she won't give them and tossing a little business in their direction is just part of it—just like the brothers look to each other before hiring someone outside the club.

And she's not all right. Breaking down and crying.

It isn't hard to guess what's going on. Throwing herself into work, distancing herself from her friends. She's blaming herself for this. Maybe worried she'll put a target on Zoomie just by being close. Probably real scared the Eighty-Eight will come for me again. If that's the case, nothing will help her but getting out to the Eighty-

Eight's compound and finishing this.

And I'm the stupidest fuck that ever lived.

I write a response. *She'll be all right. Get your ass here ASAP. I need to hire your bird.*

Bottlecap's still waiting. I give him the phone. "That'll send when you get back out there, yeah?"

"Yes, sir."

"Then get back out there." I look to Red. "We'll get eyes on the compound. They're just not going to be on the ground."

Blowback will be going up with Zoomie tomorrow night. She'll fly, he'll scope the place out. Easier than nabbing a Henchman—and less likely to go balls up. I'd rather it be earlier but it might be best this way. I pushed too hard today. I can deal with pain but my shoulder stiffened up. If I don't get a full day of resting this arm I won't be any good when the time comes to go after Reichmann.

But I'm already damn sorry I took those painkillers before coming to the ranch house. I'm feeling almost drunk and didn't put up much resistance when Jenny pushed me down onto her big bed and told me to stay put. But she's not here with me. Instead she's putting away the clothes that she picked up from my house. So I'm just lying here, my body heavy, watching her make room for me in her place. Though in truth, it's an easy fit. I don't have much and Jenny's basically got the whole upstairs floor to herself. They've opened up and expanded the rooms, so she's got a huge suite with big windows overlooking the orchard out back. Nothing girly, either. I'd have been fine with that if it was. But instead there's lots of browns and golds and greens, like she took the colors from her hair and eyes and made a room of them.

And I don't think I was wrong. She's distancing herself. Blaming herself. It's subtle, but she doesn't look at me as often as she usually does, and sometimes when she does she glances away quick. She's moving stiffly, too, back and forth from the bench at the end of the bed to the closet big enough to be its own room, holding herself really careful so she doesn't break.

Seeing how this weighs on her hurts more than being shot does.

"Zoomie said you asked her about pilots."

"I did." She's paying close attention to my jeans as she refolds a pair that were already folded. "I'm thinking of pushing the local angle. You know, hops from local fields, supporting the local farmer. That kind of thing. So I'll get photos of some nearby farms."

"You rolling out any organic beer?"

"No, but that would be smart. Eventually I will."

"I get asked all the time to put more organic stuff on the menu at the Den."

She shoots me a surprised look. "The Riders ask you for it?"

Shit. Laughing hurts like a motherfucker. "Nah. The lunch crowd. Especially tourists."

Her smile comes and goes too quickly. She turns toward the closet again. God damn it.

I get up and go after her, my feet bare and my arm stuck in a sling. Every muscle seems to weigh a ton. "You're feeling guilty, aren't you?"

Her whole body freezes up. Her widened eyes shoot to my face. "What? No. Guilty about what?"

"No? Then why are you running around here all skittish?" I know she's not afraid of *me*. Which means she's just afraid. "Am I gonna have to fuck the answer out of you?"

Her jaw sets. "I hate it when you do that."

"But it works." Because she never keeps distance between us when I touch her. But I don't ever warn her that's what I'm doing—and I'm not going to do it now. Her breath is already shuddering. I like it when she's mad but right now she's closer to crying. Gently I slip my free arm around her waist and bring her in against my chest. "You know what I'm thinking?"

She's hiding her face. Her hair tumbles over her shoulders when she silently shakes her head.

"I'm remembering sitting in my cell and getting a letter from you. Just pages and pages of how sorry you were for getting mixed up at that rally and walking into the Eighty-Eight's territory. Of how sorry you were that you couldn't get away from Reichmann by yourself. On and on, because you were sorry for every step that landed me in jail—even those steps that you hadn't taken. So now

I'm thinking that maybe you're feeling the same way, but you haven't written it out, and you've got pages and pages of 'I'm sorry' building up in you right now. But I don't want them. You remember what I wrote back to you and said?"

"I do," she whispers. "So let me go, Saxon."

I don't want to but I do, and watch her walk around the bed and open up a drawer in the nightstand. She pulls out a note and unfolds it. The creases are tattered. The paper's all but falling apart. She hands it to me and it's a punch to my chest. There's my response to her. My writing.

Don't you EVER be sorry. I'm not.
—Sax

My throat feels thick as hell. She kept this. And by the state of the paper, I guess she must have unfolded and read it hundreds of times. I swallow hard and say, "My answer this time is just the same. Last night? That was on Reichmann, not you. And I'm not sorry. I wasn't sorry for going to prison when I didn't know you, and I'm sure as hell not sorry for being with you last night. Even if it had killed me. All I care about is whether you're safe."

She flinches when I say it might have killed me. "You think I care less whether *you're* safe?"

"No. But would you be sorry for taking a bullet for me? That's never going to fucking happen. But just saying. Would you be sorry?"

Her eyes close. "Are you saying you wouldn't feel guilty if I did?"

Fuck. I walked right into that. "It's *never* going to happen," I say again and she smiles a little.

But despite the curve of her lips, her eyes are haunted when she looks up at me again. "So there's nothing I should ever be sorry for?"

I can't think of a damn thing. With a shake of my head, I give her back the note. "No. But I'm sorry I didn't write you a better letter."

"There's nothing better," she says quietly and opens the nightstand drawer again. I slide up behind her and love her ragged little sigh when my lips press against the side of her neck. She turns and her mouth is soft and trembling against mine. I take a long, deep taste, and when she moans low in her throat, I tease her, sucking on the tip of her tongue until she shivers, tugging her plump bottom lip between my teeth and licking my way back inside.

Need burns through the heavy warmth dragging down every muscle. It's only a step to the bed, then I'm pulling her over me. She weighs almost nothing, her thighs straddling my stomach as she follows me down.

"Wait." All at once she pulls away, her pink lips swollen. "You can't even smile. Kissing has to hurt."

It's fucking agony. "I don't care."

"I do." She pushes at my chest, sitting up. "If it was the other way, and you knew kissing was hurting me—"

"Jenny." I catch her chin and make her look at me. "It's

not the other way. And I'm already hurting. So hurting while kissing you? That's a good option."

Her green eyes narrow. Her gaze drops to the bandage on my jaw, then my neck. "Just tell me if it hurts more, then," she says before she slips farther down and begins tugging at my belt.

Shit. My cock's so fucking stiff when she pops the first button, *that* hurts more. But a damn good hurt. A groan rumbles up through my chest when she uses the edge of her teeth to tease my shaft through the straining denim, and her focus flies to my face, as if she's trying to decide whether that was a good pain or a bad one.

"It's all good, princess." So fucking good.

Though it shouldn't be. I'm lying in a bed I haven't earned, with a woman I don't deserve, and who's eaten up with guilt though *I* haven't protected her like I should.

Fuck. That hurts more than anything.

"Jenny," I say hoarsely. "Come back up. Just lie here with me."

Her brow creases with concern. She's immediately at my side and her hands are everywhere, gingerly touching my face, the edges of the bandages. "Why? Are you okay?"

"I'm all right." I tuck her head against my good shoulder. "I just realized that holding you was an even better option."

She snorts a little and snuggles closer. "The Percocet kicked in, didn't it?"

"I'm feeling it." No lie. Except I've been feeling it for a while.

Her hand smooths over my chest and comes to a rest over my heart. "Then sleep."

"You, too." I know she barely got any the night before.

"I will, too," she says. And it's not long before I'm being dragged down, but she's not with me. Instead of relaxing she just seems to be stiffening against me, as if bracing herself.

As if she's still wondering when she'll break.

I WAKE UP WITH AN aching cock and Jenny's mouth all over it. I can't see a thing in the dark but I don't need to. She's sucking hard, making those sexy little sounds in the back of her throat that turn into hums whenever she takes me deep.

"Fuck," I grit out the curse between my teeth. She pauses. I know she's going to ask if I'm hurting, but I'll only hurt if she stops. I tangle my fingers in her hair and hold her in place before she can come up off me. "Keep going, princess."

She moans and I know her pussy's soaking wet right now, that her cunt's just as hungry for my dick as her mouth is. Then she's sucking my thick cock to the back of her throat and I have to fight not to shove deeper.

My fists tightens. "All the way."

And she takes me. She can't swallow my full length but she swallows me as far as she can, her throat squeezing the head of my cock before she pulls off me, hauling in air, and I can't hold back any more.

I sit up and drag her over my lap. My right arm wraps around her waist. She automatically braces her hands on my shoulders then gasps and jerks her hands away.

"Oh, my God, Saxon—"

I don't want to hear anything about hurting me, and whatever she's about to say comes out as a strangled cry as my cock slides through her drenched slit and pushes deep.

Not deep enough. She's so damn tight. And I don't have any leverage.

"Lean back, Jenny." My need makes it a growl.

Her shifting weight shoves my cock deeper when she does. Fuck, yeah. Her head falls back on a moan and she goes even farther, bracing her hands on the mattress beside my thighs, her legs spread wide over my hips, her feet planted on the bed behind me. Her back is arched. In the dark, her nipples are tight shadows against the pale of her skin.

I need to taste them. "Ride me now."

She hesitates only for an instant—figuring out the position. The first rock of her hips is unsure. I steady her with my arm around her waist and lean forward to suck on her sweet little tit, then groan as her next thrust surrounds the full length of my cock with tight hot pussy.

"*Oh, God,*" she breathes and shifts her feet, digging her heels in, and this time she's got leverage to slam onto me, spearing her cunt and then grinding her pelvis against mine. "Oh, God. I need you so much. So much."

I catch her nipple between my lips and let go of her

waist. She's spread wide, completely exposed. Her clit's slippery with juices, and my thumb strums over that tight little knot as she fills her pussy with my cock again. Her cunt clenches with every surge of her body, her moans rising into screams. So fucking hot. The way she loses herself. The way she gives herself. The way she gives everything.

To me.

"Jenny," I say her name hoarsely. Then I'm pushing her back and onto her right side, scissoring her legs apart and straddling her thigh. I shove her left knee up toward her shoulder and then sink into her slick heat again, driving deep. She cries my name, and this fucking sling doesn't let me get to her clit. Her pussy's stretched tight and her inner muscles clutch the length of my cock, she's close, so close. I pound into her as hard as she was fucking herself onto me. Her fingers wildly grip the sheets like she's trying to pull away but she's shoving back against me, her hips making tight spirals with every stroke. Suddenly her whole body locks up, she's not breathing, not moving, but her pussy's squeezing me hard, so hard, over and over again.

I can't last after that. My balls seem to fill with hot lead then cum shoots out of me. Jenny shudders softly and her pussy clenches again, as if triggered by the heavy pulse of my cock inside her.

"Fuck." I can't catch my breath. Chest heaving, I brace my right arm behind her back. "God *damn*."

A little laugh shakes through her, and her pussy

muscles ripple around my dick. Jesus. I could stay buried in her warmth forever but I gently pull out, using the tail of my shirt to wipe away the cum. With a satisfied little sigh, she rolls onto her stomach. I come down next to her on my good side.

Her head's turned toward me, her cheek pillowed against the sheet. She's watching me move. "Do you need another Percocet?"

"I'll get one in a minute."

She nods. Her hand slides up and her fingers slip through mine. "I'm so scared that I'm going to lose you both."

Her dad and me. I can't say a damn thing, because she *is* going to lose one of us. Saying that it won't be both isn't really reassurance.

"I know you'll say you won't leave. But that doesn't mean you can't be taken. And I thought I *did* lose you," she continues and now her voice is just a thick rasp. In the dark, her eyes glitter with tears. "For a minute the other night, I thought you were dead, and it hurt so much I wanted to die, too. And I keep seeing it over and over. So I can't even—I can't—"

Her breath catches again. I pull her closer but she doesn't cry. She just shivers like she's cold and heaves another sigh.

SIX

JENNY

I might lose him if I do this. I might lose him if I don't.

In my email is a link from the photographer that takes me to a digital gallery. They're big, hi-res photos, and when I zoom in, it doesn't take long to find what I'm looking for. An outbuilding. Unremarkable on any spread of land in this part of Oregon, except for the burned patches on the ground behind the building. All around it, the grass is yellow and dried. Those burn patches aren't from a fire;

they're chemical burns. Some nasty shit's being dumped behind that outbuilding. A little farther back, a hole dug in the ground is filled with trash. A skid loader sits next to it—probably so they can cover the trash up quickly if they need to.

I print out the set and stuff the batch into a manila envelope. I just need to type up some fake anonymous note and send it to Sheriff Landauer. He'll know who it's from. I won't give him the info he wants about the night Saxon was shot—that's Saxon's to deal with—but giving him the shooters wouldn't have been enough, anyway. It would just be taking out two Henchmen. Something like this can take down the whole club.

And if I do it, I'll be taking that from Saxon. I'll be breaking every rule I grew up learning. Clubs take care of their own shit.

But I just want to take care of my man.

SAXON

I took it easy. I only visited the Den to sign the paychecks and do the little work that needed done before heading back to the ranch house. The truck Jenny's using is already parked out front and it's the one good thing I've seen most of the day. My jaw is bugging the fuck out of me. The drugs and the sling are bugging the fuck out of me. Everyone and everything's bugging the fuck out of me.

Except Jenny. She's just worrying me. Her body wasn't hit but she still took a beating the other night. Thinking I'd died. In some ways, she got hurt worse than I did. And if it was me, thinking I'd lost her—even if it was only for a second?

I'd rather be shot again.

Hashtag's at the door. He pounds my fist on the way out and says, "She's upstairs, boss. She's been real quiet all day."

I nod and head up. She's got all that upstairs floor to herself but it doesn't take any time to find her. Wearing a tank top and little shorts, she's curled up on the window seat, all long legs and golden skin with the sun streaming in over her. But her face is bleached-sheet white, and she's holding herself like she hurts.

"Jenny? You all right?"

With a shuddering breath she sits up and points to a thick envelope lying on the bed. "Not really. You should look at those."

"What is it?" Frowning, I pinch the clasp open, expecting some legal papers, or maybe something to do with her dad's funeral or all the other plans that come accompanied by a kick to the face when a parent is dying. Instead there's a bunch of pictures. "Where are these from?"

"The Eighty-Eight's compound."

"What?" That doesn't make any sense. Zoomie and Blowback aren't heading out until tonight.

She's watching me, her expression like an eggshell. Carefully smooth but looking real easy to crack. "I thought of it a while back. After I started hearing about Reichmann threatening me, and just after I heard that my dad was sick but before he went to you. Because I was afraid I'd have to leave, right? There wouldn't be anyone to protect me anymore. So I was trying to think of anything I could do that would get them off my back."

Jesus Christ. She's got the fucking meth kitchen circled in red. But I doubt she was planning to go in and burn it down. "What were you thinking?"

"That I'd send these in to the state police."

My chest seems to hollow, like a razor went in and scraped everything out. *Send these in.* To the cops.

To get the Eighty-Eight off her back.

She keeps going. "I didn't follow through before because I thought it wouldn't do anything anyway. I mean, *someone* has to know these guys are operating out there, and no one has done anything yet. But Landauer's asking for info from me. These guys aren't even in Landauer's jurisdiction because they're a county over, but I think he'll push it. I think he'll make sure Reichmann goes down."

And she's not wrong. Landauer would. But the razor keeps scraping more out of me, and my chest is hurting like any second I'm going to spit up blood. I can't look at her. I can't look at anything in this fucking room. I should have earned my place here before stepping a foot in.

My throat is raw. "Did you think I couldn't handle it?

You think I couldn't take him down?"

"I know you can."

That's not what these pictures say. And the anger's coming, so fucking hot. "You *know* we're planning to go out there."

She slips her arms around her belly like she's holding herself. Her eyes are huge and filling up. "Yes."

"But you do this. *Fuck.*" I toss the pictures back to the bed. "Now you're crying? You aren't the one who just got stabbed in the fucking chest—*and* in the fucking back. You're the one who screwed me here last night, who told me you fucking needed me, all the while knowing you were taking away the one fucking reason I'm here."

Her eyes close, tears slipping out under her lashes. "It didn't seem to matter. I knew I'd lose you one way or another."

"Lose me?" My laugh rips at my guts and I go to her. I catch her chin and make her look up at me, and the misery in her eyes makes us a goddamn perfect pair. "*Lose* me? No, Jenny. You go ahead and stab me in the back and turn me into a worthless piece of shit. I still won't let you go. I don't care if you don't fucking need me anymore."

Because I still need her. So damn much. I need her taste and take it now, her mouth salty with tears. She's pushing at me but I'm not done. I go in deeper, until she's clinging to me, kissing me back with her hot velvet tongue.

My fist in her hair, I pull up and snarl, "And least you still need that."

She shoves at my chest. This time I let her go. She spins away from me, her small breasts heaving, but she's not crying now. She's good and pissed. "What the hell does that mean? You think I don't need you anymore? For what?"

"To protect you, Jenny. But you sure as hell don't seem to think I can." And knowing that is killing me.

She stares at me. "I *know* you can."

"Then why the fuck would you ask Landauer to do it?"

"I'm not. If I sent those in, it would be to protect *you*."

That doesn't make any fucking sense. "What?"

"I know you can take them out. But I also know Landauer's going to be looking right at you when you do. And I don't…" Her breath hitches before she steadies again. "You already spent five years locked away because you were protecting me. I tried to help you then but nothing I said made any difference. But it will now. And I don't want to lose you for the rest of my life. So if you want me to send this in, to get rid of the Eighty-Eight that way, I will."

"To protect *me*." It still doesn't fit in my head but it's filling up the emptiness in my chest. "I protect you, Jenny. It's not the other way around."

"It is now. But only if you want it." She takes a shuddering breath. "Because you gave me a choice when my dad came to you. You let me decide whether to let you protect me. That's why I didn't just send the photos in. So you could choose, too."

"I don't want it." Reichmann's mine to take out—and

I need to earn my place at her side, not hide behind her. I know Jenny wouldn't agree, and when her eyes tear up all over again, I cup her cheek in my palm. "I don't want it like this. But knowing you were trying to look after me? I like that a hell of a lot. You don't need to protect me, though. That's what my brothers do. We watch each other's backs, I watch out for you."

"There wasn't anyone watching your back the other night."

Shit. Yes, there was someone. "You did, Jenny. You got me out of there and saved my life. Now I'm going to have to eat every word I just said."

She smiles a little, then sighs. "I know that's how the club works. I know they have your back. I'm still afraid."

"I guess that's not going to go away until it's done. But I'll be careful. Because I need to come back to you."

"And I need you here." She pulls at the front of my shirt as if to make sure I have her attention. "Not just for protection, either. That's *not* the only reason you're here. I hope."

"The sweetness of your pussy might have something to do with it." And me loving her so much I can't imagine living without her.

She grins. "Good. Because I kind of like your big cock."

"Bullshit. You love it."

Her fingers fist in my shirt and she pulls me back toward the bed. "That I do."

JENNY

Saxon has the Riders and Titans who'll be going out to the compound meet at the ranch house instead of the lodge. They're spread out around our rec room, listening as he sketches out the plan. I'm standing at the back wall and just keeping quiet. Normally he wouldn't talk business in front of me—not just for the club's protection but for mine. If anything goes wrong, the less I know the better. My dad's standing up next to him. Though he doesn't say anything to Saxon in front of the others, I can tell he's not happy that I'm here. Then Saxon tells them I got the daylight photos of the Eighty-Eight's spread, so I'm already in this balls-deep and suddenly my dad's pissed at me, instead.

I can handle him, though. I have all my life.

And I know why Saxon's doing it this way. I'm not going out with them—but it helps to hear them talk it over. Because they aren't going in like I imagined. They won't be riding in on their loud bikes with a bunch of shotguns strapped to their backs. Instead it sounds a lot like a military operation. Something most of these guys are familiar with, I guess.

Beside me, Lily raises her hand. Earlier she gave me a dirty look when I told her why I'd hired someone else—so that the photos couldn't be traced back to the Riders—but I guess flying over the compound last night and getting the infrared shots smoothed out her irritation. Those heat signatures are probably more useful anyway. It gave them a good idea of where the Henchmen will be around 3 a.m. on any given night, and how many will be standing guard.

Saxon spots Lily's hand. "Zoomie?"

"Are we bringing our own weapons, boss?"

He looks to his veep. "Blowback?"

The big man opens a long crate he wheeled to the front of the room earlier. I can tell there's some automatic rifles inside but I don't know what kind. The others do, though. A few of the guys suck in their breaths and look to each other like they need confirmation of what they're seeing.

"Jesus fucking Christ," Lily mutters beside me. She raises her voice. "Where the hell did you get all those, Jack?"

Blowback catches her in his cold stare. "I crossed paths with someone who shouldn't have had them—and he's the only one who would know that I have them now."

"Is that someone still able to talk?"

"No."

"All right, then." Lily eases back.

Blowback looks to the others. "These can't be traced to me or the Riders. Nothing out of this crate has been used before. And there's two rules that come with them now: You don't touch them without gloves on, and you leave them behind at the compound."

"Wait. Leave *those* behind? Just get rid of them?" Gunner actually sounds pained.

"That's what I said."

"A dick in a rubber," my dad adds, like he's reminding them. It's one of his favorite sayings. *Go in clean. Come out clean.* This time, so that the weapons can't be traced back to them.

"We're planning for two nights from now," Saxon says. "The moon's going to set around two-thirty. Three teams. Blowback's will be taking out the kitchen and the cook. I'll be leading mine in to find Reichmann. Red, Hashtag, and Zoomie are on the perimeter. Hashtag's our eyes and communication; Red and Zoomie are going to be flying."

Flying her helicopter? "Won't it be loud?" I whisper to her.

"Not my bird." She mimes lifting a rifle and pulling a trigger. "Up high. On a roof or in a tree."

Oh. Covering the others' backs. The knot in my chest eases a little more. It's not untangled by the time the meeting's done, but when Saxon comes to me afterward and asks quietly, "All right?"—for the first time, I think it might be.

SEVEN

SAXON

We're waiting to hear the kitchen blow, but so far there's nothing but crickets and dogs.

Blowback's team veered off at the north end of the compound. In the two days since our meeting, he's been out here a few times with Stone, checking our access routes for the rumored booby traps. Nothing yet, but we're still stepping carefully. I'm of the mind that all of the Eighty-Eight's security is more talk than show. There's dogs all over the compound, and at the meeting we thought we'd have to put them down to keep them from waking up the Henchmen before we were in place, but they're all just barking all the time. The quiet would be more of an alarm.

Dogs without training, rumors of booby traps that aren't there, a compound that's really just a bunch of mobile homes on an old farm. It's easy to spot the clubhouse in the photos—all the bikes were parked around it—but the rest of the place is littered with junkers. Real security would be cleaning that shit out so a team of three men couldn't make their way toward the houses without exposing themselves. Instead we've got dozens of rusted vehicles to hide behind.

Crouched behind the tail of an old Ford, Gunner glances at me. We're all wearing greasepaint so our faces aren't targets in the dark. I can't read his expression, just see the movement of his eyes. "Blowback's running late," he says quietly.

"Give him another minute. Having a team probably slowed him down."

Stone huffs out a silent laugh and says, "You still got us?"

Not speaking to us but into the mic against his throat. Hashtag's answer comes through the receiver in my ear—one of Gunner's toys. Between him, Stone, and Blowback, we're better equipped than I ever was during my short stint overseas.

"I'm looking into your pretty eyes now."

Grinning, Stone flutters his eyelashes just as bright

orange lights up the sky. An explosion pounds through the air. His grin drops away. "Here we go. Masks on."

To filter out whatever toxic shit is being blown into the sky right now. I pull mine up, gritting my way past the pain in my jaw. I've healed enough over the last couple of days that I can take my sling off and move my arm around, but everything is still as sore as fuck.

"Holy shit!" The shout comes from the left.

Some laughter. "It's the fucking Fourth of July all over again!"

Hashtag tells us, *"Runners are coming up on your nine. They're not looking your way."*

Because a meth house blowing due to a chemical spill or fumes building up is as expected as fleas on a stray dog. They're simply running out to see what happened. It's just human nature. And that nature will pull them all out into the open.

"I got eyes on Burke."

The Eighty-Eight's enforcer—the motherfucker who shot me and would have grabbed Jenny. God damn it. I wanted eyes on Reichmann before we start firing. Right now the Eighty-Eight are thinking it was just a chemical explosion. As soon as the first shot goes off, the whole game changes. They'll take cover and start shooting back.

A sharp *crack* splits the night. The game changer. Zoomie, covering Blowback's team. The tone of the shouting around us changes. Not just surprise but alarm.

"Red?"

"I got him."

Another *crack.*

"Shit!" Hashtag says in my ear. *"I just got eyes on Reich-mann but he saw Burke go down. He ducked into House Nine."*

House Nine. We numbered them all on the map we made from the photos. It's a one-bedroom northwest of us.

"Are we clear?"

"Keep low and behind the junkers. You'll have about twenty yards from the last one to the back of the house."

We move quick. Everyone's still scattered, probably heading for weapons. Zoomie and Red will keep most of them from poking their heads out. We pause behind the last junker. One short sprint with no cover.

"Are we okay to go?"

"I got infrared on the house. There's no one at the windows, but— Shit. There's either women or kids in the bedroom on the north side of the house. I think they're women, though. Six of them. No one real little."

Fuck. "Is Reichmann in the same room with them?"

"No. There's two other men in the house. They're all in the living room. And—" He hesitates for a second. *"Boss, I think the women are chained."*

Chained? Only one reason for that. The rage is quick and hot, but I make it cold. So fucking cold.

So they're not just running meth and guns. They're selling girls, too. And if they'd ever gotten to Jenny, there's no fucking doubt what they'd have done after they'd finished with her. "The bedroom's north?"

"*Yeah. They're sitting on the floor against the south interior wall. Other side is a bathroom. There's a window in the west wall but it's boarded up.*"

I look to Stone. "If we take out those other two, Reichmann'll go for the girls and hide behind them."

His nod is short, his face hard. "So we'll be quick, yeah?"

Hashtag comes in. "*He must have got on the horn for help because there's five men headed your way, coming from the north.*"

The other side of the house. So we're still covered for now.

"*I've got the five, Red, if you want to light up the clubhouse,*" Zoomie breaks in. "*Blowback's team is out and heading for the meet point.*"

I look to Stone and Gunner. "And we're heading in."

Only twenty yards and the night around us sounds like a battlefield. Zoomie's taking out the five Henchmen on the other side of the house but they must have grabbed cover behind more junkers, because they're firing back. I don't know if they can see her or if they're just shooting into the night. A streak across the sky is one of the flares Red's using to hit the clubhouse. Burning it all to the ground.

We're at the house quick and get our backs against the south wall, crouching low. There's still gunfire coming from the other side. "Zoomie?"

"*Almost got 'em.*" Her voice sounds strained. "*And the*

rubber on our dick broke. I need some bleach over here."

"You're bleeding? How bad?"

"*I'll pull her out,*" Blowback comes in.

"*Back off, Jack. I've got these fuckers and I'll walk out. Just bring me some goddamn bleach.*" She pauses and the noise from the north suddenly quiets. "*Okay. They're down.*"

"Pull her out and clean it up, Blowback," I say. "Hashtag?"

"*Two men on either side of the front door. Reichmann's farther back in the same room. They're all armed. Shotguns or rifles.*"

"You're sure it's Reichmann?" Infrared doesn't give that detailed a picture.

"*I'm sure, boss. His wrist's in a splint and his foot's in a cast. I figure that's because someone cut his fingers off and someone else busted his ankle.*"

"Blowback can claim the ankle," Stone says quietly. "But I'd like to point out that I got some teeth."

From the beating that was coming to him after he touched Jenny. The fingers were Red's.

His life is mine.

I point toward the front of the house. Immediately Stone and Gunner move out like they were sharing a brain, every step like they were two parts of one whole. They served together a long time—longer than they've been Riders—and don't need words to communicate and know what they'll each do, so they'll go through first. They're razors. I'm just a big fucking fist.

Long dried grass crackles under our boots. No avoiding that. It's thick around the house. But there's still enough shouting and dogs barking—and now engines revving in the distance—that no one inside should be able to detect the sound. There's no lights on. Someone inside is smart enough not to stand in plain sight, then, but the second we move around to the front the glow from the clubhouse fire will let them see us.

Raising his brows, Stone looks to Gunner, who says real low, "Hashtag, are they still by the front door?"

"Affirmative."

"Standing?"

"Yep."

"And the girls are sitting? You double check now."

"They are."

Gunner looks to Stone, who shrugs. "Hold off a sec, boss," he says, and as one they're striding out like the two ballsiest assholes I've ever seen and open fire on the front of the house with two of the assault rifles from Blowback's stash. The automatic weapons shred the upper half of the door and rip through the siding like a chainsaw. Jesus Christ. Even if the guards who were standing by the door are still alive there's no chance they're still upright. They're either cowering or running. No doubt Reichmann's running—but there's only one room to hide in.

I head for the door. Stone and Gunner stop firing and are right ahead of me, sweeping through together. One of the guards is groaning on the floor, bleeding from his shoulder and his gun in hand. Gunner barely looks down, capping him with a short burst. I expect to put on my night vision lenses but there's faint light coming from the narrow hallway now—coming through the bedroom door.

"He's got one of the girls. Dragged her into the bathroom Looks like they're standing in the tub and he's got her in front of him."

Like a shield. Shit. Eyes on the bathroom door, I point Gunner and Stone to the bedroom. "Get the others unchained and out."

Stone nods and covers Gunner as he slips down the hall.

"Not arguing," Red says over the radio, *"but this ain't going to be getting out of here clean. Blindfold them if you can and we'll drop them off at the Episcopalian church in La Pine. And watch your mouths. Don't use each other's names now."*

Gunner flips off the bedroom light—using the night vision so that he can see but the girls can't see him. There's still a strip of light under the bathroom door.

Muffled shrieks come from the bedroom, shrill with terror. Gunner's voice is low and reassuring. I cover Stone as he heads in to help.

"Does Reichmann have his weapon on the girl or the door?"

"On the door."

A rifle or shotgun. That's gotta be real hard to hold when one of his hands is still healing. But if I go through the door, I might be a dead man. If I shoot through the door, there might be a dead girl.

That's not going to happen.

Bare feet slap the floor. Four women, looking terrified and holding onto each other. Stone's carrying a fifth over his shoulder.

"I got two brothers coming out with five women. Do they have a clear path outside?"

"Yes, sir."

I gesture for them to go. "Head to the meet point."

Gunner hesitates. "Boss—"

"Get the fuck out." I say it easy, but if I have to say it again, it's going to go down real hard. "I've still got eyes watching my back."

They head out. I watch the strip of light under the bathroom door. Reichmann's got a shotgun and a gimp hand. Unless he's using a semi-automatic, it's going to be damn hard for him to work the action after he fires his first shot. And even if he's got a semi-auto, he's holding onto both a girl and the gun. The kick is going throw his aim off and if he's not steadying it with both hands, he won't be able to aim quickly again.

And he's a fucking coward. He won't hold steady. He'll panic.

In the living room, I grab one of the guards' phones. The screen is cracked but I don't need to use it. Returning to the hall, I crouch low. I put the bathroom door in my sights and aim the assault rifle at the top of the frame. I'm not looking to hit anyone inside; I'm just going for the light.

The recoil jackhammers against my right shoulder and the bullets rip a hole through the drywall above the door, into the bathroom ceiling. The light winks out. Plaster dust and wood splinters rain across the hallway floor. The woman's screaming but I can barely hear it through the ringing in my ears.

I toss the phone at the remains of the door. It hits with a *thunk*. An instant later, the center of the door blows apart and Reichmann's shotgun blast booms through the house.

I'm thinking of Jenny as I charge down the hall and kick through the remains of the door. Thinking of how he had her crammed against that wall in that booth, thinking of the fear and anger on her face. Thinking of the bruises on her arm and her thigh. Thinking how she hadn't seen him coming.

He doesn't see me coming now. He's dropped the pump-action shotgun and is fumbling for the blade sheathed at his waist, trying at the same time to hold onto the woman pulling away. Her tears are ghostly tracks over her cheeks through the night vision lenses.

I knock away the knife and slam my fist into his face.

That's all it takes. His head snaps back against the tile wall and he crumples into the tub. Fifteen years ago, I killed his brother with one kick. I didn't mean to—and I didn't even know that he'd gone into a coma and died until the cops showed up.

I don't know if I killed Reichmann now with that hit. But this time, I mean to. Grabbing his head, I jerk his chin around until his neck snaps.

Now I'm sure.

JENNY

THERE'S NO MOON IN THE sky. Only darkness outside. My heart lodged in my throat when Saxon left; the lump hasn't moved yet. I haven't moved either. For hours now, I've been sitting in window seat in my room with a burner phone in my hand. Scarecrow is standing at one of the other windows. Bottlecap's out in the orchard, making the rounds. Uncle Thorne is downstairs.

Just in case it all goes wrong and Reichmann comes straight for me.

Light suddenly fills the window alcove. The phone. I blink against the sudden spots in front of my eyes and try to read the message. It's from the second burner that Saxon picked up.

It's done.

My heart clenches tight. I'm not supposed to respond. I'm just supposed to toss the phone. But I'm going to hold onto this message until he gets home.

Scarecrow pokes his head into the alcove. "That was them? Is everything all right?"

I let out a ragged breath. "I think it is."

EIGHT

SAXON

LANDAUER COMES BY THE RANCH HOUSE TWO EVENINGS later. Red goes out on the porch to greet him. I stay with Jenny in the kitchen, where she's chopping tomatoes. Her dark hair's up, so I kiss her bare nape before drawing her back against my chest. Her heart is racing.

"All right?" I ask softly and she nods.

Good. I kiss the side of her neck before grabbing a couple of beers from the fridge. I offer one to the sheriff as he comes through.

Hat in hand, he shakes his head. "Still on duty."

I nod and open one for Jenny. Landauer looks us over. I'm pretty damn sure what he's looking for. But the only one who walked off that compound with an injury was Zoomie—a flesh wound in her upper arm—and the women we found chained up.

I didn't look back as I walked away from House Nine. I simply told Red to burn it down.

Landauer's gaze settles on Jenny. "My son tells me that you've been showing him around your place, teaching him a little about brewing."

"Hashtag?" Her brows shoot up. The prospect isn't shadowing her anymore but he's been showing up at her barn for a few hours every day. She's already asked me if hiring him will create any conflicts within the club. "I didn't realize he was your son."

"His mom and I haven't been together for a while." He clears his throat and shifts his hat from his right hand to his left. "Anyway. He seemed real interested in what you were doing."

She grins. "Every guy that age is interested in beer."

"True." His amusement tightens into a grave expression. "You probably know the reason for my visit."

"We can guess, or you can make it real explicit," Red says.

"You heard about those six women who showed up at that church in La Pine?"

Jenny grimaces. "I read about it this morning. Are

they all okay?"

"I suppose in cases like that, 'okay' is relative. They're better off than they were." He scratches the side of his jaw but he's watching her close. "They came off the Eighty-Eight's farm."

Her pink lips part in sheer surprise. Brow creasing, her gaze shoots to me, then back to Landauer. Her shock's genuine. Red and I haven't said a damn word about it. "They were trafficking women?" Then surprise bleeds into anger. *"Women?"*

"Seems like." He shrugs. "It's just what I hear. Like the rumors that the investigation's going to be taken away from Deschutes County and put into federal hands. Something about them finding weapons that suggest a big cartel was all mixed up in it, and the women saying that they thought it was law enforcement or military who came for them."

A cartel? Jesus H. Christ. "What cartel?"

I'm not faking my surprise, either. Blowback has some goddamn giant balls, that's for sure.

"That's all I hear. Except for what I came to tell you about." He looks to Jenny again. "The medical examiner just confirmed that some of the remains they found in a burned-out house belonged to Luke Reichmann."

Her face stills. She stares at him for a long second, then her eyes fill. "Are you sure?"

"We're sure."

Her breath catches and shudders. The next second

she's in my arms, burying her face against my chest. "You don't have to do it," she whispers and her tears soak into my shirt. "You don't have to."

"I would have fucking liked to," Red says, his voice hard and rough, and I don't think he's acting. He doesn't resent that I did it, but he'd have liked to.

I don't say anything. There's no hiding my satisfaction and I'll let Landauer make of it what he will. He's got his suspicions but he's got his doubts, too. But there can be absolutely no doubt that it makes me damn happy to think about Reichmann dead.

And this woman in my arms—she's protecting me, even now. Having my back, even now. My back, her dad's, and every one of my brothers. Crying against me, but so damn strong.

"Anyway." Landauer dons his hat. "I just wanted to let Miss Erickson know that Reichmann won't be bothering her again."

She turns toward him, sniffling and shuddering and wiping her eyes. "Thank you. Thank you *so* much."

Just fucking amazing.

JENNY

I'm reading in the window seat when Saxon comes out of the shower with just a towel around his hips. God. I let my book fall to my lap and drink in all that thick, gleaming muscle and tanned skin. He went in to get his wounds checked out today and the bandages are smaller now. Just a patch against the side of his neck and a square over the worst part of his shoulder. His dark hair's still damp. He doesn't have it pulled back, and the ends fall even with his strong jaw. For now, he's been shaving instead of growing his beard back, and I can't decide which I love more. He looks big and mean and sexy either way—and all mine.

I'm about to get in so much trouble.

I come up off the seat. "So are you taking off now?"

"Taking off?" He stops in front of the closet. His gaze slides down over my tank and sleep shorts, and a hot shiver races across my skin. "Where?"

"Back to your place, I guess. Since I don't need protection anymore and that's the only reason you're here."

Dark blue eyes shoot up to meet mine. His face is like granite and he's got that old look in his eyes, the one that says it'll be dangerous to take another step.

So I step closer. "But I suppose there's probably a bunch of other girls now who might want your protection. Especially since you apparently have this need to go around saving girls in trouble. But I'm not in trouble anymore, so…"

I trail off with a shrug. I'm close enough now to feel his warmth, to breathe in the clean soapy smell of him. His eyes are still locked on my face.

His voice is rough. "I told you I liked your pussy, princess."

"So you're going to stay for that?"

"Fuck, yeah, I am."

All at once his strong arm snags around my waist and he hauls me up against his broad chest, striding toward the bed. He tosses me into the middle and comes after me, catching my ankles as I scramble back. Excitement sizzles every nerve. The friction of the sheet against my skin is a warm burn when he drags me toward him again.

"And because this is all mine now. This bed. My place here with you." Hard fingers rip my shorts and panties down my legs. "And especially this sweet pussy. So, yeah, I'm going straight to my place."

His hands grip my knees and spread them wide, pinning them to the bed. Oh, my God. I'm displayed like a butterfly and his head lowers without hesitation, licking a slow path from my entrance to my clit. His hot mouth closes over that aching bud of flesh and sucks hard.

I scream, my hips bucking. He growls and goes for another slow taste followed by a rough lick, lashing his tongue over my clit. It's so good, too good, I almost can't bear it and then almost cry when he lifts his head.

"So wet. You want my cock, Jenny? Isn't that what you're here for—my big cock?"

Filling me. Because I'm empty and aching. "Yes. *God,* yes."

"Get on your knees, then."

But he doesn't wait for me to move. Hard hands on my hips, he turns me onto my stomach and drags me up to my knees. I come up on my elbows but he pushes my upper body back to the bed, his palm between my shoulder blades holding me down.

His long fingers slick through my pussy. Helplessly I moan, my hands curling against the sheets. Anticipation is a hot burn.

"Look at you, so ready for me." Each word is strained, his voice harsh. At the edge of control. "So fucking pretty. You want my cock?"

My body's shuddering in desperate need. "So much."

"I'm going to make you take every inch, Jenny." He slicks the broad crown between my pussy lips, parting me. My hips rock back and the pressure of his hand between my shoulder blades increases. "No fucking moving. You just *take* it. All right?"

"Yes," I gasp into the sheets, shaking, then tensing as he pushes against me, into me, stretching my sensitive flesh.

"Fuck, that's so hot," he groans and I know he's watching his big cock sink slowly into me. "How much do you want, princess?"

Everything he has to give. "All of it."

"You can't take all of it yet," he says and begins to withdraw. Oh, God. It feels like he's catching every nerve, pleasure sparking through my need-swollen flesh. He groans and pauses with the head of his cock lodged just inside me, and I know he's looking at the wetness coating his taut skin and the stretch of my pussy lips around his shaft.

"Spread your knees a little more—oh, fuck, yeah. You like that, too? Your pussy's clenching all around me."

I can't answer, my breath coming in gasping little sobs. At this angle the head of his cock feels huge, pressing harder against my inner walls. I cry out as he begins to push deeper, and the sensation intensifies with every inch, until I can't feel anything but that thick length wedged inside me.

"No, princess. You fucking keep still and take it," he snarls, and I realize that I'm bucking against him again, crying and writhing against the hand holding me down and the cock stuffing me full. He bottoms out and then pushes deeper, because he knows I come hardest that way, but I'm already almost there and don't know if I can take that now, too.

But I know he's going to make me. Because his fingers dig into my hip, holding tight, and that means he's going to fuck me hard.

Oh, God. "Saxon—"

He pulls back and shoves deep and I'm screaming, need and pleasure like a rocket burning through every nerve inside me, and he just gives me more, fucking into my clenching flesh with long deep strokes, hitting the end of me and going deeper until I can't take it, can't take it anymore. The orgasm detonates through me, throwing my head back and arching my spine. My pussy clamps around his thick cock, still sliding back and forth inside me. Saxon groans and pumps harder, harder, falling forward over me, his chest heaving against my back and his mouth hot against my ear. He slams deep and his every muscle goes rigid, shaking against me as he comes.

"Love you." His breath shudders against my neck and he gently kisses my sweaty skin. "I love you so fucking much, Jenny."

My heart full, I reach back and slide my fingers into his damp hair. "That's a good reason to be here."

"I've got more." His blue eyes dark, he rolls to the side and takes me with him. "It doesn't matter if it's here or at my house or in a tent—I've never had so damn much. I have everything. I'm like a fucking king, just because I'm holding you."

Throat clogged with emotion, I pillow my head on his chest and hold him tight.

"Don't you start crying." Lightly, he swats my ass. "Go check your nightstand."

Lifting my head, I give him a narrowed look, but he just says, "Get to it, princess," so I grin and slide across the bed. Inside the drawer, a new note lies folded beside the old tattered one.

I'll NEVER leave you. And I'll ALWAYS love you.

Now put this back in the damn drawer and get over here and kiss me.

—Sax

So I do.

Please note: If you are a stickler for reading order and plan to read the rest of the Hellfire Riders series, skip this novella for now and come back to it after you've read **BLOWBACK***. If you're just here for Saxon and Jenny, keep going!*

—Kati

GIVING IT ALL

ONE

SAXON

The Hellfire Riders' warlord did *not* just say what I think he said. There's nothing but silence in the office as I stare at Blowback, trying to figure out which word I misheard. But the big bastard's not giving anything away. He just sits in the chair in front of my desk, staring right back.

I shake my head. "Say that again?"

Voice flat, dark eyes inscrutable, Blowback says the same damn thing he said before.

"I married Lily."

Married. To another Hellfire Rider, Zoomie—the only female Rider. They hooked up a few months ago, and he's living at her place, so maybe it's not so unexpected…

No, it's still not sinking in.

Blowback might be crazy about her but he's completely fucked up, emotionally. I never figured he'd risk marrying anyone. And Zoomie, shit. She's never held on to a man—or a woman—for much longer than a single night.

And now they're married?

I glance at the only other man in the room. My veep, Thorne, has got twenty-five years on both Blowback and me. He's been around, seen some crazy shit. I don't know if he's seen anything like this. Two patchholders, married.

But if he's surprised, there's no sign of it on his weathered face. Instead he's sitting back in his chair, grinning.

Hell. I pinch the bridge of my nose, trying to ward off a headache. "So what does this mean for the club? There's no clause in the Constitution that covers this situation, that's for damn sure."

"It means nothing," Blowback says. "I've no intention of telling the brothers and it won't change a thing for me and Lily here. But as you're the prez, I figured you should know."

"It means nothing? Bullshit. You can't marry a woman and tell me that doesn't change your priorities."

"I *can* tell you that." There's nothing in his eyes when he answers. "Married or not, my priorities are exactly the same."

A chuckle has me glancing at Thorne. Apparently amused as hell, the older man says, "Which means Lily is first, either way."

Yeah, I figured that. I can't give Blowback shit about it, either. There's a lot of words in the Constitution that talk about the club always coming first for the members, that say a patchholder should always put his brothers above everyone else, even their own blood. But we all know there's some who wouldn't, and that includes me. Because there's a dark-haired, green-eyed woman who could make me walk away from the Hellfire Riders, if she ever asked me to—and if my being in the club was hurting her, she wouldn't even need to ask. Jenny is *always* first for me.

Since Zoomie's got the club up high on her list of priorities, though, I can't see how their marriage will change much.

"All right, then," I say, as if that approval means shit. There's not much I can do about the situation now.

After throwing a wry glance at me, Thorne adds, "Congratulations, Jack."

Blowback accepts that with an abrupt nod.

And I'm being an asshole. Typically I don't care if I am. But Blowback's been at my side for years. There's not one brother I trust more at my back. I just don't like surprises, because too often they're the kind that land you in the emergency room with a doctor digging shotgun lead out of your shoulder. And Blowback's usually the one who makes sure nothing sneaks up on me, so I doubly didn't expect the surprise coming from him.

But all that aside, this is the best fucking news I've heard in a while.

"Congratulations, brother," I say, then reach over the desk. Blowback shakes my hand and I pull a smile out of him when I add, "So you locked Zoomie down tight, huh? Smart man. I'm not sure which of you is luckier."

"I am," he says. No doubt in his voice at all.

And he's probably right. Zoomie is one hell of a woman.

"One thing for sure, you're not going to have a single boring minute." I settle back into my chair. "So how are you going to keep this quiet?" Pine Valley is a small town with a lot of big mouths. "Did you go to the county clerk's office? Because you know Grasshopper's old lady works there."

"We did it in Vegas," he says.

Vegas? Zoomie and Blowback were there the first week of November and I know they haven't gone back since. I stare at him, once again thinking I didn't hear him right. "That was almost two months ago."

"That's right."

"And you *just* got around to saying something?" So much for *As you're the prez, I figured you should know.*

He shrugs. "At least I got around to it."

With a snort of laughter, Thorne gets up. "I'd say this calls for a drink. Give me a minute."

Yeah, a drink. I get up, too. Not to head out of the office, as Thorne's doing, but because my booted feet are suddenly restless and my lungs are tight, as if something thick got lodged in my chest. I head over to the big windows overlooking the woods behind the clubhouse. There's snow all over the place. It only started this morning, but a good four inches have already piled up, with more fat flakes drifting down. If this keeps up, it's going to be a fucking white Christmas. Pretty as hell, sure—if what it looks like mattered. All I care about is how ice and snow make for the worst goddamn weather to ride a motorcycle in. We'll all be driving around in cages for a couple of weeks.

Without glancing around, I tell Blowback, "Make sure the brothers who rode their bikes out here this morning have a lift home."

"I'll arrange it," he says.

"And tell them to read a motherfucking weather report next time."

"I will. You got something else to say?"

The goddamn bastard can read me like no one else can. Like he can see right into me, see the shit clogging up my chest. Maybe he doesn't know exactly what it is, but he knows it's there.

I know what it is. Jealousy. Or envy. Or whatever the fuck it's called when your brother puts a ring on his woman's finger, not just making her his but making her *HIS*, in goddamn capital letters on a legal dotted line. And you can't claim your own woman the same way. Instead you can have her smile and her heart and her warm body next to yours every night and you tell yourself that's all you need when you sink your cock into her, when she's coming and crying your name and every part of her is squeezing you tight. The truth is, though, you want more—and you can't have it.

Yet.

But fuck me if I'm going to talk about my feelings. "No."

"Good," he tells me. "Because I'm so fucking pleased with myself for marrying Lily, I don't want to hear any of your bullshit."

The look I give him would have sent just about any other Rider scurrying away. Not Blowback. He only sits there, wearing a smug grin.

And any other Rider, I'd be knocking out his teeth for speaking to me with such disrespect. But Blowback, he's got allowances. I rely on him to call me on my shit, to pull me back to level. And he does, but he's careful to never yank my chain in front of the others, to never undermine my position.

That's why his expression rolls straight back to inscrutable when Thorne returns, carrying three lowball glasses in a cloverleaf between the fingers of his right hand, and a black box topped with a big red bow in his left.

"A Christmas present from a client." He sets the tumblers on my desk and starts opening the box. "He put in over five million on an irrigation project Red and I finished up for him this year, so either he's so fucking broke now we're about to drink pig swill, or he's still flush with cash and we're about to drink some mighty fine scotch."

I'll go with mighty fine. We carry that label at my tavern. One bottle. And it doesn't go on the top shelf—instead it's locked up. "It'll do."

Thorne pours two fingers into the first glass, hands it to Blowback. "We ought to invite Zoomie in, too. But maybe that'll be the second round. I've got something else to put in front of you."

"Then put it," I say before rolling a swallow of scotch over my tongue. God *damn*, that's smooth. Something Jenny might love. At her brewery, she mostly makes beer, but she's got a real appreciation for fine liquor. So a bottle of good Scotch whisky might be something I can wrap up for her and give Christmas morning. Otherwise, I can't figure out what the hell to get her. There's nothing she wants that she doesn't already have.

Except for her father. But that's one thing I can't give. Cancer took Red from her only a month ago. The shadows haven't left her eyes since and she's built up a wall of pain and grief.

I'd give anything to ease it for her. Knowing how she's hurting, I've walked around with a solid ache in my chest. But I can't tell if anything I've done for her has helped or if I've just made it harder. One day, I'll do something to make her smile, and the next day, doing the same thing will make her burst into tears.

And Jenny's tears, Jesus. They rip my heart out.

I just don't know what the hell to do. Fucking useless to her, that's what I am. I can't even come up with a goddamn gift worth giving. What am I thinking—after losing her dad, is an expensive bottle of liquor supposed to mean shit to her? Is it supposed to make it all better? Fucking hell.

Just fucking hell.

The next swallow doesn't go down near as easy. His eyebrows pinching together, Thorne eyes me but doesn't say anything about how I just tossed back the scotch like a cheap tequila shot. Instead he starts talking business.

"I got a message from the Sand Demons' prez," he says. "You know him?"

"I know of him." From seeing that club at rallies and just because knowing about other MCs in the state is part of doing business. The Sand Demons are a small outfit from a town on the southern Oregon coast. Low-key, they stay mostly out of trouble with the law and with other clubs. That doesn't mean they aren't doing shit that could get them in trouble, though. It only means they've done a good job taking care of any trouble that comes up. "Name is Anthill, yeah?"

"That's right."

I flick a glance at Blowback. I've got a general handle on the other clubs in the state, but it's his job to know the details of their operations. Right now the warlord is just listening, not sitting forward as if he intends to say something, which tells me there's nothing about the Sand Demons he thinks is worth mentioning yet. "What was his message?"

"He wants to call in an old favor—wants the Riders to do a little babysitting. They've got an asset in trouble and Anthill wants to hide it away for a few days while they take care of the threat."

An asset. Thorne's not being vague on purpose. Anthill probably didn't tell him exactly what that asset was. But it's not hard to guess. Clubs like to protect their money-makers. Babysitting means that moneymaker is a person.

Babysitting also means they don't expect the threat to come here. Anthill's not asking us for protection, just to keep the person out of sight.

Easy enough, unless whoever they want to hide away will be a problem.

I look to Blowback. "What are they into? They pimping out girls? Selling them?"

Because if they are, I'm not touching that shit.

"Meth," he says immediately, his flat gaze steady on mine. "High quality, large quantity. So if they're looking to hide someone away for a while, it's probably their cook."

Because a good meth cook brings in a hell of a lot of money. "You think he's being poached by another club?"

Blowback hesitates just an instant. It's enough to make the skin on the back of my neck tighten. Hesitating isn't in Blowback's nature.

Waiting isn't in mine. "Spit it out."

His jaw clenches, then he says, "If it's their cook, I suspect it won't be another club coming for him. It'll be someone he owes money to."

Enough money that he has to hide away? Combined with Blowback's reluctance to tell me more about this cook, I'm starting to suspect the name he hasn't said yet. "Who is it?"

Blowback looks me square in the eye. "Frank Carlisle."

My father. Huh.

I glance at Thorne. Carlisle used to live in Pine Valley, so my veep probably recognizes the name. His eyes narrow as he puts two and two together, and a flush rides up under his jaw. Goddamn pissed, because even clubs holding info close to their chests should know better than to keep their mouths shut regarding that sort of detail. It's real hard to believe Anthill didn't know of my relationship to one of his men and he should have said something.

"Tell Anthill," I say softly, "Merry Christmas, and he can go fuck himself."

Thorne's jaw works. Pissed off at Anthill, maybe feeling like he was played, but there's more than anger that I'm reading on his grizzled face. There's steel resolve, too.

"I can't," he grates out. "Anthill's calling in a favor."

And if a club owes a favor, then a club pays up. Usually, I'd honor that. But I've no intention of honoring this one—and, thank fuck, I've got a way out. "From the Hellfire

Riders or from the Steel Titans?"

I ask, knowing the answer. The Riders don't owe shit to the Sand Demons. And although I folded the Steel Titans MC into the club a few months back, bringing in all their patchholders—including Thorne—they're not Titans anymore. No one's going to hold the Hellfire Riders accountable for promises the Steel Titans made.

Though if it were anyone else asking, I'd pay those debts. Hell, if someone else walked through the door with a Titan IOU in hand, I'd pay it this second. But I'm not paying this one. Let whoever's looking for Frank Carlisle find him. I don't give a fuck.

"From the Titans," Thorne confirms what I already knew. "But this favor was for Red, personally. He just used the Titans' name to secure it."

Red—Jenny's father.

Something tightens in my chest. Red was the Steel Titans' president. When he got sick, he was the one who came to me, asked me to fold the clubs together...and to take care of Jenny.

Fuck. I push up out of my chair, stalk to the window. Red's dead. No one can call in any favor from him. And it's not my responsibility to pay Red's debts...but I can't turn my back on this.

Maybe Thorne thinks I am, though, because he adds quietly, "It was about Jenny."

Everything in me goes rigid. About Jenny? That doesn't make any sense. What kind of favor would Red need to ask? Jenny's father had money of his own and a club behind him. If Jenny had been in trouble, he wouldn't have asked for any favors—he'd have taken care of the trouble himself, even if it meant dying for it. The same way Thorne would.

The same way I would.

My blood rises straight to a boil. I've got 'Jenny' and 'danger' in my head now, and everything in me is ready to tear apart anything that *ever* threatened her.

I face Thorne again. "Tell me."

The older man was close enough to Red that Jenny grew up calling him 'Uncle.' And whatever he's about to tell me has him wound tight, the smoker's rasp in his voice deepening. "It was about when Reichmann got her down."

Just the mention of that is a jagged screw in my heart, twisting hard and ripping me open. Fifteen years ago, Jenny was at a rally with the Steel Titans and she accidentally wandered into a part of the field claimed by a skinhead club. The head of that club, Reichmann, got his hands on her, shoved her to the ground and was about to rape her in front of his men.

I didn't know Jenny then. Had no idea she was the daughter of the Titans' prez. But I was hanging out nearby, saw what was happening, and charged in. I kicked the fucker off her—a boot to the head that ended up killing him.

I got five years in prison for manslaughter. I've never regretted a second. And I know Red only regretted *he* hadn't been the one to kill Reichmann.

Thorne pours another scotch, then refills mine. Blowback's still nursing his first. "There wasn't nothing left for Red to take care of. Reichmann was dead. That ate at him, but it was what it was. And he didn't see anything of what happened. Just heard about it after, from what little Jenny said and what others told us. But all that mattered then was making sure she was all right. That meant keeping her away from the cops, trying to see that she never had to think of it again. Even when it looked like you'd be going away for worse than you did."

I nod. The county prosecutor went after me with all guns firing, because no one was talking about what had really gone down or naming the girl I'd saved—by then, I'd known who she was, but I didn't name her either. I wasn't opening my mouth beyond the basics of it: seeing a girl getting hurt and kicking Reichmann off her. But the prosecutor had been putting together a tidy little story about Reichmann's death being part of a territorial war between the skinheads and the Hellfire Riders, and how I was ordered to kill him. If I'd been on a jury and he'd spun that tale, I might have bought it.

Until Jenny came forward. Red hadn't wanted her to, knowing how testifying would reopen those wounds—but she did, believing it would help me, the stranger who'd saved her.

Thorne says, "It wasn't until we were listening to her testimony that Red realized there was more that needed taking care of. Because she'd told us she'd been hurt, but she hadn't really said what Reichmann had…what he'd done." His voice cracks and he takes a sip, holding it in his mouth for a few long, deep breaths through his nose. "But we heard it all there in that courtroom."

I remember. Because I hadn't known the details, either. I'd seen her on the ground at that rally, then I hadn't seen her again until she'd taken the stand. And I sat at the defense's table and watched this girl, sixteen when she'd been hurt and barely seventeen when she exposed herself in that courtroom, and I saw her—so brave and scared as she talked about what he'd done, how he'd made her bleed—and I'd have killed Reichmann all over again for her. I'd have killed anyone for her.

Fresh anger and the old memory taste like bloody acid in my mouth as Thorne continues, "And there she was, describing how she can't hit him or scratch him because he's got her on her belly and he's pinning her wrists behind her back. Then he gets his fingers inside her, and she hears him unbuckling his belt—"

"Too many hands," Blowback says.

I barely hear him over the sick pounding in my head. "What?"

"Too many hands," he says again and Thorne nods. "He's got his fingers in her, he's unbuckling, and he's pinning her wrists. That's three hands, at least, so there was someone else holding her down. You never saw?"

Probably. I don't fucking know. Before I saw Jenny in

that courtroom, I'd been spiraling hard. The day of the rally, I was flying high on a line of cocaine and Christ knows how much booze. I remember hearing shouting, the skinheads hooting and cheering Reichmann on. I remember a girl under him.

I shake my head. "I was a fucking mess. And it was chaos after I went in."

"That's why it took a while before Red found someone who saw and who wasn't loyal to the skinheads." Thorne's voice is like iron. "That was Anthill. He told Red who it was holding her down."

My fingers clench on the glass. "Who?"

The older man's gaze doesn't waver. "One of the Eighty-Eight's rabid pups. Anthill knew him by the swastikas inked on his forearms. And Red made sure that fucker was the same one who held her down before he took care of him."

Killed him. "Good."

Now I don't have to do it.

His face grim, Thorne nods. "So this favor—"

"We'll babysit," I say. No question about paying what we owe Anthill now. "And if it *is* Carlisle, he'd better fucking keep his head down while he's here."

"He can stay in one of the cabins," Thorne says, referring to the old log cabins that used to be part of the tourist lodgings when the property was a dude ranch. "With Bull and Duke keeping an eye on him. They were Titans and it's our debt."

It's my debt now, too. But I'm not going to argue. The less I see of Carlisle the better. It's Anthill I'm wondering about now. "You think their prez is pulling some shit by bringing him here? You think he knows who Carlisle is?"

Blowback answers that. "He might know, but Anthill wouldn't waste a favor on bullshit. If he says he's looking for a place to hide an asset, then that's what he's doing. And Carlisle probably *is* in over his head."

Gambling again. "Find out with who."

"I will. If there was bullshit," he adds, "it probably came from Carlisle. He might have suggested to Anthill that they come to us, and to cash in on that old favor before any Steel Titans who still care about it are gone."

Probably. Carlisle always was an opportunistic fucker. Time to swing by, drop in on his flesh and blood, see if there's any weak spots to mine for cash.

Carlisle won't find any weak spots in me. They all hardened over the first time I understood my mom wasn't crying because he always left, but because he always cleaned out everything we needed to live on when he went.

"All right," I say. "Anything else?"

Thorne nods, but I'm not expecting his, "My Molly wants to know if you and Jenny are coming over for Christmas dinner."

I have no idea what Jenny plans. Or even if she's up for it. We got the same invitation for Thanksgiving, but I don't think Thorne was surprised when we stayed home. Red had only been in the ground a little over a week then.

"I'll ask her," I tell him.

"Good enough." He rises, capping the bottle of scotch before holding it out to Blowback. "For Lily," he says. "Married to you, she'll probably need it."

"That she will." Blowback's lips twitch as he gets to his feet. "Need anything else, boss?"

"If I did, would it take you two months to get around to doing it?"

"Maybe. I've got a demanding wife to keep satisfied."

Thorne huffs out a laugh before giving the warlord a curious look. "How long has Frank Carlisle been with the Sand Demons?"

"Four years. Since he got out of the Walla Walla pen."

The state penitentiary up in Washington. I still don't know what he was in for—and I don't really give a fuck, either. The only reason I even knew the bastard was in prison was because he wrote my mom a letter of apology while going through some gambling rehabilitation program the state put him in. I didn't care about my father then, and I sure as hell didn't care when he got out, but it doesn't surprise me Blowback has kept tabs on him.

My veep looks to me. "You don't want us to babysit him somewhere else?"

Hell, yes, I do. But this ranch is as out-of-the-way as it gets. Most of the time we can't even get a damn cell phone signal out here. And if Carlisle only hangs around the cabins and the clubhouse, I can avoid him easy enough. No need to put any brothers out for this, holing them up in some shitty motel room over the holidays.

I shake my head. "Just make sure he doesn't expect some jolly Christmas reunion."

"I'll do that," Thorne says, then his expression turns grim. "Maybe don't say anything to Jenny about what Red did. She's never been squeamish about that side of the life, but considering."

Considering. Yeah. He doesn't need to say the rest.

Considering that Red just passed. Considering that Jenny's emotions are all over the place and she might take on a load of guilt, knowing Red killed someone for touching her. Considering that mentioning it will bring up all that old shit with Reichmann.

"That favor is club business," I say. "I'm not sharing it."

He nods and heads out. Blowback follows him, bottle of scotch in hand. Off to share it with Lily.

That thick envy clogs up my chest again. I glance at the phone. Jenny's at work, at her brewery on the other side of the ranch, and just like this place, the only way to reach her is by landline. No easy texts, no quick calls, because the ringing phone drags her away from work, and keeping busy is one of the ways she deals with her grief. But after thinking about Reichmann, I need to hear her voice. I need to know she's all right.

I reach for the phone and stop. Her voice isn't enough.

I grab my coat and head out.

TWO

JENNY

Shipping out three hundred gift baskets before Christmas Eve? Not my best idea ever.

No, that's not right. It *was* a great idea. The Kick-Ass Christmas Bucket from Black Boots Brewery, including his-and-her (or his-and-his, or her-and-her) T-shirts—black, with my logo on the pocket and "Have a kick-ass Christmas!" across the back—a pair of pint glasses etched with my logo, and a twenty-two ounce bottle of my limited-edition Cherry Xmas soda, all nestled in an old-fashioned tin pail.

I came up with the concept last year and sold almost thirty gift baskets in December—half through the storefront, where customers can choose to replace the soda with one of my craft beers, and half online, where I can only ship non-alcoholic drinks. This year, I expected to sell fifty buckets, but I was on track to ship seventy-five by Wednesday, the last date I can guarantee delivery by Christmas.

Most of those seventy-five orders were out of here by last night. I expected a few more to trickle in over the next two days, so I assembled a dozen buckets in advance, thinking that would cover the remaining sales. Instead I woke up to over two hundred new orders, because a popular food blogger listed it as a "great last-minute gift idea."

I should have prepared for something like this. I don't do *anything* last minute, but apparently, at least two hundred other people do.

So here's the *real* great idea: Software that integrates my online store and my on-site inventory. If we hadn't sold out of tin pails and the gift basket hadn't clicked over to "out of stock," I'd be screwed right now.

Another great idea currently saving my ass? Hiring my first employee, Hashtag. He started hanging around last summer, acting as my personal bodyguard when the trouble between the Hellfire Riders and the Eighty-Eight started going down, but he showed a strong interest in the brewery itself, helping out while he was here. And after my dad got sick, I couldn't devote as much time to working, so bringing Hashtag aboard was a no-brainer.

I don't think he imagined that learning the ropes would include slapping two hundred shiny black bows onto cellophane-wrapped pails, but even though his shift is about to end, he cheerfully volunteered to stay as long as necessary tonight and tomorrow.

Very cheerfully. He's humming "Jingle Bells" as he uses a tablet computer to scan a shipping label. Twenty pails sit on the long folding table between us. Since the only difference between any of the orders is the sizes of the T-shirts, we've set up an assembly line. If I had more room, I'd do more pails at a time, but most of the free space in the old barn is taken up by the shipment of Lionheart stout that's going out to a distributor next week. So we crammed the table in between cases of ale stacked on pallets and the stainless steel brewhouses standing behind us.

I look up when Hashtag's humming suddenly stops.

He's tall and cute in that fresh-out-of-the-military way—erect posture, short hair, close shave. Since hiring him, I've noticed an upswing in the number of college-age girls coming out this way, and I can't say I blame them, given how his black T-shirt clings to his fresh-out-of-the-military chest. Currently he's wearing a Santa hat that should look silly, but I suspect more than a few women volunteer to sit on his lap when they see that puffy white ball dangling between his eyebrows.

Right now, though, he's looking down at the tablet and that puffy white ball is hanging over a slightly sick expression. "Uh…there are still orders coming in. Almost a hundred more."

My stomach drops. "What?"

Sliding his finger down the screen, he scrolls through the list. "Looks like they're buying things individually. Especially the pint glasses. And the Xmas soda. It's…sold out."

Oh, Jesus. I reach for the tablet. "Let me see."

So stupid. Why didn't I change the estimated processing time when we sold through the pails this morning? But I wasn't thinking of individual orders. I was panicking and trying to figure out how to get all of the buckets out.

Stupid, stupid. But that stops now.

"Okay," I say and show him what I'm doing on the screen. "Global change here, see? We'll increase the processing time for every item in the store to…"

I pause to consider.

"How about a week?" Hashtag suggests. "That'll give us a breather through Christmas."

I was thinking something shorter, just a few days so that anyone who wanted their stuff delivered by Christmas would know it wouldn't arrive in time, but his suggestion is better. Not because I need time off over Christmas, but because I'm losing almost three days packing all of this stuff and I'll have to catch up on my other work.

"That'll do," I say, submitting the changes before popping over to the website. I click on an item and check the estimated delivery date. Well after Christmas.

"Phew." Dramatically he passes a hand over his brow. "What now, boss?"

God, I don't know. Can I do this? I scroll through the list of new orders. I *can* do this. "Buckets first," I say. "But we're going to need more shipping cartons for these new orders, and I don't want to try scrounging them up last minute. So can you—"

The jingle of the bell over the storefront door interrupts me.

"—go take care of that customer?" I finish.

"On it," he says.

As soon as he's gone, I exhale a long, shuddering breath and try to rub the aching tension from the back of my neck. God. What a mess. And my own fault, because I wasn't prepared.

Next year, though. Next year, I'll make sure—

Saxon.

Everything inside me stills as the Hellfire Riders' prez strides in from the storefront, a six-foot-three walking brick house of muscle and steely eyes that warn the world to stay out of his fucking way.

Once upon a time, I hated how everything seemed to stop when I saw him. I hated how my entire world seemed to narrow until Saxon Gray was the only thing that existed. I hated how I couldn't force myself to look away from him, how a glimpse of his tall, strong frame and rugged beauty stole my breath and my sense. I hated knowing I could never have him, because he was a Hellfire Rider, and for a long time, there was too much bad blood between my dad's club and his.

Not anymore. And he still leaves me breathless. But I love the quiet he brings now, love how everything else falls away. Until there's just Saxon.

And me.

I can't stop my smile as he comes straight for me, his blue gaze locked on mine. I can *never* stop my smile. Who could?

He's big, he's mean…and he's mine. I've got a lot to smile about.

But he's not smiling. His eyes are dark and intense, his expression like stone. I know that look. He's holding something back. Something's got him wound up, though he's trying not to show anything—but because he's not showing it, I know.

What would he be hiding from me?

Unfortunately, growing up around a motorcycle club means that I can think of a million dangerous possibilities. With quiet alarm, I scan his powerful frame. He doesn't seem hurt. Each step is long and sure. His boots leave wet tracks on the concrete. It must be snowing, because a few white flakes cling to his wide shoulders and dark hair. The rest have melted away.

Then even the stragglers disappear as he comes to a halt in front of me. I feel the cold coming off him, inhale the clean smell of winter he brought in from outside, but it's not the cold that sends a shiver racing over my skin when his icy fingers tip up my chin.

I manage to breathe out a "Hello" the moment before he captures my mouth with frigid lips that instantly warm against mine.

And his kiss. God help me. What Saxon does to me now isn't *kissing*. Instead he takes me and breaks me and remakes me with every stroke of his tongue past my lips. A shudder rips through me and I push closer, hands gripping the iron strength of his arms, my body heating in a fiery rush.

On a rough groan, his fingers tangle in my hair and he drags me up closer for a deep, deep taste. Delirious need sears my every nerve, burning low and raging higher. A greedy whimper sounds in my throat.

At the sound of my whimper, suddenly he eases back, his lips softening.

No, no, no. *Saxon.* He's hard against me, his cock like a pillar of stone, but when I reach between us to palm that thick length, he draws farther away.

Still kissing me, but now it's sweet—and like every time he kisses me, it's perfect—but the wild heat felt *so* good.

I sigh when his lips release mine. Lately he acts as if he's afraid I'll break. For the past month, he's been like this. Ever since my dad died. Always being careful, always keeping a tight leash on his control, even after I tell him that I don't need tender, that I still love it rough and hard.

Not that it's his fault. Some nights, I *have* needed tender. A few times, I've cried so much and felt so lost, I didn't want anything more than to lie in his arms. Other nights, the sex is still *so* good—so hot and sweet. I miss his rough edges, though. I just don't know how to prove to him those edges won't make me bleed.

That roughness isn't gone. He simply has it locked away. But whatever brought Saxon here made him forget to be careful for a few seconds.

I don't think that's a reason to rejoice, though. Shadows slip through his eyes when he looks at me. Gently, I trace the sculpted line of his jaw. He's growing in his beard again, a ward against the winter wind while riding, but it's still short enough the whiskers are bristly rather than soft. The beard suits him.

"You're all right?" I ask him. "You look like you got some bad news."

He shakes his head. His voice is like midnight, dark and deep. "Just club business, princess."

At least he doesn't try to tell me it's nothing, but I know he won't tell me more.

"Okay," I say and touch my thumb to the side of his mouth. "It couldn't have been all bad, whatever it was. Because you taste like you've been drinking something yummy."

His eyes gleam. "Yeah?"

"Mmm-hmm." I hum an assent. "Let me taste again. I was distracted the first time."

He grins and lowers his head, and I breathe his breath, taste him through that smile before drawing back. Notes of oak and honey. As smooth as Saxon's own flavor and just as sharp. Delicious.

"What kind of whiskey was that? Because I want more."

"It'll be a surprise," he says, and I can't interpret the strangely flat look in his eyes when he adds, "Here's another: Blowback just told me he and Zoomie got married. In Vegas."

Oh. I press my lips together, trying to stop my laugh. But of course he reads me easily.

"You knew?"

"Lily told Anna and me." And told us to keep it quiet. "About two months ago."

His face goes dark, but I can tell the difference between when he's playing at being mad and truly angry. Truly angry, his expression wouldn't change much at all.

He looms over me, big and menacing and so, so sexy. "And you didn't think to say anything to me, princess?"

"Well, you know. It was club business. *Girl* club business," I tell him and my laugh bursts out when he catches me up against him. I assume he's going to make me pay for being so sassy but he suddenly stills, holding me so close, his face buried in my hair.

"Jenny." His voice is rough against my ear. "I love you so damn much."

My heart overfills in my chest, emotion tightening my lungs and throat. I wind my arms around his neck, my fingers sliding into the thick hair at his nape. He doesn't have it pulled back today. Usually he keeps it in a short tail—except in bed. Right now I feel as close to him as I do there, even with layers of clothes between us, because he strips me naked with those words.

I never thought I'd hear Saxon Gray say them. Only a few months ago, I thought I was losing everything.

And I *have* lost so much. But I still have so much, too.

My eyes are burning when he raises his head to look down at me. His body goes utterly still when he sees my tears.

Oh, no. I know what he thinks. I *do* miss my dad. His absence is a deep, ragged hole in my heart. But these tears aren't because I'm hurting.

"I love you, too. Sometimes I'm overwhelmed by how much," I tell him. "And by how lucky I am."

Saxon presses a hard kiss to my lips. "The luck's all mine, princess." But he's already being careful again, his gaze searching mine when he adds, "Thorne asked if you want to visit his place on Christmas."

Oh. Uncertainty slips through me, and I pull away, turning my face so he can't see the grief and doubt that follow.

Sometimes holding it together *is* hard. Since my dad

died, I've been working almost constantly, and I know part of the reason is simply because it helps me to keep busy. I'm not avoiding the grief, I'm just trying to get through it.

But I *have* avoided thinking about the holidays. Because every time I see the lights or a tree or hear the music, I can't help but think of my dad. Sometimes it's okay. Other times I end up bawling.

Maybe I'd be fine, going to Uncle Thorne's. Maybe it would hurt too much to bear. I just don't want to spend the whole time crying and worrying Saxon, until he's looking at me as if I'm as fragile as a glass ornament.

But I'm not sure what Saxon wants. A holiday isn't just about one person.

Hesitantly, I glance at him. He's waiting, his expression tense, his fists buried in the pockets of his jeans. "What do you usually do?"

Surprise slides over his face, as if that question didn't occur to him. Or as if what he wanted to do never mattered.

"Nothing special," he says. "Go to the clubhouse, watch a game."

Really? "What about when you were a kid?"

"Nothing much," he says but this time there's a warm undercurrent that tells me *nothing much* means a lot more than *nothing special*. "We didn't have much, so there wasn't ever a big to-do."

"You and your mom?"

"Yeah." Something cold flickers through his eyes. "She was always scraping by after Carlisle left. We didn't have a tree, some years. But she said it was important to always have *something*. So she made sure we did."

My throat aches. The ice in his eyes that formed when he mentioned his dad melted by the time he got to the end of that. I didn't know his mom, but I know he lost her about six years ago to cancer. The same way I lost my dad.

She sounds like a woman I would have enjoyed knowing. "So do you want to do something?"

"That's up to you, Jenny." His gaze and his voice are so even, I can't tell if he has an unspoken preference. "What did you do as a kid?"

"All of it." And, oh God. I'm already hurting for him and now the thickness in my throat is growing tighter and tighter. "Lights all over the house, the big tree, the stockings and a pile of presents. My mom always started playing Christmas records on December first, and we'd watch those…those specials on TV, you know? Rudolph and Frosty and…Charlie Brown."

My breath is shuddering, and I'm almost crying, desperately trying not to. Then Saxon catches my face in his hands, so warm and strong and solid that it's utterly natural to cling to him. To lean on him.

"We watched those, too," he says. "I always liked the Bumble."

I give a watery laugh, imagining that. Saxon, as a kid, sitting in front of the television, entranced by the Abominable Snow Monster.

His fingers tighten and every word is a low rasp when

he asks, "And after your mom's accident?"

Oh, God. The tears well up again. That was sixteen years ago, and the pain of losing her never really went away. But this time it hurts because I know why he's asking. I've already been through this once. And now my dad's gone, too.

"My mom…" I choke up, and have to swallow hard past the lump in my throat. "She would go all out for Christmas. My dad would tease her for it, but always made sure to give her just the right thing. Or maybe anything he gave her would be right. And after…the year she died, Dad went all out for me. But everything just hurt. Everything reminded me she was gone. Reminded him, too. And nothing we gave each other was the right thing because what we both wanted most was her."

"Princess." His voice is a raw ache. "I wish I could give you what you want."

"I know." I drag in a long breath, and another—steadying myself. I'm still on the edge of crying, but this is good. Talking about it. "The following year, it was a little easier. We still missed her but it was…not so hard. So maybe this year, if you don't care, maybe we can skip it all. And don't get me anything."

"That's what we'll do, then." His lips brush mine. "You all right?"

"Yes," I say—and I am. I draw in another long, shuddering breath.

He gives me a few seconds to wipe my face, then

gestures to the table covered in tin pails. "What's this? It looks like a cow-milking party."

A short laugh escapes me. "*That* is unexpected media exposure combined with blind panic. We got slammed with orders today. In two weeks, I'll be glad of it. But today…" I trail off with a sigh. "I'll have to work late. I probably won't be home before ten. That also goes for tomorrow."

He nods. Working late is nothing new—for either of us. "I've got payroll and bonuses to take care of tonight, so I'll be at the Den late, too. Are you set for dinner?"

Yes, unfortunately. "Helena brought by a lasagna."

"Jesus." Saxon pinches the bridge of his nose. "You didn't tell her we had ten more in the freezer?"

That's a small exaggeration. Since my dad died, we've received an average of two casseroles and one lasagna a week. And that doesn't count the turkey dishes and pie that came in the post-Thanksgiving rush.

But it's not as if I can turn them away. Most of it comes from the club's old ladies, and getting on their bad sides will never be in my best interest. "She brought it here to the barn," I tell him. "It's in the office fridge now. Do you want me to send a piece with you?"

His hard stare answers for him and sends me into a fit of giggles. I guess not. And I can't blame him. Helena's a fine cook, and she means well, but I'm so tired of eating food I'm not in the mood for out of a sense of obligation. Saxon must be tired of it, too.

"All right," I say, "but I guess that means there's something I need you to do for me." Or else we're going to end up with a hundred post-Christmas ham dishes.

Immediately he says, "Anything."

"Maybe spread the word we don't need more food? *Gently,*" I stress, because knowing Saxon, he'll straight-out forbid anyone from bringing anything, and then the ladies will feel as if they've done something wrong. "Just let everyone know that our freezer's full, and that we appreciate all they've given, because it took away the burden of cooking this past month."

He nods and kisses me again, preparing to go. "I'll let Widowmaker know."

The club's secretary, who'll spread the word—because Saxon isn't going to say all of that nice and appreciative stuff himself. The prez of the Hellfire Riders doesn't say shit like that. He's got a hardass image to maintain.

Except it's not an image. He *is* a hardass. A big, mean motherfucker.

And so damn sexy as he turns and walks away. The sight of his hard ass in those jeans is a gift to women everywhere—but especially to me.

My heart thumps. "Saxon!"

He stops at the door and looks back, waiting. Maybe I'm crazy, deciding this last-minute, but suddenly I don't care. I need more of him than I've been getting lately.

"How about nine o'clock, instead—and do you want to bring pizza from Jimmy's? Even if it gets cold before we eat it, it'll reheat well."

Instantly electric heat charges the air between us. His dark blue gaze drops to my lips. "And why would it get cold?"

"I dunno. Maybe when we get home we'll do something other than eating."

"Would we? I suspect I'll be eating, either way." The look he slides down my body starts a low, burning ache. Eyes gleaming with hunger, his gaze lifts to mine again. "What about these buckets?"

Screw the buckets. "I'll come in an hour earlier tomorrow morning."

"And what if you're too worn out to wake up an hour early?"

Oh, God. Even as a shiver runs through me, I give him a look of innocent doubt. "If you really think you *can* wear me out…"

His eyes narrow in response to that challenge—and that's all the response he needs to make. That expression is a promise. Or a threat. I'll take either one.

"All right, princess. Pepperoni on your half?"

"Yes." Anticipation makes my reply sound breathless. "See you at nine."

"Just be ready. I'll be *real* hungry by then, Jenny."

"I'll be ready." God, I'm ready now. So is Saxon, his face a taut mask of arousal, his eyes burning with blue fire, his erection straining against the denim of his jeans.

When he turns and goes, I know he only manages to

leave because of his iron control—but there's nothing soft in the last lingering look he gives me. There's nothing but rough edges and hard need. Oh, thank God.

Celebrating or not, I suddenly suspect that I'm going to have a *very* merry Christmas, starting at nine o'clock.

THREE

SAXON

By the tire tracks in the snow I know Jenny's home even before I see her pickup sitting in the garage. She hasn't been here long, though. Those tracks haven't filled in even though the snow is still falling. Almost a foot deep now. It made for a slow drive from town and the pizza sitting on the passenger seat passed 'cold' about five miles back.

But it'll get colder. Because I've spent my whole damn evening imagining what I'm going to do to Jenny as soon as I get inside. On her back or on her knees, it doesn't matter as long as my cock is pumping deep into her wet heat.

My dick's been aching since I left her brewery. I need her tight pussy clenching around its thick length, need to taste her sweet mouth, need to hear her scream.

I need *her*.

Thinking of finally getting into her pushes me past aching. My cock's hard enough to break as I park Red's 4x4 next to her truck. Chrome shining under the halogen lights, my bike sits in the garage's third bay, where it'll probably stay for the next few weeks. When I lived in town, I managed to get around well enough without a cage. In the winter, the streets are always plowed and my house wasn't far from the Wolf Den or the Hellfire Riders' clubhouse. Since moving in with Jenny and relocating the clubhouse to the other side of the ranch, I've relied on Red's rig more and more.

It's a hell of a thing, driving around in his vehicle. Living in his big house. I expected it to be real fucking awkward—and not just awkward for me. For Jenny. For Thorne. For the Steel Titans. As if I'm taking over a dead man's place.

But it's been smooth. Some of that is because of Red. When I moved into the house this past summer, he made sure I had my own space, not just rooms I'd be taking over when he died. And when we folded the clubs together, he made sure the Steel Titans became Hellfire Riders in truth, not just name.

But most of it's because of Jenny. Not only because she welcomed me in but because this house is nothing without her in it. When she's not here, I don't care whether I am. So it hardly matters what room I'm in or if I have my own damn space. Whether it's a place like this—a big old house that looks like something out of a magazine—or a rathole motel, it doesn't make a difference to me.

As long as she's here, it's where I belong. It's my home. And there's no feeling awkward about it.

In the kitchen, the light's on over the stove. She's already got a new log burning in the brick fireplace by the breakfast nook. I drop the pizza box on the counter and head for the stairs.

I have to cross the great room to get there. Passing beneath the vaulted ceiling, I toss my coat onto a leather chair. My mother raised me better than that, taught me to hang my shit up, but this is a time of *need*.

I pull my shirt off while climbing the stairs. Jenny likes looking at my chest, likes running her tongue along the ridges of muscle, and if she's not hot already, I want to get her there fast.

But not too fast. I love kissing her, teasing her nipples, sucking on her clit. All of it's good. So fucking good. She gets so goddamn wet.

Dragging open my belt, I give my cock a hard stroke, already picturing her fingers on me, then her lips. Oh fuck, and her hot little cunt. There's nothing in the world like sinking into her warm pussy, hearing her shuddering breath as she takes me in, feeling her tighten around me.

Soon. Her bedroom isn't a room, but a big open suite taking up half the second floor. The bedside lamp's lit, its soft yellow glow washing over the golds and greens and browns on the bed.

There's steam in the air.

She took a shower. So she's warm and wet and smelling good and I'm going to come in my hand like a fucking teenager if I don't find her in a second.

The bathroom door's open but she's not in there. Neither is her robe, so I head for the closet—shit, it's not even a closet, but more like some royal dressing room, with more shelves than any man could ever need and a fancy sofa for sitting on while you put on your boots.

A fancy sofa that's perfect for fucking your woman. I've had Jenny on it so many times, sometimes on her back, sometimes bending her over, sometimes riding me. Seems like I'm about to do one of those again.

Or maybe all three.

She's sitting on the sofa with her back to me, her silky blue robe clinging to her slim curves. Her long dark hair's twisted up in a messy bun that I'm going to pull apart as soon as I get my fingers in it—

The sound that reaches me freezes me in my tracks.

Not crying. Just the shuddering breath that follows a storm of weeping, and she's not looking around but jerkily pushing something away. A box. I don't know what. It doesn't matter.

I just know she's hurting again.

"Princess." My voice is thick.

"I'll be right out!" It's chirpy—she's never chirpy. "I'm just getting ready. I wanted to put this on first. A surprise."

She holds up some red lacy thing but I barely even see it. Instead I see how she doesn't turn toward me, and how she's wiping at her face.

"Just wait for me out there," she says, and some of the cheerful chirp is gone, probably because she knows how fake it sounds. "I'll only be a second."

Maybe. But the last thing I care about now is my cock. She's hurting, and I'm supposed to think about fucking her now? Maybe just ignore how she's choking back tears and make her choke on my dick, instead?

"Forget the underwear, Jenny." It rips at my heart when her shoulders curl forward, when she drops her face into her hands. I slide onto the sofa, draw her into my arms, and it's like a knife in my chest when I realize she must have been in here sobbing for a while. Rimmed with pink, her light green eyes glitter like shattered jewels. Her face is pale and splotched with red.

And still so beautiful.

"I wanted to look sexy for you," she whispers, and there's a sad little laugh in it, her breath hot against my neck. "Put this on and wait for you on the bed. Then I saw *that*."

The box. Just cardboard, about two feet long and half

as wide, still sealed with shipping tape. "What's in it?"

"A pair of antique dueling pistols. I got them off eBay back in May. My dad's Christmas present." A shudder runs through her and her voice breaks as she says, "I never…do anything…last minute."

I press a kiss to her hair because there's nothing to say. Nothing to do except hold her tighter.

Clinging to me, she draws a ragged breath. Already calmer. She does that. Grief breaks over her like a summer storm, then she settles again. But it blows her out when it goes. Soon she'll be leaning heavy against me, then falling asleep.

"I forgot I hid them in here. I mean, I *saw* the box all time. I just…didn't think about it." Already she's sinking deeper into my arms. "Maybe I should give them to Thorne. Or put them with the other things to donate. Unless you want them?"

"No." I don't want anything but her.

Working my arm under her knees, I lift her up. She barely weighs anything at all. With a sigh, she rests her cheek against my shoulder and I carry her to the bed, where I slide in behind her.

She turns and snuggles in tight against my chest, her eyes already closing. "This isn't what I planned for tonight."

"I've got no complaints." I'm here in her bed. She's curled up against me. "We'll head down and eat after you nap."

"Okay." It's just a breath. Then, "I'm sorry."

Fuck that. "Don't you *ever* be sorry, Jenny."

My cock will never matter more than her heart. Having her in my arms is more than I ever thought I'd get, and a hell of a lot more than I deserve. So whether I'm deep inside her or just holding her as she falls asleep, it doesn't make any difference to me.

As long as she's here. As long as she's safe. As long as she's mine.

I don't need anything else.

FOUR

SAXON

I ENJOY SEEING CARLISLE MORE THAN I FIGURED I would. But then, I didn't know whoever's after him had already delivered a warning and busted up his knee with a crowbar. Watching him hobble around the clubhouse's garage with a brace on his leg and a crutch under his arm is the most fun I've had since putting Zoomie up against the Devil's Hangmen's prez.

And I'm enjoying it all the more because, when Jenny's hurting, I just want to tear the whole fucking world apart.

Tear it apart and remake it, and create a world where she's never crying.

But I can't. All I can give her is the little I have. I can kiss her awake and make sure she eats. At least that's something. Last night we ate the pizza together, and while we were talking over her glass of red wine and my beer, some of the light was back in her eyes. And since she only eats one slice to my three, she finished before me, then licked her way down my stomach and made up for lost time.

But I still felt the hurt in her. Even as she rose up over me, took my cock deep—riding me, kissing me, her mouth and her pussy so hot and sweet. Even as I gripped her hips and set a pace that had her scratching at my shoulders and crying out as she came. I gave what I have, being careful not to be too rough or demand too much. Still, I can tell she needs something I'm not giving.

And it's fucking killing me. So seeing Carlisle's pain is the one goddamn thing I'm happy about this morning.

"You should marry Jenny soon," Blowback says quietly.

I did *not* just fucking hear that.

I tear my gaze from Carlisle and look to the Riders' warlord, who's crouching beside a snow blower with a socket wrench in hand. The garage is another leftover from the old dude ranch—it used to be a horse stable, and instead of large bays that open to the outside, a wide center aisle separates a dozen stalls, each the perfect size for working on a motorcycle.

Today, the stalls are all occupied by motorcycles.

Since the snow's keeping everyone from riding, many of the brothers are using the downtime to tinker with their bikes—especially since Zoomie and Blowback are around to advise them if any repairs require a more knowledgeable touch. Zoomie's in the stall across the aisle, poking at Grasshopper's ride. Blowback got tapped to fix the snow blower after it puttered out this morning—although leaving it broken would have been just fine with me, because if all the walkways from the clubhouse to the cabins are a mess, it means Carlisle will have even more difficulty getting around than he already does.

Now Blowback's not even looking up at me. After saying I should marry Jenny.

"What the hell did you just tell me?"

He spares me a glance, his eyes flat and empty, then returns his attention to the machine. His voice is pitched low enough that no one can overhear. "As warlord, I've got two jobs. The first is to make sure nothing comes at you or yours. The second is to make sure you get what you need. And you need to marry her."

I do. That doesn't mean I can yet. "We just put Red in the ground. She's still hurting."

"And neither of those situations will change anytime soon. He'll always be in the ground and him dying will always hurt her."

That's true. But this is one of the ways Blowback is fucked up. I don't think I'd understand that so well if I hadn't spent time in a cell with his brother. I'm not sure whether Blowback is aware of how much I know—or if he would care that I do. But some of the shit I learned there about him and his family explains a whole lot. He doesn't always pick up on the gray areas of emotional shit that other people absorb easily. Everything's literal, cut-and-dried, black and white. But he understands well enough as soon as it's put in his terms.

I glance at Zoomie. She's healed up now. But I remember how, only a few months ago, Blowback barely touched her. "It's just like kissing a girl with her lip busted and bleeding," I tell him. "Maybe she wants you kissing her, maybe she likes it, but you know it's hurting her at the same time. So you wait until the swelling's gone."

He sits back on his heels, regards me with that dead stare. "Or just like when someone stabs your cock. You don't fuck a girl while it's still bleeding. Or even when it's scabbed over. You wait for it to scar. No matter how much you want to get inside her."

Jesus. I stare at the crazy bastard before it hits me. "You're just fucking with me."

He grins and reaches for the coffee balanced on top of the low wall at the front of the stall. The old ladies have been in and out all morning, carrying hot drinks and platters of cookies. Through the wide, open doors at the end of the garage, I can see kids playing, and the noise from outside sounds like a schoolyard. The Hellfire Riders never had any young ones around the clubhouse when we were located in town, but this was apparently a tradition out here on the ranch—as soon as the schools shut down for the holiday break, Red allowed the Titans' kids and grandkids to come out to ride their sleds and mess around in the snow.

It looks like the Hellfire Riders took to that tradition real well. And, Christ, it's a lot of kids. No one's ever going to claim the Riders don't get their share of fucking in—though a good number of the brothers could stand to wrap a rubber around their dicks a little more often.

Blowback regards me seriously again. "So you think you know when to ask her?"

"I'll know," I tell him.

It'll be when she starts listening to music again. It used to be—in the brewery, in her truck, at home—she'd always be blasting something. Or using music to make me laugh, like putting on a cheesy ballad by Air Supply and betting me I can't get through a blow job without pushing her off and changing the song to something else.

But lately, she turns her music on, listens to a song or two, then turns it off. Maybe she thinks I don't notice, but I do. And after living with Red a while, I know the songs she turns off are by the bands he listened to.

So when listening to those songs doesn't cut her so bad, when she can sing along with her music, when she dances around the kitchen again—that's when I'll ask.

Blowback nods. "You need a reminder?"

"No." I'll be counting down the days, waiting. But since he's having his fun fucking around with me, I guess

I'll do it right back. I nod toward the door and the kids playing outside. "So are you and Zoomie going to start popping out some babies?"

Blowback huffs out a laugh. "I'm too fucked up to risk raising a kid."

At least he knows it. Hell, I'm probably too fucked up, too, but I'm still looking forward to seeing Jenny pregnant with our baby. Looking forward to holding a little boy or girl in my arms. We've talked about having two or three, someday.

"We're thinking about a dog," he adds, pressing the start button on the blower. The engine coughs then catches, quickly rolling to a roar and blowing dust around the stall.

When he powers it down, I tell him, "You're probably too fucked up for a dog, too."

"Probably," he agrees easily.

Still, he'd do a better job than some. I've seen him snap necks using as much effort as other men use to eat French fries. If I told him to finish my father with a crowbar, it wouldn't be anything different than asking him to fix my bike's engine. Killing doesn't touch him like it does most people. It doesn't leave a stain he can't wash away. But as fucked up as he is, Blowback takes care of his own. If he had kids, he'd lay down his life for them, sacrifice everything he has to make sure they have everything they need.

Yeah. He'd make a hell of a lot better father than some men. Especially the one hobbling down the aisle in this direction.

I stand at the low wall, watching Carlisle come. In his face, in general appearance, I suppose he looks like me, although grayer, leaner, and a few inches shorter. But I can't say I'd have recognized him, passing on the street—and that's not just the age difference between when he took off and now. I haven't thought about what his face looks like in thirty years. I couldn't have said what color hair he had.

It's dark, like mine. He's got blue eyes, like mine.

But I don't see a bit of myself in him. I didn't know how much of a relief that would be—and it's the only good thing to come out of seeing him, a bonus addition to the entertainment.

Blowback pushes the snow blower out of the stall and leans back against the low wall, coffee in hand—settling in to watch Zoomie, I realize. Across the aisle, she's straddling Grasshopper's ride while leaning over and helping him adjust the height of his apehangers. Her blond hair's covered with a stocking cap. She's got knee-high boots on, and some skinny jeans, and the considering the way her ass looks in them, I guess I'd settle in and watch, too, if she were my wife.

Instead I watch Carlisle slowly making his way closer. "You get that info on who's after him?"

"Yup," Blowback says. "Nothing we didn't expect. He owes a bookie up in Portland a quarter million. Lowery's the collector who'll be coming after him."

"Is Lowery someone we ought to worry about?"

His gaze on Zoomie, he shakes his head. "I'm pulling in a favor. If Lowery or his crew comes this way, I'll know."

"Carlisle's not worth a favor."

"Lowery has a reputation for using family to get to his target."

That family would be me. So Blowback's just doing his job. Like when he kept tabs on my father. "What was Carlisle in for?"

"Fraud. He persuaded a handful of widows to hand over bank accounts, their kids' college savings, property. Then lost it all at the track."

Jesus. I'm no fucking saint. I've done some pretty low shit. But preying on anyone weaker—preying on women and kids—is about the lowest it gets.

Behind Carlisle follows Bull, his babysitter for the day. The Titans' former enforcer is moving in closer to the old man and eyeing me, silently asking whether I want him to keep the bastard out of my way.

Nah. Might as well listen to what Carlisle has to say. It might be entertaining, too.

"Bull," I tell him, "why don't you give Zoomie and Grasshopper a hand."

The big man nods and heads to the other stall. Carlisle's worked up a flush crutching his way over, and now he stands looking me from head to toe.

"Been a while," he says.

Too long to care now. So I wait for him to say something worth hearing, but even before a few seconds pass,

Thorne's wife Molly comes by with a tray of snowman cookies and a fresh coffee for me, her cheeks rosy from the cold. Carlisle lights up when she turns her pretty smile on him, and in his smooth compliments I see the man who persuaded all those women to hand over their money.

He's nodding as he watches her walk away. "This place isn't what I thought it would be. You've built something real good here. All these kids, the beautiful womenfolk."

What we've built is a goddamn biker club. We drink, we fuck, we fight, and we ride. But if Carlisle wants to believe this snowy holiday scene is what's usually here, he can go on thinking it.

"And that one, Jesus. I don't know whether to look at the bike or the girl." He's gazing into the opposite stall, then swings back to say, "I guess I wouldn't mind riding either one."

Now that's something worth answering. "The last man who said something like that about her, she straddled him and used her fists on his big fucking mouth until he didn't have a tooth left."

And she did it at my request. But that's not worth mentioning. Zoomie might have done it anyway.

Carlisle tips his head as if considering that. And all my life, I held the impression he was smart, if nothing else. My mother used to say that was the worst thing about him—that he was so damn smart, but so damn lazy, so he only ever put his brains to use while trying to find the easiest way to get by.

So until he says, "Having no teeth might be worth it," I didn't know how fucking stupid my father is.

I look to Blowback, but I suppose if the warlord was going to kill him, it'd have been done by now. Instead he just levels that dead man's stare at Carlisle. "The boss is mistaken. The last man who said something like that, the teeth were all that was left when I was done."

I'm not sure if he's telling the truth. He might be. A whole lot of shit went down in the past month, after one of our brothers went missing. I didn't see most of it, but Blowback did, and it's possible he took out some fucker who insulted Zoomie along the way.

But it probably isn't true. Or at least, not completely. I easily believe he killed a man. It's harder to believe he left teeth. Blowback always gets rid of the evidence.

And it's like a cold wind blowing past when he walks away now. Carlisle watches him go, shaking his head.

"That one doesn't have a sense of humor."

"He does." Just not regarding things most people find funny.

Carlisle nods and gives me another once-over. "Jesus, you really grew up into something. That size must come from your mom's side. I was real sorry to hear about—"

"No." I stop him there. "You mention her, you won't need a brace for that knee. Instead you'll need a plastic leg after I shove your foot through that snow blower. You got me?"

I don't raise my voice, I don't change my tone. And he

may be stupid, but not so stupid that he doesn't see that I mean every word.

He nods and shifts his gaze away from me to skim a look around the garage. "This ranch is a nice spread. About a hundred acres, yeah?"

Just the property we consider belonging to the clubhouse. Jenny's entire spread is another five hundred forty acres. But I nod because he doesn't need to know that.

"This is where the Titans used to hang out, yeah?"

"Yes."

His gaze settles on me again. "And you a Hellfire Rider. Did you have to kill Tommy Burns to get him out of the prez's seat?"

The Hellfire Riders' former president. "A truck killed him."

"That sounds like a bit of luck for you."

"Not for him."

Across the aisle, Zoomie glances over, a frown creasing her brow. Tommy Burns was her dad, and there was no love lost there, any more than there is between me and Carlisle. She still doesn't like overhearing that his dying was luck.

Oblivious, Carlisle just keeps on going. "Yeah, I'd say you've been real fortunate. I looked you up a while back, saw you spent some time in Snake River. Following in the sorry footsteps of your old man, I thought."

He can think what he likes. There isn't a bit of comparison between my stint in prison and his.

"But I hear that turned out lucky for you, too. That helping that girl is the reason you have all this now—"

Fuck this. His jacket balled in my fists, I whip him around and slam his back up against the wooden post between the stalls. The clatter of his crutch falling against the concrete floor echoes in the sudden quiet. Not a single brother says a word as I stare the fucker down. The only sound in the garage is the shouting of the kids floating in from outside and Carlisle's coughing as he tries to draw a breath.

I wait until I'm sure he can hear me, because I'm only going to say this once. "I'll take your leg for my mother. But for Jenny, I'll rip out your tongue and replace it with what's left of your cock when I'm finished with you. *Nothing* that happened to her that day was luck."

And the stupid bastard just doesn't know when to shut up. Instead he stares back at me with a defiant jut to his jaw. "I'm just saying, your life turned out real well. Maybe it wouldn't have if I'd been around. If I hadn't left, your life might have gone completely different, and you wouldn't have any of what you do now. So maybe you can show a little generosity to your old man instead of holding on to a fucking grudge because of something I did over thirty years ago."

He thinks this rage is because he *left*? Oh, hell no. This rage isn't thirty years old. It's twenty-eight years old, stoked while watching my mom weep in despair over a foreclosure notice. It's twenty-five years old, seeing her blistered arm, because she was so damn tired from working three jobs that she slipped and burned herself on a fryer. It's twenty years old, trying to help her out of bed because her back is hurting so bad after a decade of cleaning hotel toilets, she can't even get to the bathroom without me holding her up. It's fifteen years old, seeing her stricken expression as I'm found guilty for manslaughter and knowing she's blaming herself because she couldn't afford a better lawyer. It's seven years old, with the doctors telling her she's going to die, and making it a comfortable death is all the state insurance will cover, and the first thing she does is look to me and make me promise I won't take out loans or do any stupid illegal shit, trying to get enough money or meds to save her.

This rage isn't because my father left. It's because he took everything she had when he went, and threw her into a hole so deep, she never managed to crawl out of it. And this rage will *never* go, because I ran out of time. If she'd only lived another year or two, I could have helped lift her out of that hole. But I never got that chance, so every single fucking day is another day I can't help her.

So my generosity? It's this. Instead of killing him, I'm walking the fuck away.

I drop his feet back to the ground and leave him there, coughing and stumbling, trying to get his balance. To Bull I say, "Take him for a ride until I've left for town. And make sure I don't lay eyes on him again."

Because seeing that bastard just isn't as entertaining anymore.

FIVE

JENNY

Just before noon, Hashtag and I start wrapping up the last twenty buckets. We've still got all the individual orders to get through, but we're far ahead of where I thought we'd be. We'll still be working late tonight, but knowing the buckets will all be out early feels so damn good, and I can't stop smiling every time Hashtag breaks the silence by singing along with the Christmas music playing in his earphones. A few minutes ago his attempt to hit the high notes in "O Holy Night" doubled me over with laughter—but he didn't even blush. He just grinned and sang harder.

I'm humming along with his off-key "Here Comes Santa Claus" when the jingle of the storefront bell makes my heart skip. It might be Saxon. I didn't expect him to stop by today, because he knows I've been slammed with orders and he's so careful about not pulling me away from work. But this is about the time he usually heads out to the Wolf Den, and sometimes he swings by the brewery on his way to town.

So, maybe.

It's not. But it's hard to be disappointed when I see Bull. Of all the men who were Titans before joining the Hellfire Riders, he's one of my favorites. He's big and gruff, and I've heard his fists are like hammers—but he's also like a big old teddy bear. A big teddy bear with a wicked sense of humor.

But he doesn't look as if he's about to crack any jokes now. I glance at the older man wearing a knee brace who came in with him, and who is still standing by the door— as if either waiting to leave or waiting for permission to come all the way in.

I know Bull's father and that's not him. Yet there's something familiar about this man's appearance, and I can't quite place it.

Then Bull's right in front of me, and I can't see anything beyond his giant shoulders.

"Jenny." His deep voice is quiet, his expression hesitant. "Can I talk to you for a second?"

Instantly my pulse starts racing. It's never a good thing when a biker comes to me, worried about what he's about to tell me. "What is it? Is Saxon okay?"

"The prez is fine," he says quickly, but I barely have a second to take that in before he adds, "It's just that I'm babysitting his dad and—"

"*What?*"

I step to the side and my gaze flies to the other man. Oh my god. Frank Carlisle. That's the resemblance. Saxon's dad is thinner than he is, and not as tall. But the face, the eyes.

Those blue eyes are sizing me up in return. Noting my shock, probably, and I scoot back in front of Bull, blocking Frank Carlisle's view of me until I have a second to think this through.

Saxon's dad. Holy shit. Saxon never really mentions his father—the only thing I really know about him is that he ditched his family when Saxon was just a little kid, and that Saxon's mom struggled afterward.

Why didn't he say anything to me about his dad being here? I don't know.

But remembering the darkness on Saxon's face when he came in yesterday, remembering how something was bothering him, suddenly I have a good idea what that 'club business' he mentioned might have been.

"Carlisle wanted to meet you." Bull sounds apologetic for telling me this. "And we were driving around, doing nothing. Then he asked to stop somewhere and grab a beer, but I can't take him into town."

He gestures to the bar at the side of my store, where I usually serve samples, but it's not unusual for someone to buy a pint and sit for a while. Bull himself does it now and again.

But why can't they go into town? "Why are you babysitting?"

A flush stains his neck. "I can't say."

"Club business?" I ask dryly, and when he nods, I add, "Club business usually means there's a threat to me."

His flush deepens. "I wouldn't bring him here if there was."

I know. And I know what babysitting means—that the Hellfire Riders are just keeping an eye on someone. Maybe hiding him away. But since it's Saxon's dad, I'm not sure what to think.

But I can't deny that I'm curious. "Why don't you go back and say hi to Hashtag, then, and I'll get Carlisle a drink."

It's practically a demand for Bull to leave me alone with Saxon's dad, but he hesitates again. "You sure?"

"Yeah. Give me a couple of minutes."

"All right." He turns to Carlisle, tilts his head toward the bar. "The lady says to have a seat."

Carlisle smiles, and it's so strange to see. Despite the resemblance, it's nothing like Saxon's smile, which is more like a wolf baring his teeth. Carlisle's is warm and friendly and *so* smooth.

I prefer Saxon's rough edges.

Quiet falls over the storefront as I make my way behind the bar. There's just the tread of my boots and the tap of Carlisle's crutch, the humming of the coolers.

His eyes on me, he leans the crutch up against the edge of the bar and levers himself up onto a stool. "So you're Red's girl?"

Hearing my dad's name strikes a soft pang over my heart. "Did you know him?"

"Only by name and appearance." He studies mine. "You must take after your mother."

"I do."

"She must have been a beautiful woman."

That pulls a little smile from me. "She was. So are you an IPA man this early in the day or do you prefer something heftier?"

"I'm a stout."

"Then I'm your girl." I move behind the taps and start pulling a pint of Lionheart, but can't stop myself from glancing at him over and over. Searching out all of the differences in those features. Being struck by the similarities.

A soft chuckle rolls from him. "I see you looking at me. I suppose he told you what I worthless father I was?"

"He didn't say worthless," I reassure him. Saxon said something more like *piece of shit bastard.*

"I can guess what he said." But whatever he's imagining Saxon told me, it doesn't seem to dim his mood. "I'll tell you, though, seeing him makes me real proud. I know I've got no right to be. But he's done well."

"He has." And worked his ass off to get it all, turning the Wolf Den into a thriving business, leading the Riders, investing in a new gym downtown.

Carlisle nods. "A man always wants his son to do better than himself. And me, I did real well in school. Everyone said I was going to be something. And I suppose I could have been, but instead I kept letting go of what was important. And as smart as I supposedly was, it took me too long to figure that out."

I wonder if he *has* figured it out. Because he says letting go, yet from what little Saxon has said, his father wasn't letting go. He just kept reaching for something else. There's a difference.

But I don't say anything and Carlisle takes my silence as a cue to continue.

"It damn near broke my heart when I heard he was locked up. I thought it meant he wasn't on that path to being better than me. But then I heard it was because of what he did to the skinhead who grabbed you. That he basically got put away for being a hero."

Something inside me stills and settles heavy in my chest. My arms feel weighed down by more than a pint as I set his glass aside to let the foam rest.

Carlisle's watching me expectantly. Waiting for an answer, I realize. Or confirmation.

Despite the ache inside me, I keep my voice even. "That's right."

"You were real lucky he was there."

"I was."

"It must be rough. Knowing he spent five years locked away for that."

"It is."

Carlisle nods and lets out a deep sigh. "Knowing all he did since he got out, knowing what he made of himself, imagine what he could have done with five more years?" Quickly he shakes his head, looks at me pointedly. "I'm not blaming you. I'm just thinking."

"Sure," I say quietly. And I hadn't been thinking of *blame* at all until he mentioned it.

Which makes me wonder if that's why he mentioned it. Some people are like that. They just poke and prod, but claim they don't mean anything to hurt, so they can keep thinking of themselves as the good guy.

And if it *does* hurt…well, it must have touched something sore, right? But that's not their fault.

"I just mean, I know it's a hell of a burden, wondering what could have been. I think it myself sometimes— wondering how much more my son could have made of himself if I'd stuck around. If he'd had more opportunity. It's the kind of thing you wish you could make up for somehow. Make reparations for the hurt you did. But someone like me, what do I have to give now? My trailer?" He scoffs. "I've got nothing worth giving."

"Saxon wouldn't take it from you, anyway," I tell Carlisle and when his eyebrows shoot up, as if he's surprised by how blunt that was, I shake my head. "Regardless of your history or however you think he feels about you. Saxon feels a man is only worth what he earns, not what he's given."

"That's a fine code to live by." Carlisle nods his approval, eyes narrowing as he scans the shop, then turning back as I slide the pint across the bar. He blows back the head before taking a sip, then gives a low, appreciative whistle. "Shit. Now that's a hell of a stout. You must have a magic touch."

More like a degree in organic chemistry and three years spent perfecting the brew. "Thank you."

He takes another drink and nods though the swallow. "That's damn good. And thinking about only being worth what you earn—is that why you haven't given him any of this? Because he wouldn't take it?"

"Take what?"

"Well, all this property is yours, isn't it? Even the clubhouse. But you haven't given it to him—even though it wouldn't really be *giving*, would it? Because he earned it when he helped you out."

I'd give Saxon anything he wanted. But that's the thing. "He wouldn't want it."

"It's not always about what someone else wants. It's about what *you* owe. Trust me, I know about debt. I also know that when you don't pay up, it always comes back on you. So it's best to pay." Though his eyes have been locked on mine, now Carlisle shrugs as if what he's saying is nothing, as if it's just all casual conversation. "And if he's too stubborn to take what he's earned, well…that would be one hell of a Christmas present."

Yes, it would. But I'm not sure how to respond, or even if I *want* to respond, because it feels as if I'm in the middle of a hard sell by a used car salesman. Except this salesman loads up all your baggage in the front seat, so you've already got your emotions invested in buying what he's selling, because if you don't, you might lose something important.

So I think it's time for this conversation to end. I stick my hand across the bar for him to shake. "It was good meeting you, Frank. But I'm afraid I have a ton of shipments waiting for me, so I have to head out back again. Do you need anything before I send Bull your way?"

"There is something." His brow furrows. "Bull tells me he doesn't have any connection on his phone. I need to make a call but there's no service out here, is that right?"

"Unfortunately, yes."

"Then do you mind if I use that landline?" He gestures to the phone behind the bar. "Just a quick call to my prez, to see how things are going."

I reach for the wireless handset. "Of course."

"It'll be long distance, but I'll leave a couple of bucks—"

"Don't worry about it. Or about this pint. It's on me. And feel free to pop on back to say good-bye before you leave. I'll give you a case of that stout to take with you."

He huffs out a laugh. "I don't know about that. I haven't earned it."

"It's Christmas." And if he has a case of beer with him, he won't need to come back. "So it'll be my pleasure."

"Well, then," he says and raises his glass to me. "Thank you. For the phone, too."

I smile and nod, then head through the door leading to the back of the brewery. I make my way through the stainless steel brewhouses and find Bull packing buckets into shipping cartons.

"Oh, Bull. You don't have to do that."

"I recruited him," Hashtag says.

Bull eyes me, then looks toward the front of the brewery, as if he can see into the shop. "Everything all right?"

"Yes. But as you can see, we've got a lot more orders to go. Hang out in the shop as long as you like, though. Grab yourself a beer."

He nods before pulling out his phone and checking the face. Out here, it's worthless for calls and texts, but it's a great clock. "We'll be heading out pretty soon, anyway, because I'm getting hungry. The prez just wanted Carlisle gone until he left for town."

Somehow, I'm not surprised. "What do you think of him?"

Bull snorts. "He's a slick motherfucker, yeah?"

"Yeah." So it's not just me. "Oh, and hey—if you're

hungry, there's lasagna in the office fridge. It's homemade. Helena brought it by, but I don't think Hashtag and I will get a chance to eat it. So there's more than enough for you and Carlisle if you want to heat it up in the microwave."

"Helena's lasagna?" His eyes light up with interest and he rubs his big hands together. "That does sound like it'll hit the spot."

"Take some home, too, if you want."

"Maybe I will. Thanks, Jenny."

Hashtag's got his head down, hiding his face as the other man walks away, and his entire body is shaking. "Someone around here is slick," he says on a laugh. "But it's not just Carlisle. Bull's probably going to eat that whole damn thing."

Grinning, I flick the white Santa ball dangling in front of his nose. "God, I hope so."

SIX

SAXON

I'm in the weight room, in the middle of a series of bench presses when I hear Jenny come home. Earlier than I expected, but I'm sure as hell not complaining.

My cock's not complaining, either. Just knowing she's home gets the blood spooling south.

Then she pokes her head through the weight room door and the blood stops spooling and starts rushing. Her light green eyes sparkle when she sees me laid out on the bench in my sweats and my sleeveless T-shirt. While she takes a long look, I set the bar in the cradle and tug the headphones out of my ears.

"Thanks for sending dinner out to the barn," she says.

"It's nothing." The ranch is far out of any restaurant's delivery range, so I had a prospect run takeout from the Thai place to the brewery. "You finish up early?"

"Yeah. We've got a few more orders to finish up tomorrow but we're set." Her gaze slips over me again, lingering on the erection tenting my sweatpants. "You almost finished? You look so…sweaty. I was thinking about taking a shower, but maybe I'll wait for you. It'd be bad to waste all that water on separate showers."

"It'll be more of a shame to shower twice when we just get sweaty again."

"True." Heaving a sigh, she bites her bottom lip in the way she has when she's trying not to grin—and she has no idea how fucking sexy that is. "So we'll either be naughty and waste water, or I'll just wait for you naked upstairs and we'll shower after."

"Both options sound naughty to me, princess."

"You should spank me, then."

"Jesus." Those words are like an electric jolt through my cock. I pause at the bottom of a lift, with the bar a few inches above my chest, praying I can find the strength to raise it again now that she's killed me by mentioning a spanking. Christ, as hard as her being here has made it, my dick could probably lift the bar. "Just give me one minute."

Her grin finally breaks through, and she steps farther

into the room. The black skirt she wears to the brewery gives me a good look at her legs and I see the way she's clenching her thighs together. Beneath that skirt, I know she's already wet. "One minute," she warns. "Or I'm starting without you."

"If that means I'll walk in on you fingering your pussy, that's not a threat, princess."

Not a threat at all. More like the sweetest dream.

With a grunt, I push the bar up.

"We'll see." She turns away from the door, as if to run off upstairs, then swings back again, curiosity tilting her head. "Why didn't you mention your dad was around?"

Fuck. I drop the weight into the cradle and sit up, frowning. "How'd you know that?"

"Because he came out to the barn. Which was fine"— it's not, it's fucking *not* fine, but she's telling me—"although a heads-up would have been nice. Especially since I wasn't sure what to think. I know he bailed on you and your mom, but I didn't know the circumstances of him coming back. So I didn't know whether you invited him, or what your intentions were while he's visiting."

"I don't have any intentions. And I sure as fuck didn't invite him."

She goes still, watching me warily. "All right."

Shit. I need to dial my anger back. Knowing Carlisle sought Jenny out has me seeing red, but I'm worrying her now. More evenly, I tell her, "If he comes around again, just let me take care of him, princess."

"Take care of him—you think he'd hurt me?"

"It doesn't matter. This is what I'm telling you to do."

Ah, hell. That was a mistake. Her chin goes up and her eyes flash venom. "You're *telling* me, are you?"

"I am. This is club business," I say because she grew up around her dad and she knows not to question that—and so this should end it. "It doesn't concern you."

"Fine," she says tightly.

Then she's gone. God damn it. I head out after her, but she's fast. So fucking fast. By the time I get up the stairs she's sitting on the bench at the foot of the bed and hauling off her boots.

One goes whizzing by my head.

I jerk to the side and stop short. "What the fuck is wrong with you, Jenny?"

"Nothing."

"Bullshit."

"*Nothing* is what's bullshit," she spits back. "Because that's what you're telling me. Nothing. But you call it club business to shut me up even though this obviously *does* concern me, because he showed up at my goddamn door! So fuck you and your 'Just let me take care of him, princess.'"

She whips her other boot at me. Her aim is shit but she might as well have drilled me right through the chest. Taking care of her is *all* I've got to give. And it fucking kills me when it's not enough.

My blood pounding, I grit out, "I didn't want his

coming here to hurt you."

"Oh?" Her brows shoot up and she's still pissed. "So you *do* think he'd hurt me. Yet I don't get a heads-up for that, either? No, 'Jenny, hey, my dad's around and maybe he'll come up and smack you—so if you see him, go the other way'?"

White rage bursts through my head. "Did he fucking *smack* you?"

"No!" She throws her hands up. "I'm just saying, I had no idea what to expect! Because you didn't say anything, even though you're telling me now he might hurt me!"

"Not hurt you like that. Fucking Christ!" I rip my hands through my hair, stalk to her closet and back. "It's the fucking holidays, Jenny. Red's gone and you're still bleeding over it. What am I supposed to say? Sorry, princess, I know your dad's gone but *my* worthless piece of shit dad just showed up?"

Her eyes are huge and her jaw tight as she stares at me. "Trust me that I would never resent you having something I lost." Her breath shudders. "So is this your plan? You'll just keep me ignorant of everything you think might hurt me?"

Is that so fucking bad? "I will if I figure I should."

"So maybe you'll tell Hashtag's dad to stay away, too. Or Uncle Thorne, because he reminds me of my dad *all the time.*"

A hot burn fills my chest. That's shit I would *never* do. I can't fucking believe she's saying I would. With anger vibrating through me, I head for her. Next time she's going to look me right in the goddamn face as she says it. Arms crossed beneath heaving breasts, she tilts her head back as I come, her cheeks flushed and her jaw set.

"You're skating real close to the edge, princess," I warn through clenched teeth. "I'm not talking about Thorne or anyone like him. My dad's a diseased dick who cons women out of everything they own."

"And you think I'm stupid enough to fall for his shit?"

Fuck, no. I don't think the women he takes advantage of are stupid. I think they're probably too trusting. Or generous. Or hurting. And Jenny is two of those. "I just don't want you to have anything to do with him. *I* don't want to have anything to do with him, but we owe his prez a favor so my hands are fucking tied."

"Then say that! Just tell me you hate him and hate knowing he's around, and I won't go out of my way to be friendly. *Jesus,* Saxon. I'm not going to get into your business. I'm not going to ask what the favor is." In frustration she shoves against my chest but I don't go anywhere. "Just stop wrapping it up in some nice little package about club business and telling me it's for my own protection!"

I just don't see how it's any different. I tell her it's club business and she's pissed at me. I tell her my dad's a fucking asshole and she's pissed at me. All I care about is that she knows to walk away if she sees that bastard coming.

"It *is* for your protection. Maybe not the way you like

it, but I'll look after you the way I see fit, princess."

"You will?" And fucking hell, there go her eyebrows again—two elegant 'fuck you's arching high over her glittering green eyes. This time her thin smile joins them, cutting right through my throat, slicing me open. "So maybe you think I really am a princess. Just *so* delicate. *So* fragile. I can't handle anything without big ol' Saxon Gray here to protect me and tell me what to do."

That's not what princess means to me. "You're twisting shit around, Jenny," I tell her hoarsely. "You know you are."

"Then stop treating me like I need to be coddled! You think I couldn't see how he's poking at me about your time in prison? You don't think I couldn't see through that shit about my debt to you being a burden I need to pay?"

All my boiling rage turns to ice. "He was doing *what*?"

"Playing off my guilt, trying to persuade me to give you the clubhouse property. I don't know *why*, but—"

"What guilt?"

She blinks and looks at me in momentary confusion at the abrupt change, trying to shift gears away from my father. Because I don't give a shit about Carlisle and what he said. I need to know what the fuck she meant by her guilt.

"Um, you know," she says with a frown. "For when you went to prison."

Oh, *fuck* no. Roughly I ask, "And you feel guilty for that?"

Her green eyes widen at my tone. "Saxon—"

"Answer the goddamn question, princess."

"Sometimes," she whispers and the icy rage splinters through my chest, ripping and tearing. "I can't really help it."

"And what about this debt that's such a burden? You think you owe me something, too?"

"Saxon." Her tongue darts out to moisten her lips. "I *know* he was manip—"

"He can't manipulate what's not there." Catching her face in my hands, I snarl, *"Do you believe you owe me?"*

Her breath is coming in harsh pants. "Saxon—"

"God damn it, Jenny, just answer—"

"Yes!" she shouts, then quiets on a shaky little, "Sometimes."

That rips me right open. I pivot away from her, feeling my guts spill out. "So you're just going to hand over your property to me because of it?"

"No, I told you—"

"You think I'm here for your money, Jenny?"

"No! I never thought that." Her body's trembling when I turn back, her eyes glistening, her fists clenched. "But I'd give it to you if you wanted it. Not because I owe you, Saxon, but because I'd give you anything."

"You don't fucking *owe* me!" Anger and pain blows it into a roar, but she doesn't back down. She's so small, just a tiny thing next to me, yet my Jenny still stands so fucking tall. "And I only want one thing from you. Just one fucking thing."

Her heart.

But it's my heart that slams to a halt when Jenny suddenly sinks to her knees.

Her lips parted, she looks up at me through those long dark lashes. Her nipples are twin points beneath her black T-shirt, and the glittering in her jade eyes isn't anger, isn't tears. She's worked up and hot as hell.

Her voice is husky with arousal when she says, "Is this what you want?"

Jesus. No. That wasn't what I was thinking. But now I'm not thinking at all, my brain just fucking blowing away, taking with it a little part of me that says I have to be soft and gentle.

"Yes." It's a growl from deep in my chest. My fingers sink into her thick dark hair. I shove my sweatpants down over the jut of my erect cock and drag her closer. "Right now. You claim to owe me, princess? Then I'll show you *exactly* how to pay me. Open that pretty mouth."

She already is, leaning in and bracing her hands on my thighs, so eager for my cock. Need shaking through me, I fist the base of my shaft and aim for those lush lips. Pink tongue extended, she slides a teasing lick over the swollen tip before her hot mouth takes me in.

Ah, fuck. I groan as her scalding heat surrounds me. My fingers tighten in her hair, ruthlessly pushing my cock to the back of her throat. My head falls back when she moans, her tongue working along the bottom of my shaft as if she can't get enough of my taste.

God help me. I can't get enough of her mouth.

"Like that, Jenny." My voice is a hard rasp. "Take me deep."

Immediately her cheeks hollow. Slowly she draws back and the pleasure of Jenny sucking my dick explodes through my head. Every single thought goes, and all that's left is just the feel of her mouth, her tongue, the sweet painful scrape of her teeth when she tries to swallow me too deep.

Some days she teases with light kisses and licks. Not today.

Her fingers dig into my ass cheeks as if she's trying to force my full length into her mouth. But there's too much, and instead she takes in all she can and sucks hard, pulling back to swirl her tongue over the head again and again.

I'm fucking losing it with every stroke. Thrusting into her mouth, squeezing the base of my shaft so I don't come too fast—but those sounds she's making, those hungry moans, Jesus. And she's looking at me. She's got those beautiful green eyes locked on mine, those pretty lips stretched around my cock, the veined shaft glistening from the wetness of her mouth.

As I watch, she pushes the bottom of her shirt up, exposing her pretty tits. She cups the soft weight in her palm and her thumb flicks over one rosy nipple before pinching it between her fingers and tugging hard.

So fucking beautiful. "Don't forget your pussy, Jenny."

On a moan, her eyes close and she sucks harder. Her

hand slides down and dips under her skirt. Her hips rock forward, the fingernails of her left hand digging into my ass, her hungry mouth drawing me deeper.

I groan and can't look away. Fuck me. The sight of her playing with herself puts me on a fucking razor's edge. I pull harder at her hair, shove deeper past her lips.

"Now." It's a guttural command. "Suck me down."

She hums and I feel her throat working around the wide head of my cock even before I start to come, and the feeling's like fucking heaven, her tongue like hot lightning. A long groan rips from me as my dick jerks in her mouth, filling her with my cum.

She swallows every drop, then keeps going back for more, licking the sensitive little slit and swirling her tongue around the thick tip.

It's sweet fucking torture. My chest heaving, I drag her away. She resists for an instant, her fingers curling against my ass and her mouth sucking hard on my cock. Jesus Christ, she takes my goddamn breath away. Eyelids heavy, lips swollen.

And I intend to see all of her. Hauling Jenny to her feet, I take her mouth in a long kiss, tasting myself, tasting her hunger.

When she's whimpering with need and pushing up against me, I let her go.

She stares up at me, her lips glistening. "Saxon—"

"You take a step over there, princess." My voice is gruff and hard, and I've seen men sidle away, looking for escape when I use that tone. Jenny just shudders and catches her breath, because she knows there's no danger here. For her, that tone means she's about to get good and fucked. "Because you say if I want something, you'll give it? Hell, no. If I want something from you, Jenny, I'll *take* it. You understand?"

With a hectic flush staining her cheeks, she nods and whispers a breathless, "Yes."

"Good. Because I'm going to take what I want now."

And I want every goddamn inch of her.

SEVEN

JENNY

Despite the heat racing through my blood, I can't stop shivering. This is exactly what I wanted, needed—my whole world narrowing down to Saxon, and instead of bringing in all those outside cares by being so gentle and soft, he's demanding everything. My body, my attention, my heart.

And I want to give them.

He turns away from me, stripping off his sleeveless shirt. Oh, God. Just looking at him makes me hotter, wetter. His shoulders are heavy with muscle, his arms like thick steel. The Hellfire Riders' emblem inked across his back seems to flutter to life with every rippling movement under his skin. He hauled up his sweatpants again but they sit low on his hips, his thick cock still half-hard beneath the gray cotton.

His dark blue gaze sweeps over me, his expression carved from stone. He sits on the upholstered bench at the foot of the bed, using the mattress as a backrest that he leans against, spreading his arms along the top of the bed.

Just as if he were on a couch in the Hellfire Riders' clubhouse, surveying his domain. Instead he's looking at me like he owns me.

He does.

His gaze skims down my length, from my hair to my bare toes, which curl nervously into the carpet. I'm trembling in my Black Boots' shirt and skirt, my nipples drawn into tight aching points, my inner thighs slick with my arousal.

Saxon's eyes meet mine again. "I'll take that shirt, Jenny," he says.

Taking what he wants. A shudder rips through me and for a second I think about turning and running—not because I'm afraid but so he'll have to catch me before taking me. But this time, that's not how I want to play.

I don't want to play at all. I just want to give him everything he wants.

He draws in a long breath, his eyelids going heavy as

I draw the shirt over my head. My breasts are small, my nipples rosy and tight, and I know he loves everything about them. They aren't always sensitive, especially before he's played with them, but sometimes he sucks on the hardened tips until I'm screaming with frustration and on the edge of coming.

I hope he does that now but instead I just hear his gruff, "And I'll take that skirt, too."

Making me strip in front of him. My fingers shake a little as I push the tight skirt down over my hips, then kick it away.

His hard gaze follows the flight of the skirt, then returns to my panties. Almost absently, his big hand goes to his cock, gripping the bulge of his erection through the sweatpants.

"Are those panties wet, Jenny?"

I can't stop the flush crawling up my face. I'm not embarrassed. But, Jesus. They're not just wet. They're *soaked*.

"Yes," I answer softly.

"Then I'll take those, too. *But*"—his sharp tone stops me with my fingers hooked in my waistband—"don't you just toss all that pussy juice aside like it's nothing. You bring those panties to me."

Biting my lip, I slide them down. I don't have any sexy stripper moves but I know one way to drive Saxon crazy.

My gaze locked with his, I slowly fold the panties into a neat little bundle.

The growl he makes in response has a hitch in it, like

a laugh. But his voice is hard as he says, "Get your pretty little ass over here."

The cool air in the bedroom teases the wetness between my legs with every step. Sharp prickles of awareness tighten every inch of my skin. He's so beautiful, his abdomen defined even in that relaxed posture, bisected by a happy trail of rough hair over tanned skin.

His steely gaze follows me, lifting as I stop directly in front of him. "Now you hand those panties over."

Not that easily. "I thought you planned to *take* what you wanted."

He moves *so* fast. His hand hooks around my waist and he snatches the panties, then he drags me forward and his hot mouth latches onto my breast. I cry out, my fingers diving into his hair, but it's over just as quickly.

Drawing back, he leaves me panting, my nipple wet and aching for more. Panties dangling from his fingers, he brings them to his nose, watching me over the silk as he breathes in deep.

His voice is a rough growl. "These are *sopping* wet, princess."

"Sorry?"

His short exhalation sounds like another silent laugh. Watching me, he pushes the bunched silk beneath his waistband—using the wet panties to stroke his dick, I realize. God. I'm entranced by the movement of his hand, imagining his fist gripping his shaft and rubbing my arousal all over his cock, feeling the answering stroke of need deep inside me.

"You step up here now," he says.

Onto the bench. Heat stains my face, but I step up, my feet on either side of his hips. With him leaning back against the bed, the position forces me to part my legs right in front of his face. His warm breath skims across the wetness painting my inner thighs. I close my eyes as his deep voice shivers over my skin.

"You're dripping all over, Jenny."

I can't respond. Instead I stand with my eyes closed, shaking with tension and waiting for his touch.

It doesn't come. Instead he tells me, "Now spread those pussy lips. Use both hands. I want to take a good, close look at what's mine."

All his. My pussy's hot and wet and slippery. I can't stop my whimper when my fingers brush my clit, dying to go back for another touch, to rub and rub until I come, but I slip my fingers deeper into my slit and expose myself to him.

An endless second passes, the silence only broken by the sound of our harsh breathing before he says, "Such a pretty cunt, Jenny. Now, I intend to take a long taste—"

Anticipation quakes through me.

"—but I better warn you, first."

Warn me? My eyes fly open and meet Saxon's. Head tilted back, he's looking up at me. Hunger draws his rugged features into stark, unyielding lines.

"I came so fucking hard when you sucked me off, I'm

not in a rush to come again. And I'm pretty damn comfortable here with your hot little cunt in my face and your sopping wet panties wrapped around my cock." A hard smile curves his mouth. "So it'll be a long while before I'm done taking what I want from you."

That didn't need a warning. With my heart in my throat, I tell him, "I hope you're never done."

His smile drops away. His voice is a thick rasp when he says, "I won't ever be. Now you keep holding those pussy lips open for me. You stop, I stop."

I nod, trembling. "Okay."

"And you keep those beautiful green eyes on me. I want you to see what I'm taking."

I'm not even sure the response I make is a word. Just a sound, escaping on a rush as he slowly draws me closer, urging my left leg up so I can brace my knee on the bed behind his right shoulder. I'm completely spread over him, shaking uncontrollably when his lips open against the slick skin of my inner thigh.

Oh, God help me. Because what he takes then is his *time*. Kissing his way up to my cunt lips, his beard scratching my sensitive skin. Licking my slippery fingers, his tongue sliding between them, teasing my flesh but never my clit, never pushing inside me.

Until I can't take it anymore. "*Saxon.*"

My voice is a hoarse plea. And I think he intends to keep torturing me, because he simply kisses my shaking fingers, his steely gaze on my face, watching me.

Then watching my reaction as he takes a long lick up the length of my slit.

I cry out, my knees almost folding as his tongue swirls lazily over my clitoris. And I thought it was torture before, but nothing is like the torture of Saxon taking his time now—the teasing graze of teeth against my labia, the slow thrusts of his tongue at my entrance, the soft, suckling kisses over my clit. All of it making me hotter, winding me tighter, but never hard enough to come.

And it doesn't end. He licks me until my chest heaves on sobbing breaths, ecstasy and tension waging a painful war inside me, my body shaking so hard I can't support myself anymore. I curl forward over him, bracing my left hand on the mattress, barely coherent enough to keep my right hand between my legs and holding myself open.

There's nothing else here, nothing but Saxon as I'm spread over him, rocking my hips, riding his face. Nothing but his tongue and teeth and lips, and the hungry wet sound of my pussy against his mouth.

And still years pass before he lets me come, and he takes what he wants then, too, licking and sucking, his open mouth locked onto my cunt, his ravenous groan reverberating through my convulsing flesh.

Finally spent, I fall forward against him, his beard painting a wet streak across my belly. My legs have turned to trembling mush and I can only laugh breathlessly when he says in a steel voice,

"Now, Jenny, you get up on that bed."

"I can't move," I tell him.

A sharp smack against my ass jolts through me, stiffening my legs. "Will that get you moving?"

It will. Grinning, I crawl forward onto the bed. I love it when he spanks me, though I can never take too many before the pain overloads the pleasure. But a single sharp slap? God. It gets all my nerves firing again.

"On your back," he orders harshly. "Legs spread."

Saxon drops my panties onto the bench. My heart racing, I fall back against the pillows and watch him come after me. His mouth is reddened, his bearded chin wet. Sweat glistens over his broad shoulders and chest. The bulbous head of his rigid cock peeks out above the waistband of his sweats, the taut skin ruddy and slick.

"Legs *spread*," he repeats.

On a shuddering breath, I open my thighs—knees bent, my feet flat on the bed.

"Wider."

Anticipation rocking through me, I spread my thighs as wide as I can. His burning gaze locked on my pussy, he lowers himself to the bed on his stomach, his powerful biceps bunching as he stretches his long length out—with his head between my legs.

"Saxon?" His name passes my lips on an uncertain breath.

He looks up at me with a smile playing on his hard mouth. "I told you it would be a while, princess. And although I had a good taste of you, my hands sure didn't get in on any of the action."

Oh my god. I barely have a moment to brace myself before his head lowers, mouth taking possession of my too-sensitive flesh. My body bows, a ragged cry escaping me, and he doesn't take his time but devours my pussy, as rough and fast now as he was gentle and slow before. Long fingers push inside me, thrusting deep as he sucks hard on my clit, his tongue lashing the slick bundle of nerves with ruthless precision. I scream his name, my hands fisting in his hair. Saxon groans and crowds closer, forcing my thighs up over his shoulders, tipping my hips up for a deeper taste.

And I come and come and come, bucking beneath him, trying to push him away but he takes more and more and more. Until I fall back, his name a hoarse chant on my lips.

Brutal satisfaction gleams in his eyes as he rises over me, his shoulders pushing my limp legs higher, until my knees are pressed against my chest and my heels resting in the hollows above his collarbones.

He lifts my right hand to his lips and gently kisses my fingertips. "I'm going to take what's mine now, princess."

A long, hot tremor rolls through me. "Good."

A smile touches his dark eyes, but his grip is hard and relentless as he bracelets my wrists with his strong fingers and pushes my arms over my head. "Can you move?"

I try, but between his weight over me and his hand pinning my wrists, I can't wriggle more than an inch. "No."

"Good." His big body shifts against me, and my breath catches when I feel the blunt head of his cock sliding through the slick folds of my cunt. "You look down and watch me take you, Jenny."

I already am, mesmerized by the sight of his massive length lodged against my entrance, my pussy lips plumped with arousal and flushed a deep pink. He's huge, and with his big cock poised above me like this, seeing how many of those inches will soon be buried inside me, it seems impossible. But I know it's not. And I know exactly how good this is going to feel.

"Please, Saxon," I whisper in a voice raw from screaming. "Do it hard."

With a groan, he pushes into me—not hard, not yet, but he never is right away. Not while I catch my breath and struggle to adjust to his size, my pussy stretching around the thick invading shaft relentlessly driving deeper and deeper. On this first long thrust he's always slow, no matter how wet I am, no matter how desperately eager, no matter how I whimper and beg for him to just go harder, harder.

I shudder helplessly when he bottoms out, my pussy gripping his hard length. Then frustration burns every nerve when Saxon still doesn't begin fucking me, but grinds his pelvis against mine, his big cock massaging my clenching inner walls.

"I'm in there real deep, Jenny." Each word emerges as a guttural bite, his face a rigid mask of control. "You're so goddamn tight, but my cock's filling you up and I'm taking every single inch of you. You like that?"

"Yes!" It's almost a sob. Oh my god. He's *so* deep and I can't move, can't push against him, can't reach my clit and ease this agonizing tension.

His fingers tighten around my wrists and he begins drawing back, his thick cock dragging slowly across every nerve inside me. Almost completely withdrawing, he stops with just the broad head nestled between my swollen pussy lips, his shaft glistening.

"Look at those sweet juices all over my dick. Your little cunt's so hot and wet and greedy. It needs to be fucked, doesn't it?"

"Yes! Please." Now it is a sob, a cry of desperate need. "Please."

His chiseled abdomen flexes and that's all the warning I get before his thick cock suddenly spears into me, slamming deep. My ragged scream is pure pleasure, ecstasy searing the inner walls of my pussy and radiating outward on a wave of erotic heat, then he fucks into me again, again, again. Pinned beneath him, I can't move, can't do anything but watch the slick plunge of his shaft into me, each deep thrust drawing more wetness from my pussy and shining the length of his dick.

Then Saxon rears back slightly, changing his angle, his cock digging deeper and rubbing hard against that spot inside me that seems to pull everything tight, tighter, until I'm screaming and writhing in constrained little circles under him.

"Fuck, yeah." Saxon's voice is a rough, urgent growl in my ear. "Come all over me, princess. You want harder?"

He doesn't wait for an answer but gives it to me, hard and rough and I can't even breathe, my entire body tense and awaiting each deep plunge. Then he fills me up with a savage thrust and the orgasm explodes through me, my inner muscles convulsing in sharp agony, in desperate relief, and I can't move or cry out but just come and come and come.

Saxon doesn't.

And that must have been one hell of a blow job, if *that* didn't make him come again.

I laugh breathlessly when he eases out of my pussy and rolls me onto my side, settling in behind me. Even as a stinging slap on my ass makes me tense and gasp, he lifts my leg and pushes deep inside me again.

And he feels so damn good. I moan and arch my back, utterly spent but I can never, ever get enough of him. Each thrust is long and slow now, and I glory in his touch as his callused palm slides up my side. His fingers tease my nipples, his mouth hot against my temple. I reach back, fisting my hand in his hair, craning my neck and turning my upper body toward him until he can take my lips.

His kiss is long and hot and sweet. Then hotter, as his pace quickens and each stroke pushes deeper, harder. His hand drifts down over my belly and his long fingers begin rubbing my clit, and I can't come again, I *can't*.

I whimper into his mouth, then a sharp slap against my pussy stiffens my every muscle. I freeze for an instant, then all at once I have to move, have to grind back against his cock, to ease the pain or seek more, I don't know.

Saxon groans, fucking deeper into my clenching heat. "You like that, Jenny? You're going wild on my cock."

I *feel* wild, my breath coming in feral pants, my fingers twisting in the covers, my hips rocking back against his.

All at once his body stills behind me, but his slick fingers continue working my clit, rubbing, rubbing. "You want it again?"

Oh, God. Yes. No.

"Once," I whisper, biting my lip before adding, "But harder."

"Fuck, Jenny," he groans, but doesn't slap my pussy again. Instead his cock plunges into me, and his harsh ragged breaths deepen to grunts with every hard thrust. He's about to come, I realize, his body stiffening, and I can't stop moving, trying to push him into me deeper and faster.

Then the stinging pain comes, a slap directly over my clit that bursts across my nerve endings in shocking waves that spread and spread until I'm coming, crying out as my pussy clenches again and again. Behind me, Saxon grips my hip with bruising fingers and slams his cock home, his harsh groan ripping from his chest as his thick shaft pulses deep inside me.

With another groan, he rolls back and pulls me

over him, his chest heaving against my side. Aftershocks shudder through me.

From somewhere far away, I hear his ragged, "You all right, Jenny?"

"Oh my god." I laugh against his shoulder. "Stop talking or I'll probably come again."

"That's not likely to put me off talking." His fingers skim down my spine, and even exhausted, my body responds to his touch. "If you've got another one in you, we can deal with the fact that I've still never taken your ass."

Hardly my fault. "You're the one who always says your giant cock will tear my ass apart."

"Maybe next time, then."

"You always say that, too."

His chuckle is low and deep. Pulling me closer, he presses a warm kiss to my temple, and I'm pretty sure I'm smiling as I fall asleep.

EIGHT

SAXON

It's still dark when I feel Jenny practically bounce out of the bed and skip into the bathroom to get ready. I lie half-awake, listening to her take the shower we never got around to last night, followed by the gentle clink of her bottles on the vanity, knowing she's putting on all those lotions and moisturizers that make her smell and feel so damn good. She disappears into her closet and comes out a minute later in the sexy uniform she wears to the brewery, carrying her black boots and tiptoeing to the door.

My sleep-roughened "Good morning, princess," sends her on a detour in my direction.

Smiling, she leans over the bed and kisses me, soft and slow and tasting of mint. With her lips hovering over mine, she says, "Coffee in a few minutes, if you're getting up."

I'm definitely up. But although I'd love to pull her back into bed with me and bury my cock inside her, I know she's up so early because of work. "I'll be down," I tell her.

"Okay," she says, and my chest tightens when she adds in a rush, "I need to tell you, Saxon—about you saving me from Reichmann, I want you to know I don't feel *guilty* guilty. It's more like—"

"Me feeling guilty for not being able to save my mom when she got sick," I interrupt gruffly. Because, yeah, I know.

I also know I'm a fucking asshole. But she's smiling at me like I'm not.

"Exactly," she says. "Or me with my dad's cancer. Neither one of us likes feeling helpless, and there's always that guilt because we couldn't do more. And whatever I say I owe, it's not something I can slap a number on. It's just feeling that if I could go back and change what happened, I would in a heartbeat."

"I'd change you getting hurt," I tell her gruffly. "But not the rest of it. And I don't want you feeling like you should."

"Well, I know I *can't*. So there's that. And since it's the reason I'm with you now, I wouldn't want to change much, either."

Fuck. She's so goddamn sweet. "What I'd change, Jenny, is going after you when you said you felt guilty. I don't want you thinking you can't say how you feel without me turning into a fucking asshole."

She grins. "You *are* an asshole. And I'm not afraid of you." Before I can respond she drops a kiss to my mouth and starts backing away. "Anyway, I like how fighting with you always turns out."

Yeah. That *was* pretty damn good. I chuckle to myself as she scampers away, but my smile fades fast, remembering how I went after her last night. Hell. I sit up, scrubbing a hand over my face. She's already got enough emotional shit to deal with and I pushed her so fucking hard.

Too fucking hard, if the first thing she does this morning is try to explain what she meant—even though she didn't say a damn thing wrong.

But I've done it before. So many times. She tells me 'thank you' and I tell her I don't want to hear it, because I've done nothing she needs to be grateful for. Not saving her from Reichmann. Not stopping the trouble with the Eighty-Eight earlier this year. I'd do anything for her, and none of the trouble that came at Jenny was her fault, so I don't need thanks.

Now I wonder if tossing those thank-yous back in her face is any different than getting after her for saying she feels guilty. What Reichmann did wasn't her fault, but she feels guilt for what happened to me anyway. My mom's cancer wasn't my fault, but I sure as hell feel guilty for what I couldn't do. Jenny was right about that.

So I've got to stop this shit I'm doing. I've got to stop telling her not to feel something, just because I don't like it. And I've got to stop throwing her words back at her, whether it's guilt or a thank-you.

I won't be able to say 'you're welcome.' That would stick in my throat like barbed wire. But I'll find something to say that's right—and hope I don't make it any harder for her.

My chest is heavy as I haul on my sweatpants and make my way to the kitchen. Jenny's humming under her breath, pushing down the plunger on the French press. Her hair's up in one of those fancy twists that makes her bare neck look so vulnerable and exposed. God, she's just a little fucking thing.

She glances up as I come in. "Thermos or mug?"

"Thermos. I'll be heading out. I've got to run through the checklist at the new gym before the building inspector comes next week," I tell her, watching her pour the coffee into two insulated cups, and feeling sick all of a sudden when I spot the dark circles around her wrists. Bruises from my fingers. Because I pinned her, and held her down, and fucked her.

It's not the first time she's bruised a little. But, Jesus. She's already so damn fragile.

"Saxon?" She's watching me warily. "Is everything okay?"

I nod but can't look away from those dark circles. My

voice is raw as I say, "I was rough with you last night."

A shadow moves over her face and pain twists deeper inside me. Maybe I shouldn't have reminded her.

Her gaze don't move from mine. "I liked you being rough."

And she came hard. But an orgasm doesn't seem as if it's enough to make up for those marks on her skin. My throat's a burning ache as I tell her, "But it was too much. And I'm sorry."

Her eyebrows pull together in a frown. "Are you sorry for the bruises or for fucking me as hard as you did?"

"All of it."

She stares at me for a long second, then quietly looks down and screws on her coffee lid. Oh, Christ. I know that carefully blank expression. She's hurt—and pissed.

"Princess—"

"You know what, Saxon?" The explosion comes hard and fast. "Fuck you. And fuck your 'Sorry.'"

God damn it. "Jenny—"

"I got on my knees without you telling me to," she snaps at me. "I told you to slap my pussy. I *wanted* it. I *asked* for it. You want to protect me from dangerous assholes, from the Reichmanns of the world, and I'm glad of it. I've needed it. But I don't need you to protect me from myself!"

"I wasn't—" Was I? Christ, I don't know. And I don't know how this just went so fucking sideways. "You've been hurting so much since your dad died. I never want to add to it."

"Yeah? Well, I *am* hurt. Right now. But not because of my dad." She lays that on me like a roundhouse to the heart, and as I'm standing there, trying to absorb the pain of it, she grabs her coffee and heads for the door. "I'll probably be working late again. So I'll see you when I fucking see you."

WHEN I WENT INTO THE kitchen, she'd been humming.

That's the only thought in my head as I pound the heavy bag at the new gym. The place is dark and empty, not open to the public yet, and I'm supposed to run through that goddamn checklist but I can't stop thinking about Jenny, and how she'd been smiling and humming and happy, and how I ripped that away.

And hurt her.

Never again. I vow it with each strike of my fists. *Never again.*

Never. Fucking. Again.

And I'll make it up to her. Somehow. Because that's the only thing that will make this pain go away. Not this sweat, not this burning ache in my shoulders and fists.

Just seeing her smile again. Just hearing that happy hum.

I don't hear Blowback come in. The bastard's quiet, like a goddamn mouse. Any other time I'd ask if he wanted to go a round up in the ring, because he'll draw blood and I deserve to bleed, but the look on his face tells me shit's about to go down.

I catch the swinging bag, my chest heaving. "What is it?"

Flatly he says, "Your father is the stupidest fuck who ever lived."

Only if you don't count the stupid shit I said this morning. But like father, like son. I start pulling off my gloves. It's probably too much to hope Carlisle slipped on a patch of ice and cracked open his head. "So what's the old bastard done?"

Blowback's answer freezes my blood. "He pointed Lowery straight at Jenny."

I can't fucking breathe. "Is she all right?"

The warlord nods. "We've got time."

There's never time enough when it comes to Jenny. And that's a question answered. *What's the old bastard done?* What he's done is kill someone.

He just better pray it won't be him.

NINE

JENNY

When Saxon comes to the brewery, I know something's gone wrong. Not just because a half dozen Hellfire Riders roll up behind him, but because the expression in his eyes tells me he's beyond pissed—and it's not the hot and dark anger that flares up when we fight. This rage is a frigid howling wind and Saxon's the wolf at the center of it. Ice seems blow off him, sharp and feral.

I glance away from his face to look outside again. Frank Carlisle's sitting in the passenger seat of Saxon's 4x4.

That might explain his rage but it doesn't explain what he's doing here.

I meet his eyes. "What's going on?"

With a sharp nod, he gestures to the bikers who came in with him. "You said you were busy. So I'm bringing in some extra help."

Bullshit. I sigh and shake my head. "Saxon."

His jaw tightens and he grasps my hand, leading me through the door to the back of the barn. Hashtag glances over, then takes off when Saxon says, "Get the fuck out."

"Saxon, damn it. Is he my employee right now or is he a Rider?"

"Today, tomorrow, he's a Rider. This is club business," he says, and just before I explode—"but it concerns you, Jenny."

I settle back, waiting. So that's why he brought me back here. So he can tell me what he needs to tell me without the others listening in.

His chest rises on a long breath, and I see now—his control is on a thin leash. So damn thin. He's on a killing edge. "Carlisle used your phone yesterday."

Frowning, I nod. "To call his prez, he said."

"Well, he did. Then he called a bookmaker in Seattle about Friday's game. And that bookmaker called the man in Portland who Carlisle owes money to. A reverse phone lookup ain't hard, Jenny."

Oh, shit. "So you think someone will be coming *here*?"

"Probably not. Don't you be scared." He catches my

face in his strong hands, his intense gaze locked on mine. "The most I expect is he'd come in, maybe ask if you'd seen Carlisle around. But it's not hard to draw a line from you, then to the Hellfire Riders on your property, and then to me. So I don't know, maybe he'd look at you as leverage. At the very least he'd be looking hard at the ranch, and I don't like thinking of him being anywhere near here."

I don't either. "So what will you do?"

"I'm going to leave some men with you. What you do with them, I don't care. Tell them to stay out in their trucks, or put them to work wrapping your orders. Just so I know you're safe here."

Though I don't think he'll tell me, I ask anyway. "And you?"

"It's the holidays, and since my father's visiting me, I'm having lunch in town with him." A faint snarl rolls through the reply. "Someplace real visible. Then I'm going to take him to a motel and make sure people know he's staying there through Christmas."

Using Carlisle as bait. Or making sure that whoever's after him doesn't have a reason to leave town and look for him out at the ranch.

Saxon's voice softens as he continues, "I don't know how long it'll take, Jenny. A couple of days, maybe. I intend to send Thorne and Zoomie to stay with you at the house tonight."

Not just any Riders, not when I'm at home. He's making sure they're the two I'm most familiar with—a man I call my uncle and one of my best friends. "All right."

I see his relief as he nods. "Good. And tomorrow's Christmas Eve. Were you planning to open the store?"

"I *was*." I always get last-minute customers coming in to buy kegs for their holiday parties. "But do you think I should—"

"Don't close up. Just, maybe you could let Hashtag mind the front if anyone comes in."

"I can do that." Lifting my hand, I lay my palm against his jaw. "And thank you for looking out for me."

His jaw clenches tight, and even before he opens his mouth, I know what he'll say. *Don't thank me.* Because he'll say it's his fault Carlisle is here in the first place. He'll say it's his responsibility to clean up any trouble the Hellfire Riders get into. He'll say he doesn't want gratitude from me.

But I don't care *why* he looks out for me. It just matters to me that he does.

Then all at once he drags me close, burying his face in my hair. "Jenny," he says hoarsely. "I love you so fucking much."

My heart shoots up into my throat, huge and aching—but before I can say a word, he pulls back and kisses me hard.

Hard, but not nearly long enough. Lifting his head, he searches my face for a long moment, his thumb tracing my tremulous smile. "Stay safe, princess."

"You, too," I say softly, then watch him go.

And know that nothing will be right until he's back again.

TEN

SAXON

After more than twenty-four hours of sitting in a motel room and watching the parking lot, I don't know if I'm snowblind or if I'm just so damn tired my eyes are telling my brain to fuck off.

Checkout time was a few hours ago, so the traffic through the motel parking lot slowed in the early afternoon. But now it's picking up again as holiday travelers start checking in. It's a shitty place to stay over Christmas Eve, but I suppose most of them will be going out again to spend time with friends or kin.

Thank fuck I haven't had to spend much time with my kin. The motel has two levels and is shaped like a "U" around a parking lot—so from my room on the second story of the north leg, I've got a direct view of Carlisle's room on the south leg. I've pushed the table over to the window, kept the sheer curtains open just enough to look out without giving anyone a good look in, and have seen a whole shitload of nothing all day.

Until a truck pulls in to the parking lot below. Not Lowery. Thorne.

He knocks on the door a minute later, a caddy of coffee cups in hand. I take one, and after a glance at Bull, who's snoring away on the bed, Thorne sets the caddy down and takes the other cup for himself.

He eyes the motel room door across the way. The windows are dark, the curtains drawn. "Anything yet?"

"Not yet."

"You sleep at all?"

"Not much." I tried to rest the night before while Bull kept watch but I didn't get a wink. Instead I just kept thinking about Jenny.

I know she's fine. The brothers looking after her have checked in regularly. But it's hell lying in any bed but hers.

He pulls up the extra folding chair we brought in. "Jenny left the house pretty early this morning."

"She's been working hard."

"Girl works harder than almost any other I know," he

agrees, still looking out the window. "Is that why you two didn't put a tree up? I couldn't help but notice the house looks pretty damn bare this year. Just didn't have time?"

Anyone else, I'd probably tell him to fuck off and keep his eyes on his own business. But Thorne knows Jenny—maybe better than anyone else.

"She didn't want it," I tell him. "And I didn't want to push her."

He hums low in his throat, nodding again. I figure he's got more to say, so I wait, and for about five minutes the only sound in the room is Bull's snoring.

Finally he says, "I've got two Christmas stories for you. Now, you can take them as your veep giving you advice or just take them as an old man's ramblings."

I know better than to take anything Thorne says as ramblings. He's been around too long, seen too much. And he wouldn't be my veep if I didn't trust what he said.

"All right," I tell him.

"The first one is about Red and Angela and Jenny. And how the first year after Angela died, Red tried to give Jenny a Christmas that was exactly what Angela'd always given. But it wasn't the same. And he was fucking miserable. He would have been anyway, but trying to make their Christmas just like it was made it worse. Because it wouldn't ever be the same again."

"Jenny knows that. It's why she's skipping this year. She said the next year was better."

Thorne shakes his head. "It wasn't better. Angela was

still gone and it wasn't ever going to be better. But what made it *different* was that Red didn't pretend it was the same. That year, he made a Christmas for him and Jenny. And they started making their own traditions. Now there's no Red and Jenny. There's *you* and Jenny. And of course she knows it won't ever be the same—but my point is, you've got to start making your own traditions, too."

My chest is aching. "We will."

"And that brings me to my second point. You've got to be careful what traditions you make, because they'll sneak up on you. The second story I'll tell you is about me and my wife. Our first year, we ended up snowbound out at our place. We couldn't get out to buy groceries, and by the time Christmas Day rolled around, Molly was down to tomato soup from a can and some grilled cheese sand-wiches. So we're eating them for our Christmas dinner, and all the while we're making plans about the next year. That we'll buy everything ahead of time, we'll have that ham she'd been hoping to make, even if we have to kill our own damn hog. And being with her, making those plans, was so damn perfect. I wouldn't have traded that first Christmas for anything."

He pauses for a long moment, his gaze staring out the window, but I'd bet he isn't seeing anything but his wife and that long ago day.

"Now, the next year comes around, and it's all just like we planned. A big ham dinner, a big fucking tree. But it didn't feel right—though I wasn't saying anything, because I didn't want to hurt her by telling her something was missing. Hell, I didn't even know *what* was missing. Then that night she came to me with some tomato soup and grilled cheese, and all at once it was right. And we still make those soup and sandwiches. We do our thing with the kids, all that traditional shit—like that dinner I invited you to—but every Christmas night Molly and I have our own dinner, and until that moment it's not Christmas to me."

Stopping to take a swallow of his coffee, he glances over. "So you can make traditions without meaning to. What you've gotta be careful of is that you and Jenny don't make a tradition out of grieving Red. She's gonna grieve for him, regardless—but skipping a year might not make it better. Instead she might just end up feeling guilty next year, because maybe she'll feel like resuming celebrations means his death doesn't matter as much as it did the year before. And you know our girl."

"That she'll take on loads of guilt real easy? Yeah."

He nods. "So that's all I have to say. You make your own traditions. And you be careful which ones you make. All right?"

"All right." Though I doubt it's that easy.

We sit in silence for a few more minutes—and both notice the new arrival at the same time. A tall blond man getting out of his car with a pizza box in hand. He covers his hair with a red delivery cap.

Thorne gets up. "Is that our guy?"

"Looks like," I say, then shake my head when Thorne reaches for the gun holstered at his back. "You won't need that. Blowback's over there."

He frowns, watching Lowery climb the stairs. "A fucking pizza delivery. Is anyone stupid enough to open a door for that?"

"My father probably is." Which reminds me of the last time food showed up at that door—a story I enjoyed too damn much. "When Bull went over there to take them lunch, he said Blowback had Carlisle tied to a chair and his mouth taped shut."

Glancing away from where Lowery's knocking at the other door, Thorne shoots me a look that's half amused, half disbelieving. "Was he worried Carlisle would say something to tip Lowery off?"

"Just tired of listening to him, I guess."

The room door opens a crack. Lowery shoves his way inside. The door slams.

Then nothing.

Thorne begins pacing, watching the windows across the way. No movement. No lights showing through the curtains. "You sure about this?"

I nod. "I figure Blowback will probably wait until dark to get rid of the body. So you can call Anthill, tell him we took care of his problem—and to come and pick up his baggage. I don't want to see Carlisle around here again."

We both go quiet as the door opens across the way. Blowback comes out wearing a Santa hat and carrying a bulging red sack over his shoulder. Judging by the size of that bag and the way the contents are heavy enough to make the warlord stagger a little going down the stairs, it's not hard to guess he's got Lowery's body in there.

"Sweet baby Jesus." Thorne whistles through his teeth. "What the hell do you say to that?"

Fuck if I know. "Maybe he's in a rush to get home to Zoomie."

Yawning and scratching his belly, Bull joins us at the window. In the parking lot below, Blowback loads Lowery's body into the back of his rig, then reaches into the red bag and fishes around until he pulls out a crushed, blood-stained pizza box. Opening it up, he scoops out a slice and takes a bite while walking to the cab of his truck.

With another yawn, Bull looks to me, then to Thorne. "Merry fucking Christmas," he says.

And heads back to bed.

ELEVEN

JENNY

I don't park my car in the garage when I pull up to the house—the overhead door rattles too much as it opens and is directly beneath my bedroom. Saxon's a light sleeper and I don't want to wake him. Judging by the exhaustion I saw on his face when he came into the brewery to kiss me and tell me everything was taken care of, he probably drove straight home to rest.

And it looks as if he did. When I tiptoe up to my bedroom, he's sprawled facedown across the bed. For a long moment, I just look at him, my heart filled *so* full. I don't know how I ended up with this man. I don't know what I did to ever deserve him. But I am *never* letting him go.

I will let him sleep, though.

Quietly, I head back downstairs. The house is silent. Almost too silent after days spent working with Hashtag, listening to him caroling along to all of those Christmas songs. Now it's Christmas Eve and the house is dark and cold.

In the kitchen, I try to warm up by starting a fire and making some hot apple cider—the same kind my mom used to make for me on Christmas Eve. She and my dad would drink mulled wine but she'd give me hot spiced cider. After she died, my dad continued making the cider, but for both of us. No more mulled wine for him. After she died, I don't think he ever drank it again.

Though my heart aches with the memory, thinking of it doesn't bring real pain. Instead it brings soft heat to my cold skin, comforting warmth with every sip.

My gaze sweeps around the kitchen. No lights, no tree. I thought they'd hurt too much to have, but it almost hurts worse to know how heartbroken my mom would be if she knew I was huddled in a cold kitchen, how sad my dad would look if he walked through the front door.

It's too late to do much. But I should do *something*. Not just for me. For Saxon, too. What was it his mom said? *It was important to always have something.*

So we will.

No gifts, though. I already told Saxon not to get me a present and there's no time left for him to order anything. Christmas decorations, then. And dinner tomorrow. I check the fridge. One of the prospect's duties is picking up groceries for the prez, and a glance assures me it's stocked with everything we need—including a pecan pie. Perfect. I'm going to kiss Bottlecap the next time I see him.

A tingle of excitement grows in my chest. I grab my coat and head for the garage. My dad kept the Christmas lights above the—

The ringing of the doorbell shatters the quiet. Oh, shit. I race to the front door, stopping just long enough to glance through the peephole—Frank Carlisle, shit, *shit*— and see his hand rising as if he's about to knock.

I pull the door open but don't move out of the doorway. "Frank."

"Jenny." He looks relieved to see that it's me. I don't blame him. "Merry Christmas."

"Thank you. Merry Christmas to you, too." I look beyond him, where a truck sits in the driveway next to mine, its headlights off but the dome light on. Whoever's inside doesn't seem to care what's going on in my doorway. The way he's frowning down at his lighted screen, I guess he's having difficulty getting a connection. "Just passing through on your way back home?"

"Maybe." He looks past my shoulder into the interior of the house before meeting my gaze again. "I was wondering if I could come in and talk to you for a second."

I've got a feeling that even if I say no, he's going to eventually talk his way inside, anyway. "For a minute," I agree, stepping back. I hold up my coat as if I was headed somewhere other than my chilly garage. "But I'm afraid I can't be long."

"It won't take long." He limps his way inside on his crutch and leg brace. As I shut the door, he removes his stocking cap and regards me with serious eyes. "I wanted to apologize to you, Jenny. I understand that using your phone created some problems for you, and I'm sorry for that."

"Thank you," I tell him. "I appreciate that."

He offers an abashed smile. "I just figured, you know, that if I won big on that game, I could get myself out of that mess I was in. I didn't imagine it'd just pull me in deeper."

Was this an apology or an excuse? Does he expect me to say it's fine? Because it's not.

So I wait, watching his gaze dart to the great room and linger on the big fireplace.

"It's a nice place you got here. But no Christmas tree? No stockings?"

I'm not going to explain myself. "Not this year."

"Because it wasn't long ago you lost your dad, isn't that right? Must be hard to feel festive."

My spine goes rigid. "Sometimes."

He nods again, then draws a deep breath. "I know

I messed up with that phone call, Jenny, but I was wondering… You know what it's like not to have your dad around—and Saxon's had a father missing his whole life. Maybe I could change that now, if he gives me a chance. And I think he'd listen if you put in a word for me."

Frank Carlisle hasn't earned a word from me. And does he think reminding me of my grief will engage my sympathies?

Instead it's just pissing me off, and I'm struggling to think of a polite way to get him out of here when politeness goes flying out the window.

"What the *fuck* are you doing here?"

Expression thunderous, Saxon strides in through the great room wearing nothing but his sweatpants. His eyes sweep me from head to toe, as if making sure I'm all right, before his furious gaze shoots back to his dad.

"Hold up, son." Carlisle lifts his hands. "I'm just talking to your girl and appealing to the spirit of the season."

As if protecting me from the sight of his father, Saxon grabs my hand and draws me around behind him. "You think I don't know what you're appealing to? Maybe asking her if she'll give up her house to me."

With a tight little laugh, Carlisle shakes his head. "I'm just looking out for you. I've been gone, I know that. So now I'm just trying to do what a father should."

"Then walk out that goddamn door. Right now."

A flush rises over the older man's cheeks. "That girl owes you five years of your life. I just want to see my son get what he deserves."

Every muscle in Saxon's powerful body tenses. His voice deepens, suddenly quiet. Cold. "You look at her again, and you'll get what *you* deserve. So get the hell out. And don't you fucking come back."

His fingers linked with mine, Saxon pulls me forward with him. He throws open the door and stands, waiting. Carlisle doesn't move to leave but just looks at him.

"So this is who your mother raised you to be? You're just going to toss your old man out into the cold?"

A cruel little smile touches Saxon's mouth. "I'd really fucking enjoy that. But it looks like you've got a ride. So go catch it."

Carlisle looks to me. "And this was how *you* were raised, too? I heard Red was a better man than that."

My fingers tighten on Saxon's, stopping him when he growls and steps forward, as if intending to beat the shit out of his old man.

"You're absolutely right, Frank," I tell him. "This *isn't* how I was raised. The way my dad raised me, if someone won't leave when asked, I'm supposed to go grab the shotgun. So maybe you ought to go, because I really don't want to shoot anyone on Christmas Eve."

His jaw tight, Carlisle glances from my face to Saxon's. As if finally realizing he's not ever getting anywhere, he gives a tight nod. "All right, then."

Saxon and I are silent as he crutches his way past us. Carlisle barely steps onto the porch before Saxon slams the heavy oak door behind him, hard enough the solid frame shivers under the impact.

"Goddamn *fuck!*" he grinds out, then turns to me, his expression gentling. His big hands capture my cheeks, his dark gaze searching mine. "You all right?"

Pretty good, considering. "Your dad's a dick."

"Yes, he is." His thumbs slip over my cheekbones in a gentle caress. "I'm sorry he brought Red into it."

"Me, too. But the whole shotgun bit was pretty awesome, wasn't it?"

Saxon doesn't smile, but continues watching my face… as if waiting for something.

I catch his wrists. "What's going on?"

His voice roughens. "I don't like knowing he hurt you."

"But he didn't." I stare up at him, and abruptly recognize the tender way he's looking at me, holding me. As if waiting for me to break down and cry.

And *that* makes me want to cry.

Abruptly I pull away from him. "I'm okay. Really."

His jaw clenches, his hands curling into fists. Raw torment lines his face as he says hoarsely, "I don't know what the fuck to do, Jenny. I don't know what I'm doing wrong. The other morning. Now. I know you're hurting, and I don't want to—"

"I *am* hurting!" My voice is tight, my throat burning. "But I've hurt before, and I survived. My mom died, and I survived. Reichmann hurt me, and I survived. You went to prison, and I survived. My dad died, and I *will* survive." My breath hitches. "But what I won't survive is *you* building a wall out of my grief!"

"*I* built the wall?" He throws his arms wide, his expression a mask of disbelief. "I didn't build any fucking wall. If there's any wall, it's built out of your hurt—and I don't want to hurt you more by smashing through it!"

"Oh, God, Saxon." Understanding wipes the fight from me. Shaking my head, I let out a shuddering sigh. "My grief isn't a wall for me. It's something I *carry*. And sometimes I let that burden down, or forget how heavy it is. And one day, maybe it won't weigh so much, or maybe I'll build up more strength so carrying it becomes easier." I hold his gaze with mine. "But when you keep that hurt *between* us, because you're afraid I'll break if you're too rough or too hard—then it's a wall that I can't climb. Not while carrying this weight, too."

"All right, princess. All right." He moves closer and his long fingers slide into my hair, tipping my head up until I meet his eyes. His gaze is gentle as it searches my face. "I get it. And I know I can't carry this hurt for you, Jenny. But when you need me to, I'll carry you *and* the hurt. All right?"

My eyes burn with tears. "Yes. Although I don't like being a burden."

Saxon huffs out a short laugh. "I know that about you, Jenny. But I love carrying you."

"Because I'm your princess? The girl who's always needing rescue?" I say it lightly, but there's hurt there, too.

I love it when he calls me his princess. But lately it's felt like another way of saying I need to be coddled.

"Jenny." It's a soft reprimand. "You notice I don't use my father's name? Even though it's right there on my birth certificate and my parents were married. But when my mother went back to using Gray, I did, too."

"But—"

"Now think of who raised me. Cancer got her in the end, but before that, my mom never stopped fighting. She got knocked down again and again, but she kept on surviving. And we didn't have much, but as far as I was concerned, she was a queen who deserved so much better." His long fingers skim across my trembling lips. "You're much like her. So strong and so damn smart. And when I say you're a princess, it's because you're the girl who deserves so much better than me. You're also the girl I'd fight dragons for. You're the girl I'd die to kiss just once. And you're the girl I'm afraid will wake up and see I'm no fucking prince."

"I know that." I can barely speak past the ache in my throat. "I've always known that. But I love the man you are."

"And you made me that man."

I shake my head. "No—"

"You listen." His hands tighten, stopping my denial. "*You made me that man.* I should have been that man before, should have been how my mom raised me to be, but back in those days all I could see how I was nothing. Just a coked-up asshole who couldn't even lift his mom out of the hole my father threw her into. But seeing you in that courtroom, Jenny, seeing how you were so fucking brave…" His throat works as he looks down at me. "Carlisle talks like those were five years wasted, but it was in prison when I became the man I needed to be. I educated myself, got my shit together. And when I got out, those few years with my mom still alive, she looked at me with so much pride, Jenny. And it's all because you looked at me in that courtroom like I was worth something. But I'm *nothing* without you."

"Saxon—" My tears spill over and I desperately try to stop them. "Shit. After I just tried to convince you I'm not all weepy and don't break so easy."

His laugh is low and deep, his lips warm as he kisses the tears from my wet cheeks. "Then I've got no choice but to take you upstairs, Jenny. To put you in that bed and treat you like a princess."

I sniffle and laugh, wrapping my arms around his neck. "What did you treat me like the other night?"

"Like a woman who could take me." He sweeps me up against his chest. "But I gotta tell you, princess—that means the same damn thing."

I cling to him, smiling against his shoulder as he carries me up the stairs. Halfway up I remember—"Before your dad showed up, I was thinking we should do a little something for the holiday. Like your mom said."

"I was thinking the same thing." His voice rough, his

strong arms tighten around me. "But we'll do it in the morning. Right now, I'm going to start the Christmas Eve tradition of licking your pussy until you scream."

That sounds *almost* perfect—but much too far away. "Why not the Christmas Eve tradition of fucking me on the stairs?"

Abruptly Saxon stops, letting my feet swing to the step above his. Anticipation rockets through me as his head lowers and he presses closer, mouth hovering just above my lips, his thick cock wedged between my thighs. "I think we're going to have a lot of traditions, Jenny."

I think so, too.

TWELVE

SAXON

I feel like some little kid as I kiss Jenny awake. She sighs and her lips soften, then yelps and jolts up to sitting when the ice of my freezing hands and cold cheeks sinks through her sleep-warmed skin.

"Saxon?" Sleepily she blinks up at me, so fucking sexy with her long rumpled hair and heavy eyes. She clutches the sheet to her chest and takes in the coat and hat I'm wearing. "Were you outside?"

"I was."

And because I'm as impatient as a little kid but a hell of a lot bigger than one, I scoop her up, sheet and all. She shrieks and laughs, desperately pulling up the bed sheet's trailing end before we hit the stairs. Clinging to me, she's still giggling wildly as I carry her into the kitchen.

Her giggles abruptly stop. Her mouth open, she stares at the tiny tree standing in front of the brick fireplace.

Not even a tree. Shit, the truth is, I was hoping to find a seedling, but the snow out there's too fucking deep. So I settled for hacking off part of a pine branch and sticking it into a pot. Then I found a red ribbon and tied it around the top.

The ribbon's almost bigger than the tree.

She turns to me with a tearful smile. "Oh, Saxon."

"Christ, Jenny." I grin and carry her over to the breakfast nook, where I set her ass down on the wooden table. "Only you would cry over that twig."

That makes her laugh, and that's good. Because she might really be crying soon.

I cup her cheek in my cold hand. "Now, listen. That tree is tiny and not even worth the name. But maybe it had a rough start. Kind of like you had a rough year. But next year, we're going to pick out a twig that's a little bigger, a little stronger. And the year after that, one that's even a little bigger. I figure by the time we've got kids running around, we'll have a sturdy little tree to put some lights on. And by the time *their* kids are running around, we'll have one big enough to reach the ceiling in the great room. All right?"

She nods, her green eyes huge and glistening. "All right."

It's just a whisper, like her throat is clogged up. And, fuck me. Mine's lumping up, too. I reach into my coat pocket. She goes utterly still when I pull out the ring box.

"Now, listen. This isn't from *me*. You said not to get you anything and I didn't." My hand's shaking when I open it up, and there she goes, her breath catching on a ragged sob. "Red gave this to me and he said to give it to you when the time was right."

"Saxon." Her tears are streaming now. Her trembling fingers touch the gold band. "That's my mother's wedding ring."

"I know it is. And you must know what I would have asked if I'd given it to you later. You must know why your dad gave it to me. But I didn't want to hurt you, or rush you. This soon after Red…it's not right."

She's silent, her tears dripping down her cheeks as she lifts the band from its velvet cushion. Her fingertips trace the inscription inside the band, almost worn away:

Always.

My voice is a thick rasp as I say quietly, "But this is the right thing to give you now, I think. So you have something of both of them today. Something that's *from* them. And you can put it on a necklace and wear it that way, or put it on whichever finger you like. In my heart, Jenny, I've already married you. So you can put it on your left hand and hold its place until we make that official. Or you can put it on your other hand—"

And I choke up completely when she slips the band onto her left ring finger. Because I can't talk, I kiss her, tasting the salt of her tears and the heat of her mouth.

When I pull back, she's still crying, but they're soft and happy tears, glistening through her beautiful smile.

Cupping her face in my hands, I tell her, "Now, you didn't want any gifts from me. And I'm not giving you anything you can hold. I'm not giving you anything you didn't already have from me yesterday, or the day before. And that's this promise: I'm never leaving. I'll marry you tomorrow or I'll wait forever, it doesn't mean anything to me. I'm here until the end. Forever and always. All right?"

"All right." Nodding, she wraps her arms around me and releases a long, shuddering breath against my neck. "This was exactly the right thing, Saxon."

Good. And, hell—maybe this isn't the right thing, but she's soft and sexy and almost naked against me, and when I kiss her again she tastes so damn sweet. Then she moans low in her throat and she's got a ring on her finger, and I need to make her mine, only mine. My fingers slide beneath the sheet, and she's so fucking hot and wet, I lose my goddamn mind. She cries out my name as I push my cock into her scalding heat. I'm rough but she takes every hard thrust, her fingernails digging into my shoulders and begging for more. I give her more, and more, give her everything, until her pussy's clenching around me and I'm coming deep.

And I don't even think of saying 'sorry' for being so hard and rough when I collapse over her. Instead I just try to catch my breath as her legs wrap me up tight.

After a long while, I lever myself up off the table, taking her with me. She looks up into my eyes, her teeth worrying her lip.

"Now, you stop that," I tell her.

Her eyebrows go up. "Stop what?"

"I know you, Jenny. Even though this ring didn't come from me, you're feeling guilty for not getting me anything."

A laugh slips from her that she quickly stops, pressing her pretty lips together. She stares up at me for a long second, her green eyes sparkling, then says, "Oh, Saxon. You know me better than *that*."

Shit. I do know her better than that. "You've got a present stashed away in a closet, don't you?"

"I never do anything last minute," she says with a laugh. "I started buying them in July."

"*Them?*"

She nods.

"Well, save them all for next year, then." Because I'm probably going to need a whole damn year to catch up.

Smiling, she rises up and kisses me. "This year, I'll just give you the same promise that you gave me. I'm yours, Saxon. Always."

"Always, princess," I tell her.

And that might almost be long enough.

THE END

ABOUT KATI

Kati Wilde is a tight-lipped, loose-hipped woman of indeterminate age and low breeding. She writes romantic fiction to assuage her darker urge to write Transformers erotica. You can reach Kati at kati@katiwilde.com or any of the Club authors (Ella Goode, Ruby Dixon, and Kati Wilde) at 1theclub1@gmail.com.

www.katiwilde.com

Facebook: www.facebook.com/authorkatiwilde
Instagram: www.instagram.com/authorkatiwilde
Twitter: www.twitter.com/katiwilde

www.katiwilde.com/newsletter

CONTENT WARNINGS

All of the Hellfire Riders stories include swearing, violence, explicit sexual content including references to group sex, sex in public and voyeurism (some main characters only watch while others participate), references to alcohol and drug use, sex trafficking, illegal cage fighting, and murder (mostly only bad guys, but there are exceptions.) There are no cliffhangers and no cheating.

For this particular book:

- heroine was sexually assaulted as a teenager
  - threats of sexual assault continue
    - a parent has cancer
- death and grief (mostly in the holiday story)
- the bad guys deal in sex trafficking and have women chained up in their clubhouse
- the bad guys are white supremacists whose club name, the Eighty-Eight, is a reference to "Heil Hitler," and they are obviously terrible people with a racist/misogynist agenda.
- I don't know if this actually needs a content warning, but I know some readers can't enjoy a book where the main characters engage in any sexual activity with other people, so I will mention that there is a brief m/f/f scene — the hero touches the heroine only while another woman also touches the heroine only. There are no "other woman" or "other man" scenes, however.